Dear Reader,

Firstly may I thank you for all your letters and the questionnaires you have returned? If you haven't yet completed a questionnaire, we'd be delighted if you could fill in the form at the back of this book and let us have it back. It is only by hearing from you that we can continue to provide the type of *Scarlet* books you want to read.

Perhaps you'd like to know how we go about finding four new books for you each month? Well, when we decided to launch *Scarlet* we 'advertised' for authors through writers' organizations, magazines, literary agents and so on. As a result, we are delighted to have been inundated with manuscripts – particularly from the UK and North America. Now, of course, some of these books have to be returned to their authors because they just aren't right for *your* list. But others, submitted either by authors who've already had books published or by brand new writers, are exactly what we know readers are looking for. Sometimes, the book is almost perfect when it arrives on my desk, but usually we enjoy working closely with the author to give their book that essential, final polish.

What you'll notice over the coming months are more books from authors who've already appeared in *Scarlet*. Do let me know, won't you, if there's a particular author we've featured who *you'd* like to see again? See you next month and, in the meantime, thank you for continuing to be a *Scarlet* woman.

Best wishes,

Sally Cooper

SALLY COOPER,
Editor-in-Chief – *Scarlet*

About the Author

Jean Saunders has been writing for 30 years and is the published author of 70 novels, 600 short stories, numerous articles and five 'How To' books for writers. You may already have read and enjoyed books by Jean under one of her other pseudonyms: Rowena Summers, Jean Innes or Sally Blake.

Jean is very involved with writers' organizations such as the Romantic Novelists' Association. She is the Chairman of the Southern Writers conference, has appeared at seminars and conferences, and on radio and television talking about her life as an author.

Married with three adult children and ten grandchildren, travel is listed as one of Jean's major interests and she has visited many countries around the world including the USA.

*Other **Scarlet** titles available this month:*

CARIBBEAN FLAME by Maxine Barry
THE MARRIAGE SOLUTION by Julie Garratt
UNDERCOVER LOVER by Sally Steward

JEAN SAUNDERS

WIVES, FRIENDS & LOVERS

SCARLET

Enquiries to:
Robinson Publishing Ltd
7 Kensington Church Court
London W8 4SP

First published in the UK by Scarlet, 1996

A copy of the British Library Cataloguing in
Publication data is available from the British Library

ISBN 1-85487-700-3

Printed and bound in the EC

10 9 8 7 6 5 4 3 2 1

PROLOGUE

1985

It wasn't a time for giggling, but as the long wait dragged on, the tension in the small, makeshift dressing-room became unbearable; their only release was in laughter. Jonesy, the Welsh music tutor, coming backstage to check that they were ready for their number, glared at them, bristling at their flippancy, his brow already beaded with sweat over this end-of-year concert with a fifties theme that had seemed such a good idea at the time . . .

'You three just behave yourselves now. I've given you the finale because I thought you were capable of it, so don't let me down. And Gemma Grover,' he added, giving weight to his words by using her full name, 'I'm relying on you to hold the other two together.'

Since they were finding it hard to even hold each other up, in their ridiculous bouffant blonde wigs and shimmering jelly-pink dresses, they all but dissolved into a mass of shrieking hysteria at his words.

The short, stocky tutor threw up his hands in disgust and left them, muttering that he hoped next year's intake of young ladies would have more decorum than this lot.

But next year's intake of girls at the Cheltenham boarding school which Laura, Gemma and Penny had attended for the past five years, wouldn't be as immediately close as they had become. Friendship took time to develop. The newcomers would be strangers to one another, scared and bewildered, like the three of them had been, before they had gravitated together like homing pigeons and began sharing all their late-night secrets, all their hopes and dreams.

'We really should try to calm down,' Laura advised, wriggling her ample shape more comfortably into the tight-fitting pink dress.

'Why?' Gemma asked, always ready to argue.

'Because I'll never be able to sing otherwise. I *know* I won't, and it'll be a disaster. I can't sing anyway, and I don't know why I let you talk me into this!'

As her voice rose in panic, Laura knew she was quickly losing all the confidence of the past weeks, when they had rehearsed every spare minute of the day, and the song had seemed so perfect for the three of them.

'You'll be fine, Laura,' Penny said, giving her a hug. 'And as long as Gem belts it out in the middle of us, all we need to do is remember the harmony. Lord knows we've practised it often enough.'

'But the *Beverly Sisters*!' Laura protested, as if the realization of it was only just hitting her. 'We must have been mad to think we could do it.'

Gemma spoke sharply. 'We *can* do it, and we *will* do

4

it. It's always been our motto, hasn't it? No matter what.'

'The Three Musketeers and all that,' Penny added for no reason at all. 'All for one, and one for all. We'll show them.'

Without warning, the atmosphere in the dressing-room changed. They were all conscious that it was very nearly the last time they would be like this – so close in friendship that when one hurt, so did the others. When one was in love, the others warmed for her and ached for her, and shared in all the vicarious delights of touching and holding and kissing that they were only just dis-covering when the rare opportunities arose.

'Sixteen, and never been kissed, at least not the way you have, Gem,' Penny had moaned on the night of her birthday several months ago. 'Where did I go wrong?'

'If you didn't spend so much time on the sports field, and more time on your appearance, you might find out,' Gemma had replied; she was always the pithy one, always giving a straightforward answer. 'Anyway, Laura's no better off than you. The couple of twits she's had recently wouldn't turn anybody on, and I'm not surprised she dumped them just as fast.'

'Well, maybe that's because I'm choosey,' Laura had objected, not prepared to let Gemma get away with this . . .

Oh Lord, if ever they needed to be in harmony, it was now, tonight, when they were about to give their own hopelessly inadequate version of 'Sisters' by the Beverly Sisters. Laura's blue eyes felt salty.

'For pity's sake – we'll be on in a few minutes, and

we'll be rotten if we don't calm down and get it together.'

'You're right,' Penny agreed readily. 'Just remember to follow Gem's lead, Laura, and don't go off-key.'

'Oh, thanks! That's all I need!'

'You'll be fine,' Gemma said firmly. 'We'll all be fine. If we didn't feel nervous before going on, we wouldn't be proper *artistes*.'

The exaggerated word threatened to bring on another fit of the giggles, and simultaneously all three reached out their hands and linked them together.

'Sisters,' Gemma's voice was suddenly and unusually as soft as Laura's. 'Right?'

There was no time for anything more, because they were called to the wings then; the act before them was taking a bow – a pair of double-jointed twins in spangles and tights who had done a circus acrobatic turn. Mr Llewellyn Jones, music tutor and self-appointed compère, then introduced Laura Robinson, Gemma Grover and Penny Bishop as a well-known trio. They received thunderous applause, and Laura got the most horrendous attack of cold feet.

'I can't do this. I just can't,' she whispered.

She felt herself being gripped and held, and she tried not to notice the sea of faces beyond the footlights. It was only an end-of-year concert, for God's sake, she kept telling herself. The end of their year. The end of five wonderful years of friendship. She gritted her teeth and swallowed the lump in her throat, trying to concentrate on the moment and not looking beyond it.

But she was not an extrovert performer like Gemma,

nor like Penny, who excelled at every sport she under-
took. She was just Laura, tuneless and ordinary – and
petrified at being thrown to the wolves like this, when
she'd far rather have been wardrobe mistress, or
prompt, or –

'We're on,' Gemma hissed, as the opening introduc-
tion of 'Sisters' was bashed out on the school piano by
the heavy-handed Mr Llewellyn Jones.

She was propelled forward by the other two, holding
hands and taking a preliminary bow. Gemma was in the
middle, the other two by her sides, and it dawned on
Laura that they were getting a great ovation as their
costumes and wigs, together with the music, identified
them immediately. Gemma's velvety brown eyes
sparkled, loving every moment of glory, while Laura
sagged, knowing that this adulation couldn't last. Once
they began to sing – or rather, once *she* began, and
nothing came out . . .

Penny would cope, of course. She always coped with
everything. She was one of life's survivors. Laura felt
one final squeeze of Gemma's hand before they loo-
sened, and as the audience hushed, a rush of determi-
nation rippled through her. Gemma wanted this so
much. Gemma had longed to be a star tonight. She
had thought up the idea of them being the Beverly
Sisters, and it was up to Laura and Penny to support
her. They couldn't let Gemma down.

The tune was familiar to everyone, and as always,
Gemma gave it everything she had. But even to Laura
and Penny, who had heard her sing so often, her pure,
clear, beautiful voice soared out that evening, and

7

somehow it lifted the other two, so that they gave it everything they had too. They were in perfect harmony, as they had been for so long in other ways. And when the song ended it was almost an anti-climax to hear the applause, and to realize that they could have gone on singing for ever . . .

As they took their bows, they were joined by the rest of the cast. And then Jonesy came on stage in his role as musical director, and singled Gemma out, pulling her forward to centrestage.

'They've all been wonderful, haven't they? And if my instincts serve me right, I'd say that this young lady is obviously destined to have a singing career.'

From the applause, it was clear that the audience agreed with him. And later, backstage, they were all flushed and excited, glowing with the congratulations of the other performers and tutors alike. And with the seeds of ambition already planted firmly in Gemma's mind.

The boys in their final year at the adjoining boarding school had been invited to the concert, and would be returning for the disco in a couple of hours' time that evening.

In the room the girls shared, that held so much of them all, they took turns in the shower, and changed out of the frothy pink dresses into jeans and shirts. School uniform was no longer an essential at last, and nobody needed to dress up in party frocks tonight. It was to be informal and casual, like a breath of fresh air blowing through the rather stuffy corridors of the Wellesley

Boarding School for Girls, named after its founder a hundred years ago.

They all tried to calm down a little. But nothing could stop Gemma swanning about the room, clearly still charged with adrenaline at all the compliments she had received. It didn't bother Laura. She was glad and pleased for her. She'd only gone along for the ride, to be with her best friends, and it had all turned out spectacularly well – better than she had expected.

Laura took life easily, never expecting too much, and never being disappointed. If that made her a blob, she was a popular blob. She didn't really excel at anything, but everybody loved her – and even if she sometimes thought with rare cynicism that her popularity was due to the fact that she wasn't a threat to anyone, that didn't bother her unduly. In her introspective moments she had sometimes wondered why the other two had taken up with her, but it was pointless to question such things.

What did it matter, anyway? After tonight, they would all be going their separate ways, and that was something Laura simply refused to think about until she absolutely had to.

'Haven't we had enough singing for one night, Gem?' Penny said suddenly, living up to the reputation of her green eyes. Not that she had any real need to be jealous. She had her own adoring fans who wanted to emulate her performance in the gym or on the hockey field. But there was a spark of competitiveness between them, all the same.

'I can't stop!' Gemma said, laughing. 'I'm so hyped up I think I shall go on singing for ever.'

'Yes, well, some of us would prefer that you didn't.'

'Jealous, Pen? You've no need to be. You did all right,' Gemma said generously. 'Even Laura hit the right notes most of the time. And I'm sorry if we couldn't have a hockey match on stage so that you could shine.'

Penny's eyes flashed. 'Well, it was pretty obvious why you wanted us to be a singing act.'

'What's that supposed to mean? For God's sake, lighten up. We were great together, like we always are. Don't spoil it now. I don't want to leave here tomorrow with your resentment ringing in my ears.'

'I don't want to leave here at all,' Laura said.

They both turned to look at her, sitting mouselike on her bed while they wrangled. And suddenly seeming as small and vulnerable as she had been when they all arrived at the Wellesley five years ago.

'We all have to go on, Laura,' Gemma smiled sympathetically, softening at once. 'We can't remain as we are for ever.'

'Gem's right,' Penny agreed at once. 'What would we do here, anyway? Become the oldest trio in the place, or turn into the Misses Haley and Grimes?'

Laura grinned at the thought of the three women tutors who lived together, as string-beaned in shape and literary in mind as it was possible to be.

'I can't quite see that,' she said, acknowledging Gemma's dark-haired beauty, and Penny's bouncy red curls that she desperately tried to straighten every morning. And herself, rounded and nice-looking enough, she supposed, and never in a million years

10

destined to be one of the intensely serious Misses Haley and Grimes variety.

'Let's stop getting maudlin,' Gemma took charge briskly. 'We're going to a disco, and nobody's going to stop us making out with any guy we fancy, because what can they do to us? They can't suspend us, or put us on report, because we've finished here for good. So let's make the most of tonight and leave tomorrow to take care of itself.'

The disco was held in the main hall, cleared now after the concert, with chairs and tables placed around the sides, and a bar of soft drinks set up at the far end. It was to be held strictly under Wellesley rules – 'with no alcohol, smoking, drugs or sex,' Gemma said solemnly. At which they all doubled up, remembering their last sociology lesson, when the unlikely Miss Grimes had tried to advise them on the evils and temptations they might encounter in the future. And ending up declaring grandly that the whole wide world was a voyage of discovery for them, and to be sure to travel it wisely.

'What does she want us to do? Try it all out, or live like nuns?' Penny had whispered.

But unexpectedly, Gemma had shivered. The Bermondsey flats in London, where she lived with her grandmother, had been the scene of a vicious, drug-related gang attack just recently, and she had vowed there and then that she was never going to be part of that scene. That was one thing Miss Grimes need never fear. It still left three vices, anyway . . .

But she wasn't going to think about that tonight. By

11

the time they reached the main hall the music had begun, and the on-duty tutors were trying to look as if they were enjoying themselves. It was a scream, really. For one moment, Gemma was tempted to pull old Jonesy onto the floor, but he'd probably expire if he had to do anything more than a fox-trot or a waltz. Laura, of course, wouldn't see anything wrong in what the kids derisively called joined-up dancing. Smooching was hardly any different, and there was certainly nothing wrong with that, though she doubted if they'd get many of those thrown in tonight. But it was a sure bet that they'd have to have the occasional strict-tempo stuff as well, just to satisfy the tutors.

'This is stupid,' Penny said irritably a while later. 'It's just as if the fifties theme has overlapped into the disco.'

They looked around, seeing how so many of the girls hung about in groups, and the boys were in no hurry to get up and dance.

'It's too bright in here, that's the trouble. I'm going to turn most of the lights off –'

'Gemma, you can't!' Laura said. 'You'll get –'

'What? Slung out? They can't do that, dummy. And whoever went to a dance where all the lights were full on?'

Determinedly, she marched over to where the light switches were, and without making it too obvious, selected the ones that she knew would put out all but the ones above the recording equipment. The room was immediately plunged into a more intimate atmosphere, and a great cheer went up from all the students. As if it was right on cue, the wild music currently on the tape ended, and a slower melody came on. For anyone who dared to do it, and who had a partner, it was perfect for smooching.

'Laura?'

She jerked up her head as the male voice sounded close to her, and her face flushed.

'Oh, Tommy, hi.'

He held out his hands. 'Are you dancing, or what?'

God, what finesse. She could hear the other two giggling behind her, and damn it, they both knew that Tommy Hall had originally sought her out because their fathers were farming neighbours, and he'd had some daft idea of looking out for her. He was hardly God's gift – but even as she thought it, another thought swept through her mind. Nobody had asked the glamorous Gemma to dance yet, nor Penny. But somebody had asked her, ordinary Laura.

She allowed Tommy to pull her to her feet, and let herself be pressed close to him. He smelled faintly of body odour and she couldn't miss the sweaty feel of his palms on her back. Obediently, she clasped her hands around his neck, and pretended that she was in the arms of some terrific hunk . . . but that was a rotten thing to do, when he was nice enough, and she wouldn't want to hurt his feelings.

'I really like you, Laura,' he mouthed against her hair. 'Maybe when we get back home, you'll come out with me sometime.'

'Oh, I don't know about that,' she said hastily. 'Dad was against the idea of me coming away to school in the first place, and it was only Mum who persuaded him. He'll be keeping his eyes on me from now on.'

It was the feeblest excuse, and she knew it. It should put anybody off. But amazingly, she felt Tommy's arms tighten around her. She could feel every bit of him. She could feel the buckle on the belt of his jeans pressing into her. And not only that. She swallowed, her mouth suddenly dry, feeling the hardness of him, and knowing he was becoming horny. And it was the last thing she wanted. Not *Tommy Hall* . . .

'See what you do to me, Laura?' he muttered hoarsely. 'When we get back to the village, I'll ask your Dad if I can take you out, if it bothers you so much.'

'Let's just wait and see, shall we? Anyway, I'm not planning anything for the next few months. After this hectic last term I just want to relax and do a bit of work around the farm until I decide what I want to do.'

'OK. But you're not thinking of university, are you? It wouldn't be your style, Laura.'

She felt a flare of annoyance. 'Why not?'

He shrugged. 'You wouldn't cope with it. You're too sweet and natural to be in among those types.'

'You make me sound as boring as a sugar lump.'

Tommy laughed as heartily as if she'd made some hugely witty remark, and squeezed her even tighter.

'I love the taste of sugar,' he whispered, in what was obviously meant to be a sexy voice.

'None of us intends going to university,' she snapped. 'We've all had enough of school.'

'I'm not interested in your friends. They're not as brainy as you, anyway.'

14

She refused to rise to this, whether it was supposed to be a compliment or not. She extricated herself from his octopus embrace as soon as the music ended, and walked back to where she'd left the others. By now, Gemma was tightly wrapped in some guy's arms on the dance floor, and seemingly unable to tear herself away from him.

Penny sat with her arms crossed, glowering, and just as Laura was wondering what was wrong, and how to handle it, the lights were snapped on, and everybody groaned with the shock of it. But it had the desired effect of breaking up the tightly-locked couples still on the floor, and Gemma returned to them, hot and bothered, and with a love-bite on her neck.

'Let's go to the cloakroom,' she said, grabbing their hands. 'I have to tell you about Dirk.'

'*DIRK*!' Penny shrieked. 'That's a made-up name if ever I heard one. Why is he going under an alias?'

Gemma wouldn't say any more until they reached the girls' cloakroom, and saw thankfully that they had it to themselves.

'Shut up and listen. He's got some booze with him, so we're going up to our room, and I want you to cover for me. If anybody asks, just say that I'm somewhere around, and you saw me dancing just a minute ago, right?'

'Gemma, this isn't a good idea,' Laura said at once.

'Yes, it is, little Miss Puritan, so don't try to stop me. We can only disappear for a short while, so nothing much is going to happen.'

But from the excitement in Gemma's eyes, they all knew she was hoping that it would.

'Gem, be careful,' Penny warned, suddenly. 'You know damn well what I mean.'

'Don't worry. He's got something else with him too,' she grinned. 'It won't be the first time, and I do know how to be careful.'

She was the only one of them who'd sneaked out with boys on a regular basis, and had graphically completed their sexual education on her return. She did them a favour, she said grandly, because now they knew what to expect. Though if Laura ever imagined doing some of the things Gemma described with Tommy Hall, it was enough to turn her off the thought of sex permanently. And Penny was more interested in sport, and the prospect of the horse her parents were buying for her as soon as she got out of this place.

But if this was what Gemma wanted, they'd fight tooth and nail to see that she wasn't caught.

'You know we'll cover for you, Gem,' Penny promised. 'It's our last chance, after all.'

They looked at one another, and the enormity of this day, and the future that began tomorrow, overwhelmed them simultaneously. The ready tears filled Laura's eyes. Penny looked stricken, and Gemma's high colour faded a little as they clutched each other's hands.

'I'm going to miss you both so much.' Laura spoke in a choked voice.

'Well, it's not as if we'll never meet again, is it?' Gemma asked, her voice shaking for once.

'Yes, it is,' Penny said. 'We'll all go our separate ways, like everybody does. Laura will hibernate on that Somerset farm of hers, you'll go back to London and be swallowed up in the crowds, and I'll just concentrate on my riding. But Gloucestershire's miles from any of you, and boarding school's hell for that reason. We all come from different parts of the country, and when we split, we'll forget each other.'

'No, we won't!' Gemma was ferocious now. 'We won't let that happen to us. We mean too much to one another. We'll keep in touch . . . but let's do more than that. Let's make a pact here and now to meet up every two years, come what may. We can make it here in Cheltenham, or anywhere you like, but let's just *do* it, even if I become a famous pop star and Penny turns into a super athlete, and Laura ends up with a husband and a houseful of kids,' she finished wildly.

And suddenly, their super-charged emotions were becoming more than they could bear, so they all agreed on it quickly, and turned to leave the cloakroom before they all cracked up completely.

CHAPTER 1

LAURA

The wonderful smell of newmown hay drifted into Laura's bedroom, tantalizing her senses. This was the very best time of the year on the farm, when everything was warm and blossoming and green, and looking at its most spectacular, as if it had been painted by a magic hand. She adored the rural life, from the fields surrounding their own white-washed farm buildings nestling in the Somerset countryside, where their own cattle softly grazed, to the soaring, hazy Mendip Hills beyond. There was a continuity and a completeness about it all that touched Laura's romantic soul.

And this was her favourite time of day. These waking, private moments before the work of the day began. When she could lie on her bed in the bedroom where she had been born; lie and stretch and just *be*.

But she wouldn't be doing any work today. She felt a sliver of excitement run through her veins. Today she was driving up to Cheltenham in the new-to-her second-hand Mini, having just passed her test. She was meeting Gemma and Penny for the first time since leaving the Wellesley two years ago, and she still didn't know how she'd managed to contain herself from even telling them she'd been taking driving lessons.

Not that you needed too many lessons when you were born and bred on a farm. On private land you could drive around in whatever vehicle was available, and she'd driven a tractor under her father's tuition before she ever sat behind the wheel of the Mini.

'Laura, are you up yet?' she heard her father bellow from the yard below, and she got hastily out of bed, knowing how he needed her presence over breakfast.

The biggest shock of her life had happened a month after her return from boarding school. After all those years away from them, living a separate life from her parents, she'd been looking forward to settling into family life all over again. And then her mother had died from a heart attack, and her father had gone to pieces.

From then on, Laura's future had been decided. She was no academic, and her dearest wish was to stay on the farm and help out. And after those first long weeks of disbelief and desolate grief, when her dad had clung to her so inconsolably, it was obvious that it was his dearest wish as well. He didn't pressure her, but it was what they both wanted, and somehow they had come to terms with a heartbreaking situation.

And one thing Laura's mother had never failed to do was to be up early to share as leisurely a breakfast as was possible on a busy working farm. Now Laura had taken over her mother's role, and was happy to do so.

'I'm coming, Dad,' she called out, scrambling into

the shorts and T-shirt she wore first thing. He would already have done an hour or so's work before coming in for breakfast, as most farmers did. Once the meal was over and he went outside again, she always took a quick shower and changed, ready for the day ahead.

'Today's the day then, is it?' he greeted her when she arrived downstairs in the huge flag-stoned kitchen they had never tried to update. The old Aga exuded a welcome warmth in the cool kitchen, and the mouth-watering smell of sizzling bacon came from the heavy blackened pan on top of it.

She gave her father a quick kiss on his leathery cheek, ruddy from years of exposure to the Somerset winds, and told him he should have waited for her to start breakfast.

'I know you, girl,' he said with a grin. 'Your head will be up in the clouds today, and when the day comes that I can't sling a few rashers into a pan, I'll hang up my boots.'

The kettle was singing now, and Laura quickly made a pot of tea, as strong as he liked it. For a moment, she had a quick flash of forward vision, seeing herself and her best friends drinking delicately-flavoured tea out of china cups in a posh Cheltenham tea-room. And almost defiantly, she took down the two thick pottery breakfast mugs with their homely pictures of Dartmoor ponies on them, and the jug with its patterned willow design that she had so loved as a child.

'Don't you go hurrying back today,' her dad ordered. 'Take as long as you like with your friends. We'll have plenty of helpers to get the rest of the hay in.'

'You're sure?' she asked a trifle guiltily, even though she knew it was true.

The Somerset farmers had a tradition of helping one another when it came to hay-making or lambing or any tasks that took a concerted effort. Despite the balers and the new, sophisticated machinery that replaced many of the old, back-breaking methods of farming, it was how many smaller farmers managed to stay afloat, in defiance of all the government restrictions and low profits. Their fierce love of the land was stronger than any petty rules and regulations.

'I'm sure. Farmer Hall's coming over with his boys, and the Johnsons and Millers have promised to put in an appearance. We should be finished here today, and we'll all be over at the Halls' tomorrow.'

She was just glad there were no obstacles to stop her taking off at this busiest time of the farming calendar.

'And at the end of next week, when all the hay is in, we'll have a great supper,' she promised him. It was their turn to be hosts.

And that was another tradition that was unique to the farming community. When the work was done, the celebrations could begin. The continuity of it all had always charmed Laura. It was almost spiritual. Whatever else happened in the world, the story of life that was encapsulated in a farming community never altered. Life, and death, and all the dramas in between, were part and parcel of it all.

She felt the touch of her father's finger on her cheek. 'I know,' he said gruffly, misunderstanding the sudden softness in her eyes. 'Your mother should be here with us. But she'll be present in spirit, Laura. She always will be.'

And for a down-to-earth farmer with seemingly no poetry in his soul, that was poetry indeed.

Laura swallowed the lump in her throat and turned to the Aga to put the fresh-that-morning eggs into the frying pan before her eyes threatened to fill completely. And that would do neither of them any good at all. Her dad had work to do, and she was meeting the two best friends she hadn't seen since that last day at the Wellesley when they had made their pact.

There had been letters, and Christmas and birthday cards, of course, and the occasional phone call. Especially from an ecstatic Gemma, who had met an agent in London who was going to do wonderful things for her in a future singing career. She admitted that nothing much had happened yet, but the signs were good . . . and since her zodiac sign for the coming year had promised great and wonderful professional opportunities for her, nothing could dim her optimism!

They would all have changed, though. They were two years older, for one thing. They were eighteen now, and so far, none of them was romantically attached. Not that Laura expected Penny to be too bothered about that. Penny had phoned her just last week to assure her that she'd make it today, come hell or high water, despite the most exciting news imaginable. And nothing was going to make her divulge it on the phone, so Laura could just whistle for it.

'You're a prize pig, Penny Bishop,' she had laughed into the phone, reverting so easily into their old

Wellesley jargon it was almost impossible to believe that two years had passed.

'I know,' Penny said cheerfully. 'But don't let it worry you. I'll tell you all when we meet.'

'Can't you just give me a hint?'

'Not likely – and spoil my big surprise? Anyway, we'll all have plenty to talk about and a lot of catching up to do, so you'll just have to be patient. You usually managed that all right, didn't you?'

After Laura had hung up she went about her chores, laughing at the busily clucking, feed-hungry hens and chicks as they followed her about the yard as if she was a Pied Piper. And then her smile gradually began to fade as it dawned on her that the other two obviously had exciting news.

Gemma – well, God only knew what Gemma had been up to lately. Her letters were always full of suppressed excitement about this marvellous agent and the people he introduced her to, and the singing career that wasn't yet taking off, but which was always just on the brink . . .

And Penny – whatever she had to tell them, there had been the same brimming excitement in her voice. New scenes, new people, new adventures. They both had them in abundance. While Laura . . . what the hell did *she* have to tell them?

She'd learned to drive, and she'd passed her test a week after her eighteenth birthday. She was quite into jam-making, simply because her dad loved home-made apple and blackberry jam so much, and because she adored the way the old kitchen became so filled with the heavenly scent, bringing her mother's presence back to her so poignantly . . . She could queen it with the best of them at village fêtes and local events when required. And at the drop of a hat she was happy to provide open-air suppers on any occasion, with their own home-cured hams and scrumpy cider for their neighbours.

But suddenly it all sounded so dreadfully dull, and more than that. It was just so *rural*. It couldn't compare with the high life in London that Gemma was enjoying, by all accounts. Nor the horsey set into which Penny was now moving in Gloucestershire, aided and abetted by her well-heeled parents. Though if the Bishop parents were looking for a similarly well-heeled marriage for Penny, Laura thought they could probably forget it. By now, Penny had decided that riding was her thing, and she didn't intend getting involved with a man for years yet, if ever. Nor with a woman either, she added with a grin, just in case her best friends thought she was going slightly off-centre.

Of course, Laura thought, she could always invent a boyfriend. Her soft mouth twisted. Why invent one, when that dope Tommy Hall was still hanging around and driving her mad? She'd gone out with him a number of times, especially when she'd needed a partner for a village dance. Once or twice, well into the scrumpy, he'd tried to put his hand up her sweater, and once or twice she'd let it stay there for a few minutes, just to see what it felt like.

But it did absolutely nothing for her, except for the mechanical reaction of sending her nipple shooting outwards. And since that got him panting his scrumpy breath all over her, she soon squashed any ideas of that nature. But it was ridiculous, she sometimes thought angrily. She was as innocent of sex as a kitten, and at eighteen years old any girl had a right to be no longer a virgin.

Damn it, all the magazines told you so. And she had yearnings, like any normal girl. There was nothing odd about her. Nothing frigid. At least, she hoped there wasn't. She felt a frisson of anxiety whenever her thoughts got to that point. Because she wanted to love and be loved, and to have as satisfactory a marriage as her parents had done. She was a conventional girl, and if that meant being a virgin until marriage, so be it. All the same . . . all the theory in the world didn't tell you what the actual practice was like. And maybe she wouldn't be *that* conventional if the right man came along . . . and there was one thing she *was* bloody sure about. It wasn't Tommy Hall.

Once she was on the road for Cheltenham she put all such thoughts behind her. She was looking forward eagerly to this first meeting. She and her friends would have changed physically, but inside, they'd still be the same. The Three Musketeers, all for one and one for all. She grinned, thinking how daft and solemn they must have seemed when vowing such things, and got a passing whistle from a couple of lads in an open-topped sports car who thought she was grinning at them.

''Ello, darling!' they yelled out.

And because she felt so good and so happy, she

laughed back and waved at them. Her spirits were lifting by the minute, but she was still quite new to driving this car and knew she'd better keep her wits about her. She wasn't yet used to the motorway, so had kept to the old roads, pulling into a wayside café when she was about halfway there.

A quick cup of coffee and a call at the ladies' cloakroom was all she needed. And when she looked in the cracked mirror above the washbasin, even she could see why those yobs had whistled and yelled at her.

She was flushed with excitement, her generous mouth pink and mobile. Her eyes, complemented by the blue dress she wore, were larger and bluer than ever. The fair hair that she normally kept tied back in a pony-tail for work had been left loose for today, and it streamed out over her shoulders in the summer breeze. She looked good, she thought, with pleasure. She'd never be a sex-symbol like Gemma, nor sophisticated like Penny, but she looked good, and nobody needed more than that.

It was almost lunchtime by the time she found the small tea-room where they'd arranged to meet, with thankfully a car park at the rear. They did lunches as well as teas, and the friends planned to eat here, then maybe take a wander around some of their old haunts, although the last thing they intended was to turn up at the Wellesley. They had always despised those Old Girls who couldn't seem to stay away, clinging to the past like limpets. But it would be fun to take a walk around the perimeter, and remember.

Laura was the first to arrive, which didn't surprise

her in the least. She was always on time, whatever the occasion, while Gemma always had to re-do her make-up half a dozen times, and change her dress and her shoes . . . and Penny was always late for everything. She couldn't think why it annoyed her now, even more than it had done before. But it wasn't so much the tardiness of the others; it was more the predictability of herself.

'This is Miss Grover's table, isn't it, Miss?' the waitress asked her for the third time when the tea-room began to fill with middle-aged, blue-rinsed matrons and classy younger women, awash with jewellery and designer clothes. 'Only she did book it for three people, and we're getting rather full.'

'I'm sorry, but my friends must have been delayed, and yes, it is Miss Grover's table,' Laura said, as the thin-faced woman looked at her with disapproval written all over her. Out of the corner of her eye she saw a taxi pull up outside, and to her immense relief, Gemma stepped out of it.

'Miss Grover's here now,' she told the waitress coldly, 'and I'm sure Miss Bishop won't be far behind.'

God, but she sounded as if she was acting out some stupid melodrama, Laura thought, as the woman swished away. And then she didn't give a damn what anybody thought, as Gemma swept into the tea-room as if she owned the place.

'Bloody train from Paddington got held up for thirty minutes,' she greeted Laura, uncaring how loudly she spoke. She hugged her wildly, and then stepped back a pace to look her over. 'You look wonderful, darling!

28

The country evidently suits you, and I want to hear *everything* about all those gorgeous young farmers.'

She took Laura's breath away. For one thing, she was so self-confident, and that theatrical 'darling' placed her firmly in a professional mould. But it was far more than that. The once-wild glossy black hair had been slicked and moulded about her face, and the perfume she exuded was sexy and strong. Her red tight-fitting trousers and shiny cream shirt, with the top buttons left casually undone, shrieked that she was a city girl, as if anybody could mistake the fact. The heavy make-up was perfect in its almost grossly exaggerated effect, but she *was* beautiful. God, but she was so beautiful. And Laura felt totally inadequate beside her.

'So come on, darling,' Gemma was saying now. 'Tell me all your news and then I'll tell you mine.'

'Not yet!' Laura said, knowing she was stalling for time. 'We have to wait for Penny. Otherwise we'll have to say it all over again.'

Though God knew what she had to say that could remotely compare with the expected thrills of this girl's life. You only had to look at her to know that she would make a success of whatever she set her mind to do. She had always been the strong one of the trio, and she was strong now. The glint of ambition that had been in her eyes when old Jonesy told her she was destined to have a singing career, was now a burning light.

There was a sudden stir of interest from the other clients in the tea-room. Their alcove table was at the back of the café where they could talk relatively undisturbed, and several ladies craned their necks to see the sleek black Daimler purr up to the kerbside. Even the Cheltenham dames were intrigued to see who was being driven around by a uniformed chauffeur. Maybe royalty . . .?

Penny alighted from the back seat with a brief smile at her driver, and glanced at her watch.

'I think you'd better call back for me in about three hours, Andrews. I can't be definite about the time, and if I'm not ready to leave by then, you can always come back later.'

'Right you are, Miss,' the man said, touching his cap.

She spoke to him with the ease of someone well used to dealing with such a situation, and he responded in a like manner. She was well aware of the stir of interest on her arrival, but ignored it. All that mattered was seeking out her two best friends.

They fell on one another with screams of delight that set some of the matrons tut-tutting, and others wistfully wishing they could be as young, as frivolous, as joyful in meeting one another as these three. There were no inhibitions, and no shortage of chatter from the alcove table.

'You look marvellous, Gem,' Penny said at once. 'But it's no more than I expected. And so do you, Laura!'

Was it an afterthought, or was it genuine? Laura was annoyed at even thinking it. And even more annoyed at how her pleasure in her second-hand Mini was diminishing by the second. After seeing Penny's arrival in the swish, chauffeur-driven Daimler, it would be the anticlimax of all anti-climaxes to show it off.

But her chin lifted. Damn it, it was *hers*, and she'd bought it herself by scrimping and saving, and with the aid of a few generous birthday and Christmas presents. And she hadn't been born into money, like Penny, who could have anything she wanted just by a casual mention. Neither had Gemma . . . though she always looked like a million dollars anyway.

That irritating sense of inadequacy was starting to seep into Laura's veins again, and she quickly smothered it.

'So what's been happening to you, Pen?' Gemma asked eagerly. 'Is there a man on the horizon yet?'

Penny's snort would have done justice to one of her beloved horses in her father's stables. She had developed into a tall, elegant girl, her red curls finally tamed into a wet-look style, which made her appear more sophisticated than ever. She was very slender, almost angular, and her slightly aloof air made her intriguing to every man who met her. Which was just unfortunate for them, she always concluded in her caustic manner.

'I'm not wasting my time on men,' she retorted. 'I prefer horses.'

'Good God, Pen, you can't go to bed with a horse,' Gemma put in at once.

'Who said anything about going to bed with them? There's more to relationships than that!' Penny's green eyes were beginning to sparkle.

'Is there?' Gemma said innocently, and Laura could see all the old warning signs between these two. The sparring, the teasing that sometimes veered into taunting and occasionally into outright bitchiness. It wasn't what they were here for, but it was so like the way they had always been that she found herself laughing out loud.

Gemma looked at her in surprise, as if only just registering that she was there.

'What's tickling you, for God's sake?'

'You two! We might never have left the Wellesley from the way you're carrying on. If we're not careful, these old ducks will think we've skipped classes for the day.'

'Not looking like this, they won't,' Gemma grinned. 'And not many Wellesley girls skip classes in a chauffeur-driven Daimler, either.'

Laura suddenly saw something she had never perceived before, in all their five years together. Gemma truly resented the fact that Penny had had everything handed to her on a plate, while she had been sent to the boarding school through a bequest from a grateful patient her grandmother had nursed back to health. She would never have made it otherwise. But it was extraordinary how the resentment had never been quite so obvious as it was to Laura right then.

Penny laughed. 'Remember how we used to do that?' she said good-humouredly. 'Especially Gemma, sneaking out to meet the boys from next door.'

Gemma shrugged her shoulders. 'What the hell else were they there for, if not to meet us?'

Laura said, 'I don't think that was the sole purpose!'

'Well, you wouldn't, would you?' Gemma's words were softened by a smile. 'Anybody who was satisfied with the likes of Tommy Hall – '

'I never was! I told you I was choosey, and he just happened to be around. Besides, I couldn't very well snub him. His farm is next to ours, and it would have been very awkward if we weren't on speaking terms.'

'Have you seen him since, Laura?' Penny asked.

'I can't miss him!' Laura said, trying to suppress a groan. 'He's always hanging around our place giving my dad a hand at something or other.'

'And giving you a hand too?' Gemma grinned again.

Laura felt her fair skin go hotter. 'Not in the way you mean. I told you, I don't fancy him. He's just always been *there*, like the wallpaper.'

'So you'll probably end up marrying him and having a dozen kids, just like we said,' Gemma replied.

'I will not. Tommy Hall's the last person on earth I'd marry. Let's talk about something else. You don't usually spend this much time talking about me, anyway.'

She was the pithy one now, knowing it was true. But what did it matter? she thought generously. These two had far more glamorous and interesting lives than she did, and for the next couple of hours, while they ate their way through lunch (frugal for Gemma because of her figure; strictly vegetarian for Penny; and joyfully calorific for Laura), and then avoided the waitress's disapproval by drinking endless cups of coffee, they compared notes of what was happening now, and their future plans.

Penny's plans were vague after all. It was a bit of a let-down. There was talk of show-jumping and hunt balls, and a world which neither Laura nor Gemma could

33

remotely envisage. None of them had ever visited each other's homes, and Laura fervently hoped it would stay that way. The thought of hobnobbing with upper-crust folk who spoke with plums in their mouths was enough to make her quail. How the hell had three such unlikely companions ever become so close? she found herself marvelling. But close they had been, and close they were. And the fact that they could wrangle and bicker and still remain so intimate was proof of their feelings for one another.

'My agent's getting somebody important to come and hear me at the Blue Parrot Club next month,' Gemma burst out at last, careful to let them in on the best bits without mentioning the sordid undertones of the club in question. 'If it goes well, who knows where it may lead?'

'That's fantastic, Gem!' Penny exclaimed. 'Will we be able to come and hear you?'

'Why not?' Gemma said, smothering any thoughts of their reaction at the location. 'I'll let you both know a suitable date, and maybe we could have a night together in London. How about it, Laura? Can you get the hayseeds out of your hair for long enough?'

'I might just manage it.' Her tone was deliberately cool.

'So what's new with you? You've said next to nothing,' Penny said encouragingly.

'That's because I couldn't get a word in edgeways,' Laura replied smartly. 'Well, I've learnt to drive and passed my test, and I've bought myself a second-hand car. I drove here today in it, as a matter of fact,' she added as nonchalantly as she could.

34

'My God, our little Laura's coming out of her shell at last.' Gemma's voice was rough with affection. 'Good for you, kid. Do we all get a ride in this jalopy?'

This cut her down to size at once. For of course, in Gemma's eyes, Laura's car would have to be a jalopy, a run-around – the kind of heap a housewife drove to the shops or used for dropping off her kids at school.

And oddly enough, the thought of all that didn't seem half-bad to Laura at all. But she was damned if she was going to admit her longing for such a humdrum, ordinary lifestyle to these two ambitious best friends.

CHAPTER 2

GEMMA

Once she left school, Gemma took whatever singing job she could get, in pubs or retirement homes, or the occasional amateur musical production. She was prepared to sing anywhere and to go where there was work. And the small-time agent she met, Rube Steiner, was prepared to help her on her way. *Have voice, will travel*, she sometimes thought with a grin.

She was well used to travelling by train. She enjoyed it, at least on the mainline trains. She liked the attention she got from fellow travellers, whether it was a surreptitious look from a stuffy businessman at her long, slender legs, or the lecherous, bolder stares from younger men. She was vivacious and beautiful, and very aware of her own sensuality. Her dark hair was rinsed now into a glossy frame for her oval face, her velvety brown eyes heavily fringed with mascara to make them wider and more luminous. And her voluptuous shape was always accentuated by figure-hugging clothes.

The one thing she didn't like about all the attention she got, were the leering gestures and catcalls from some of the building-site workers she had to pass every day on her way to the modest flat which was the only home she could afford for now until she went upmarket. In particular, she loathed the uniform of low-slung jeans showing half their backsides, and their sweaty sleeveless vests. One day, as soon as she could, she intended getting right away from Bermondsey, but right now everything she earned went on the necessary clothes and make-up and publicity photographs to promote her image.

'It goes with the territory,' Rube told her in his lisping voice. 'You look like a star, and people will believe you're a star. You need the image, kid, and the rest will come later. And so what if you attract the wrong kind of guys? Sex is what it's all about. If you ain't got sex-appeal, you're in the wrong business, ain't yer? You got to get the punters panting with lust so they can't wait to get home and bang merry hell out of their wives. And you know how to keep 'em from getting too fresh.'

Gemma also knew by now that he never minced his words, and the last bit was said more sharply. Once, when he'd thought he was dazzling her with all his exaggerated talk of making her a star, he'd tried to paw her, forcing his leg between Gemma's, and expecting sex as a favour in return. Instead, she had kneed him where it hurt most, bruising his most sensitive parts as well as his ego.

'Who the bloody hell do you think you are, kid?' he'd shouted, shocked fury in his eyes. 'Right now I'm your bread and butter – remember?'

'I'm not in it for kicks,' she'd shouted back. 'I'm in it to make a career for myself, and if you won't help me without all this, I'll find somebody who will.'

But later on, talking to other artistes on his books, Gemma quickly realized that the general feeling was that if an agent like Rube Steiner was prepared to take on a little nobody with potential, then the least the little nobody could do was to drop her knickers for him. That went with the territory. If she chose not to co-operate, well . . . he could dump her so fast she'd never be heard of again.

'Well, then, I'll be the first to dump *him*,' she retorted, and she made it clear she meant every word.

But whatever Rube's feelings, he left her alone after that. Maybe, as the same club managers began asking for her to return time and again, it began to dawn on Rube that he could be onto a winner after all, and he needed her as much as she needed him. He still couldn't resist the odd dig though.

'In the music business, anything goes, kid, and you'd better believe it,' he was forever telling her.

But she was stubborn, said she didn't see it that way. Yet he'd bet his bottom dollar that she wasn't a virgin. He could smell 'em a mile off. She'd been around, even if it was only with some of the snot-nosed kids at that fancy school of hers that she never talked about, and where only Gemma knew she'd had the rough edges of her accent knocked off.

But then he'd thought more generously about her. The voice, speaking as well as singing, was part of what made her so smoulderingly sexy to the clients in the small clubs where he'd fixed gigs for her so far. That earthy, sexy look, and the way she gazed at every guy as if she was singing only for him, and that unexpectedly beautiful diction that went with it, lifted her way out of the ordinary . . .

Oh yes, she had something all right. Rube had a nose for success, and this one was definitely heading for it. But not yet. She wasn't ready for the big time yet. She had to be moulded, to learn patience, and to work her way up. Too many so-called stars had come and gone overnight, and it wasn't what Rube wanted for Gemma. She had to be a stayer. And the lure of the big bucks she was going to earn for him in commission was part of the reason he didn't push the sleeping arrangements, much as he'd like to.

In fact, even thinking about it gave him a surge of pleasure in his loins, and sent him into his den to concentrate on gigs and fixtures for his other clients, instead of lusting over the delectable Miss Gemma Grover.

Gemma didn't care for the Underground any more, even though it was quick and she'd often used it to cross London. But she'd turned her back on it since the time she'd been travelling back late at night from a gig, still in her stage-gear and make-up, and feeling pretty wrung out. There were few people on such a late train, so it was hardly worth worrying about her appearance. For once, Gemma didn't want to be noticed, and she didn't even look up when a man sat beside her and tried to strike up a conversation.

'Nice dress,' he said.

Gemma ignored him, and closed her eyes. It was late and she was tired. And he smelled none too savoury. Why the hell couldn't he have sat somewhere else, when there were dozens of empty seats?

'Go away,' she muttered.

'Unfriendly,' she heard him say disapprovingly. 'Shame. Nice tits too.'

Gemma felt a stab of alarm. But she wouldn't look at him. If they once made eye contact she'd see the kind of man he was, and she already knew enough about that. She allowed her eyes to open just a fraction, looking down the length of the carriage, and seeing that there were only a few passengers on it besides herself and the man.

There were several giggling girls, huddled together and no doubt recounting their night's adventures; an elderly man waiting to get out at the next stop; and a couple of muscly men with the close-cropped haircuts that suggested they might be Army types. If she had any sense, she'd go and sit near the girls.

Before she could put the thought into action, the train drew up at a stop, and the girls got out. Gemma was tempted to get out too, but she must have dozed off before the man sat beside her. She wasn't absolutely sure where she was, and the train had stopped on the platform between signs. Besides, if she tried to get out, she'd have to step over his sprawling legs, and he might follow her.

Without warning, her nerves got the better of her. She could scream, but he hadn't actually done anything, and she'd make herself look such a bloody fool. She decided to ignore him, and pray that he got out before she did.

'What do you think of this?' he said suddenly.

Alarm bells screamed through her head, but an irresistible instinct, curiosity, or just plain compulsion, made her turn her head. She still wouldn't meet his eyes, and so her gaze went downwards to where his flabby penis lay exposed outside his trousers.

It was ugly, disgusting, and even as it revolted her, the instinct of self-preservation took over. Hardly stopping to think what she was doing, Gemma bashed down on it hard with the heavy leather bag that contained all her make-up and towels and daytime clothes, and she kept right on bashing as he howled out in pain and rage.

'Somebody help me!' she managed to shriek, and at the sound of her voice the Army types leapt to their feet. They were beside her in an instant, while the man screamed at her.

'The bitch asked for it. Flaunting herself with her tits like that – '

Gemma scrambled past him then, shamed and humiliated. She crouched back against the farthest seat on the other side of the carriage as the two men held him down, while she sat snivelling in a state of shock.

Then, to her horror, she saw the Army types start to beat the man up until his face was a bloody pulp. She heard herself whimpering. She hadn't wanted this. He might be a pervert, but he didn't deserve this. Not this savagery.

'Are you OK, love?' one of the Army types finally turned to her and said. She could see the pervert's blood on his hands, and she felt sick. She nodded.

'Where do you want to go?'

He sounded concerned enough, but by now she wasn't prepared to trust anyone. There were two of them, and they were big and powerful, and for all she knew they might think she was as easy as the pervert had done. All too late she realized what a mistake it had been to travel so late at night in her glittery stage-dress, but if she'd stopped to change, she'd never have got home tonight.

'This is my stop,' she said quickly, as the train slowed down, even though she still had no idea where on earth she was. 'Somebody's meeting me here, so I'll be perfectly OK now. And thanks. I'm very grateful to you both.'

But not that grateful. Unconsciously, she had allowed the Wellesley vowels to slip into her speech, and if they had suspected that she was a tart, she prayed the accent would have stopped them in their tracks.

'Well, if you're sure . . .' the first guy said. The other one flexed his fingers, making the knuckles crack.

'Leave it, mate. This one's out of our league.'

Gemma felt doubly humiliated, wondering if they now thought she was a high-class call-girl with that plummy voice. But if it meant she could get out of this stifling carriage unmolested, she didn't care what they thought.

'Thanks again,' she gasped, without another glance at the pulpy mess of the man who'd sat beside her. Her legs were shaking so much she had no idea how she made it up to the surface of the tube station into the London street outside, but when she did, she gulped in great breaths of night air, feeling as if she'd run a hundred miles.

And when she saw the wonderful, welcome orange light of a cruising taxi, she waved like a madwoman, falling into the cab, and vowing never to take the Underground late at night again. In fact, she would only take it when she could get into a carriageful of women. From then on, as long as she could afford it, and especially when she could charge it to expenses, she took taxis everywhere.

Gemma knew she should just put it down to experience, but the memory of that night never left her, even though she never told anyone. And ironically, she was thinking about it on the morning she travelled by Underground to Paddington to catch the train to Cheltenham. Crammed and strap-hanging among the morning commuters, without enough space to put a pin between them, the situation could hardly have been more different from her nightmare, even if there were always men who used this forced intimacy to press up tightly against women.

The horror of that awful night had almost threatened to put her off sex for a while. But not for long. Not once she began a torrid and on-going thing with the sexy pianist in the band at the Blue Parrot Club.

She didn't expect it to last for ever. She wasn't that naive. Nor was she looking for the kind of commitment

Laura would want out of a relationship. Gemma needed to be free to pursue her career. Once she was on top, no pun intended, then she might just think about moving in with a guy on a semi-permanent basis.

But it had surprised her to discover how much Rube disapproved of their affair.

'Don't waste yourself on trash, kid,' he'd lisped. 'The guy's a bum. He'll never make it, and he'll drag you down with him. He's too fond of the juice, and once he gets the shakes in his fingers, he'll be finished. You'll be supporting him before you know it.'

'No, I won't. We're not talking marriage here, Rube.'

'Who's talking marriage, for fuck's sake? He'll drain you, kid, and believe me, I know what I'm talking about. I've seen it all before, and once he gets you to move in with him, it'll be the end of your independence.'

'Well, I've no intention of moving in with him, either,' she snapped, 'so you can stop worrying.'

It had never been her intention. And nor had she reckoned on Eddie moving into her flat. Sure, she'd invited him there on a number of occasions, and they'd had a high old time, but she'd never allowed him to stay until breakfast.

And then, the night before she was due to meet Laura and Penny for the first time in two years, Eddie came hammering on her door in the early hours. She pulled her dressing-gown around her and looked through the peep-hole in her door before opening it and letting him stumble inside. He was drenched to the skin from a downpour of rain, and shut out of his boarding-house because his landlady was fed up with his drunken ravings and the state he was in.

Gemma let him in because he simply had nowhere else to go. She scolded him as if he was a naughty child, stripping him out of his wet things while he stood as docile as a mouse, and drying him with a bath towel in front of her electric fire. There was no more sexual intent in her mind than flying to the moon. He was too drunk to notice, anyway. Or so she thought.

Until suddenly his arms wrapped themselves around her in a vice-like grip, and she knew he was no more drunk than she was. And that this was all a set-up.

'You've no idea how erotic and how bloody frustrating that was, having you undress me and dry me while I stood like a statue, pretending not to notice,' he grinned.

Gemma drew in her breath half-angrily. It wasn't the first time she'd undressed him, though never like this. Never while he stood so passively, nor without him undressing her as feverishly as she tore the clothes off him. He'd never come here uninvited before, either.

'What the hell do you want, Eddie?' she said.

He grabbed at her so hard that her knees buckled and they fell to the floor together. He was on top of her before she could protest . . . but suddenly the wantonness of the situation wouldn't even let her think of protesting. He was her lover, and he could excite her so fast that she felt dizzy with wanting him. Dizzy and wild, and uncaring . . .

His hands pushed aside the silky dressing-gown and

palmed her breasts for a moment, before sliding down the length of her thighs, squeezing and moulding her as his lips followed the trail of his hands. His fingers moved quickly inwards, feeling her, parting her, until she felt the rush of excitement flooding through her at his touch.

'You know what I bloody want,' he said hoarsely. 'Can't you feel what I want?'

He grabbed her hand and clamped it around his erection, and her legs parted so involuntarily she hardly knew it was happening. And then he was inside her, filling her. She was scorched by the electric fire, and scorched by his passion, and after a few furious thrusts he suddenly came. She gasped and clung wildly to him, her long fingernails scraping weals down the length of his back as her climax matched his.

'By God, girl, that was good,' Eddie muttered at last. He was completely spent, still inside her, but dwindling fast, and in no hurry to move away.

But Gemma was. She had long ago decided that she had a short orgasmic life. Once it was over, however spectacularly, it was over, and all she wanted to do now was sleep. Whoever these Amazonian women were who had one climax after another, she was never likely to be one of them. But quality, not quantity, suited her fine. She wriggled away from Eddie, with the excuse that her side was going to be red raw by morning if she didn't get away from the fire.

'And not the only thing, eh, babe?' he said with a wink and a leer.

It was the one thing she didn't like about him. He

could be crude at a time when she didn't want crudeness. She could spin a dirty joke with the best of them, but at moments like these, it wasn't what she wanted to hear. She remembered one of Laura's favourite words. *Finesse*. That was it. She wouldn't mind a bit of *finesse* now and then . . .

'You'd better go, Eddie, since I'm damn sure your landlady hasn't chucked you out at all,' she said quickly. 'I've got to be up early in the morning to catch a train to Cheltenham, and I don't want to look as if I've been out all night.'

She just managed to avoid saying *up* all night, knowing the interpretation he'd put on that.

'Cheltenham!' he echoed, as if he'd never heard of it. 'What the fuck do you want to go to Cheltenham for? That's a place for old ladies, not a luscious chick like you.'

'I went to boarding school there,' she told him, knotting her dressing-gown tightly around her again and flinging his clothes at him now. 'And before you say anything else, there was nothing snobbish about it. At least, not about me and my best friends. We're all meeting up again tomorrow.'

She remembered at once that Eddie knew nothing about her past life. All he knew was the image she presented at the Blue Parrot Club when she did her sexy numbers. He didn't know, and he didn't want to know. Theirs was a transient kind of relationship, requiring no background details, and no future plans, despite what Rube thought. There was only the here and now, and what they could both get out of a relationship. Gemma knew that well enough. She'd just never stopped to analyse it properly before.

On the train down from Paddington the next morning, Gemma wondered if she'd made a mistake in wearing the bright red skinny trousers and flashy shirt. But the outfit attracted plenty of attention, and she liked that. And she'd worn it in a kind of defiance against Cheltenham and all the stuffy things the town stood for.

Unfortunately, she had become all too conscious of the tarty image she presented. That bloody Eddie had made her start to think, and she resented him for it. He'd come to her flat last night, too damn cocksure of her response. And, as usual, he'd been right. But he didn't respect her. It had never bothered her before, nor had she stopped to think about it when she was having fun, but she was thinking about it now.

In particular she was thinking about Laura and Penny. They'd meet again in a couple of hours, and she hoped to God there wasn't going to be a terrible awkward silence between them as they all attempted to assess each other. She tried to imagine what they would look like, and how much they had changed.

Laura . . . had she turned into the typical image of the farmer's daughter – apple-cheeked and wearing chintzy, homespun dresses?

And Penny . . . despite her arch avowal that she had no interest in women, and preferred her horses to men, there had always been a tiny doubt in Gemma's mind on that score.

But why should she care? In showbusiness you met

all sorts. Damn it, she'd even performed in a pub full of transvestites one evening, and it had been oddly exciting to see men dressed as women and looking so unbelievably beautiful.

And while it didn't bother her one bit if somebody was AC/DC, or completely the other way, for some reason she didn't particularly want it applied to Penny.

'Is this seat taken?' she heard a low voice say on the train to Cheltenham. She groaned. Not another Underground-type pervert, please God . . . And then she turned to see a sweet-faced nun smiling down at her.

She said no, and thought that if ever there was a case for prayer, it was to pray right now that the nun wasn't a thought-reader. She felt a grin tugging at her lips, and tried to compose herself. It was funny how nuns made you go completely tongue-tied. You just didn't know what to say to them, but the nun was evidently keen to while away the journey in conversation.

'I'm Sister Clementine,' she said. 'On my way to retreat for a month.'

'Oh,' Gemma said, wondering what the hell that entailed. 'I'm sorry, but I don't follow you – '

The nun smiled again. 'And why should you, a pretty young woman of the world like yourself? It's no more than a time of silence and penitence, with time to think and pray.'

'I see.' It sounded ghastly to Gemma. Boring and ghastly. To her astonishment she heard the nun laugh softly.

'You don't need to hide your feelings from me, my dear. It's not a life that suits everybody, and I'm sure

49

yours is the right one for you. Tell me what you do.'

Well, sometimes I spend half the night fornicating with a man I'm not as crazy about as I thought I was, Sister . . .

'I'm a singer,' Gemma explained in a choked voice, thanking her lucky stars she hadn't said the words aloud.

'A singer! Are you now?' the nun said admiringly. 'We do a lot of singing at the convent, but I've no voice at all, I'm afraid. Can't get the right pitch, no matter how hard I try, and I admire anybody who can.'

'I have a friend like that,' Gemma told her companion, 'though she's not too bad if several of us sing together. We once did an act as the Beverly Sisters at a school concert.'

Now why the heck had she said all that? She stopped abruptly for two reasons. One, because she didn't expect Sister Clementine to have the faintest idea who the Beverly Sisters were. And two, because she was suddenly overcome with the most ridiculous sense of nostalgia for those other days. How crazy that was.

'Oh, I used to like the Beverly Sisters,' the nun said, and to Gemma's amazement she began to hum the melody of 'Sisters' beneath her breath.

It was horribly out of tune, but it had the effect of reinforcing all the feelings Gemma hadn't really expected to have for today. Of course she was looking forward to meeting Laura and Penny again, but privately she had wondered if this pact was such a good idea after all. Now she knew that it was. Some ties were just too strong to be severed.

Sister Clementine got out of the train first. Gemma

watched her black-clad figure walking along the platform, to be greeted by several more as they moved out to a waiting mini-bus. Going on retreat. Renewing their spiritual feelings. It sounded good, if you were into that kind of thing, Gemma thought, with a return to her more normal frame of mind. For a few minutes, she'd been almost carried away . . . and now, she began to wonder what kind of a high old time they really had.

Were there midnight feasts at the convent, the way there had been at the Wellesley? Or clandestine meetings with monks from a neighbouring Order . . .? Or bottles of booze brought into their cells until they were all blotto . . .?

The nun turned to wave to her as the train pulled out of the station, and Gemma felt her face flame. She knew she was becoming far too cynical by half. But as Rube would say, it went with the territory.

CHAPTER 3

PENNY

The eighteenth-century mansion deep in the Gloucestershire countryside was known to everyone in the locality as simply 'the Bishop place'. It had an air of history and gentility about it that couldn't be bought – the kind that only arose out of generations of the same family inhabiting its walls. The house was well hidden among the dips of its parks and woodlands, so that its relative proximity to motorways, and railway stations, and the trappings of commercial life, passed almost unheeded over its serene head.

That it was also within metaphorical nodding distance of more well-known establishments such as Highgrove, hardly ruffled the inhabitants of the Bishop place and their equally wealthy neighbours. Most of them had lived out their own personal dramas in the area for those same generations, and with a smugness some hardly bothered to conceal, they were well-used to the fact that royalty and nobility chose their own God-given county for rest and relaxation.

There was little thought of such relaxation in Penny

Bishop's mind on that late Saturday morning when she was getting ready to meet her closest friends for the first time in two years. She'd been glad of a long lie-in after last night's social activities, knowing she didn't have as far to travel into Cheltenham as the others. But she had been on the phone to Laura the previous evening, just to check that the plans hadn't changed.

'I can't get through to Gemma, so I think she must be out performing,' she'd said in the low, pleasing voice that had needed no smoothing out in the way Gemma's had.

Laura had never tried to upmarket her accent. If they couldn't take her as she was, then they needn't take her at all, she had said cheerfully on that first day at the Wellesley when they had eyed one another up so cautiously.

But why should she try to change herself, Penny had said generously, when she had such a lovely, well modulated, peaches and cream accent that reminded one so deliciously of the freshness of country air?

'And the pigs,' Laura had grinned, unable at eleven years old to take such a compliment without turning it into a joke, and not too sure what the word modulated meant anyway.

Penny had found herself smiling at the memory as she heard Laura's soft voice over the phone last night. She could detect the other girl's excitement, and that she was brimming over with something she obviously wasn't going to tell her just yet.

'Something's got you sparkling,' Penny said at once. 'And I'll bet it's something in trousers.'

Laura laughed. 'Why does everybody think it has to be a guy who makes you sparkle? You of all people should know differently, Pen!'

'I'm not sure what you mean by that – '

'I mean your beloved birthday horse, of course. What did you think I meant?'

Penny could hear the grin in Laura's voice, and she laughed back, even though she wasn't so sure that she cared for the growing reputation she had now of being a one-horse woman. But her parents' wonderful eighteenth birthday gift of the black thoroughbred had taken even Penny's breath away.

Since that day, two months ago now, she'd overheard one of the stable-lads say that she and Midnight Sun had become as inseparable as lovers. The comment had both charmed her and slightly annoyed her. It was perfectly true she had more time for horses than for the indolent and Porsche-driving young men in her circle, most of whom revelled in the luxury of squandering their daddy's money, and doing very little else. The very thought of marrying one of them, and having to pretend to enjoy his sexual pantings, turned her off even more. But sometimes she wondered uneasily if she was frigid, and just how far you had to go with a fellow to find out . . .

She could almost imagine Gemma's juicy and instructive voice, advising her . . .

'*All those upperclass twits you socialise with wouldn't turn anybody on, Pen. Maybe what you need is a bit of rough. One of the horny guys on the building-site near my flat would probably oblige.*'

Penny shuddered fastidiously. Not in a million years, she thought.

The thoughts were flitting through her head as she realized Laura was still chattering like a magpie at the other end of the phone, and she still didn't know what news she had to tell. But one thing was certain. There would be no big secrets there. Laura's emotions were always plain in her face for all to see.

'Come on, tell me what gives,' she said quickly to Laura now. 'Whatever it is – '

'No, I can't. You know we said we'd always keep something to spring on one another, otherwise we'd have nothing to talk about.'

'After two years? You must be joking!'

'Yes, well, they've hardly been lost years, have they? Your phone bill must be enormous, and the scrappy postcards from Gemma have piled up – '

'And you're the sweetest letter-writer I ever knew,' Penny said, 'and I'd better stop while I'm ahead, or you'll think I'm going loopy over a collection of soppy letters.'

'I know,' Laura apologised. 'It's just that when I start, I can't stop. It's like writing a private diary, really, where you bare all your feelings, sure that they won't go any further. While I'm writing to you and Gemma, I feel as if I'm actually talking to you, and it brings us close again. Daft, isn't it?'

'Coming from anybody else, it would be, but it's so, well, so *Laura*, I guess it's OK.' Even if it did sound suspiciously like too much clinging to the past . . . and she just didn't have the time to indulge in being maudlin right now. 'Look, Laura, I've got to go – people are coming to supper. I'll see you tomorrow.'

She hung up before Laura could start to think that she was getting soft or less sophisticated than she liked to appear. You had to be tough in the world of sport. It wouldn't do to let people think she had a soft centre. That was one of her secrets.

As she took her shower and tried to decide which dress to wear for this evening's supper, at which a dozen local big-wigs would be arriving in an hour, Penny found herself wondering about secrets.

She'd bet a hundred to one that Gemma had plenty of secrets that they weren't going to hear about tomorrow. Gemma was always destined to have a secret life. It was part of her mystery, she'd once told the others grandly. You never tell people everything. *You always keep part of yourself private*. It was one thing on which she and Penny, with her privileged background, totally agreed.

But at the ironically-timed remark from Gemma, they had all fallen about with shrieks of laughter, since she had just crept into their room at the Wellesley after a hot and steamy half hour with one of the boys from the neighbouring school. And wasted no time in telling them all that had happened, in great and gleeful detail.

Even so, Penny knew shrewdly that Gemma would always have secrets, things she was too ashamed to tell her friends about.

She felt a sudden unease for the life Gemma led. It was glamorous, yet it was also risky. Anybody who put themselves in the spotlight automatically became a target for cranks and perverts. Such things were common enough in their own circles. No, compared with the racy life Gemma led, Penny's own was very ordinary – at least by her upper-middle-class standards.

She'd been born into money. She never had to ask for anything twice, she had parents who indulged her, and an older brother in the Foreign Office, a diplomat abroad who brought home endless and costly gifts for them all. She wanted for nothing.

And yet . . . And yet . . . There was still a restlessness in Penny that was only ever subdued when she was racing Midnight Sun against the clock, or crouching low over his back with the wind in her face and soaring with him over the jumps into space. She adored him. And she wouldn't let anyone but herself perform the final, almost sensual act of rubbing him down when he was profusely sweating; calming and soothing him; and bedding him down for the night herself.

She found herself thinking: *The stable-boy's right. I am thinking of him in terms of a lover. And sometimes, just sometimes, dear God, I wonder about myself. Just like people grow to resemble their dogs, and certain men take on the persona of the cars they drive, I've seen those women who grow to resemble their horses, and Heaven forbid that I should turn into one of them. Or that I get the reputation for being a strident, mannish woman, with all that that implies.*

As if to emphasize all that was feminine in her, Penny chose her clothes with feverish care for the meeting with the girls. She discarded her designer wardrobe, not wanting to be too ostentatious, although fashionable Cheltenham wouldn't turn a hair at anything from a

Christian Dior ensemble to a trendy Jean Muir outfit. In the end she decided on a simple silk dress in palest peach that did marvels for her auburn hair and green eyes, and didn't emphasize her almost painful slenderness too much.

Her make-up was subtle and pale, as befitted someone of quality . . . and her mouth twisted at the unconscious snobbery of the thought. She clasped a single rope of pearls around her neck, and madly resisted the temptation to wear the beautiful little brooch her brother had miraculously managed to acquire for her special birthday in May. This wasn't the occasion.

Though at the time she had been beside herself with excitement when she realized what she was holding in her hands. But there it was, authenticated as one of the smaller of items from the Duchess of Windsor's fabulous Collection of jewels, that had been sold for millions in April that year. There was romance and history in every precious stone. And now it was hers. She was so lucky. Yes, she really had everything . . .

'You haven't told us *your* extra-special news yet, Penny,' Laura prompted, trying desperately not to feel disappointed at the reaction to her beloved Mini.

Not that she could have expected anything else, she thought practically. With Gemma taking taxis everywhere, and obviously making a success of her chosen career; and Penny being chauffeur-driven like Lady Bountiful wherever she needed to go; her own modest achievement was like comparing a minnow to a whale.

Still, wasn't there an old saying – 'little fish are sweet'? Laura's ready smile emerged at the thought, as she waited for the inevitable thrilling news from Penny.

'All right. I can't wait any longer to tell you anyway,' she said, her eyes shining, almost choking with excitement.

She wasn't as beautiful as Gemma, nor as softly pretty as Laura, but at that moment she practically glowed. 'My parents have got tickets for all the family to go to the World Athletics Championships in Rome at the end of August and into September.'

'Gosh,' Gemma said without expression.

Laura looked at her quickly. There was a wealth of meaning in that word. It said: why on earth would anybody want to sit in sweltering heat looking at a lot of sports-mad men and women, racing and sweating and each trying to outdo the other . . .? Even if the thought of those muscly guys could be a turn-on, a fat lot of good they'd be when they'd done their 100 metres or chucked their javelins about, or whatever.

'Oh, I know it's not your scene, Gem,' Penny continued, unconcerned. 'But it's something I've hoped for for ages, and tickets are like gold dust.'

'Except when your daddy has the wherewithal and the contacts to get them,' Gemma muttered.

'Well, we all know it pays to know somebody on the inside, don't we? You probably wouldn't have got as far as you have today without your agent.'

Sensing the prickles, Laura spoke quickly. 'I think it's wonderful news, and I know it's something you've always wanted, Pen. Not quite the Olympics, I suppose, but the next best thing.'

It was odd, but it had always been Penny who was slightly jealous of Gemma's chances, though Lord knew why, with all that she had. But now, it was clear as the nose on her lovely face that Gemma was resenting the chances that wealth put in Penny's way. Gemma had to work damn hard for her money, playing up to the punters who mentally raped her with their eyes every single night, while Penny sat back and had it all on a plate.

Penny looked at Laura gratefully. Laura the Peacemaker, she thought fleetingly. Funny. They had always accepted Gemma as the one who held them all together. Gemma, the strong one, the leader. But until that moment, Penny had never registered how often they had looked to Laura for appeasement. There was more strength in that quality than people realized.

'That's not all, either,' she went on recklessly, seeing she'd got their attention now. 'We're all off to Ohio as soon as the Rome trip is over, to watch the Ryder Cup at Muirfield. I'm putting my money on Eamonn Darcy to retain it for Europe, though I suppose you're both going to say you've never heard of him. It doesn't matter. Then, if I can persuade Dad to go for it, we may go on to Los Angeles for a few days.'

She spoke of a sporting world the others didn't know, and couldn't have cared less about. It was obviously important to Penny, but Gemma couldn't contain herself any longer.

'And that's it? You're going to Rome, and rubbing

shoulders with all these athletes, and then you're going to America to watch some old golf match and off to the West Coast.' She examined her scarlet fingernails with studied nonchalance. 'It rather puts my prospect of a TV spot in the shade, doesn't it?'

She felt a rush of adrenaline in her veins, knowing she had kept the best bit up her sleeve until last, and that it would make them both sit up and take notice.

'TV?' Laura almost yelped. 'You haven't said anything about that before.'

'Of course I haven't, dummy. It's my big surprise. Anyway, it may never happen. Rube says we have to play it very cool, but a couple of TV people are coming to hear me at the Blue Parrot Club in a fortnight's time, so I'll keep you posted.'

She was as level headed as it was possible to be in the circumstances, but by God, it was so exciting she was nearly wetting herself just thinking about it. This was her big chance – her road to stardom and the Big Time. She just knew it, and she'd staked two weeks' wages on a gloriously sexy scarlet dress to impress the TV people.

'Gem, that's wonderful,' Laura said sincerely. 'You just be sure and let us know when you'll be on so we can watch you and tape it. Imagine being able to say, "That's my friend on the box". I'll be able to bask in reflected glory.'

'Well, it may never happen, but you'll both be the first to know if it does, as long as Penny's not swanning off around the world at the time.'

'If I am, I'll be sure to get it recorded so I can see it the minute I get back,' she promised.

'Good,' Gemma responded briefly. She didn't know why she was so annoyed with Penny. There was no reason for it. They all knew each other so well. She could have predicted that Penny would be immaculately dressed, with the essence of old money and background oozing out of her. She knew Laura would be country fresh and looking like a china doll with those great big beautiful blue eyes.

So why did she suddenly feel so seedy, as if she was tainted by all the guys she had known, and the blatant intimation from Rube that she had better be prepared to be nice to the studio guys he was bringing to the Blue Parrot Club, if she wanted to get ahead.

She'd been furious at the time. He made it sound as sordid as the old Hollywood casting-couch arrangements, she had raged at him.

'So it is, doll. So it is,' he'd grunted. 'You're in a cutthroat business, and you'd better believe it.'

'You're not telling me it's the only way to get to the top, are you?' she'd said scornfully. 'What about all the big stars, the big names? They didn't have to go to bed with any creep who blinked at them, did they?'

Rube shrugged. 'Not all of them,' he conceded. 'But what's wrong with a little friendliness? The age of the sugar daddy ain't dead yet, babe.'

Gemma looked at him with savage dislike. 'You're living in the past, Rube,' she snapped. 'If you think I'm letting some lecherous old man touch me up for the sake of a TV spot – '

'Of course you don't have to,' he said in his silky, lisping voice that always made her think of a lurking reptile. 'Anybody with star quality from the outset wouldn't have to. The rest of us may just have to try a little harder, and take any help we can get, kid. It all depends how much and how fast you want success.'

'Are you all right, Gem?' she heard Penny say. 'You've gone a bit pale. Do you want some more coffee?'

'What I want is some fresh air,' she muttered, seeing the future stretching ahead of her in an endless round of toadying up to men who disgusted her, and not liking what she saw. These moments hit her now and then, but she knew she'd be perfectly all right when she got back to the flat and had a few drinks to settle her nerves.

She was fine when she was up on stage performing, when nothing else mattered but the song and the music, and all the erotic seduction she could put into it. Then she could play a part, hiding behind the smouldering sexiness of Gemma Grover, *artiste* . . . She was fine when she was cavorting on her bed with the very inventive Eddie . . . and she was mad to let herself get in such a state over something that would probably never happen.

It wouldn't, as long as she kept her head, and didn't let herself be screwed by every unscrupulous guy in the business, in every sense of the word.

'Why don't we get out of here then?' Laura suggested. 'I thought we were going to take a walk around our old haunts, and it's so hot I'm starting to stick to the chair. Are you sure you're all right, Gemma?'

'I'm fine. Don't fuss. I'm not one of your blasted farmyard chicks.' But she gave her a quick hug to show

63

that she wasn't really being bitchy, just recovering from a nasty, secret bout of nerves.

This was Laura's moment. The Wellesley was some distance away from the tea-room where they had met, so they all climbed into the Mini and she drove them out through the imposing tree-lined streets of the town, peppered with their quaint old tea-rooms, and on past the race-course and recreation ground by the old Evesham Road.

Then she parked the car and they walked through the park adjoining the Wellesley Boarding School for Girls, and leaned on the perimeter fence, mentally breathing in the aura of the old redbrick buildings, the rooms they had shared, the gym and the dancing lessons . . .

They were half-nostalgic for times gone by, and more than thankful to be out of the restrictions it had imposed on them. They leaned on the fence and watched the distant tennis courts, where girls clad in the obligatory white shorts and shirts were going through their paces. Except for the occasional shouts when a point was won, their voices were muted from here, as if a television set was tuned to the lowest volume.

'Laying ghosts, Pen?' Gemma grinned, seeing the way her shoulders moved almost involuntarily with the swing of the rackets.

'Maybe, just a little. They have good sports facilities here, and they were good years.'

'My God, you sound like Methuselah,' Gemma said.

'She's right, though. They *were* good years,' Laura agreed. 'A slice of our lives that we'll never find again.'

Gemma spoke crisply. 'Who would want to? It's a mistake to spend all your time looking back. You can't ever go back.'

'I know!' Penny said, nettled. 'I'm not living in the past, any more than you are.'

'But memories are what hold us together, aren't they?' Laura put in. 'If we didn't have those, and if we didn't think they were important to us, then what are we doing here?'

The other two looked at her, and Gemma leaned forward and touched her soft face with a scarlet-tipped finger.

'You're right, of course, and I'm a prize bitch for belittling it all. You've got a wise head on those shoulders, Laura.'

'Thanks. That makes me sound about as attractive as an old Chinese soothsayer.'

'Christ, where does she get these odd ideas from?' Gemma said, grinning now. 'Do you do all this philosophizing when you're out in the cowshed, or whatever it is you do all day down on the farm?'

'Hey, we're not all yokels! Maybe you should come and visit sometime, and see for yourself!' Laura flashed at her.

'Not likely. The country's not for me. All those smells and cowpats, and guys with hayseeds coming out of their ears, and God knows where else! No thanks.'

Laura rarely lost her temper, but she was close to losing it now.

'Do you ever stop to think how stupid you sound,

Gemma?' she snapped. 'There's more to life than standing up in front of a crowd of gawking strangers and singing sloppy songs for their entertainment. Once they go home, they'll have forgotten all about you. However great you are today, you could be a has-been tomorrow, but the land and the people who care for it go on for ever.'

The other two stared at her in shocked amazement. Laura was never bitchy. It was left to the other two to spar and taunt, knowing it meant nothing. But coming from Laura, it had meant something. It had meant a great deal.

'Well, now I know just what you think of me, don't I?' Gemma said at last. 'Destined to be a has-been – providing I ever get to be a star first, of course. Or does your crystal ball tell you that's never going to happen, as well?'

At the sound of her own words, she looked suddenly stricken. She wanted this so much, and with a few short sentences from someone she had always thought totally loyal, she was back in that no-man's-land of still trying to make it.

None of them spoke for a moment. There was no sound, other than the metallic scraping wheels of a boy on a skate-board racing through the park. Then Laura's face crumpled.

'Oh God, just listen to us! Gemma, I didn't mean it. And of *course* you're going to be a star. You've always had star quality written all over you – hasn't she, Pen?'

'Of course she has. We always said so, didn't we?' Penny was appalled at the suddenness with which this longed-for day had begun to disintegrate. And from such an unlikely source.

But it couldn't end like this. It mustn't. And there was one thing that was guaranteed to cheer Gemma up.

'Look, let's change the conversation. Let's tell each other secrets about the guys we've met recently, like we used to,' she said recklessly. 'No holds barred, now. We want all the gory details.'

'Well, that won't take long as far as you're concerned, will it?' Gemma responded, but looking a little less ruffled, and already wondering just how far she could go with her tales of the cavorting Eddie.

'Oh, I've met one or two who are worth a mention,' Penny said, hiding a groan.

'Me, too – even if they are all young farmers,' Laura said defiantly, and then she laughed. 'But you'll obviously have the best stories, Gem, so let's find somewhere to sit under the trees and you can go first.'

And without knowing quite how it happened, they walked to a nearby park bench in the shade of an old oak tree, their arms closely linked. Anyone watching them would have said it was almost symbolic. All for one, and one for all.

CHAPTER 4

'Laura, come and say hello to my cousin. He's staying with us for a week, and I've been showing him how to get his hands dirty with some real work.'

The kitchen door at the Halls' farmhouse had been flung wide open to let in the morning sunlight, and on hearing Tommy Hall's voice, Laura turned around without too much enthusiasm. She and her father had driven over to their neighbours' farm straight after breakfast, and a small army of men was already out in the fields with the haymaking.

Laura and Mrs Hall had spent a chatty hour preparing mid-morning beef rolls and flasks of tea in the farmhouse kitchen that was a near-replica of the Robinson farm. And amid all the farming chatter, there had been the briefest mention of a cousin coming to stay, and the comment that Mrs Hall was sure Laura would like him.

She had thought briefly then that if Tommy's cousin were anything like him, she'd find him just as irritating. But the moment she turned to greet him, the thought died immediately. She found herself looking up into a pair of dark eyes with attractive creases at the sides when he smiled, and with her hand being clasped in a handshake that was firm and friendly.

'So this is the lovely Laura that Tommy keeps telling me about. She sounded so wonderful that I began to wonder if she really existed, but now I see that she does.' The newcomer spoke in a voice that made Laura's toes curl.

From anyone else the words could have been unbearably chauvinistic and cringe-making. But not from this man. He didn't have a Somerset accent, nor was his speech affected, either. It was just an accent with the edges smoothed out, though she thought she could just detect a touch of Scottish in it. And she found herself laughing back at his words.

'Whatever he's told you, don't believe it!' she said lightly. 'I'm just the girl next door, and you are – ?'

'Our Nick's a doctor,' Tommy boasted proudly, just as if he'd had a hand in his achievements himself. 'Dr Nicholas Dean, newly-qualified, no less.'

The information took Laura by surprise. They'd kept this particular relative a great secret, she thought! Though she knew the Halls had many distant relations all over the country that they rarely saw. She could see at once that Nick was older than Tommy, as he would need to be to have gone through medical school.

He was a tall, ruggedly self-confident man, and she found herself thinking he probably charmed all the old ladies in his practice with that warm, sexy voice. The unexpected thought made her nervous, and as always, when she was nervous, she made an involuntary joke of it.

69

'It's nice to meet you, Doctor, and actually, I've got a little pain right here,' she said with a giggle, and pressed her hand to her forehead in a theatrical gesture.

Seconds later, she knew she was blushing furiously, and wondering why the hell she'd said such a daft thing and sounded so stupidly naive . . .

To her surprise Nick stepped forward and gently removed her hand from her forehead. It had been a silly joke, no more, and one that he'd probably heard a thousand times before. She was sure he'd think her a complete idiot, and as juvenile as his cousin. But then she felt his sensitive doctor's fingers pressing gently on her temples and slowly moving to the back of her neck to massage it gently. And she had to force herself not to give a shiver of pleasure at his touch.

'Tension,' he declared. 'My recipe for a cure is for you to get out in the fresh air for a couple of hours, and then come out for dinner with me tonight.'

Laura's mouth dropped open. The teasing had been one thing, but this sudden invitation was something else. He grinned at the startled look on her face, and went on speaking as his aunt laughed openly at his nonsense. It was clear to Laura that she was going to indulge him in anything he said.

'All right, I'll come clean, before you think I'm the fastest worker in the world. My aunt and uncle and cousin have invited me out for a meal this evening, and we'd very much like you and your father to come with us.'

Laura managed to drag her gaze away from Nick Dean to look at his aunt. It was a most unconventional invitation, and it came from a most unconventional man. She couldn't imagine what his family must think of him. Then she heard Mrs Hall chuckle again, her comfortable body shaking inside its voluminous overall.

'You'll have to get used to our Nick, Laura love,' she said easily. 'And I reckon you've met your match there. I was going to ask you about tonight myself, but we've had too many other things to talk about, and Nick got in first. We thought we'd go to that new place on the Bridgwater road. It's really Nick's party, to celebrate his becoming a real doctor, and our Tommy said we should include our best friends.'

'Oh! Well, I'll have to ask Dad, of course, but I know we'd love to join you, if you're sure you don't want to keep it all in the family.'

For some reason, Laura felt a small pang of disappointment. Stupid, of course, but just for one glorious moment, she had allowed herself to believe that this lovely man was asking her out on a sudden whim, and intending to keep her all to himself. She hadn't even considered that it had all been Tommy's idea, nor did she want to have her name linked with his in any way. She had always known she could never feel remotely romantic about Tommy, and nothing had changed in that respect, nor ever would.

And she didn't believe in love at first sight, either. That was for novels, not for real life. But as she let herself watch the cousins bantering together, and the way Mrs Hall was obviously so fond of Nick, she found herself wondering if fiction was so very far removed from real life after all.

'You two boys had better get back to the others,' Mrs Hall said eventually. 'We expect everybody to sing for their supper on a farm, Nick, and you're no exception. Though it'll be a change from doctoring, I daresay.'

'Just a bit,' Nick grinned. 'Anyway, I've got some news for you. I was waiting until tonight, but I'm not sure I can keep it to myself any longer, now that I've seen some of the delights around here.'

He didn't look at Laura as he spoke, but she felt the words reach out and touch her as if they were tangible. He lounged against the kitchen dresser while Tommy sprawled out on a chair, and the contrast between them was marked. One was still a boy, while the other . . .

'Come on then. You've got to tell us now, Nick,' Tommy said at once, seeing nothing untoward in his cousin's words. But then, he wouldn't, thought Laura. He didn't have that kind of perception and never had done.

'I'm moving down here in a couple of weeks,' Nick announced calmly. 'Part of my reason for being here is to finalize the interviews with the practice management. I'm joining a country practice near Blagdon on a six months' trial, and if it all works out well, I hope to get taken on eventually as a junior partner and settle here.'

'That's wonderful!' Mrs Hall exclaimed. 'And you won't miss Scotland?' she added, confirming what Laura had suspected.

Nick shrugged. 'There's nothing there for me now. When Dad died, I decided to look around to see where I could make a fresh start after I qualified. But there was no point in letting you know until I was certain of my plans.'

'So where will you live?' Tommy put in. 'There's plenty of room here – '

'Thanks, Tom, but there's a flat going with the job, so I shan't impose on you indefinitely. It's great that I'll be near enough to see you often, though.'

This time he glanced Laura's way. It was no more than a fleeting glance, but to her awakening senses, the look spoke more than words. She wondered if she was going slightly mad, to feel this sudden empathy with a man she hardly knew. Or was this the way love affected you, when it hit you with the force of a tornado? Having never been in love before, Laura had no way of telling. All she knew was that the feeling was a little scary, and more than a little marvellous.

And Blagdon wasn't so far away. She knew the village above the lake, where fishermen spent long, quiet hours in summer, and cursed the newly-allowed speedboats for disturbing their rituals. Blagdon was less than fifteen miles away, and she had a car . . . She found herself breathing more quickly, and was glad when Mrs Hall shooed the men out of the kitchen, saying that she and Laura would bring the food and drinks out to the fields in due course.

'You've never mentioned Nick before,' Laura said at once, when the two women were alone.

'Haven't I?' Mrs Hall said vaguely. 'Well, I suppose there was never any need. We didn't ever see much of him, and he's my cousin's boy, really, so he's not a close relative. More of a second cousin, I daresay you'd call it. And he lived so far away, of course.'

'In Scotland,' Laura prompted, suddenly wanting to know everything about him.

'That's right, love. His dad married for a second time when Nick was small, but it wasn't a good marriage, and Nick had an unhappy childhood, though he never talks about it. Then last year his father died, and there was no love lost between him and his stepmother. We knew he'd gone in for doctoring, but that was all, until he phoned us last night to say he was in the area and wanted to visit us. It was quite a shock, I can tell you, and now this news is an even bigger shock.'

'A nice one, though, isn't it? I know you always like to keep in contact with your family.'

'Oh yes, and he's a lovely boy, of course. Well, you can see that for yourself, Laura. He'll be a popular doctor, I've no doubt, and it's always useful to have one in the family,' she finished with another chuckle.

Laura felt the most extraordinary range of sensations then. On the one hand she welcomed everything Mrs Hall was saying, wanting everyone to like Nick . . . and on the other, she felt a sting of jealousy at the thought that he'd be a popular doctor, with all the nubile young women in the district rushing to register their names with Dr Nick Dean.

'Are you all right, love? You don't really have a headache, do you?' Mrs Hall said, peering at her. 'You do look a bit flushed.'

'I'm fine, really. But I think I'll follow Dr Dean's

advice and get out in the fresh air as soon as we've got this little lot ready.'

She continued packing the mountain of beef rolls and flasks of tea, the scrumpy cider and the pickled onions, and the home-made fruit cake, into the cardboard cartons, and helped the farmer's wife load them onto the Land Rover. Mrs Hall was an erratic driver, gripping the wheel and thundering along the lanes as if her life depended on it, and the cartons always had to be loaded securely. But Laura knew better than to suggest she drove her Mini out to the fields – a suggestion which would have been met with scorn.

When they arrived, the scent of newmown hay was sweet and overpowering as the teams of men forked the great bales of hay onto the wagons. Mechanical balers and loaders would have made life much easier and quicker, but these were traditional farming men, and the close camaraderie of working together was what made them strong.

Laura saw Nick at once, working with the best of them. His checked shirt had the sleeves rolled up now, and he looked the part in his working jeans. His dark hair was tousled in the breeze, and his skin was tanned as if outdoor work was nothing new to him. He was talking and laughing with Laura's father, and the sight of them together made her catch her breath. Despite the difference in their ages, they were oddly alike, both tall and sparely-built, with the same intense dark eyes and ready smile.

And wasn't there something somewhere that said men frequently fell for women who reminded them of their mothers? And girls fell for men who reminded them of their fathers . . . Laura had always found it a slightly incestuous thought, but it didn't seem so any more. It seemed a right and natural continuation of love and respect . . .

'Come on, Laura. Stop daydreaming and bring on the grub! You've got a dozen starving men over here,' she heard Tommy shout, and Mrs Hall gave a snort as she began unloading the Land Rover.

'The day that boy starves it will be a miracle,' she grumbled affectionately. 'I never saw anybody pack so much food away at every meal. Lord knows how he ever managed when he was away at school.'

'We didn't exactly get Scrooge-like proportions, Mrs Hall,' Laura grinned, remembering how the Halls had always brought food parcels for Tommy whenever they visited his school, as if he desperately needed feeding up. 'Things were quite civilized, honestly.'

And from the look of Tommy's paunch now, and the flabbiness around his jawline, too much good farmhouse food and scrumpy cider wasn't going to do his blood pressure much good in a couple of years . . . Laura pulled her thoughts up short. She was reacting like a doctor now, for God's sake! And one doctor around here was quite enough.

All the men had stopped work now and were making for the shade of the trees where they would eat their midday lunch. And she watched Nick as he walked towards her, tall and lean and beautiful, and she was lost.

'So we're invited out tonight.' Laura's dad spoke sociably from the armchair in his own parlour when the day was finally over, and the farmers and helpers had gone their various ways. 'I'd have thought the Halls would have waited until the haymaking was over to go out celebrating with young Nick.'

'I think they wanted to make this a special night, before we had the usual farming suppers after the haymaking, Dad. Just for the family – and close friends.'

'We're the only other ones invited, by all accounts.'

'I know. I can't think why,' she said.

'Can't you?' Farmer Robinson asked shrewdly. 'You know as well as I do that they've always had you earmarked for young Tommy, so putting you in the picture might make it seem a bit more official.'

'Well, I've no intention of being earmarked for Tommy Hall or anyone else!' she snapped, annoyed at the thought that Nick might have already got the same idea. 'I'm never likely to marry him just to please his folks, either. I don't love him, Dad, and I never will. He's just a friend, like he's always been. You wouldn't want me to marry somebody I didn't love, would you?'

Remembering the comfortable and abiding love her parents had shared, she was certain he wouldn't. But now, tonight, she needed that reassurance in words. Before she had to listen to some excruciatingly embarrassing hints from the Halls about herself and Tommy.

'Of course I wouldn't want it, love. You don't need to protest so heartily to me on that score. Besides, you're young yet. There's time enough for falling in love when the right one comes along, and anyone with half an eye can see that Tommy's not the one. T'other one would be more your style.'

Laura's heart jolted. It was no more than a throw-away remark, and it meant nothing. Not to her father, anyway. But to her, it was something to hug to herself, and to know the truth of it. Nick was *definitely* more her style . . .

'I bet he's aching all over by now,' she said, knowing weakly that she was doing what all women in love did. Talking about the beloved and keeping his image alive in her mind by speaking his name and picturing his smile – and feeling the touch of his hands on her neck . . .

'Who? Oh, the doctor fellow. Not used to hard graft, you mean? Don't you be too sure about that. He was telling me he'd done some skiing in Scotland, so your man don't spend every day sitting on his backside.'

'I thought he'd be the athletic type,' Laura murmured, though she hadn't expected the mention of skiing. She'd never been to Scotland, but yes, she could see him in her imagination, soaring down the snowy slopes, crouched low over his skis with the wind in his hair and his muscles tensed . . .

'You liked him, didn't you?' Farmer Robinson said with a smile. 'I could see that you took to him.'

Oh yes, she liked him, if liking was a word that could ever describe such an intense flood of emotions . . .

'Of course. Didn't you?'

Please say that you did. I want you to like him. He's going to be important to me, you see . . .

Her father got to his feet and kissed her lightly on the

78

forehead before going upstairs to wash and change his clothes for the evening out. They didn't kiss often, and the contact took her by surprise.

'I liked him, Laura. I approve. And I'll say no more.'

She felt a ripple of excitement surge through her veins. It was just as if something was settled already, even though she knew very well it couldn't possibly be. It was just as if her future had been decided, and the course of it couldn't be changed, because fate, or destiny, or karma, or whatever you cared to call it, had decreed that it was so.

Gemma would scoff at such a thought, and Penny would look at her as if she'd gone cuckoo, but Laura had always maintained that there were things on Heaven and earth that were far more mysterious and inexplicable than the mere logic of science. Someone far cleverer than herself had said something of the same, and she was utterly convinced of it. She believed in horoscopes and the influence of the stars, and the changing seasons that could produce such marvels of new life after the deadest of winters.

Anyone reading her thoughts now would probably think her a total nutcase, she thought ruefully, a hopeless romantic who was seeing things that weren't there, just because she wanted to see them so much. And most likely, this Nick Dean had a string of girlfriends at his beck and call. Maybe even a fiancée, or a wife . . .

Laura felt suddenly chilled at the thought. And what had he said to her after all, to bring about this feeling of empathy between them? He'd merely given her an invitation to dinner, which included his entire

Somerset family, and her own father. Yes, she was a complete idiot.

When the phone rang she was jerked out of her sudden misery. She leapt to her feet, sure it would be him, however unlikely. She heard Penny's voice and had to gulp twice before she could answer.

'What's wrong?' she asked.

'Nothing's wrong, at least not with me. But you sound funny. Have you got a summer cold or something?'

'I'm OK. Just a bit of a sniffle,' Laura lied. 'So to what do I owe the pleasure of this call?'

She forced herself to inject some warmth into her voice. This was her friend – her best friend – and she knew she must have sounded less than pleased to hear from her.

'I thought you looked a bit peaky when we met, Laura, and I wondered if you'd care to spend a few days up here. I'd love to show you around.'

Laura's heart jumped with fright. Penny's home was reputedly so grand, and she was sure she'd never fit in. And it was an impossibly bad time of year, with the haymaking still not finished on the local farms. And Nick was here.

'Laura? What do you say? My parents are gluttons for punishment, and they're off on a week's cruise before we fly out to Rome. So we'd have the place to ourselves, if that's what's worrying you. I could even teach you to ride.'

'No thanks,' Laura said at once. 'You stick to your horses, and I'll stick to the farm. Metaphorically speaking, of course. It's sweet of you to ask me, Pen, but I'm not sure. We're still in the middle of haymaking – '

'Surely you don't have to be tied hand and foot, do you? You need a break from it sometimes, Laura, and you really should get out more.'

'Look, can I call you back tomorrow? We're going out to dinner tonight as a matter of fact, and I'm in a bit of a rush. I'm sorry, Pen, I don't mean to appear ungracious,' she added, realizing how it must sound.

'That's all right, sweetie. Call me tomorrow, but you can tell your father that I'm in need of your company by the end of the week. Don't let him boss you about.'

Laura smiled as she put down the phone. Penny could be the bossy one when she chose, which was something her Dad had never been. He was an indulgent father, which was probably why she never needed to ruffle the harmony of their life. She didn't bother too much about holidays. A few days at the seaside up or down the coast, or the occasional visit to Taunton or Bristol were enough, and she was always happy to get back to the tranquillity of the farm.

But listening to her own thoughts, she knew how *dull* she sounded. How provincial and elderly, and stuck in the most terrible rut for an eighteen-year-old to admit to. She should see a bit of LIFE in capital letters, and not be content with the Saturday-night hops at the village hall or the life of a woman twice or three times her age. Penny was so right. She should get out more.

That evening, Laura dressed carefully. Dinner at a smart new roadhouse wasn't an everyday occurrence for busy farmers, which was why she wore more make-up than usual and plaited her long hair while it was damp. When it was dry and she released it, it fell about her shoulders in rippling waves. She wore a flattering blue dress and her favourite silver locket and long earrings. She wasn't dressing for *him*, she told herself, knowing very well that she was.

And his eyes told her that he approved of what he saw. Tommy's father complimented her in his bluff farmer's way, and Tommy told her she looked good enough to eat, which was about the limit of his *finesse*. She smiled faintly at the word her best friends always called 'Laura's yardstick of approval'. But Nick merely raised his glass of wine to her and said it was good to share a celebratory meal with friends and family.

'I've been invited on a visit to Penny's,' she said to no one in particular, when she knew she couldn't stare at Nick Dean all evening. He looked so different now, wearing a dark suit and immaculate white shirt and brightly patterned tie. He looked what he was: the successful junior doctor on his way up, and she was suddenly tongue-tied with him.

'You didn't tell me,' her father said now. 'When did this happen?'

'She phoned me while you were getting ready. I forgot to mention it, mostly because I'm hardly likely to go.'

'Why on earth not?' he asked at once.

At this Tommy gave a guffaw, and at the taunt in his eyes she knew why she had always disliked him so much. Beneath that puffy bland face was a small spiteful streak.

'Laura's afraid she'll be out of her depth in that great mansion Penny's always boasting about. That's right, isn't it? You'll never know which fork to use and end up in a right old state.'

'That's unkind, Tommy,' Mrs Hall protested. 'You could learn a thing or two from Laura's table manners – and get your elbows off the table.'

He was too thick-skinned to even take offence, Laura noted furiously, as he plonked them further onto the table for a second or two before removing them. Then Nick spoke.

'I can't imagine Laura being out of her depth anywhere. I haven't known her more than a day, but I'm already convinced that she'd grace anyone's home.'

'Well said, Nick,' Mrs Hall approved, but Laura wasn't listening, and nor did she heed the way the older woman continued scolding her son for his bad manners.

All she was hearing was the rich timbre in Nick Dean's voice, and startling thoughts were surging through her head now. She hadn't known him more than a day either, but such trivialities meant nothing at all when you felt you had known someone for always.

CHAPTER 5

'You know I want to see you again, don't you?' Nick said, under cover of the general conversation after the meal.

By then, the other three men were deep in noisy farming talk, and Mrs Hall was quietly dozing in a corner seat of the roadhouse lounge. And Nick and Laura had been getting to know one another.

'Do you?' she whispered.

'I thought I'd been telling you so all evening. Not with words, perhaps, but with everything else. Don't pretend you haven't been aware of it, Laura.'

If she had been Gemma, she would have been able to answer him with some flip remark. She would have encouraged him, or flattened him with a crude comment, or been as provocatively sexy as only Gemma knew how, while remaining completely in control of the situation.

If she had been Penny, she would probably have put that cool, autocratic note into her voice that had the effect of quelling any man who dared to think she had an interest in anything that wasn't on four legs.

But she was neither of them. She was Laura, and she didn't have an ounce of guile in her.

'Of course I've been aware of it,' she murmured, her hands held loosely in her lap. The roadhouse was crowded, and they sat close enough to one another to touch, but they didn't touch, at least not physically. In every other way, Laura had the strangest feeling that they had been touching each other's mind and body all evening. She swallowed, wondering if she had drunk a little too much wine, to feel so light-headed and intoxicated.

'So when can I see you again?' Nick pressed urgently. 'I'm only here for three more days, then I have to go back to Scotland to clear up everything there. In a couple of weeks I'll be back to stay, but I don't want to wait that long to see you again.'

'I shouldn't think I'd arrange to go to Penny's for at least three more days,' she heard herself say. 'There's still work to do here, and I can't leave Dad in the lurch.'

'He'll have to get used to it one day. You'll be leaving him when you get married.'

'Who said I was ever going to get married?' she asked with a nervous laugh.

'I did. Didn't you know – ?'

The three other men suddenly bellowed out with loud laughter, waking Mrs Hall from her slumber. She glared at them crossly.

'You three should be ashamed, making such a spectacle of yourselves in such a nice place,' she said. 'Just you stop talking about farming for once, and remember you've got guests. I don't know what Nick and Laura must be thinking, if you've been ignoring them like this.'

Laura looked at Nick, and a small smile curved around her lips to match his. And the sweet telepathy between them told her that he had been no more aware of anyone else in the place than she had herself. For both of them, there was only each other. And what they had so recently said to one another ran round and round in her head like a litany.

'Who said I was ever going to get married?'

'I did. Didn't you know – ?'

Laura knew it could have been just a line. It could have meant nothing – or everything.

By the time she left Somerset for Gloucestershire, most of the haymaking was over, thanks to the smoulderingly hot summer weather. The celebration suppers had been gargantuan as always. And Laura and Nick had spent every minute together that they could.

On their last evening, he asked if she'd care to see the small furnished flat that was going to be his in a couple of weeks' time. It was empty now, and according to Nick, it had a splendid view of the lake.

'I'm not sure that I should,' Laura said. If their relationship had already been intense, taking her much farther than she had ever expected to go in so short a time, she hadn't made the final commitment. They hadn't made love, and she wasn't sure she wanted to spoil the sweet innocence of their relationship by rushing things.

If that was old-fashioned, then so was she, but there

was a fragile beauty about taking things slowly, and savouring every moment they spent together. Taking things step by step . . . But since he was so much more worldly than she was, she didn't know how she could explain those feelings to Nick without sounding unbearably young and silly. He was so much more sophisticated than she, and he was also eight years older.

'Why aren't you sure?' he said gently, as they sat in the car he had hired for the duration of his visit.

'You know why,' she answered, without feeling the need to explain.

He leaned towards her, caressing her cheek with his finger, and his kiss was gentle on her lips. There had been far more passionate ones, but Laura was discovering that a gentle kiss could be as erotic as any other.

'Trust me,' he said, his lips moving against hers. 'I'm a doctor.'

The idiotic phrase that was the butt of so many television sit-coms started her giggling. She knew he meant her to take it that way, and he'd said the words solemnly to take the heat out of the super-charged atmosphere between them. For if they once went back to his flat, they both knew what was likely to happen. But she could no longer deny or resist the sexual tension between them.

'All right,' Laura whispered huskily. 'Just for a little while. Remember you have to leave early in the morning.'

'I'm not likely to forget,' Nick groaned, starting up the engine and reversing out of the lane in which they were parked, 'since I'd much prefer to stay here with you.'

'And your family,' she reminded him.

'No. Just with you,' he said, matter-of-factly.

He kept one hand on the steering-wheel and the other one held Laura's as he drove back towards the outskirts of Blagdon. There was little traffic on the country roads, and his careful driving belied his burning need to reach the flat as quickly as possible. Nick was a passionate man, but he had surprised himself with the speed with which he'd fallen in love. But now that he'd found this beautiful fair-haired girl, he knew he could never let her go. And just how this evening was going to turn out, he was still uncertain. He wouldn't push her, but he wanted her. God, how he wanted her . . .

He showed her the practice buildings, which were all in darkness now. It was a new practice, since the area had grown so much recently, and could support more than the old one-man family doctor system. The traditional GP still existed, for those who didn't like change, but the doctors in the new practice were all young and keen and with different skills to bring to the community.

The flat was a little distance away from the main part of the village, on the upper floor of a two-storey building. Nick had already been given the keys for it, and once they were inside the small sitting room, he pulled back the curtains in the long picture window to show Laura the view of the lake in all its serene beauty.

The moon was full tonight, brilliant in an indigo, starlit sky, and threw a sheet of gold across the dark waters. She drew in her breath.

'Oh, it's so beautiful,' she said softly. 'I've never seen

the lake at night before, nor when it's been so – so lonely, if that's the right word for it.'

'It'll do,' Nick agreed. 'And when you've gone away, I'll think of your words, and be lonely too.'

She didn't speak for a moment, and then: 'Nick, you know I can't stay very long,' she said in a low voice.

'Would you want to, if you could?'

Would she want to? Every part of her ached to say yes. To be with him, to be a part of him, in a way she had never known before. To lie together, exploring each other, to be as close as if they were one person, and to awaken still in each other's arms . . . She felt a sudden fright as the wanton thoughts swept through her.

'What I want, and what I know I should do are two different things,' she murmured.

'They needn't be. As I said, I'm a doctor. Trust me.'

But the words were clumsier now, and no longer said in jest. Yet for all that, they were somehow more endearing, because she sensed that maybe he was a little afraid too, of the way passion was threatening to overtake commonsense.

'*Can* I trust you, Nick?' she said, almost inaudibly.

'Always,' he assured her.

Without speaking, their arms became entwined around one another, and he was leading her towards the bedroom. The moonlight streamed in through the curtains and gave them enough light to undress by. She fumbled with her clothes, and then his hands were helping her, easing straps from her shoulders and caressing the smooth, velvety skin before moving downwards to her rounded breasts.

She knew she should feel embarrassed, but she didn't. Even so, they had been given to understand at the Wellesley that nice girls didn't do this sort of thing . . . especially after knowing a man for only three days . . . but those schooldays were gone, and she wanted this too much to feel anything but love and desire for him. She lay back on the bed and waited for him, and her heart beat painfully fast in her chest as his questing fingers sought and found her.

'I'll try not to hurt you, my darling,' he said comfortingly.

And although it was the first time, she was so ready for him that the pain was of little duration, and then he was slipping inside her and filling her, and she arched her back and rose to meet him with an instinctive and primitive passion.

When they finally lay passively in each other's arms, she felt bound to ask in a small voice if everything was all right. She didn't know too much about the mechanics of love-making, but she had been aware of some small delay before he actually entered her.

'Everything is all right in the way that you mean, and everything's wonderful in every other way. Laura, I want you to know that I'm not a man to take things lightly. You mean a great deal to me, and I hope you're going to mean even more in the future.'

'I hope so too,' she whispered.

It was far too soon to be thinking about happy endings when this was just their beginning. But the feeling of well-being that had spread through every part of her while they made love, didn't diminish, and she was warmed by his words.

They were reluctant to end the evening, but she knew she couldn't stay all night. They had to be practical. Her father would be waiting up for her, and besides, Nick had to be away in the morning to catch a very early train from Bristol. This would be their last time together for several weeks.

'You won't forget me while you're away, will you?' she said, joking, when she suddenly felt more like weeping.

'That's the last thing I shall do,' he said. 'You'll be in my thoughts and my heart every moment from now on.'

He held her to him a moment longer, and then she said she really had better go. After they had dressed, he drove her back to the farm in silence, and it was only because his hand still held hers that she felt any contact with him at all. It was frightening, she thought, how you could feel so close to a person one minute, and strangely isolated from them the next.

'I'll call you when you get back from your friend's house,' Nick offered when they had reached the farm, and their parting was imminent. 'And I'll let you know exactly when I'll be returning here.'

'Promise?' she said, still close to tears.

'I promise,' he told her, holding her in his arms for one last, sweet kiss.

Penny could see at once that something was different about her. Laura had driven to Gloucestershire almost as if she was on auto-pilot, hardly heeding the road signs and with her mind still in a daze from all that had happened so quickly between herself and Nick.

And now they were apart, and in the cold light of day, she wondered if she had been stupid in giving herself to him so easily.

And just how gullible would Gemma think her, if she knew? But Gemma didn't know, and it was going to stay that way, Laura thought determinedly. But Penny knew, even without being told. It must have been written all over her in large guilty letters, Laura thought in alarm.

'So who's the boyfriend?' Penny asked, when she had shown Laura all over the sumptuous house, and they were finally sprawled full-length together on Penny's bed, on what seemed to Laura to be acres of white satin-covered bedspread.

'What boyfriend?'

'Oh, come on, you can't fool me! And I couldn't bear it if you told me it was that little creep, Tommy Hall, who's put those stars in your eyes, so it has to be somebody else.'

'What are you, a private detective or something?' Laura asked with a grin.

'Stop messing me about, and *tell* me, Laura. You know I'll get it out of you in the end, and it had better be *right now*, or I won't tell you my big surprise.'

To Laura, Penny's plummy voice always sounded screamingly funny when she resorted to the kind of slangy talk her parents would definitely disapprove of. She ignored the thought of whatever surprise Penny had in mind, and couldn't contain herself any longer.

'All right then. His name's Nick, and he's a doctor, and I'm madly in love with him. There. Does that answer your question fully enough?'

'Good God, no, it certainly doesn't!' Penny practically screamed, sitting up in bed and gazing down at her pink-faced friend. 'I want to know every detail. Where and when did you meet him, and how come you're so madly in love when you haven't mentioned a damn thing about him before now? And a doctor, for God's sake. Is he some kind of aging Svengali or something?'

'No, he's not,' Laura said crossly. 'He's twenty-six, if you must know, and I met him a week ago – '

'And you're already madly in love with him? This sounds more like Gemma than you, Laura. I hope you know what you're doing. He hasn't had his wicked way with you, has he?'

She grinned as she spoke, not believing it for a minute. She was just making conversation to cover her surprise at the extraordinary fact that Laura seemed to be so besotted by this man. But when there was a continuing silence, the grin faded at the guilty look on Laura's face now.

'My God, he has!' Penny squeaked. 'You definitely *don't* know what you're doing, you idiot. I just hope he was careful, that's all.'

Laura sat up quickly, and hugged her knees.

'You're spoiling it and making it all seem so sordid, and it wasn't like that at all,' she muttered. 'And yes, he was careful. He's a doctor. Of all people, he knows about these things.'

She bit her lip. If Penny was insensitive enough to say

the joke they'd so often screeched with laughter about, she knew she'd hit out at her, guest or no guest.

I'm a doctor. Trust me. And she had.

But she should also have trusted Penny's perception.

'Do you want to tell me any more?' she said after a moment. 'And I'm sorry. I didn't understand how much this meant to you, and knowing you, I should have done. You'd never have gone into it lightly, so he must be Mr Wonderful.'

'Yes, he is. He's also Tommy Hall's cousin. And before you say it, that's the only thing they have in common!'

She caught the glint of laughter in Penny's eyes then, and her own mouth twitched. And suddenly they were rolling with laughter on the bed, each with her own image of what Nick Dean was like, and the remembered picture of Tommy Hall.

'Well, I must say you've surprised me,' Penny gasped at last, when they'd used half a box of tissues to wipe away the tears. 'Though it was always on the cards that it would happen to you sooner or later. The Earth Mother syndrome, and all that. What was it like, by the way? Don't tell me if you want to keep it private.'

She sounded so casual that Laura knew she was really dying to know. She wasn't interested in men, but she was intensely curious about the need for this thing that seemed so all-important to other people.

'Yes, I do want to keep it private,' she smiled dreamily. 'I'm not going to describe it, but it was the nearest thing to Heaven I've ever experienced, and that's all I'm going to say about it.'

'Fair enough,' Penny said, sliding off the bed. 'Now I'll tell you my big surprise, shall I?'

'Yes, please.' Laura was half-glad to get away from the subject of Nick and herself, and half-reluctant to let the sweet imagery go.

'We're going to London tomorrow night.'

'What? What do you mean, we're going to London?'

For a moment Laura couldn't concentrate her mind on what Penny was saying. She'd come here to relax, and now there was talk of going to London, where she'd never been in her life before.

'Gemma called. She's had endless delays about this audition thing, but it's finally going to happen at this nightclub of hers. The TV people will be in the audience tomorrow night, and that's the real reason I had to get you here by this weekend. I knew you'd never make it to London from deepest Somerset under your own steam. So we're going together, and Andrews is driving us.'

Laura remembered the long, swish Daimler that had brought Penny to the tea-room in Cheltenham, and the uniformed chauffeur driving it.

'I don't believe it,' she said at last.

'Which bit? The fact that Gem's actually got an audition, or that I inveigled you here under false pretences? I'm not leaving you behind, so you can just make up your mind that you're going to see the bright lights tomorrow night, kid.'

'That doesn't bother me. I just never thought of being driven by car to London, that's all.'

She had to say something, since her thoughts were in

such a whirl; Penny had jumped so swiftly from delving into Laura's personal life, to this sudden announcement that they were off to the Blue Parrot Club, whatever that was. It could be a marvellously sophisticated place, or the most awful dive. Either way, it was something out of Laura's experience.

'Does Gemma know we'll be there?'

'She suggested it when we met in Cheltenham, remember? But it's taken longer to set up than she anticipated, and she sounded pretty cut up about that. Gemma was never good at dealing with disappointments.'

'I should think she's in the wrong business then,' Laura said.

Penny laughed. 'That's a very profound remark, coming from you.'

'Why is it? Do you think I'm so dumb I'm unaware of what a cut-throat way of life the music business can be?'

Penny looked at her thoughtfully. 'You know, you've really grown up in two years, Laura, in more ways than one.'

'I should damn well hope I have.'

And I've overtaken you in one respect, she found herself thinking. *I've got a lover, and I'm just as wild about him as he is about me.*

'When are you going to show me around your stables and introduce me to your wonderful Midnight Sun?' Laura felt her brief antagonism fade away as erotic thoughts of Nick invaded her mind instead.

'Right now,' Penny said briskly. 'But I'll make a bargain with you. If I show you Midnight Sun, you've got to promise to show me Nick.'

'The comparison sounds slightly obscene to me, but I think I know what you mean,' Laura grinned. 'And of course I'll want you to meet him one day, but he doesn't actually move to Somerset for a couple of weeks.'

And right now I want to keep him all to myself . . .

'Well, I'm not going to wait two years before we meet up again to find out what he's like,' Penny declared.

Laura smiled. Much as she loved her two best friends, there were some things that were best kept private. And she wasn't prepared to share one iota of Nick with anyone just yet. She'd never thought of herself as being possessive, but when it came to love and war, she was already learning things about herself. And she had no idea why such a weird thought should come into her head just then.

The following evening, Laura acknowledged that Andrews was a superb driver. The car edged smoothly onto the motorway and sped towards London with the minimum of effort. She and Penny sat in the comfortable back seats, and a glass panel was drawn across the car between themselves and the back of Andrews' head, which kept them completely private. It was like something out of a Hollywood movie, she told Penny.

'You get used to it,' Penny said.

'But didn't you ever want to learn to drive yourself?' queried Laura curiously.

'Why should I, when there's always somebody to do it for me?'

And that just about summed up the difference between their two lives, thought Laura. Penny had always had everything done for her, while Laura had had to learn everything for herself.

As for Gemma . . . Laura frowned. Gemma had had it the hardest, and was to be admired the most for rising above herself and her background to get exactly what she wanted by tooth and claw. You had to hand it to Gem.

Laura half-suspected that Tommy Hall had once made a play for Gemma, and got the knock-back he deserved. It was a bit like a pauper going after a princess . . . and Gemma always got full marks when it came to ridicule. It was necessary, she used to say, to keep the lechers in their place.

'Do you know where this Blue Parrot Club is?' she asked suddenly.

'Oh, somewhere in Notting Hill, but Andrews will find it,' Penny said casually. And from the tone of her voice, Laura guessed that in any other circumstances, nobody in the Bishop place, from its pampered daughter to its uniformed chauffeur, would truly approve of the location.

'I hope it's, well – all right,' Laura went on. 'You know what I mean.'

'Gemma can take care of herself, and always has done, so you don't need to worry about her. As for us, well, Andrews is a black belt in karate, should we ever need him.'

Laura's mouth felt dry. She hadn't meant that they might need that kind of help. She'd just been concerned to know that Gemma wasn't singing in some low dive.

And the incongruity of the stuffy Andrews arriving

like the cavalry over the hill in his posh uniform to act as a kind of bouncer to defend them, was just absurd. As if she was reading her mind, Penny squeezed Laura's hand.

'Don't worry. He'll park the car in a safe place and change his gear before he follows us to the club. He'll look like an ordinary punter, and can act as our official minder,' she finished with a grin.

It sounded all right, Laura thought dubiously, but for the life of her she couldn't conjure up the kind of excitement she should be feeling for this evening. And that was bad. She longed to know that Gemma was making a success of this fabulous singing career, and she felt fiercely protective of her. But she couldn't forget that sudden look of desperation on Gemma's face in the tea-room in Cheltenham, and the way she had gone so pale.

Laura was filled with the most awful doubts about this Blue Parrot Club now, and began to wish she'd never agreed to come at all. Then, as the thought entered her mind, she felt a spurt of anger at being so mouselike. It was an adventure, for God's sake! She was eighteen years old and she'd never seen London or the inside of a nightclub before, so it was time she did.

But she found herself wishing passionately that it could be Nick who was her minder for the evening.

CHAPTER 6

The entrance to the Blue Parrot Club was down a flight of steps leading to a basement. Inside, the lighting was low and pink and intimate, with a lot of plush red-velvet seating and tables in discreet alcoves. The atmosphere was already heavy with smoke and perfume, but Laura was relieved to see that the clientèle didn't look disreputable. The two burly bouncers on the door were the only indication that life here could sometimes get rough.

Laura's only experience of nightclubs was what she had seen in films, but this was exactly the way she had imagined it. There was a table booked for them in Penny's name at the back of the room, and they were both thankful it wasn't right at the front, where the spotlight would pick them out.

They had been inside the place for fifteen minutes before Andrews surreptitiously joined them. By now he was looking less like a chauffeur and more like a professional escort. Laura would have been naturally curious as to how and where he had changed his clothes and parked the Daimler, but it was obviously not the kind of thing Penny would deign to ask her chauffeur. What he did when he wasn't needed was his business.

He ordered soft drinks for her and Penny, and a whisky for himself, the cost of which Laura assumed would be added to his expenses for the evening. It was a different world from hers, and she was only just beginning to understand it.

There was a prominently reserved table in the centre front of the dimly-lit room, and shortly before the announcer gave out Gemma's name, the clients arrived. A short, swarthy fellow ushered in three portly men wearing evening suits, lots of gold chains and rings, and smoking large cigars. Dark glasses added to the theatrical effect, and to Laura, they were simply caricatures of the way the Mafia was portrayed in films.

'They've just got to be Gemma's agent and the TV audition people,' Penny hissed, 'and from the look of them, it's they who reap the profits when it comes to promoting an unknown singer.'

The word leeches came to Laura's mind, but she refrained from saying it out loud. In this cut-throat business, she supposed an artiste had to have their kind of back-up and support.

Then at last Gemma stepped out into the spotlight, glittering in a scarlet dress with a deep, slashed neckline. Before she began to sing, she acknowledged her pianist with a smile. This was Eddie, Laura remembered, with whom Gemma had had a torrid and long-lasting fling. She had no idea if it was still going on, or if it had fizzled out by now.

But she forgot all of that as the music filled the

nightclub, and Gemma began to sing. Her glorious voice had gained an indefinable sexiness in the past couple of years, and Llewellyn Jones at the Wellesley wouldn't have recognized it in a million years now. The voice seemed to caress the words of the song as Gemma moved among the audience, and held them captive. When she reached her friends' table, she teased Andrews by pretending to make a play for him, to his obvious embarrassment.

When the three songs she had chosen were over, and the applause had finally died down, Gemma walked over to her agent's table. Laura and Penny could see the intense discussions going on there now, while a group took over the entertainment spot, and couples began to smooch on the dance floor.

'She was just great, wasn't she?' Penny enthused. 'You've got to hand it to her, Laura. She knows exactly how to milk an audience.'

'It was wonderful,' Laura agreed. And all the time Gemma had been singing one of the old ballads that were as well-suited to her voice as to the ambience of this place, Laura had been applying the words to herself and Nick.

Every time we say goodbye, I die a little . . .

'We're invited to a party later,' Penny told her.

'Oh no. I don't want to meet all those people,' Laura said at once. 'I won't know what to say to them – '

'I doubt that you'll need to say anything. Gemma will be bubbling over, and her agent will be keeping her under his thumb until he gets a contract signed up. But she wants us to be there, and so we have to go.' Her

102

voice became suddenly sharp. 'She's worked bloody hard for this, Laura, and we're not going to let her down, are we?'

Laura gave in, knowing Penny was right. And who else would Gemma want around in her moment of triumph, but her two best friends? Providing it *was* a moment of triumph, of course, but from the smiles and handshakes and kisses at the front table, she had no doubt of it. Gemma was on her way.

She heard Andrews clear his throat discreetly before he spoke to Penny.

'What are your instructions for meeting you after the party, Miss?' he said.

'We'll be leaving here quite soon, I should imagine, so I suggest that you pick us up at the agent's flat at two a.m., Andrews. Make yourself known to him, and find out the address,' she added vaguely.

'Very well, Miss.'

He obeyed at once. Laura observed all this with a kind of fascination. It was like listening to people enacting a play, in which one character called the tune, and the other did whatever was wanted, smoothing the way. She was more than thankful, now, that in their Wellesley days she'd never fully understood the kind of life Penny was used to.

'Is this party going to be at the agent's flat then?' she asked now.

'Apparently so,' Penny confirmed. 'Isn't he called Rube something or other? It's some name like that, I seem to recall.'

'Rube Steiner.'

'Oh yes, that's it. Well done, Laura. You always did have a good memory for names.'

Laura couldn't remember anything more about Eddie the pianist, though, except that he was a fantastic and inventive lover, according to Gemma. At the time, the breezy words had been said to shock and intrigue her friends, but Laura realized she was no longer embarrassed when she thought about them. Not now that she knew exactly what Gemma meant.

Gemma approached them a little later, beautiful and glowing in her scarlet dress, and she caught both their hands in hers. If ever there was a moment in time when 'stars in her eyes' was the only description possible, then this was it.

'It's going to be all right,' she said chokingly. 'I can't say any more at the moment, but Rube's certain I'm going to get a TV spot. Once he's got the finer details sorted out, we're hoping to sign the contract tonight.'

'There was never any doubt in our minds after all you put into those numbers,' Penny said.

'Congratulations, Gem. You were simply wonderful,' Laura added warmly.

Gemma looked at them both.

'I can't tell you how glad I was to know you were both here. It held it all together, somehow. And that's the one and only sentimental thing you're going to hear from me tonight.'

She let go of their hands then, and her voice became more practical. 'We're all leaving for Rube's flat in ten minutes, so come to the back room through the bead curtains whenever you're ready. Your bloke's already got the address for collecting you later, Pen.'

She blew them a kiss and was gone, but every step she took was punctuated by more praises. She really fed on it, Laura thought, and hoped fervently that it would always be as good as this for Gemma.

'Well,' Penny said, after a small pause, 'I suppose we'd better do as we're told.'

And what Andrews was going to do, and where he went, was obviously no concern of Penny's, as long as he also did as he was told.

Several cars took them to Steiner's flat. The three girls were squashed in the back of his car, while Rube and Eddie sat in the front. The TV people followed on behind in a stretch limousine with darkened windows. Leeches, Laura thought again.

'There'll be a few more people there to meet you, doll,' Rube announced casually. 'You're on your way up, babe.'

'It's the only way to go,' Gemma said.

'Aren't you the smallest bit nervous?' Laura asked.

Eddie spoke without turning round. 'Hey, don't go putting ideas like that into her head. The secret of success in this business is to be outwardly confident, no matter how you feel inside. You *never* allow nerves to show. Right, Gem?'

'That's right,' she answered.

For all that, Laura had the oddest feeling that Eddie was trying to bolster up her courage. She'd never thought Gemma would have needed it, but she supposed that even sudden fame could be a shock to the system, like winning the football pools . . .

Rube's flat wasn't over-large, but it was still spacious enough to prove that he was no longer just a small-time agent. He had clients who were Names, Gemma confided, and she planned to be one of them herself very soon. And when his clients became big, so did Rube.

He was pleasant enough, but Laura preferred the outgoing Eddie, who clearly adored Gemma. Who wouldn't, of course, when she sparkled like champagne, and charmed everybody in sight?

Laura felt depressingly ordinary beside her, and couldn't even guess how Penny felt. Penny was used to dealing with any situation and any company, and she was also adept at keeping her feelings well hidden – the way a well-bred young lady was trained to do.

The three of them were such contrasts, she thought. How the hell had they ever become close friends? And how were they going to stay friends, when circumstances were bound to separate them, and in fact, had done so from the minute they left the Wellesley.

For a few moments, Laura seemed to stand on the sidelines, watching the animated conversations going on around her. She wasn't used to parties like these, but they clearly held no problems for Penny, who could converse with anyone.

'Let me get you another drink,' she heard a male voice say beside her. 'It's Laura, isn't it? Gemma's friend?'

Eddie had taken off the bow tie he wore for his nightclub spot, and his shirt was open at the neck now, regardless of how anybody else was dressed. He was darkly bohemian in a gypsyish way – a typical musician – and Laura could see at once how Gemma was attracted to him. She also saw that his hands were far from steady by now.

'I don't drink much,' she protested.

'Neither do I,' he winked conspiratorially. 'But you have to be sociable at parties, don't you? How about a long drink then, while I get myself another whisky? Rube's paying, and that's a rare enough occurrence, so I aim to make the most of it tonight.'

He probably made a study of being outrageous too, Laura decided, but she couldn't help liking him, all the same.

'A long drink, then,' she insisted. 'And some food wouldn't be a bad idea, since you're looking after me.'

And maybe he'd have some food himself, and not drink so much. She listened to herself, knowing she was thinking like a mother hen, when she was damn sure Eddie could take care of himself perfectly well. But as she watched him weave across the floor between the other guests, she wasn't so sure.

When he returned, he was precariously balancing a huge plate of food on top of two drinks.

'Made it,' he said as he put them down, as triumphantly as if he'd climbed the Eiger. 'Now, tell me what you thought of our star tonight. Wasn't she terrific?'

He didn't need Laura's confirmation of that, but she suddenly realized he needed to talk about Gemma, in the same way she had needed to talk about Nick to Mrs Hall. And with her heightened sense of perception tonight, she saw something else too. Eddie wasn't just one of Gemma's adoring slaves. He was passionately in love with her. And she frequently treated him like dirt.

'She was wonderful. But we always knew she would be, even at school.'

'Tell me what she was like at school,' he invited, at once confirming everything Laura suspected.

But she wasn't allowed to spend all evening with Eddie. She was told by Gemma to mingle, to meet people, and so she did. By two a.m., she was mellow and relaxed, and she wasn't too sure just what had been mixed in her drinks when she saw Andrews at the door, immaculate as ever in his chauffeur's uniform once more. She almost fell into the back seat of the Daimler beside Penny, and was promptly asleep within seconds.

'Wake up, Laura. We're nearly home.'

She heard Penny's voice as if it came to her through a fog, and she felt herself being nudged.

For a moment, Laura couldn't think where home was. It wasn't the farm, that was for sure. And she wasn't with Nick.

Nick was hundreds of miles away, and she felt the most awful maudlin misery creeping over her at the thought. She wanted him so much. She needed him and ached for him, and . . .

'Are you all right?'

She started. 'I think so, though my head feels as if it's made of cotton wool and doesn't belong to me any more.'

'You're not used to the stuff,' Penny said casually.

For a moment, Laura's brain refused to function, and then it did, and she wanted to hit out blindly at this girl who was supposed to be one of her two best friends. She jerked upright in the back seat of the car.

'You're not telling me those drinks were spiked, are you?' she snapped. 'I thought the ones Eddie got for me tasted a bit odd. What the hell was in them, Penny?'

'I've no idea, for God's sake. Certainly it was none of the hard stuff, and if it was anything at all, it was probably just something to make everybody feel more relaxed. I just meant you don't normally drink, do you? Anyway, whatever it was, it worked. You've been asleep and dreaming all the way back from London.'

'I don't take drugs,' Laura yelled, not listening to anything else.

'Well, neither do I, so stop making such a fuss. I told you, it was nothing.'

'Can you swear to that?'

Penny's voice became suddenly angry. 'Don't you think it's time you stopped acting like such a little Puritan after what you told me about you and your doctor lover?'

Laura was shocked at the sudden venom in Penny's voice. They so very rarely fought, and it was always Gemma who was the caustic one and stirred up the arguments. And what Penny said wasn't fair. It was hitting below the belt, literally.

And she couldn't find the words to answer, knowing that with every utterance, Penny was tainting her one lovely night with Nick . . .

'Oh God, I'm so sorry, Laura,' Penny suddenly said,

reaching out to hug her friend as she huddled in the corner of the car. 'Just listen to us, will you? I don't know how this conversation got so out of hand, but I'd never have said anything so bitchy if I hadn't had too much to drink myself. You *do* know it, don't you?'

'I suppose so,' Laura mumbled. She was on the brink of saying it was all right, and to forget it . . . when it wasn't all right, and she couldn't forget it . . .

'Do you forgive me?'

At least she could answer that with reasonable honesty, if that wasn't a complete contradiction.

'Of course I forgive you. We've been friends for too long for me to do anything else.'

But she vowed to herself that it was the first and last time she got involved in that kind of party. And she felt a real flicker of fear over just what Gemma was getting herself into.

It was daylight when Gemma awoke very, very slowly. She was in someone's bed, and it wasn't her own. For a moment she panicked, and then she felt a familiar pair of arms closing around her, and the not-unpleasant scent of a man's body that she knew.

'Eddie,' she murmured, without opening her eyes. 'How the hell did I get here?'

'You were in no fit state to be on your own last night,' he said, his hands idly stroking her fabulous breasts beneath the bedcovers. 'Once Rube had struck the TV deal to his satisfaction, I offered to take you home in my car, but I didn't say which home. Are you objecting?'

She knew she should get excited all over again about

the TV deal, but that could come later. Right now she felt more excited by the familiar throb of desire for Eddie, and she nestled her face into his shoulder.

She was always aware of an odd mixture of emotions when she was with him. Sometimes he infuriated her, and at other times, she felt such a great tenderness for him. He could always arouse her to the point of a desperate need for him, and yet he also made her feel safe.

And since he was hardly the settling-down kind, it was something she couldn't begin to explain. It was as if he was her much-needed safety valve . . . She had told him so once, and he'd whispered some crude remark in her ear, which had sent them both into peals of laughter.

That was one of the things that was so good between them. They enjoyed one another so much, and they had fun together, which was far preferable to the intense kind of relationship most men expected from a woman. She knew where she was with Eddie. He was her friend as well as her lover, and except on rare occasions, he never demanded more from her than she was prepared to give. And she admitted that lately she had definitely mellowed towards him.

Right now she was mellow with the lovely, languid, morning-after feeling, of waking up in his arms and knowing that if she once wound her arms around him, and pressed her body into his, they would be making love within minutes.

'I'm not objecting,' she said huskily.

'Nor to this?' he whispered, his hands sliding down the length of her receptive body and kneading her belly softly before reaching deeper.

'Nor to anything,' Gemma said, drawing him down onto her, and opening up for him.

Laura slept late as well. The beds at the Bishop place were of the very best quality, and there was no traffic noise to disturb the tranquillity of the country-house setting. It was quieter than the farm, where early-morning noises from birds and animals and tractors made a mockery of the city-dwellers' idea of the idyllic pastoral scene.

When she felt someone sitting on her bed, she opened her eyes a fraction. Penny was already dressed in jeans and a checked shirt, and placing a glass of freshly-squeezed orange juice on the bedside table.

'What time is it?' Laura asked, reluctantly struggling out of a lovely dream in which she and Nick had been walking barefoot along the water's edge on a sun-kissed beach.

'Nearly twelve.'

'What? You mean I've slept until nearly lunchtime? My father would have a fit if he knew.'

Penny laughed. 'And there speaks a farmer's daughter! You needed your sleep, and I haven't been up long anyway. But since we didn't get home until after three this morning, you haven't done so badly.'

'I suppose not.' She took the glass of orange juice Penny handed her and felt its refreshing coolness slide down her throat as she sipped it.

She would have preferred a cup of tea, but presumably that would come later. Penny was always one for healthy living, and besides, Laura knew she needed the burst of energy the orange juice was supposed to give her. She felt decidedly shaky this morning.

'When you've showered and dressed, we'll have some brunch, Laura. Then, if you really can't face the thought of riding, I thought we'd go for a tramp across the fields. Though there's a very docile mare that would suit you – '

'Honestly, Penny, I'd rather not. Dad tried to get me up on a horse once, and it's the one thing I can't stand. I know it's stupid, when I was brought up with animals, but I just don't like horses.'

'It's not stupid, but I can't really understand it. I thought all little girls liked horses. Didn't you ever want to ride a pony when you were a child?'

'Not that I can remember,' Laura said.

'Most children do. Yours will, when you have some. You won't stop them, will you?'

'I'm not thinking that far ahead – '

'Not even about your doctor?' Penny said neatly.

Laura laughed. 'You said yourself I've hardly had time to get to know him, so don't start getting any ideas about wedding bells just yet.'

Penny got off the bed. 'All right. But I've got the strongest feeling about you and Dr Nick. So when the time comes, don't forget where you heard it first.'

'I won't,' Laura grinned.

But later, lifting her face to the shower and letting the soft warmth of it begin to revive her, she knew Penny was mistaken. Because she had first heard it inside herself. Some things you instinctively knew. It was like the way you doodled on exercise books when you were at school, and then scribbled out the words so that only you knew they were there.

Nick loves Laura. Laura loves Nick. Laura's going to marry Nick and live happily-ever-after . . .

Half an hour later, feeling considerably more human, she wandered downstairs and found Penny already in the dining room. And at last there were welcome pots of tea and coffee awaiting them. There was also grilled bacon and scrambled eggs, tomatoes and mushrooms and sausages, all keeping warm under silver tureens on a side table, and toast and marmalade and a huge bowl of fruit and cheese and biscuits for dessert. Brunch was no more than an elaborate word for a late breakfast, Laura thought with a grin, but her mouth watered all the same. It seemed a very long time since she had eaten anything substantial at all.

'We'll serve ourselves,' Penny was blithely unaware that Laura had not considered doing anything else. 'Do you feel revived now?'

'That's just about the right word for it. I feel great, Pen, and I'm really glad I came.'

'So am I. It just seems so silly that we've never visited one another before, any of us, when we're all within reasonable striking distance.'

Laura tried to envisage Penny fitting into the homely atmosphere of the Robinson farm, and knew she was being guilty of inverted snobbery. Besides, Penny was due to depart for Rome soon, so there was no question of returning the invitation in the immediate future. She shouldn't feel relieved about that, but she did.

'You know you'd always be welcome to come down to Somerset, if you could bear to slum it,' she said, to smother her own guilt feelings.

'Why on earth would I think I was slumming it? You do have some weird ideas sometimes, Laura. And you had better invite Gemma and me to the wedding, or we'll both want to know the reason why!'

Laura paused in spooning a mound of scrambled egg onto her plate and looked at her in exasperation.

'I told you not to go on about that.'

'Why? Are you superstitious that if you talk about it too much, it may never happen? That's no more than an old wives' tale, Laura. My governess used to say such things, and my mother was always furious with her for doing it.'

Until that moment Laura hadn't even known she had a governess. She sat down at the table abruptly, eyeing the huge mound of food on her plate, and wondering if she was being an absolute pig in taking so much.

'I'm not superstitious at all.' But Laura knew very well that she was, and so she mentally crossed her fingers at the same time as she denied Penny's gibe. Why else would she already have sussed out that Nick was a Gemini to her Aquarius, and had been childishly de-lighted to discover that they were supposed to be so compatible? And always read his stars as well as hers . . .

'Yes, you are, and you always were,' Penny said. 'I've known you too long to forget it, okay?'

But she said it with rough affection, and Laura knew they were back on the old familiar footing they had known at the Wellesley.

If only Gemma had been here too, it would have been perfect, she thought, tucking into the brunch with some relish. It would have been just like old times.

People said you could never go back, and you wouldn't want to do that, anyway. You had to go on, but the best thing of all about friendship was going on together. And Gemma would really hoot if she could hear that little bit of homespun philosophy, Laura thought with an eggy grin.

CHAPTER 7

On their last day at the Wellesley, they had made an emotional vow to meet every two years. It was the kind of arrangement that could lead to a lifelong commitment, or it might be forgotten and never be honoured. Sixteen was a vulnerable age, when feelings ran deep, but once the schoolroom doors were closed for ever, so many other things could get in the way of remembering a part of life that was over and done with.

Laura was basically an optimist, but even she had been dubious over whether they would really do as they had vowed. Initially the correspondence between them had been regular, but it had dwindled, and Laura had half-expected any number of excuses for the meetings not to take place. Now she knew she had been wrong.

Since their first meeting after a two-year gap, they all knew the friendship was as strong as ever. They kept in touch, no matter how sporadic. Penny usually communicated by phone or postcards, enthusing about the gymkhanas, the show-jumping and dressage events, and the growing number of rosettes she and Midnight

Sun were accumulating as their names became well known in riding circles.

There was talk of foreign visits and celebrity dinners, and it all left Laura breathless. It was a world she didn't know, but was happy to feel a small part of, especially when some of the events were televised, and she was glued to the TV set and willing Penny on.

'I think she's terrific,' Laura said to her father. 'She's doing exactly what she wanted to do.'

'And of course it helps that her Daddy has the money and contacts to help her do it,' he said dryly.

'Oh, you're just being an old cynic,' Laura laughed, but knowing very well it was true.

But without all Penny's advantages, she had to admit that Gemma was also realizing her own fantastically-successful dream. In a matter of months after the contract-signing in Rube Steiner's flat, Gemma's face had been on the TV often enough that nobody would fail to recognize her in the street – unless they came from Outer Space.

Rube Steiner was now her self-styled manager as well as her agent, having fully realized her potential, and discarded some of his less-promotable clients. The ease with which he did so made Gemma slightly uneasy, but since she knew none of them, she didn't let it bother her unduly.

Gemma's scrappy notes were more erratic than Penny's and far less chatty than Laura's letters, but she usually managed to let her friends know when she was going to be on the radio or TV, or interviewed on one of the morning chat-show programmes. But there was hardly any need to let anyone know. She had been photographed for the cover of a showbiz magazine, and featured in various women's magazines, for a public avid to know more about her background.

In meteoric fashion, Gemma had become a not-infrequent guest artiste on other people's TV shows, and there was vague talk of a nationwide tour with a backing group. Everybody wanted to jump on the band wagon, Rube told her, though the recording contract he had negotiated was hardly going to make her rich overnight. But with several singles and an album already in the stores, she was on her way. In less than a year, Gemma's life had been transformed, and so had she.

She had been made-over by an image-making team, and she no longer wore quite so much flamboyant scarlet and other glaring colours when she did her numbers. She was now more often seen wearing sophisticated black or white, and her always-good figure had been fined down to accentuate her small waist and voluptuous curves.

From her scrawled notes to Laura and Penny, they knew that Eddie was still on the scene. And anyway, the magazine reports were always quick to mention that she wouldn't perform or travel anywhere without her own pianist. The inference was always that they were lovers, even if it was never actually stated. And if it was intended to ensure a little mystery about the delectable Gemma Grover, it certainly worked.

Nobody was allowed to know too much about her private life. And if the friends who knew her well had a few nagging doubts about the occasional shadows beneath Gemma's eyes that the make-up boys and the close-ups couldn't hide, there was nothing they could do about it, Laura thought. Besides, she had a far more important private life of her own to think about now . . .

As Gemma's rise to fame began, Laura was waiting for her love to come back to her. She hadn't been sure of the exact day when Nick would be returning to Somerset; the two weeks apart had stretched to three, and seemed like an eternity. He had told her he wouldn't phone or write while he was away, as he'd be frantically clearing up everything before moving south, and she had accepted that.

But she couldn't help wondering if he, like herself, was unconsciously thinking of this uncommunicative time apart as some kind of testing period. That maybe they had fallen in love too fast and too soon, and it wasn't the kind of love that was destined to last. Maybe it was all lust and not love at all . . .

Not that Laura believed this for one second, and would be devastated if it were true, but she had to accept that it could happen.

By the time she was thinking desperately that Nick must surely be back in the district soon, the phone rang. It was a sunlit, mellow, late-summer afternoon, and she had been baking to stock up the freezer, so the farmhouse kitchen was warm and steamy with the luscious aroma of blackberry and apple pies. She wiped her floury hands on a towel before picking up the receiver, expecting it to be the man wanting to discuss her father's order of organic fertilizer.

And then her heart leapt wildly as she heard Nick's voice, as close as if he was standing right beside her.

'I've missed you like hell,' he said, without any preliminaries. 'I've been back at the flat for all of ten minutes now, and I can't settle to a damn thing. I haven't been able to stop thinking about you for a single minute since I've been away. So how soon can I see you?'

There was never a thought of prevaricating in Laura's mind. 'I could be with you around six,' she said, abandoning any idea of supper with her father.

'Good. We'll eat later.'

Laura felt her smile begin. 'Oh yes? And what do you propose we do first?'

'Make love. What else would we do?'

From anyone else it might have sounded brash and arrogant. From Nick, it was everything she wanted to hear, and Laura felt her knees weaken, and her skin tingle, just as so many romantic novels said they would.

For one crazy second she felt as if she wanted to shout to the whole world that it was all true. You *did* feel faint when you heard your lover's voice, and you *did* think of him every minute of the day and night. And every romantic song you ever heard could only have been written for the two of you and nobody else . . . and these few weeks apart had been absolute hell on earth for her, too.

'I'll be there,' she repeated quickly.

When she hung up the phone, she heard her father

clear his throat behind her, and her face burned. She tried frantically to remember what she had been saying, but she was sure she hadn't said anything that could have been misconstrued. Nick had done most of the talking.

'So he's back,' he said with a smile.

'How did you know it was Nick?'

He took her hands in his calloused ones and squeezed them tenderly for a moment.

'Well, it certainly wasn't the man from the supply store. I've seen you mooning about ever since Nick left, and from the look on your face now, it could hardly be anyone else but him. So I'm to get my own supper tonight, am I?'

She turned her face away from him for a moment, so he couldn't read the expression in her eyes.

'You don't mind, do you, Dad? I promise I won't make a habit of it – '

He was suddenly brisk. 'Of course you damn well will. And if he's the one for you, it's only right that you should want to spend your time with him, and not with me. So I'm going to have to get used to it, aren't I?'

She wasn't sure how he expected her to answer. He was still missing her mother, even though he went about his daily business as cheerfully as ever. But Laura knew. And although she had never tried to take her mother's place, and couldn't possibly have done so, it would be another wrench to him if – *when* – she left him, too.

'Now just you listen to me, my girl,' Farmer Robinson went on, when the silence lengthened between them. 'I've always wanted the best for you, and that includes a good man to make an honest woman of you. Damn it all, I want grandchildren before I'm too old to enjoy them, so don't you go being selfish and hanging on here any longer than you have to, d'you hear?'

She was laughing long before he had finished.

'Oh Dad, you're the best, and I love you.'

'Maybe. But I can't give you what a husband can, and that's for you young 'uns to find out for yourselves in due course. So tidy yourself up and don't worry about me tonight – or any other night, come to that. I'll be happy enough down at the Nightjar with a pie and a pint and a game of darts.'

And Laura would be making love . . .

She wondered if there would be some embarrassment when they met each other again. How long had they known one another, after all? They had come so far, so fast . . . and they might never recapture that spectacular passion again . . .

She pushed such disturbing thoughts out of her mind, as she drove feverishly through the lanes towards Nick's flat. And once he opened the door and took her in his arms, she knew nothing had changed for either of them.

'So when are you going to marry me?' he said lazily, a long while later, when they lay naked beneath the bedcovers, and were both sated with love.

She twisted her head to look at him, unsure whether or not she had heard him properly. From the look in his eyes she knew that she had. There was only one answer she wanted to give, but she wanted to give him the option, too.

'You don't have to ask me that, you know,' she breathed softly into his shoulder. 'I wouldn't pressure you into anything, and we can go on as we are for as long as you like.'

'No, I don't think we can,' he said. 'For one thing, I'm not going to start commuting to your farm every evening to see you, and I'm not having you sneaking in here all the time on a hole-and-corner basis. I've got my reputation to think of, remember?' he added teasingly.

'Are you blackmailing me?'

His arms held her so tightly that her breasts were flattened against his chest, and her legs were closely entwined in his.

'Too right I am. I'm not letting you go until you promise to marry me. I'll keep you here all night, if need be, and then we'll both scandalize the neighbourhood. The news will soon be out that their new doctor is sleeping with the respectable farmer's daughter.'

Laura felt the laughter bubbling up inside her. They had just made love as frantically as if they were expecting to hear the four-minute warning at any second. And she had behaved as wantonly as he, and learned that a combination of lust and love could be awesome and wonderful.

'I feel anything but the respectable farmer's daughter right now,' she said. 'I feel – I don't know how to say it.'

'Yes, you do. Tell me exactly what you feel, and no holds barred,' he demanded.

She spoke slowly. 'Well then. I feel loved, and

cherished, and as if no one else in the world has ever discovered love this way before.'

'They haven't. Not our love, anyway. Everything that happens in this room is unique and belongs to us alone.'

His words charmed her. 'Do you think everyone feels like that after they've made love?'

'I don't care about anyone else. I just care about us. And marvellous though this is, it's not enough. I want to fall asleep with you in my arms every night, and wake up to find you still there in the morning. And you haven't answered my question yet.'

'What was the question?' Laura said, playing for time, and wanting to hear him say it again.

'When are you going to marry me?'

She swallowed, knowing she was about to commit herself and her entire future. But knowing that the thought of a future without him was already unthinkable.

'I always thought April would be nice for a wedding,' she suggested haltingly.

'Good God, that's eight whole months away!'

'And by then you'll be a junior partner in the practice. You'll be able to look for a bigger place for us to live than this poky flat, somewhere between here and my Dad's farm, perhaps. And anyway, I'll need that much time to organize things properly,' Laura finished.

He laughed at her practical forward planning, holding her away from him and looking into her determined blue eyes.

'My God, I can see how you kept those friends of yours in order at your fancy school,' he said with a grin. 'But I like a woman who can make up her mind and doesn't waste time. Though I can't think why any woman needs eight months to organize a wedding. A special licence is all I'd require – '

She shook her head. 'That wouldn't be good enough for us, Nick. I want everything to be right, and to do things properly. The church, the dress, the flowers, and a proper honeymoon. You'll allow me that much, won't you?'

'I certainly approve of the honeymoon. And you know you've only got to ask and I'll give you the earth. I also think you've got a very mature head on those lovely shoulders, Mrs Dean.'

She drew in her breath. 'That's jumping the gun a bit, isn't it?' She felt she had to protest, while knowing how much she was savouring the sound of it.

'So is this,' Nick smiled, pulling her across his body and proceeding to make love to her all over again.

Her father wasn't in the least surprised when they told him their news. He'd made an early marriage himself, and he could see that his girl was so head-over-heels in love that it would be a crime to make any objections, as long as they kept to their eight months' engagement period. They told Nick's Somerset relations at the same time, and the Halls were delighted, all except Tommy, who sulked and stamped about, consoling himself with far too much scrumpy and the company of the village girls.

126

Penny wasn't surprised either, and was delighted for her, but Gemma thought she was completely mad. She phoned Laura especially to make her views known.

'For God's sake, think what you're doing, Laura, and don't tie yourself down before you've had a chance to see a bit of life. Bloody hell, you'll only be nineteen when you marry the guy, and you must admit you're rusticating down there.'

Laura counted to ten, but she was way too far up in the clouds to let Gemma upset her.

'Well, that's the way it is,' she said cheerfully. 'And I want you to be happy for me, and to promise to come to the wedding, Gem. It'll be such a thrill for all the hayseeds down here to actually see my glamorous friend in the flesh. You're my one claim to fame!'

'Well, of course I'll be there.' Gemma completely missed the fact that the words were said tongue-in-cheek. 'You don't think I'd miss it, do you? Nor Penny either, providing she can get off her damn horse and out of her riding breeches for long enough. God knows how I ever came to have two such countrified amigos.'

Laura laughed. 'And God knows how the hell we ever put up with you. And it's *amigas*, too. We're female, remember?'

'Just as long as your Dr Nick remembers, who the hell cares what anybody else thinks?' The grin in Gemma's voice was very evident. 'All right, kiddo. Just tell me where and when and give me enough time to arrange my schedule, and I'll be there. And congratulations.'

It may have been an afterthought, but Laura was

ridiculously glad to have her approval. Apart from her parents, Gemma and Penny had been the two most important people in her life before Nick. And she desperately wanted them to like him.

Christmas that year was one that she would always remember. Some days seemed to be etched in gold, she told Nick, and you knew you would never forget them. On bad days, you could take the memories out and polish them and remember the glow that you felt . . . and she thanked God that he didn't think such daft statements were ridiculously over the top.

Anyway, if you couldn't be nostalgic at Christmas, when on earth could you be? The two families had gone together to the midnight carol service at the village church, and everyone in the congregation held a lighted candle, so that the whole place was ablaze with light. And because she was sharing it all with Nick, it was the most beautiful and holy night she could remember. There had been a sprinkling of snow during the evening, and the temperature had dropped, so that the fields were frosted and beautiful as they made their way back home.

Nick stayed overnight at the farm, in a bedroom along the corridor from hers. And it seemed right, that here in her father's house, they should remain two doors apart.

The Halls had invited Nick and Laura and her father for Christmas Day, and their farmhouse was filled with holly and mistletoe, and she couldn't prevent Tommy giving her a great smacking kiss the minute she arrived. He had evidently got over being miffed at her preference for his cousin, and had his own girl in tow, a jolly, red-faced village girl, who was clearly destined to become a farmer's wife.

Laura listened to her thoughts, and felt immediately ashamed at being so snobbish, just because she was destined to become a doctor's wife . . . Then she caught Nick watching her, and the smile between them was secret and special. He'd bought her an engagement ring for Christmas, and it still felt unfamiliar on her finger, but every time she looked at the sapphire surrounded by diamonds, she almost burst with happiness.

Sometimes she was fearful that such joy couldn't last. The superstition she had always pooh-poohed was sometimes very strong in her head, and she could never quite ignore it. Penny wouldn't give it house-room, and as for Gemma . . . Alone and sleepless in bed that night, Laura wondered what her friends were doing now. The card from Penny had said they expected to be in the Canaries for Christmas, while Gemma's extravagant card told her she'd be working.

Gemma had engagements at several London clubs during the Christmas period. She scorned the seasonal songs that everybody else seemed so keen to perform, until the audiences must be screaming with boredom at hearing them yet again, and insisted to Eddie that they kept to the sexy ballads which had made her name.

'I think you're wrong, babe,' he argued. 'People expect a good dose of sentimentality at Christmas.'

'Well, you know damn well I'm not the sentimental

129

kind,' she retorted. 'And I'm not changing my style for the sake of a few old biddies.'

'Don't knock them, darling. Those old biddies are just as likely to be buying records and cassettes this Christmas as the kids. What's wrong with giving them what they want?'

'It's not what *I* want, that's why,' Gemma insisted. 'I don't want to be a singer who has to promote a Christmas song every year just to sell records. I'm better than that.'

She caught Eddie's thoughtful look. They were lounging in the swish new penthouse flat that her sudden wealth had bought her. Rube said it went with the image, even though the rent was almost obscene. The flat had a panoramic view of the Thames and its bridges far below the picture window. Life was better for Gemma than she had ever dreamed it could be, and she wanted to keep it that way. People adored her, and she had never felt that kind of affection from anyone in her life before. You could feel the empathy from an audience as strongly as if somebody wrapped a warm blanket around you.

The achievement was hers, and hers alone. She was sometimes jealous of sharing any of it, even with Eddie. Everybody thought he had moved in with her permanently, but she still only allowed him into her life when she chose to have him there. She used him, but although he was apparently content to be used, he was certainly no wimp, and he could still turn her on like crazy. But, in rare moments of introspection, Gemma knew she was still, in essence, the same little East End girl she'd always been, clawing to find a place in the world. But nobody but herself would ever know it.

'Besides,' she went on, 'once Christmas is over, who the hell ever wants to hear those songs again? Most of them are bloody awful, anyway. And Rube doesn't try to push me into it, so why should you?'

'Rube goes along with whatever you say these days,' Eddie observed shrewdly. 'He's too afraid of losing you otherwise. You ought to know that by now.'

'Why would he think he was losing me?'

'Because some other big-time agent will try to snap you up. They're already sniffing around, but he's kept them out so far.'

Gemma sat bolt upright. Until that moment, she had been lying on the deep-piled sofa with her feet on Eddie's lap, and his hands had been sensuously caressing her legs, encased in their silken stockings.

'You mean he's already been approached to let me go? How do you know?'

'I've been in this business longer than you have, and I know the signs, that's all. Rube wants to keep you sweet, so he'll go along with anything you want to do, providing it fits in with his plans for you and lines his pockets.'

Her indignation died down a little. Eddie was right in one respect. He'd been in the music business a long time, and he knew the sleazy, dog-eat-dog side of it as well as anyone. She had never altogether trusted Rube, although he had long ago stopped ogling her, and she knew his motives for promoting her were prompted solely by greed.

But she trusted Eddie. All the same, he should have warned her of this before now.

'What do you think I should do, then? Just supposing some other agent or manager wanted to take me on?'

Eddie shrugged. 'It's your life, babe. I'm only saying it like it is.'

His usual response infuriated her. She wanted him to *tell* her, for God's sake, not to sit on the fence and let her make up her own mind. Rube got her the work and advised her on the clothes she wore, and had people flitting around her as if she was the Queen Bee and they were all worker drones . . . but just sometimes, she wanted to put her head on somebody's shoulder and have him tell her what she should do, with no strings attached.

But Eddie was the type who never interfered. He stated the facts, and left people to make up their own minds. This notion of everybody being a free spirit was just an excuse for not getting involved, as outdated as the sixties it came from. Sometimes you needed somebody to lean on. And that was about as unlikely a feeling for Gemma Grover to admit to as flying to Mars . . .

'But what do *you* think?' she persisted.

He pulled her into his arms and nuzzled his unshaven chin into her neck, whispering sweet obscenities into her skin that made her shiver. He was no more than a damn gypsy at heart, she thought, easily dodging the issue, and relying on his undeniable sexiness to make her forget any problem, big or small. And it worked, damn it. It worked every time. It was working now . . .

'I think you talk too much,' he said finally, his tongue

132

circling her lips before foraging into her mouth. 'When we have far better things to do.'

'This doesn't solve everything, Eddie.' But his lips went lower, and she felt his fingers begin to unfasten the buttons on her dress and move inside.

'Oh yes, it does,' he muttered.

A long while later, she remembered something she'd been going to tell him.

'That ex-schoolfriend of mine is getting married in April,' she said.

'Which one? Not the horsey one?'

Gemma laughed. Anyone conforming less to the image of a horsey female than Penny, she couldn't imagine. Unless you compared her to a supple, sleekly beautiful race-horse . . .

'No. The other one, Laura. She's marrying some country doctor, and the wedding's in April. I've got to sort out dates with Rube, but I'm going to it, whatever he says.'

'Sure you are,' Eddie said with a grin. 'It'll be a great photo opportunity, babe.'

She scowled. 'I didn't mean that, and anyway, it'll be Laura's day, not mine. You can come as well, if you like. I know Laura won't mind.'

'Okay, why not? You'll need a minder.' The words were a lazy drawl, and they both knew there was nothing in it. Turning up together at a wedding was simply that.

CHAPTER 8

It was a toss-up to know who was more surprised at meeting Nicholas Dean for the first time: Penny or Gemma.

They had both declined to be bridesmaids, saying this was Laura's day, and since there were enough little girls in the village and surrounding farms eager for the job, she hadn't pressed them. Guiltily, Laura knew she hadn't really minded that Gemma hadn't agreed, for it would have been only natural for everybody to crowd around her for autographs and photos of her glamorous and well-known friend.

They would want to take photos of Penny too, since she'd just taken part in a well-publicised point-to-point event alongside royalty, and her elegant photograph had been splashed across many of the tabloid newspapers the preceding week. It wasn't that Laura was jealous of either of them, but, as they had both said, this was her day. And anyway, no matter how many important contacts they made, Laura knew she had the only one she ever wanted. She had the best.

The various Robinson relatives were mostly from

134

the farming community, and those who were attending the wedding all lived within striking distance, and would meet up at the church. Laura's special guests arrived the night before, and stayed at the farm for the one night. There would be no evening party after the wedding, as Laura and Nick were flying out to Cyprus in the early evening for a week's honeymoon, which was all the time the practice could spare him for.

Penny arrived, chauffeur-driven as usual. Gemma and Eddie roared up later in his red convertible. The girls were to share a bedroom, while Eddie had been given the small box-room in the attic, much to Gemma's amusement.

'If I dared, I'd sneak up there and give him a nice surprise in the middle of the night,' she told Penny, when they had exhausted their talking and retired for the night. 'But I wouldn't want to offend Laura's father when he's probably uptight at the thought of his one ewe lamb getting married.'

'He seems to be delighted about it,' Penny said. 'You do have some odd ideas sometimes, Gemma.'

'I always did, according to you. But look where they've got me.'

They lay in their twin beds in the companionable darkness, and they could have been back at the shared room at the Wellesley, except that Laura wasn't with them. By this late hour, they both knew Laura would be trying desperately to sleep and to think calm thoughts before tomorrow.

'Are you happy, Gem?' Penny said now.

'Good God, do you need to ask me that? Haven't I got everything I ever wanted?'

'I don't know. Have you?'

Gemma sat up, leaning on one elbow.

'What the hell's that supposed to mean?'

'Oh, I don't know. I suppose it's hearing Laura go on about this wonderful doctor of hers, and ending up doing everything we said she'd do. Apart from having the houseful of kids, of course, which will surely be the next thing. Who's really getting the most out of life, I wonder?'

Gemma was so used to keeping her private life a closely-guarded secret from the intrusive press that her reaction to the interrogation was sharper than she intended.

'Well, excuse me, but I've got no complaints! And I shouldn't think you have, either, with all the trips you make and the influential guys you meet. Oh, but I forgot. You're not interested in anything in trousers, are you?'

'I'm not interested in women either, if that's what you're inferring. I like men well enough, but they don't have to be the be-all and end-all of your life, do they?'

'You try telling that to Laura. In fact, I've been wondering if I shouldn't have told her a thing or two before tomorrow. She's such an innocent. She must be the last virgin to come out of the Wellesley.'

She began to laugh as the *double entendre* of that remark hit her. But then she stopped laughing as Penny hissed at her from the other side of the room.

'You'll do no such thing, do you hear? You're not to

spoil Laura's day, Gemma. Besides, she's not – she's not – '

'What?' Gemma was bolt upright now, her voice alive with interest. 'Are you telling me she's not so innocent after all? Well, I'm damned. Good for her – and good for Nick, whoever he is. He must be quite a guy to have got into Laura's knickers before she had the ring on her finger.'

'Sometimes, Gemma, I could really dislike you,' Penny said coldly.

'No, you couldn't. We go too far back for that. You just wish you could be as frank as me when it comes to sex. And deep down, you wish you knew what it was all about, too. The day any sane woman would be satisfied with a horse instead of a man, she might as well give up living.'

She turned her back on Penny and snuggled down beneath the bedcovers, wishing she had Eddie to snuggle up to. What was it about these two that sometimes made her feel so uncomfortable and defensive? There was Laura with her fresh-faced Earth Mother look; and Penny, who would be totally clammed up now after that little dig, and as snooty as any of the big-wigs with whom she hobnobbed. What on earth did the three of them ever have in common . . .?

The thought of getting through tomorrow and this rustic affair, and having to play up to the local photographers, was beginning to oppress her. She was far more at home at one of the after-gig parties where she could be herself, where anything went, and life was lived on a far more superficial basis.

In fact, one of the best things about her relationship with Eddie was the way he understood that. They could be wild passionate lovers one night, and practically passing strangers the next. And even when one of them had the occasional fling with somebody else, it seemed to make no difference to their abiding affection. They both liked it that way. There were no strings, no commitments . . . He hadn't moved in with her, no matter what the scandal rags suspected, and they each had their own space.

But she wished he was here with her right now, sharing a couple of bottles of wine until they were both nicely tipsy and relaxed, falling into bed together with his arms holding her tight until she fell asleep. And then she was disgusted by her own sentimentality, knowing it made her sound almost as cosy as Laura . . .

'My God, you look beautiful!' Gemma sounded awe-struck as she and Penny put the final touches to Laura's appearance by fixing the bridal veil in place and adjusting the little crown of pearls and diamanté on her head.

'Well, you don't have to sound *quite* so surprised,' Laura said, with a faint smile. 'Anyway, all brides are supposed to be beautiful. It's traditional.'

'But you look specially beautiful, Laura,' Penny repeated. 'You truly do.'

They caught sight of their reflections in the long bedroom mirror. Gemma was city-smart in a slick citrus-lemon suit that dramatically emphasized her dark colouring, and Penny was regally elegant in palest blue. Standing between them now, the bride was smaller and rounder, but with an indefinable beauty that no one could miss.

'I can't tell you how glad I am that you came,' she said now with a catch in her throat.

'I felt just the same when you both came to that awful audition at the Blue Parrot Club,' Gemma remembered. 'I was a bundle of nerves until I saw you both, and then it was just like always. One for all, and all for one.'

She grinned, to take the stickiness out of her words, and went on airily. 'But tonight, you'll be on your own, kid. Whatever you do, enjoy it – and that's all I'm going to say,' she added, catching the warning look from Penny.

'I will,' Laura promised softly.

'Well, you can stop practising your lines now,' Penny teased her. 'I'm sure you'll be word-perfect, anyway, and we'll see you in church,' she added as they heard the impatient hoot of Eddie's car horn.

She gave her a quick hug, careful not to disturb the effect of the careful make-up job Gemma had done on her. She whispered in her ear so that only Laura could hear.

'And whatever else you do, darling, be happy,' she said, and then they were gone.

Laura went downstairs more slowly, to where her father waited at the bottom of the staircase. And just for a moment, she saw the hint of a tear in his eyes, and knew exactly what he was thinking.

'I wish your mother could be here to see you now,' he said unnecessarily. 'She'd have been so proud.'

'I'm sure she knows,' Laura whispered huskily, turning from those sad eyes to bury her nose in the bouquet of pink roses and stephanotis that filled the room with its heady scent.

She willed the Rolls-Royce that was to take them to church to come right now. She didn't want to linger, allowing memories to flood her mind, and seeing her father's feelings etched on his face. But she couldn't ignore them either. She hugged him quickly.

'Mum would have loved all this,' she said. 'And she'd have approved of Nick, wouldn't she, Dad?'

'Of course she would, girl,' he confirmed, and thankfully they heard the white-ribboned bridal car arrive. A second car followed, with the four little bridesmaids and two mothers; and a small clutch of farming neighbours had walked across the fields to watch Laura Robinson leave home to be married.

Her heart suddenly settled down in its place. This was the way a marriage should begin, with friends and family to wish them well, and the sense of an enduring continuity that only farming folk knew.

In the small country church, she hardly made out a single feature among the mass of faces turned towards her as she began the long, slow walk to reach Nick's side. She only saw Nick, waiting to marry her, to love and cherish her, and to fulfil her dreams of happy-ever-after.

Only when she turned to hand her bouquet to the oldest of the little bridesmaids did she catch sight of a bright citrus-yellow suit in the second row, and register, for a fleeting moment, that even Gemma looked awed by the occasion.

'Wow!' Gemma breathed irreverently to no one in particular. 'How did she ever nail a guy like that?'

She felt Eddie dig her in the ribs and was silent as she concentrated on the marriage service. Marriage wasn't high on Gemma's list of things to achieve, though she supposed it would probably happen eventually. And she knew it was never in Penny's sights.

All the same, an occasion like this could make the toughest cynic weaken. As she caught Eddie's eye again, she grinned, knowing she was in no danger of him trying to persuade her to fall for the shoes-and-rice bit. He was as independent as herself.

Penny sat perfectly still beside her all through the service. Penny had been trained in the way to sit and stand, and to be composed at all times. Penny was a lady, Gemma thought, despite the fact that she didn't turn a hair at rubbing down a horse, and mucking out stables, and standing by when a vet had to be called in to perform unspeakable things to animals.

By the time the service was over and the photographs had been taken, they all repaired to the village hall for the reception. It was almost adjacent to the church, and everyone walked in procession, with the bride and groom leading the way, in village tradition.

'So I get to meet Gemma and Penny at last,' Nick said, when he and Laura were greeting their guests, and they had reached them in the line-up. 'I've heard so much about you both, I feel as if I know you already.'

141

'Oh dear. Maybe I should leave right now, then,' Gemma said at once. Penny laughed.

'Take no notice of her, Nick. She loves to shock people to cover her real feelings. We're both enjoying this day so much, and we hope you'll be very happy, though I only have to look at you to know that.'

Penny knew all the right words to say, but she said them with sincerity. She kissed the newly-weds, and Gemma followed suit without hesitation.

'You didn't have to spin out the bridegroom's kiss quite so long,' Eddie told her when they had found their allotted table placings.

'Don't tell me you're jealous. Everybody kisses everybody else at weddings. Look at them now, for God's sake.'

As he went off to get them all a drink, Penny spoke sharply. 'Why do you tease him so, Gem? He really loves you, you know.'

'Don't be daft. We're mates, that's all.'

'Who are you kidding?'

'Well, all right, we're more than mates, but neither of us wants to be an albatross round the other's neck, and that's the way it's going to stay.'

It was a beautiful wedding, but she knew she would be glad when it was over and they could get back to their own lives. Someone had put a programme of music together on cassette, and people were dancing in the middle of the floor now. But before Nick and Laura were to go to an upstairs room to change into their travelling clothes, Laura pleaded with Gemma to sing just one song for them.

'Why don't we all sing?' Gemma suggested at once. 'We were a hit as the Beverly Sisters, remember?'

'I do remember, and I vowed then that I'd never do it again!' Laura said with a groan. 'Please, Gem, do this for me. I don't know what the piano's like, but I'm sure Eddie will play for you.'

'What do you want me to sing?' she offered reluctantly, as Eddie nodded.

'Something romantic, of course.'

Eddie leaned towards her. 'Come on, babe, I'll accompany you, so let's give these folks a treat. How about *Unchained Melody*?'

'Perfect,' Laura said happily, and walked back to Nick, whispering to Tommy, as Best Man, to make the announcement. He stood up importantly.

'Ladies and gentlemen, by special request of the bride, Miss Gemma Grover will sing for us.'

It wasn't the normal ambience they knew, but as Eddie's fingers flew over the keys they turned a slightly out-of-tune instrument into something magical, and as always, Gemma forgot everything but the words of the song, and injected all the feeling she could into it.

Everyone crowded around her afterwards, and the bridal pair were in danger of being eclipsed. Tommy had quickly latched on to Penny, claiming an old friendship from Cheltenham days. He was well away with scrumpy cider by now, and squeezed her hand.

'That one was always destined for bright lights, Pen,' he slurred. 'But you had all the class.'

'Thanks, Tommy,' Penny said, extricating herself with difficulty.

'So whaddya think of my cousin stealing my girl away from me?' he grumbled next.

'Oh, come on, you know Laura was never your girl. She made it plain enough.'

'Yeah, just like all of you,' he scowled. 'You always thought yourself too good for me, and Gemma was only good enough for a quick – '

'You've had too much to drink, Tommy,' Penny said quietly. 'Don't spoil Laura's day, there's a good boy. She's family now, remember, and your parents wouldn't like it.'

'Yes, ma'am,' he saluted smartly, and then his antagonism faded. 'OK, I'll be good. But if you want my opinion, and just between you and me, I still think Nick had a bloody cheek, muscling in like he did and sweeping her off her feet.'

'Well, why don't we do as you say, and keep your opinion private between you and me?'

He stared at her, his face flushed and podgy now, mulling over her words.

'Did you ever think about going into the diplomatic service?' he said at last.

His remarks were still in Penny's mind when Andrews was cruising the Daimler comfortably back up the M5 in the late afternoon. It had been a lovely wedding, but maybe there was something in what the irritating Tommy Hall had said. Had it really all happened too soon? It was more than eight months now since Laura and Nick had met, so they had had ample time to get to know one another, but Penny couldn't forget the ecstatic look on Laura's face when she'd told her how quickly they had become lovers. It hadn't been what she expected of Laura. She wasn't a prude, but she had always thought Laura was, and it had taken her by surprise.

She was picturing the two of them now, remembering the way Laura had thrown her bouquet to the waiting well-wishers before they were taken off to Bristol Airport an hour ago, and how a young girl from one of the farms had caught it, to screams of laughter from her friends. She was picturing them stepping off the plane at Paphos Airport, which she knew well, and being whisked off in a limousine to their honeymoon hotel near the Tombs of the Kings, and being oblivious to the rest of the world for seven whole days and nights . . .

'Are you all right, Miss? You look a little pale, if you don't mind my saying so,' she heard Andrews say.

She hadn't bothered to pull across the glass division between them, and she could see his eyes in the driving mirror now, watching her.

'I'm perfectly well, thank you, Andrews, but I am feeling a little tired,' she said. 'I think I'll have a doze.'

She pulled the partition across to shut out any further conversation; there was no way she was going to admit, especially to her chauffeur, that for one extraordinary moment she had felt emptier than she ever had done before. As if her life was completely unfulfilled and she was going nowhere . . . which was complete madness, when it was so full and successful, and she and Midnight Sun were off to compete in a French show-jumping event near Cannes in two weeks' time.

She had everything, Penny thought. And yet, there had been a moment, when she had felt ridiculously that she had nothing. Or at least, nothing to compare with Gemma's free and easy bohemian kind of existence, with her adoring Eddie paying court, and her legions of fans; and she didn't have a loving man's arms to hold her tight, the way Laura would tonight . . .

It struck her that Gemma and Laura were very alike in one respect. Both of them had been swept along by the speed of events. Gemma with her singing and her gypsy pianist, and Laura with her Dr Nick. While Penny was virtually the same as before . . . and a succession of horsey events suddenly seemed of little more importance than the chaff in the stables.

God, she must be more tired than she'd thought, Penny decided in annoyance. There had been too many glasses of a cheaper wine than she was used to drinking at the reception, and the effect was obviously getting to her. And she reminded herself that whatever else the others had, it wasn't what she herself wanted, and never had been.

She turned on the cassette recorder in the back of the Daimler, and let the strains of Mozart's music soothe her until she reached familiar territory, in more ways than one.

'Thank God that's over,' Gemma said, kicking off her shoes after the ghastly journey back to London. To Eddie's fury, his precious car had broken down, and they'd had to spend an endless time trying to get a mechanic out to fix it. It was only when Eddie yelled at him that she was Gemma Grover and she'd send him a signed photo when she got back to London, that the guy agreed to do anything at all. It had cost them plenty and they were both in a fine old temper by the time they got to Gemma's flat.

'Are you kidding me?' Eddie snapped, pouring them both a drink. 'You were having a great time playing up to all those country yokels. The poor saps were wondering what had hit them, and you were making the most of it.'

'What else was I supposed to do? Sit in a corner and act like a mouse – or be the Lady Bountiful like Penny? Sure I was having a good time, but I'm still glad it's over,' she protested. 'There's a limit to how long I can discuss knitting patterns and jam-making.'

'I don't remember you doing much of either.'

Gemma slammed her glass down on the coffee table, slopping it over the polished surface.

'I was speaking metaphorically, if you can possibly understand the word,' she said with heavy sarcasm. 'Look, Eddie, I didn't ask you to stay, and in fact I'd much prefer to be alone tonight.'

'For Christ's sake, why? I thought weddings were supposed to make people randy.'

'Yeah, that's just what you would think. But after the hell of a time we had getting back, it all seems like a long time ago now, and all I want to do is sleep, okay?'

'Okay.' He shrugged, and drained his glass in one swallow. 'So I'll see you around.'

He was gone before she could say any more. And still in a fury, Gemma picked up her shoes and hurled them across the room. It was very late, and the flat was suddenly too silent. She usually turned on the radio as soon as she came in, just for the company, and she hadn't done so tonight. She decided to take a shower to help her unwind, without knowing exactly why she felt so unsettled.

The day had been just the way she had expected it to be. Sweet and lovely, like Laura herself . . . and the doctor lover had been unexpectedly dishy – the doctor *husband* now, she reminded herself, and wondered instantly what they were doing now. Her thoughts swerved away. Somehow she just couldn't picture innocent little Laura writhing with passion beneath that hunk of a man.

'Christ, you're becoming such a cynic, Gemma.' She spoke out loud, disgusted by her own thoughts.

The album she had recently recorded for the low-budget recording company was on the turntable, and she switched it on to hear her own voice, just as if her self-confidence needed a boost. Stripping off her clothes as she went to her bathroom, the garments fell carelessly to the floor, until she was naked. Once in the shower, she let the soothing water run all over her body, pampering herself with expensive shower gel, and then she wrapped herself in a voluminous towelling bathrobe before making some much-needed black coffee.

Only then did she notice that her answering machine was flashing. She always turned down the irritating bleeping noise, and relied on the small red light to tell her if there were any messages. There was only one.

'Gemma, I gotta see you as soon as possible, doll,' she

148

heard Rube Steiner's voice say. 'I got big news for you, kid, but I ain't leaving no message on the machine. I wanna see your face when I tell you. I know you're off rusticating today, so I'll be round at the flat sometime Sunday. If Eddie's there, you tell him from me he can keep his nose out of this one. It's got nothing to do with him.'

The message cut off. Gemma stared at the machine for a minute, then pressed the rewind button and played it again. Ten minutes ago she'd been feeling really down, and if she hadn't drunk so much she'd have taken some uppers to revive her, but she wasn't going down that road. Not that she objected to the pills, just the cocktail of pills and booze.

But she wasn't feeling down any more. The adrenaline was pumping through her veins so fast she thought she was nearly in danger of expiring. She wanted to call Rube there and then, but it was nearly 2 a.m., and he wouldn't thank her for waking him, no matter what he had to tell her. In any case, he hadn't invited her to call. Maybe it wasn't really as important as he tried to make her believe. Maybe it was only some tin-pot little engagement, and maybe she'd better not get her hopes up too much.

Gemma shrugged off the towelling bathrobe, refusing to let her imagination soar away with her, and fell straight into bed, stark naked. Whatever it was, it could wait until morning.

CHAPTER 9

Laura knew she would always remember Cyprus with a very special affection. It was aptly named 'the island of love', where in ancient times the goddess Aphrodite had cavorted with her beautiful young men in the pool named after her.

Cyprus was where legend had it that Aphrodite rose fully-formed from the sea, borne in on the foam, to enchant and entice with her beauty every man who saw her. It was where Nick told Laura that she was more beautiful and desirable to him than a thousand goddesses.

'I bet you say that to all the girls,' she said in a husky attempt at teasing, as they lay entwined on their honeymoon bed in the small hotel in Paphos overlooking the Tombs of the Kings.

'Not all of them,' Nick protested. 'Only the ones I marry.'

She twisted round in his arms, and they were so close that his heartbeat merged with her own, and she could no longer tell them apart. He stroked her soft skin with his sensitive doctor's fingers, and she had never felt so happy, nor quite so scared. Could such happiness possibly last? Or was it only borrowed . . .

'Do you think we'll always feel like this?' she asked him. 'Will we always feel the way we do today?'

'I doubt it,' Nick said, and she moved away a fraction to stare up at him, but he pulled her back to him again with a sexy laugh. 'Don't look so worried. I mean that it will only get better, darling. How can it fail?'

Laura couldn't answer such sweet logic. But she didn't know how anything could get better between them, either. Everything here was idyllic; their love-making; the warmth, and the sheer ambience of the island; and the powerful sense of past and present merging together through all the lovers who had ever discovered the magic of the ancient sites, and retraced the steps of those who had gone before.

To Laura, that lovely sense of continuity was almost tangible, and the glory of it was that Nick was aware of it too. A doctor was supposed to have a prosaic and scientific nature, but Nick always saw the poetry in things, just as she did. She was so lucky . . . and she crossed her fingers every time she thought so, just in case she was tempting fate in having more than her fair share.

'Are we getting up, or what?' she asked him now. It was already morning, and she knew that once they pulled back the heavy bedroom curtains a brilliant sun would be streaming down on their balcony outside and the day would have begun. But she was blissfully reluctant to move out of the warm cocoon of his arms.

'Or what,' he said irreverently, and then his mouth

was on hers with a demanding kiss that made her forget everything else but loving him.

Gemma knew Eddie wouldn't call round on Sunday. There was an unspoken understanding between them on that score. It was a kind of cooling-off period that they both accepted without explanation. Whenever they had had one of their spats, they kept well apart for a couple of days, unless work was involved. If it was, they were both totally professional in public, and went their separate ways in private.

Sometimes, Gemma admitted that it must be hard for audiences to believe there was nothing going on between herself and Eddie, when she always made a point of seducing him with her voice and her eyes whenever they performed together, whether it was in one of the intimate little London clubs or in the glare of the TV spotlight.

For Gemma, it was all part of the act, and nothing more, but the audiences loved the hint of romance between them. And in her heart she knew damn well it wouldn't be the same without him. He was one of her props, as much as the sophisticated stage clothes and the glittery jewellery she wore, and the sexually-charged songs she sang. And although she knew just how much she was dependent on his responsive participation in her act, she never let on. Eddie wasn't the type to want anybody feeling dependent on him.

But she was glad he wasn't going to be around that Sunday, when she was expecting Rube to call with whatever news he had to tell her. She prowled around

152

the flat like an angry cat, willing him to come. But she knew he rarely stirred himself until lunchtime on Sundays, and he certainly wouldn't thank her for turning up at his place unannounced.

Her phone rang as she was defrosting a TV dinner, since she couldn't be bothered to cook for herself, and she grabbed the receiver like a lifeline.

'Gemma, did you get back all right?' she heard Penny's cultured voice say. 'Andrews thought he spotted Eddie's car going off the motorway, and I kept wondering if everything was all right, or if there was a problem.'

She spoke delicately. For all she knew, Gemma and Eddie might have decided to break the journey and spend the night in some little hotel . . . and it was one of the reasons she hadn't instructed Andrews to take the next turning off the motorway and find out if anything was wrong.

'The bloody car only broke down, didn't it?' Gemma said brashly, to cover the sick feeling in her stomach that it hadn't been Rube or Eddie at the other end of the line. 'It took us hours to get it repaired and get back to town, but I suppose it was all worth it.'

'Of course it was worth it. Laura looked lovely, didn't she? And she'd have been so hurt if we'd missed her wedding day.'

'Who said anything about missing it?' Gemma picked up on the implied censure at once. 'I never meant that.'

'I know you didn't, but I thought it might have been all a bit boring for you, after the exciting life you seem to lead.'

It was so near the truth that Gemma found herself snapping back in self-defence.

'And for you too, Miss Show-Jumper of the Year!'

Penny laughed uneasily, wondering how a simple enquiry had turned into one of their well-remembered tit-for-tat sparrings. 'I'm a long way from achieving anything like that, Gem. You're the star among us, and you know it. And it was really sweet of you to sing for Laura and Nick at a minute's notice the way you did.'

'I know. Especially when I usually get paid a nice fat fee for my services.'

In the silence from the other end, she spoke quickly. 'For God's sake, I'm kidding! I was happy to do it.'

'Well, whatever. I know it put the finishing touch on the day, anyway. And I was just checking that everything was all right with you. Keep in touch, Gem. I don't suppose Laura will have much time for letter-writing from now on. She and Nick are going to be working all hours doing up this old place they're buying. Did she tell you about it? I gather it all happened in the last few weeks when the house became vacant. I'd hoped we could have seen it, but there wasn't time.'

'She told me, and I'd rather her than me. I don't like creaking old houses. I lived in them for too long. Look, I'm sorry but I've got to go. I'm expecting somebody any minute.'

She hung up, vaguely dissatisfied as always after talking to Penny lately; she always got the feeling Penny was disapproving of her. As if Gemma was the bad girl of their trio, Laura was the shining angel, and Penny sat in the middle in judgement . . .

Gemma scowled, wishing such a stupid idea hadn't entered her mind, but all too aware that it wasn't for the first time.

She turned thankfully when her doorbell buzzed, and spoke into the intercom to tell Rube to come on up.

'What on earth was so important that you couldn't leave a message or tell me on the phone?' she demanded, as soon as he got inside the door. 'You've kept me awake half the night wondering about it!'

He grinned his familiar sly grin. 'That's not the way I'd like to keep you awake half the night, darling!'

'Drop dead, Rube. If that's all you've got to say – '

'Of course it ain't. Jeez, but you've got bloody touchy lately, doll. You can be a real primadonna when you want to be.'

She wanted to say, 'Don't call me doll!' . . . but she knew it would only add fuel to the flame. And besides, she was too impatient to hear what he had to say to waste any more time.

'So I'll try not to be. But if you don't tell me the news I'll explode!' she said instead.

He sprawled out on her luxurious sofa, looking mighty pleased with himself. But she knew him too well, and her sixth sense told her he wasn't quite as cool as he tried to appear.

'We've been together a good while now, ain't we, kid?' he said. 'And you know I've always done my best for you, introducing you to the right contacts and getting you started on your TV career.'

'I know that.' She spoke abruptly, sure that she knew now what this was all about.

She'd been right not to get her hopes up too much. He'd got her some tin-pot little deal that was supposed to dazzle her, and he was going to demand a much heftier cut of her earnings than he already took. She could read him like a smutty book.

'I've had an offer for you, doll,' he said.

'Oh yeah? This had better be good, Rube, and if it's another club like the Blue Parrot, I don't want to know. I've finished with all that sleaze.'

She gave a sudden shiver at the calculating look in his eyes. She didn't deal in sleaze, nor did she want to be known as a singer in second-rate clubs where the other acts were usually strippers and foul-mouthed comedians. But she knew that if Rube saw money in it, he'd try to persuade her.

'You've got it all wrong, babe,' he said smoothly. 'I mean I've had an offer from a big agency to handle you.'

He'd got her full attention now. 'You don't mean you want to hand me over to somebody else? What do you think I am, an unwanted parcel? And why would you want to get rid of me, anyway?'

Don't you like me any more?

The appallingly childish question was in her head before she could stop it. He could be offering her a spectacular chance to further her career, and yet she felt an absurd impulse to cry. And she never cried. She hadn't cried since her grandmother died, and she finally realized she had to make it on her own. Her grandmother always said it was better to stick with the devil you knew than to go into unknown territory blindfold, and that was exactly how Rube was making her feel now. He was a devil all right, but he was the devil she knew. He'd always been there for her to lean on. Just like Eddie. And she remembered instantly that Eddie had tried to warn her about something like this.

'Now you just listen to me, Gemma,' Rube went on, with more steel in his voice than she'd ever heard before. 'I know what's best for you, and ain't I always done right for you up till now?'

'Yes,' she said sullenly, feeling as if she'd been punched in the stomach.

'Well, these guys can do even better. I'm not letting go of you completely, doll. Hell, would I do that? No, it's just that they can do more for you than I can – see?'

She suddenly saw all too clearly.

'You've sold me out, you bastard!' she screamed. 'How much of a backhander are they paying you?'

He was on his feet now, shaking her. 'Nobody's selling you out, you silly little bitch, and you'll have the last word on it before we sign the agreement,' he yelled back. 'But it all comes down to how important your career is to you.'

She was breathing as hard as he was now, but his words made her pause. She wrenched herself free of him, and stood stiffly with her hands clenched at her sides. Ambition was a powerful weapon, and Rube knew it.

'What's the deal?' she said at last.

Even though it was Sunday, Rube had set up a meeting with the agency people for that evening. One look at the vast Mayfair offices, and Gemma knew the LaFarge

Theatrical Agency was in a different class from Rube Steiner. She'd heard of them, of course. But she'd never dreamed that they would have heard of her. She also knew that once she signed a contract with them, she'd be in a different class too.

When she was informed of the opportunities that could come her way, coolly outlined by Desmond LaFarge and his associates, the paltry recording contract Rube had already fixed up for her seemed very small-time. LaFarge spoke of silver discs and gold discs and dates on American TV; a guest singing spot in a popular soap opera could also be a high option, once she put herself on their books.

It was light years away from anything Rube could do for her, and they all knew it.

'Of course you need to be groomed and polished, Miss Grover,' LaFarge went on, his eyes flicking over her. 'But it's time to change your image. You've done your apprenticeship with these smoochy, sexy ballads that get old ladies swooning for their lost youth. I want something more exciting for you. I want to turn you into a jazz singer; under my guidance, you could be another Cleo Laine.'

Gemma gasped. 'Oh, I don't think so! I'm no jazz singer, and I never could be – '

'You could be anything you wanted to be,' LaFarge said flatly. He was big and powerful, and everything about him and the expensively-suited other men seated around the vast desk, reeked of money and success. LaFarge had a high-profile name in the theatrical world. He was at the very top of his profession. He could smell success in a client, and when he signed anybody up, he took them to the top with him. Gemma knew that.

'I'm prepared to offer you a five-year contract, Miss Grover, on terms that you will never get elsewhere. But there's one thing I shall insist on,' LaFarge told her smoothly. 'You'll have to ditch the piano player. He's a hanger-on you no longer need. I can get you the very best musicians to back you.'

'Eddie *is* the best,' she protested indignantly. 'And you can't expect me to turn my back on him. We're a team!'

'Then I've been wasting my time,' LaFarge said, standing up to indicate that the interview was over. He held out his hand, weighted down with even more rings than Rube wore. 'I'm sorry we can't do business, Miss Grover. You could have had a dazzling career.'

She had stood up automatically, but as his words sank in and she heard Rube sucking in his breath, she felt her heart begin to pound sickeningly fast. She had worked so hard for this, and she had been in the business long enough to know that the wrong word in the right ear could ruin a career faster than blinking.

He had something of Eddie's casualness, she raged, in the way he wasted no time in clearing out any debris. If she wouldn't accept his terms, he'd find some other client who would. Gemma Grover wasn't yet indispensable. Gemma Grover hadn't yet reached the top. It was all there, as clear as daylight, and if she didn't want that stardom, he wasn't going to waste his time convincing her that she did.

'How am I ever going to face Eddie?' she muttered out loud, and the hand squeezing hers was firmer now, almost propelling her back into her seat on the far side of the desk.

They had no engagements until the end of the week, and she didn't see him for three days. The one person she wanted to tell, and the one person she didn't know how to tell, was Eddie. But within a couple of days the showbiz magazines had got hold of the news that Gemma Grover was being taken on by the mighty LaFarge agency, with Rube Steiner remaining as her manager. It was part of the deal, Gemma discovered. Rube still wanted his percentage of her, however diminished, and somehow he'd persuaded LaFarge to go along with it.

So, because of the showbiz snippet, Eddie would know, and the fact that he didn't call or phone was driving her crazy with nerves. When he finally arrived at the flat three days later in the middle of the evening, she knew he'd been drinking steadily for some time.

'Congratulations, sweetie,' he said, with the careful diction of the very drunk. 'You're really on your way now.'

'I wanted to tell you before it got out, Eddie – '

'Did you? But I understand, darling! It's tough to find the words to tell somebody there's no longer a place for them in your life, isn't it?'

She felt sick to her stomach. She loved him, and she'd always loved him, even if it wasn't the all-consuming kind of love that Laura had for her Nick. It was just that he'd been in her life for so long, and in signing the five-year contract with LaFarge, she felt as if she'd signed away a part of herself.

'How did you know?' she said weakly, for there had been no mention of that in the magazine. She looked at him in abject misery, aching for him.

'I know how these guys operate. When they take somebody on they take them body and soul, and mould them to their own specifications. And they don't want hangers-on. Isn't that the way he put it?'

'Almost exactly,' Gemma muttered. 'Eddie, you know I didn't want it this way – '

'But you've got it. You've got everything you ever wanted, darling, so don't let sentimentality get in the way. When does the new arrangement take effect?'

'At the end of the month. We've got gigs to honour until then – Eddie, you won't back out of them, will you? I need you,' she added fearfully.

She went to him and clung to him, and she could smell the whisky aroma on his breath. His arms went around her automatically, and he pressed his lips to her forehead. If it had been the other way around, it would have been like the kiss of Judas, she found herself thinking irrationally.

'You don't need anybody from now on, but don't worry. I won't let you down. I never have yet, have I?'

He never had, not even when he'd been drinking solidly all day, and it was a miracle that those fingers could find the right piano keys, let alone produce such magic. Gemma was filled with nerves, knowing she was losing so much.

'Don't go yet,' she said huskily. 'Stay with me till morning, Eddie.'

He extricated himself from her arms.

'That's not what I had in mind, babe. You've gotta get used to being without me, so we might as well start now.'

'What the hell did you come here for then?' Gemma couldn't hide her anger at this rejection.

He looked at her thoughtfully, already halfway to the door. 'If you don't know that by now, then I've been wasting my time all these months,' he said.

The honeymoon was over, and Nick and Laura had decided their new home was finally ready for occupation. It had taken longer than they'd thought to do all that they wanted to the old property, and it was nearly two months after returning from Cyprus before they were finally clearing out his flat and moving everything to Lilac Cottage. They'd practically gutted the old place that was midway between a large cottage and a small farmhouse in appearance, with a field and an orchard, and what used to be a paddock with several outhouses alongside.

The property had really seen better days, and it was badly in need of tender, loving care. Which was just what they had given it in every spare moment in the couple of weeks before the wedding when it had come onto the market. They had been there at all hours after the honeymoon too, busy with scouring brushes and bleach, pots of emulsion and gloss paint and wallpaper, and supervising the fitting of necessary new kitchen units, and the right carpets to replace the tattered remnants of the previous owners.

'It's wonderful,' Laura said on that bright summer Sunday morning, feeling a glow of pride in the first home that was hers and Nick's.

She didn't really count the flat. That had been no more than a temporary bachelor place, but Lilac Cottage was different. It was a place where a family could put down roots and raise children, and it was theirs. He put his arms around her as she gazed at it all with pleasure.

'So are you, Mrs Dean,' he said. 'I didn't know you had such a flair for interior decorating. I'm finding out all kinds of fascinating things about you.'

She wrinkled her nose. 'It's hardly a flair to know which colours don't clash with each other, and we chose the furnishings together, didn't we? I don't think I'm likely to be featured in *Homes & Gardens* just yet, Nick!'

She laughed as she spoke, loving the pale, fresh green and lemon decor that was repeated right through the cottage to give it a sense of continuity. It was so right for a country home, echoing the open spaces outside, Laura thought blissfully. And on a day like today, with the summer heat making her feel almost light-headed, the coolness of the cottage was an added bonus.

In fact, she felt hotter than the day decreed, and her exertions that morning hadn't been enough to make her feel the beads of sweat on her forehead, nor make her legs so shaky. She leaned back against Nick, suddenly limp.

'I think I'd better make us a sandwich,' she murmured. 'My stomach feels so weird I'm sure it must be lunchtime, and I feel quite peculiar all of a sudden.'

'You can't be hungry. It's barely eleven-thirty,' Nick said. 'You've been overdoing it as usual, rushing about like a mad thing as if there's no tomorrow.'

He had followed her into the kitchen. They had kept the flagstoned floor intact, since it reminded Laura so much of the big farmhouse kitchen at her old home, and just covered the coldness of the stones with serviceable rugs. Along with the old Aga cooker she couldn't bear to discard, the old and the new blended in amazingly well with the natural wood worktops that modernized the kitchen.

Laura tried to get her thoughts together. This was surely no more than a stomach bug. Unless . . . but she didn't want to consider what else it might be. She spoke quickly.

'Actually, I'm not hungry. The thought of food makes me feel worse now I come to think of it. I felt like this yesterday morning, too. And the day before when I was over at the farm with Dad. It's probably just a bug, though at the time I thought it was the cheese and pickled onions we'd taken out in the fields with us. Dad's onions are always guaranteed to take the lining off your stomach – '

She stopped talking as Nick put his fingers against her lips, and a smile began to spread across his face.

'I don't think it's a bug. Don't you know what's wrong with you, Mrs Dean?'

She felt his hand move downwards to gently palm her

164

stomach, and the beads of sweat on her forehead were even more pronounced as she got his meaning at once.

'No, I can't be, Nick. I haven't missed – '

'That doesn't always follow. Some women don't stop having periods for the whole nine months, though I admit that's rare,' he said in his doctor's voice. 'But plenty more have one or two at the beginning of a pregnancy.'

She was so jittery she knew he was talking this way to calm her sudden attack of nerves. And then he took hold of her hands and kissed her upturned palms, and his voice softened.

'We didn't do anything to prevent it, did we? We both said we wanted children whenever they came along.'

'Yes, but I hadn't expected it to happen right after the honeymoon,' Laura said, almost belligerently. 'It's so indecently soon! What will people think?'

She listened to herself, sounding so impossibly old-fashioned, and more like some guilty schoolgirl caught doing something she shouldn't. It was *legal*, for God's sake. And Nick was right. It was something they'd discussed and both wanted. She'd simply dismissed any thought of being pregnant already. She was nine-teen years old, and it scared her.

'Does it matter what people think?' Nick asked.

Laura looked into his eyes and knew that it didn't, not the tiniest bit. The only thing that mattered was themselves and the new life they were creating. It was an awesome responsibility, and the crazy thought came into her mind that Penny and Gemma always said having babies was what she had been destined for. At the time, she had laughed it off and said she wasn't turning into a breeding machine just to confirm their ideas about her.

'Of course it doesn't matter,' she smiled, reaching up for his kiss.

Anyway, there was nothing to having babies these days. It was in and out of hospital, taking advantage of whatever assistance was available to make things as easy and painless as possible, and back to normal in a couple of days. Everybody said so . . . but she crossed her fingers behind her back as she thought it, just to be on the safe side.

CHAPTER 10

'Can't somebody *do* something?' Laura screamed out, as the powerful contractions took control of her body again.

None of the ante-natal exercises, nor the breathing and puffing rehearsals had prepared her for this, and she could no longer concentrate, or remember anything she was supposed to do to make things easier.

She wanted Nick . . . not these competent hospital strangers in the delivery room at Southmead Hospital who kept inspecting her as if she was a piece of meat, constantly coming and going and leaving her alone for far too long.

She wanted Nick . . . but he'd been obliged to stop and assist at an horrific road accident while their own ambulance was taking her to Bristol, and how could she compete with that? She was only having a baby, after all . . . no, *two* babies, she reminded herself, in a brief lull from the pain. The fact that she'd turned into something resembling a beached whale these past months was due to her expecting twins.

'There were twins in a distant branch of the family

many years ago, I seem to remember,' Mrs Hall told her, when the scan had revealed the news. 'So I daresay it was always possible for it to come out again sooner or later. I doubt that Nick even knew those other folk, or maybe he just forgot to tell you.'

Laura clamped her teeth together now, to stop herself from crying out as a new contraction threatened to tear her apart. No, Nick hadn't bloody well told her, but what difference would it have made if he had? It wouldn't have stopped them wanting children. But she'd naturally expected to have them one at a time . . .

And it hadn't helped to have Tommy Hall leering when he'd found out about the twins, either.

'My God, our Nick must be more of a bull than I thought. I never knew he had it in him.'

'Don't be stupid, Tommy,' Laura snapped. 'It's what's in a person's genes that decides on the sex of a child, and everything else about it.'

'Well, ain't that just what I was saying?' he hooted, taking the wrong meaning from her words.

She gritted her teeth again now, wishing him to Kingdom Come, along with every other male in creation at that moment. It was the utmost indignity to be left here alone, feeling as if she was virtually fighting with her own body.

The pregnancy had been difficult enough, with the morning sickness continuing right through the nine months. Her usual placid nature, and the ability to take everything in her stride, had seemingly vanished overnight. And whenever she had caught sight of her enormous bulk in a mirror, she felt she had totally missed out on the bloom that was supposed to make every pregnant woman beautiful.

She felt gross and bloated and disgusting, and how Nick could ever have fancied her in the later stages was beyond her. The fact that he apparently did so only made her more irritated with him. And he was so damnably understanding.

Penny had paid them a flying visit just before Christmas, and Laura had complained bitterly about him.

'If I need anything, he jumps up to get it before I can move,' she said. 'If I yell at him, he just teases me for my bad temper and says everything will be fine once the babies are born. He's like a bloody saint, and I'm not sure how much more of it I can stand.'

'You should be thankful he cares about you so much. How else would you want him to behave?'

Laura looked at her limply, the picture of misery in her over-stretched leggings and bulky jumper as she sprawled out on the sofa at Lilac Cottage, with six endless weeks still to go before the birth.

'I just want him to act normally, the way he used to. I don't want this cut-glass treatment, Pen. I bet he doesn't act that way with the pregnant women he sees at the clinic.'

'Of course he doesn't. They're just patients. You're the most important thing in his life, and most women would envy you, so don't knock it.'

'Oh, I know you're right, but I can't help it. Nick says plenty of women get contrary or downright cantankerous at this stage of pregnancy, and I must be the worst.

I honestly didn't think I could feel so bloody-minded towards him. I hear myself doing it, and I just can't stop it. If it had been Gemma, I could understand it. Have you heard anything of her, by the way?'

She spoke listlessly, not really caring. All her energies these days seemed to be spent on heaving herself around, and the smallest household tasks that she would have flown through previously, seemed to take her for ever.

'She's in America. This Desmond LaFarge has got her some dates on a couple of TV shows over there.'

'So that's why she hasn't been in touch. And what about Eddie?' Laura said, trying to take an interest.

'I don't know. She didn't mention him in her card.'

'Oh well. And what are you doing this winter? Skiing in Switzerland or something equally energetic, I suppose?'

Penny looked at her thoughtfully. 'As a matter of fact, yes. I'm going with a group from the pony club. We're staying at Gstaad for a week or two and then moving on to the chalet of one of the club owners. I'm sorry to miss the birth, Laura, but I'll leave you a number, and you be sure to get Nick to phone me to tell me the news.'

'All right. And you can give my love to Prince Charles in passing,' Laura suggested, grimacing as one of the babies pressed on her rib cage.

Penny lived in another world that she couldn't even be bothered to contemplate right now. She just felt so full of babies that she could scream. It didn't feel as if there were only two in there. When they each fought for space and kicked her so mercilessly, she was sure there must be at least a dozen. There was no other way to describe it . . .

'*Nurse!*' Laura suddenly shrieked out now from the hard delivery trolley, frantically pressing her bell. 'Somebody had better get in here – *fast*.'

They said that once you looked at your baby's face, you forgot all the pain and discomfort of delivery, and were immediately consumed with a primitive and fiercely protective emotion.

Whoever 'they' were, they had it all wrong, Laura thought wearily. Unbelievably, it had taken another hour before the babies were finally safely delivered. The cord had been wrapped tightly around one neck, and the afterbirth had broken up, causing the hospital staff to rush around in some kind of panic. And when the babies were finally placed in her arms in their blanket cocoons, wrapped up as tightly as mummies, with their heads still damp and blood-stained, Laura looked at them, and felt absolutely nothing.

'We have two beautiful baby girls,' the Sister said, as triumphantly as if she'd given birth to them herself. 'Have we got names for them, Mother?'

Laura looked at her with active dislike. She hadn't believed such people as Sister Prole still existed. She was definitely of the old school, and looked as if she should have been pensioned off years ago.

'I'm not your mother,' Laura said distinctly. 'And would you take them away, please? They're hurting my stomach.'

Sister Prole's mouth dropped open, but she grabbed

both the babies and took them out of the room at once. Laura could hear her muttering to someone outside the labour room, but she was too tired to bother trying to hear what they had to say. She was too tired to bother about anything but the awful pains in her stomach. They weren't labour pains any more, but they wouldn't go away, either.

It seemed an eternity before she felt the grip of Nick's hand on hers. By then, she had been drifting in and out of a weird, unnatural kind of sleep, aware of needles being pushed into her arm; a drip was set up beside her now. And she felt so ill, so terribly ill . . .

'Darling, wake up,' Nick's voice said.

As soon as she heard it, she knew there was something wrong. And there was a question she would be expected to ask, even if the answer seemed to be of little concern to her.

'Is there something wrong with the babies?' she whispered, hardly able to speak because of her dry mouth and throat.

'The babies are fine, Laura. They're both perfectly healthy, and they're as beautiful as their mother.'

She opened her eyes a fraction. 'Then what?'

'I want you to be very strong, my darling,' Nick went on. 'They have to take you down to the operating theatre to do a small repair job. You were badly torn during the birth, and they suspect that there may be other internal complications.'

He stopped abruptly, and she knew he wasn't telling her everything.

'What kind of a small repair job?' she said at last, but at his stricken face, he hardly needed to tell her. 'You mean a hysterectomy, don't you?'

His eyes searched her face, seeing the slow tears run down her cheeks.

'I'm so sorry, Laura, so very sorry, but there's no other option. It would be too much of a risk for you to have another baby, but I still have to ask you to give your consent to the operation.'

She could sense his sheer torment at asking this of her. She nodded without speaking. He bent to kiss her trembling lips, then released her and went away to fetch the doctor in charge. And Laura closed her eyes tightly, thankful beyond anything that he couldn't read her thoughts.

He would think she was being so very brave, yet all she was capable of at that moment was offering up heartfelt thanks to whatever guardian angel was watching over her, that she would never have to go through this hell again.

They called the twins Sarah, after Laura's mother, and Charlotte, after Nick's. He had insisted on installing a reliable nanny-cum-housekeeper in the house for some months after the operation, since Laura was temporarily forbidden to do any lifting, stretching, or driving.

If she had felt useless before, dragging herself around before the twins were born, she felt even more so now. It was like watching a play being performed in her own home, she complained to Nick. She should have been the principal actor, but instead, she had to sit on the sidelines and watch Mrs Yard do the cleaning and attend to the babies when they cried, while Laura coped with any light duties.

The obliging helper normally insisted on staying to help prepare the evening meal, and often hung around until Nick got home from surgery. And despite all her simmering resentment at being thought so incapable in her own home, Laura still felt too lethargic to do anything about it.

'This situation won't carry on for ever,' Nick told her. 'Take it easy now, and you'll feel like a million dollars in a few months' time. Trust me. I'm a doctor.'

She couldn't even raise a smile at that any more. She supposed she was suffering from what they called postnatal depression, and she suspected that Nick was being ultra-careful not to use the words.

He knew very well she wouldn't take pills, other than aspirins for the occasional headache, so he didn't suggest them. Instead, he encouraged her to spend as much time as she wanted to at the farm with her father, or visiting his aunt to show off the twins, but this had the added frustration of having to ask Mrs Yard to drive her there, and to collect them later.

'You know I'm happy to do it, Mrs Dean,' the woman said. 'We all want you to be your old sunny self again, so you just let others do the work while you've got the chance.'

There were times when Laura thought uneasily that all this pampering and being taken care of, was distancing her even more from her own babies. She still hadn't formed any real bond with them, not even the

174

closeness of feeding them herself. And the fact that they thrived and belched so happily on their bottled milk gave her an added feeling of inadequacy.

But even though she was well aware of what was happening, she couldn't seem to raise the energy to do anything about it, which made it all the more terrible. She was guiltily *glad* to hand them over to other people.

They were six months old before Laura felt any real attachment to them. She had finally been allowed to drive again, and several times a week she drove over to the farm, where her father revelled in playing with his granddaughters on the living-room carpet.

'They've got a real look of your mother about them when they chuckle, Laura,' he said, with undisguised pleasure. 'Can't you see it?'

'Oh yes, everybody says so,' she said.

Other people had mentioned it, so it must be true, though if she was honest about it, Laura couldn't really see any great likeness to anybody. They were both fair-haired, with big blue eyes that seemed to look right through you. Sometimes Laura could swear they both gazed at her and wondered why their mother didn't like them . . .

She felt a sudden tightening in her throat, wondering where such an awful thought had come from. It wasn't true. Of course it wasn't true. She looked at the two identical faces now, and couldn't miss how their mouths curved upwards just like Nick's. Their features were more like his, she supposed. It was only their colouring that were hers and her mother's.

She watched as her father pulled faces at them to

make them laugh. Sarah chuckled and waved her arms furiously with excitement. And Charlotte mouthed her first word.

Laura's heart leapt, and then began beating very fast.

'Did you hear that, Dad? She said Mum! She did, didn't she? You must have heard it.'

'I heard something, but I'm not sure what it was,' he said, laughing.

'She said Mum. She did, really!'

Laura knew she hadn't been mistaken. And she was totally taken aback by the thrill that ran through her, that her own child had recognized her. Cleverer folk than herself would say such a thought was sheer nonsense, and it was simply a child's natural way of picking up sounds from other people, and imitating them. But Laura heeded none of that.

On a rare impulse she picked up Charlotte and held her close, nuzzling her face into the peach-like skin of the baby's neck, and hearing her chuckle with delight. Sarah gurgled, staring fixedly at Laura and punching the air with her fists and kicking her legs until she was gathered up in her mother's arms as well.

And without any warning at all, the feeling of love that came over Laura at that instant was overwhelming and spectacular, and like nothing she had ever known before.

She closed her eyes briefly, wanting to hold the moment for ever, and knowing how effectively she had managed to shut them out of her life all these months. She breathed in their sweet baby smells, and caught sight of her father's knowing old face above their heads, and saw his understanding nod.

He knew, she thought instantly. All this time, no matter how she had tried to hide it, he had known. Maybe more than Nick did, with his busy doctor's life. And he had never said anything to censure her.

'You know, I've been thinking it's probably time I let Mrs Yard go,' she said slowly, knowing it was the first sane decision she had made in all these months, and jealously wanting to guard this newly-discovered closeness with her own babies. 'What do you think, Dad?'

'I think it's more than time, my love,' he smiled.

Laura's second sane thought was to realize how crazy it was to believe she could change in an instant. Nor should she think that all the crankiness of the past months, the secret weeping and frustrations and panic attacks, could disappear just like that. Miracles didn't happen that way – or did they?

Work on the farm never stopped for long, and her father left her alone with the babies for a couple of hours during the afternoon. In any case, Laura was reluctant to leave. She felt a great need to spend time in the warm, familiar surroundings of her own childhood, and to feel as if she was getting to know these two little human beings who owed their existence to her, for the very first time.

She examined their perfect, minute fingernails, in the awed way that new mothers were supposed to do on the day their babies were born, and knew she had missed six months of enjoying such marvels. She watched their changing expressions, seeing the similarities and differences in their individual personalities, and her own eyes felt as if they had been newly-opened.

Sarah was the more placid baby, while Charlotte was the boisterous one, clearly destined to be a tomboy. How could she possibly have missed it all? She smothered them with kisses, wondering how she could have rejected them for so long. It was as if, at last, she was coming out of a long, dark tunnel, into the light.

As soon as Nick returned to Lilac Cottage from evening surgery that night, he knew something had happened. By then, the babies were asleep in their cots upstairs, and a succulent aroma of steak and onions steeped in a casserole of red wine and herbs, filled the kitchen.

Laura had showered and washed her hair and wore a red silky dress that she knew was one of Nick's favourites, even though it fitted her far more snugly now. The table was set, the lights were low, and the candles were waiting to be lit. A bowl of full-blown roses permeated the air with their heady perfume, and romantic music was playing on the record player.

'Welcome home, Nick,' Laura said, as gauche as a schoolgirl on her first date.

After he'd looked slowly around the welcoming cottage, he took her in his arms. His kiss was long and deep, and his mouth was still on hers when he spoke.

'Welcome back, Laura,' he said. 'I don't want to push my luck, but I'd say you were trying to seduce me, woman.'

She laughed. At the teasing note in his voice, she felt

the rush of excitement in her veins that had been missing for so long. Until that moment, she hadn't even realized how long it had been absent. Nor how patient Nick had been.

'I'd say you were probably right,' she told him. 'But food first, yes?'

'If we must,' Nick said with a grin. 'But I seem to remember we didn't always wait for food.'

'Ah, but I wasn't an old married woman with two children, then!'

He kissed her again, his hands sliding down the silky red dress to caress her buttocks.

'That's the very last way I'd describe you. And I trust you've sent Mrs Yard packing as usual, otherwise we might shock her. Is her absence all part of the seduction scene?' he said with a grin.

She looked up at him, her arms still around his neck, and the laughter bubbled up inside her again. She recognized his masculine impatience so well, and knew there was only way this evening was going to end. She could see it in his eyes and taste it on his lips, and she could feel it in every sinewy part of his body. She took a deep breath.

'I've sent her packing for good, though not quite so brutally as it sounds, Nick, and she was quite happy to accept it. I decided it was time Sarah and Charlotte realized who they really belonged to.'

As she referred to them by their names, instead of as 'the babies' or 'the twins', she was momentarily shocked to acknowledge how little she had done so in the past. She had so much to make up to them, she thought guiltily . . . and to Nick, who was looking at her now as if he'd never seen her before.

'Well done, my darling,' he said softly. 'This was something you had to do for yourself.'

She wasn't sure exactly what he meant, but she swallowed and tried to keep her voice light. 'Then you don't mind that I dismissed Mrs Yard without consulting you?'

'I'd mind it even more if I thought she was still around, when I want you all to myself tonight. Do you know how long it's been since we were together? Really together, I mean, not just going through the motions.'

She hesitated a moment, and then spoke softly. 'Nick, I think the dinner will keep for a while in the oven – '

She didn't get the chance to say any more, before he picked her up in his arms and carried her towards the stairs, kissing her on every step. She clung to him, sure that everything was going to be all right with her world at last.

And the best thing of all, her deep-down secret that not even Nick knew, was the sweet, guilty joy of knowing they could be the most passionate of lovers, and there was no possibility of any more pregnancies.

For the first time in a very long period, she felt the urge to write at length to her two best friends. There had been so little to tell lately, they probably assumed she was buried in blissful domesticity and had written her off. But even as she thought it, she knew it wasn't true. She had always been the keenest letter-writer, and she realized now that she'd held everyone at arms' length, these past months. Even when Penny had phoned, she had fobbed her off by saying the babies needed feeding or changing, or the health visitor was at the door.

She wondered now how she could have let herself get so low, and feeling so worthless. And if she had ever needed anyone to support her, she should have known she could always count on Penny and Gemma. She made up her mind.

'I think I might phone Penny some time,' she said to Nick at the end of August, when she was feeling on a far more even keel at last. It was a mellow late-summer afternoon, the twins were in their playpen in the garden, and Laura was lazily watching them. 'You won't mind if I ask her down for a few days, will you?'

'Of course not. Ask Gemma too, if you like.'

Laura shook her head. 'No good. She's touring in the States. I showed you the piece in the newspaper, remember?'

'Vaguely,' Nick said.

Laura glanced at him thoughtfully. 'You didn't like her much, did you, Nick?'

'I wouldn't say that. I just liked Penny better, that's all. But any old friends of yours will always be welcome here, darling, you know that.'

'I didn't really have any more. The three of us were always so close, there didn't seem much room for other friendships. It's a bit frightening, when you come to think of it. And even when I came back to the farm, it was hard to pick up relationships with people I hadn't seen for years. We'd all grown up and grown apart.'

'And then you met me,' he said.

'And nobody else mattered. And if you were angling for flattery, Nick Dean, you got it.'

He laughed, pressing a kiss on her nose and kissing each of the twins before he left on his way to the surgery. She watched him go, loving him so much, and feeling the familiar stab of anger with herself at letting six months of their precious lives slip away almost unnoticed. And because she was enjoying life so much now, she delayed getting in touch with anyone, until Penny phoned, several weeks later.

'So you're still alive down there!' came her cool voice. 'I began to think you'd emigrated like Gemma.'

'She hasn't, has she?' Laura said at once.

'Just a figure of speech, darling, that's all. As far as I know, she's still as British as the rest of us, and intends to stay that way. But how are you? And how's that gorgeous husband and my delicious god-daughters?'

Laura thought guiltily that they hadn't encouraged visitors, or formally invited anyone to stay since the christening, and Penny's impeccably correct upbringing meant that she would always wait for an invitation.

'We're all blooming,' Laura said quickly, 'and I'd really love to see you, Pen. In fact, I've been meaning to ask you to come and stay for a week, as soon as you like.'

'Oh, I just wish I could, but I'm afraid I can't. The autumn Events are starting in earnest now, and I've got very involved with organizing things. But I do have a free day tomorrow, and I could make a flying visit, if that's all right with you. I'll be there in time for lunch and we could all go out somewhere.'

'Not with two babies in tow, we won't. It's too much of a hassle to lug them in and out of restaurants. Besides, we can't talk properly in a crowd. And Nick's off on a three-day course, so I'd really love your company. Just arrive here whenever you can, and I'll make us lunch.'

'Fine. I wanted to talk to you about a proper christening present for the girls, anyway.'

'Don't be silly. You've already done that!' And the silver mugs and the two identical cased sets of spoons certainly hadn't come out of Woolworth's.

'Nonsense. Anyway, I've been thinking about giving them something special, but I'll need your approval first.'

CHAPTER 11

Gregory Bishop had been born into money. He'd inherited a vast amount of wealth from his father, and his maternal grandparents had lavished gifts of profitable stocks and shares on him from an early age, and provided handsomely for him when they died. The huge estate known as the Bishop place had been in his family for several generations, and Gregory saw no reason why his only daughter shouldn't have all the advantages he himself had received.

Being given anything she wanted, almost before she knew she wanted it, could have turned Penny into a selfish and precocious snob, but the wonder of it was that she had turned out to be so blessedly normal. Her father doted on her, and the fact that she followed in his footsteps in his fanatic love of horses was an added bonus.

Penny's mother simply tolerated the closeness between the two of them and was quite unruffled by it. She preferred to put all her not-inconsiderable energies into a social round of afternoon bridge parties and evening cocktail parties, and a more conscientious duty

184

of organizing charity events, and sitting on committees of her own choosing. She was happy to meet up with the rest of her family if and when their various activities coincided.

It all made for harmony, Helena Bishop had been heard to comment more than once to her friends. None of them got in each other's way, but all of them took a polite and encouraging interest in what the others were doing.

If Penny sometimes thought it was a rather sterile attitude for a mother to adopt, she had grown used to it from an early age, and it never bothered her. Being sent to boarding school in Cheltenham had never bothered her, either. In their circles, going away to school was a perfectly natural occurrence, while the parents got on with their own busy lives.

The two unlikely friends to whom she had become closest in those Cheltenham days had initially been singularly reticent about their own family lives. She had only gradually learned how Gemma had known nothing but a grandmother's rough and ready care. And Laura had hidden the details of what she called her boringly average life on the farm, until they had met up with that wretched Tommy Hall in the neighbouring school. Penny had accepted, then, how fortunate she was to be such a privileged person.

'I've told Andrews I want him to drive me down to Somerset tomorrow,' she told her parents when they met at dinner that evening. 'You didn't need him, did you, Ma?'

'No. I'm driving up to London myself. I can't see

why you don't have some driving lessons, Penelope,' her mother said. 'It would save you so much trouble, darling, and your father would get you the very best tutor and you could choose whatever car you wanted. You know that.'

Penny shook her head. 'We've had this discussion before. Horses don't frighten me in the least, but the thought of coping with a car on a motorway, or in city traffic, just ties my stomach in knots.'

'Leave it, my dear,' Gregory said coolly to his wife. 'Andrews is always at Penny's disposal, and she knows what's best for her. But you won't forget we have a meeting tonight, will you, Penny? You must be back in time for the election, although there's not much doubt who the new Chairman will be.'

'You shouldn't count your chickens, Gregory,' Helena told him. 'I'm not sure some of the older members will agree to the nomination.'

'Yes, they will,' he said, and from his slight smile, they all knew that whatever it took to persuade the Gloucester Pony Club that Penny Bishop was going to be their next Chairman, Gregory would see to it.

'You're going to visit that friend of yours, I take it? The one with the twins?' Helena asked now, dismissing the previous conversation with her usual ease. If there was nothing more to be said, then there was nothing more to be said.

'Laura, yes.' Penny was feeling the usual mild irritation that her mother never called her friends by name.

She had never appreciated how important a part of Penny's life Laura and Gemma had been. And it was partly because her own world consisted of such a vast number of acquaintances and fairweather friends, to say nothing of sycophants, that Penny suspected she had no concept of what a real friendship meant.

She was still thinking about that as Andrews drove her smoothly down the motorway the following morning. It had never really occurred to her before that her mother's life, which always seemed so incredibly full, was also so very shallow in many ways. The knowledge that Helena would find such an observation completely beyond her understanding, simply underlined the truth of it.

Once they were driving deeper into the country lanes leading to Lilac Cottage, the more Penny's heart lifted at the thought of seeing Laura again. She hadn't realized how much she had missed her. Life was as hectic for Penny as for her mother, but deep down she knew there was something missing. And since it certainly wasn't a man, it had to be the close friendship that had somehow never been replaced by anyone else.

Laura fell on her neck as soon as she arrived, quickly directing Andrews off to the nearest local pub. His choice of venue never worried Penny. He was well versed in the conditions about drinking and driving, and too keen to hold on to a job that paid him handsomely, to ever step over the mark.

Laura wore a simple cotton skirt and blouse, and she seemed as bubbly as ever, but Penny felt a small shock at the sight of her. She hadn't yet lost all the weight she had gained with the twins, and there were signs of strain around her eyes that presumably spoke of disturbed nights. Penny's limited knowledge of babycare was confined to those appalling TV sit-coms where tiny babies turned into screaming monsters who sent their parents demented, and kept them pacing the floor half the night.

'You look wonderful,' she lied, and Laura laughed.

'No, I don't. I look overweight and harassed. The twins are teething, and it's bad enough to have one of them doing it, let alone both at the same time. You're the one who looks wonderful, as always.'

She spoke breezily enough, and Penny felt a sense of relief. In the past few months, whenever she had phoned Laura, there had been too many cagey responses, and it was good to see there was nothing seriously wrong after all.

'I daresay you wouldn't have been so eager to have any more, after all, then.' Penny had heard Laura say several times that two were quite enough to cope with, thank you. She followed her indoors. 'So where are the little darlings?'

'They always have a morning sleep,' Laura said, over her shoulder. 'Come upstairs and have a quick inspection right away, and then we can have our coffee in peace.'

Penny knew she should have picked up something in the way she spoke, but couldn't quite put her finger on it. However, she quickly forgot it as she admired the sleeping babies and remarked on how pretty they were and how much they had grown. It wasn't hard to be enthusiastic and say all the right things about these two gorgeous infants as they lay so peacefully in their cots.

'You wouldn't think they'd been screaming half the night, would you?' Laura whispered with a grin, confirming Penny's worst thoughts about babies. 'They'll be out for the count for at least another hour, so let's leave them to it and you can tell me all your exciting news.'

'And you can tell me yours,' Penny smiled back at her friend, as they went quietly downstairs again.

'There's nothing much to tell here. Unless you count the nuisance of your husband being on call day and night – though it's not every night any more, thank God. The practice has become quite streamlined now, with a properly organized rota for night calls. At first, it was traumatic, and with Nick being the junior partner, he always seemed to get the worst of it, though he always denied it, of course.'

'But you're happy,' Penny persisted, following Laura to the flag-stoned kitchen. 'You've got everything you ever wanted, haven't you, Laura?'

'Of course! Doesn't it show?'

She filled the kettle and spooned instant coffee into two large mugs. At Penny's house they had percolated coffee in bone china cups and saucers, accompanied by delicious cream and the pretty little coloured knobs of sugar you only saw in high-class restaurants. The Bishop parents probably wouldn't recognize a jar of Nescafé if they saw it, Laura thought to herself. But she was comfortable in knowing that Penny would, because they had used so much of the stuff in their room at the Wellesley.

And of *course* she was happy, even if the ecstatic glow of realizing that she did truly love her own children after all had faded a little with the exhausting nights of the past month. She did have everything she wanted . . . and she also had a secret that she kept from everyone, even her best friends.

Even Nick didn't know how fervently thankful she was, that she didn't have to go through another pregnancy as long as she lived. There were bonuses to it that he must appreciate, of course. It had made them even freer with their lovemaking, and he could hardly complain about *that*.

But what he also didn't know, was the new and insidious sense of guilt she felt lately, because of her relief at not being able to give him any more children. He'd always wanted a large family, and she couldn't provide it for him. He never reproached her, and had insisted from the first that they were a complete family.

But he didn't have a son, and now he never would. And in all the classic novels she had ever read – and in all the rubbish ones too – having a son was of basic importance to a man.

'The kettle's boiling,' she heard Penny say. 'Are you off in your dreamworld again?'

Laura laughed self-consciously, pouring the boiling water quickly into the mugs and breathing in the lovely coffee aroma. Instant or percolated, it had the same stimulating effect, and she could do with a little more energy after last night's stint with poor Sarah, who was suffering more than Charlotte with her teeth. The trouble was, when one started, the other one yelled in sympathy. She tried to get her mind off babies for the moment.

'I don't have too much time for dreaming these days, Pen. But never mind about me. What you see is what you get, just as you always predicted. But I want to hear about you, and what's happening in the outside world.'

She hoped she didn't sound as insular as she sometimes felt. She supposed everyone felt this way when their babies were tiny, unable to go far because of feeding times and nappy changes, and then the teething problems and all the rest of it. And it never ended. Once you had children, your life changed for ever. And that was something the happy-ever-after novels never told you.

Penny's face came into focus, and she tried to concentrate, and to push down the mild rush of panic such thoughts always gave her.

'Well, the most imminent news is that I'm in line to be elected as Chairman of the Gloucester Pony Club tonight, so I have to get back in reasonable time,' she said.

'Good Lord, that's a responsibility, isn't it? All those children under your control.' But they'd be school-age children, of course, not the kind who were still comparatively helpless, and not yet crawling, let alone walking . . .

'They're not all children,' Penny informed her. 'It's really a blanket term for a whole range of riders, from novices to experienced competitors in various events. By calling it the Pony Club we encourage all ages to join, and if they start at an early age, the younger ones

191

don't feel inhibited. Especially if they're accompanied by parents or older brothers and sisters.'

'Will they accept somebody who's only twenty as Chairman then?' Laura was unconsciously echoing Helena Bishop's thoughts.

Penny shrugged. 'Oh yes. I've been a member since I was a child, and I've been on the committee for a couple of years now. My father says there'll be no problem.'

As she spoke, she felt a little shock at knowing how dependent on Daddy's manoeuvrings she sounded. She had grown up feeling independent and self-assured, but without that omnipresent parental backing, she wondered for the first time just how confident she would remain. It wasn't a comfortable thought.

'Actually, Laura, that reminds me of what I wanted to talk to you about,' she said quickly.

And the feeling that swept through her at that moment was one of mild disgust, and a swift recognition of her mother in herself. Helena so easily pushed away any uncomfortable thoughts that disturbed the serenity of her life, and Penny found herself doing exactly the same.

'Go on,' Laura prompted.

'Now, just hear me out before you say anything, because I know your first instinct will be to say no. But I really want to do this, Laura.'

'Do what? You're driving me mad with suspense now.'

'All right. Well, I know you have an aversion to horses, strange as it seems to me, especially being brought up with farm animals – '

'I wasn't exactly *brought up* with them. I'm not some female Tarzan of the Apes!'

Penny laughed. 'You know what I mean. Anyway, I don't think you should deprive your girls of one of the most enjoyable forms of exercise I know, just because of your own negative feelings. And before you say it, I'm not talking about sex.'

'Did I mention sex?' Laura said, her eyes wide and innocent.

'So because I love you all, what I'm proposing is a christening gift that is very personal to me,' Penny went on relentlessly. 'You've got a reasonable-sized paddock here, and several outhouses that could easily be converted into stables, and I want to give each of the twins a pony of their own. I'm also offering to teach them to ride properly when they're old enough. What do you say?'

Laura didn't say anything for a minute, since the statement had taken her completely by surprise.

'I say that you're sweet, and generous, and completely mad,' she said finally. 'And they're only seven months old, for God's sake!'

'So what? It pays to plan ahead. Don't tell me you haven't put their names down for infant school yet.'

'That's different. You have to do it practically as soon as they're born these days.'

'So put their names down for having a pony each when they're five. All little girls love to ride, Laura.'

'I didn't.'

'Well, most of them do. I'm sure Nick won't object. and it's a shame to let the paddock go to waste. It's crying out for children to ride in it.'

Laura gave in. Besides, it was all a long way ahead, and she knew how generous Penny was being in thinking of a gift that was dear to her heart. If she didn't have children of her own to lavish her gifts on, and presumably didn't want them, then this was the next best thing. And Laura knew her tuition would be of the very best too.

'I'll talk it over with Nick when he gets back from his course, but I'm sure he'll be pleased. It's lovely of you to think of it, Penny,' she said, trying to sound suitably enthusiastic.

'Well, since they're probably the only children I'll ever get close to, I have a special interest in them, don't I? Gemma's never been the maternal type, and it's not likely to be on my horizon in the foreseeable future, if ever.'

'Don't you ever want to get married?'

'Let's put it this way. I've never yet met a man I fancied spending the rest of my life with. If and when I do, you'll be the first to know. But don't hold your breath.'

Laura wondered privately how all Penny's riding achievements and important committee jobs could possibly compare with having a man to love. With Nick temporarily away, she was only too aware of the loneliness of sleeping alone when you were used to having a man's arms holding you until morning. She missed the closeness, and she missed him . . .

Right on cue, Sarah and Charlotte let out their breaths in loud, angry cries, and the grown-up lunches had to wait until they'd been fed and soothed, which the two of them seemed aggressively determined not to be.

Their needs dominated everything. And that was something Laura hadn't quite bargained for.

By the time the visit came to an end, it was hard to say who was more exhausted: Laura from trying to keep calm and be the perfect mother: or Penny from trying not to betray her horror at having to cope with the angelically-sleeping infants who had suddenly turned into squalling, red-faced monsters. Despite her sympathy for their obvious suffering with their teeth, Penny was glad when Andrews arrived at the appointed time, and she could decently say she had to get back. Laura put the twins in their playpen and left them screaming while she went outside to say goodbye.

'I suppose this has to count as our two-year get-together this time,' she commented. 'There was no chance of Gemma meeting us, and I know it's been difficult to pin me down lately.' She gave a self-conscious laugh. 'Just listen to me, will you? It's the two of you who lead such exciting lives, and your dates that we all have to work around!'

'Don't sell yourself short, Laura,' Penny protested. 'You've got what plenty of others would envy. But you're right about the get-together. Lord knows when Gemma will be around again, but I met one of our group in Cheltenham the other day, and I gather they're planning a school reunion sometime. We must all try and make that!'

'Just as long as they don't expect us to look the way we did then – '

'And as long as old Jonesy doesn't expect us all to burst into song,' Penny added with a grin.

They laughed, and hugged one another, each thinking how good it was to remember the carefree days at the Wellesley, but even better to be exactly where they were now. And babies didn't stay babies for ever . . .

They called it 'the terrible twos', Nick told Laura, airing his superior knowledge of paediatrics, in which he was becoming increasingly involved at the practice.

She glowered at him, too fraught from a day of wrestling with the toddler tantrums of her normally placid daughters, to feel anything but annoyance that a mere man should understand them so well, while she did not.

Today, of all days, she had wanted to stay calm and serene, and he'd promised to get home as early as possible. But she could never rely on that, Laura thought, with a rare show of pique.

There was always some patient or other wanting to see the handsome Dr Nick in preference to the other partners. Some elderly woman, or nubile teenager, wanting him to deal with their verrucas or their acne, or a young married woman wanting to discuss her sex problems . . . and he always had time for them all, which was why he was so popular.

'Don't worry about a thing,' he said now, totally oblivious to her simmering emotions. 'Go off and enjoy yourself. You look gorgeous, by the way.'

'I do not look gorgeous,' Laura snapped. 'I look exactly what I am – a boring mother who should have got her figure back in two years, and hasn't. And everybody else will be so skinny. Penny never puts

196

on an ounce, and Gemma always starved herself, anyway. And all the rest of them in our year will take one look at this podge, and think how I've let myself go!'

'My God, what's this – self-pity night?' Nick smiled. 'If you feel like that about it, take off the dress and the high heels and we'll have a quiet night in instead. I've no objection to spending an evening with my cuddly wife.'

Laura counted to ten. He wasn't being the most tactful of men. She was annoyed with herself for being so spineless about this reunion, which had sounded such a good idea at first. It had finally been arranged six years after she had left the Wellesley, and incorporated everyone who had left during that time. It was a chance to meet old friends and catch up on all the gossip. And best of all, it was knowing that the three of them, the old firm of Laura, Gemma and Penny, would be together again.

Now, Laura was overcome with nerves. It was unbelievable to think that she and Penny hadn't seen Gemma for three years, and she was presumably doing all right in America now. The times when she came home, there seemed to be no opportunity for socializing. In fact, she was becoming better known over there than over here, she'd confided in one of her scrappy notes, even if she wasn't at all sure if it was the right way for her career to be going.

Such a statement had mystified Laura, especially since she seemed to have got everything she ever wanted. But Nick had put his own interpretation on it.

'Gemma always has to be number one, Laura, and if

she's got any kind of brain in that head of hers, she'll still want most of all to be number one in her own patch, which is right here in England. If that eludes her, none of the rest will count for anything.'

'I can't agree with that! She was so ambitious, and America was always a dream ticket. And she can fit in anywhere,' Laura said in defence of her friend.

Though in a way, she could see what he meant. Even when Gemma was starting to be a success and touring clubs in the Midlands, she'd once confided her hankering to be back in London, where she belonged. And where she felt safe.

Laura remembered those odd words now. And she wondered just how Gemma felt, coming back to England on a flying visit, which coincided with the reunion at the Wellesley boarding school. But she brushed any speculation aside, sure that nothing would ruffle Gemma, especially a school reunion where she would be the undoubted star.

Laura was the one beset with nerves, every time she realized how narrow her life had become. She did the usual things with the children: took them to a play-group school twice a week and stayed as a helper for part of the afternoon; accompanied them fortnightly to some swimming baths where there was experienced tuition for teenies; joined a local young wives' group that sometimes bored her silly; got involved with the village drama group; and couldn't avoid the kind of social life a doctor's wife was supposed to enjoy.

And she did enjoy it. Of course she did. She was married to the loveliest man on earth, and she adored him.

But tonight she was meeting all those sophisticated girls from other worlds again. Who knew what some of them might have achieved in the six years since they all went their separate ways?

And when the evening came to an end, she and Gemma were to stay overnight at the Bishop place. This time, the parents would be there, and Laura knew she would be all fingers and thumbs, remembering the aloof Helena Bishop from the few occasions she'd attended school sports days, and Penny's pseudo-aristocratic father. That was Laura's real bugbear.

'You're surely not getting nervous at the thought of seeing old schoolfriends, are you?' she heard Nick say. 'For God's sake, they're only people, Laura. If they worry you that much, try the old trick of imagining them without any clothes. That usually cuts them all down to size.'

'I'm not sure that's an ethical statement, coming from a doctor,' Laura was starting to laugh. 'Anyway, it's not just the reunion. It's staying at Penny's place afterwards. I told you what it's like.'

'So? All you have to do is imagine the old boy and his stuffy lady without any clothes on too,' Nick suggested irreverently, at which she simply convulsed.

CHAPTER 12

'I don't believe this,' Gemma said.

Before the reunion, they had all converged at Penny's home, where Gemma had paid off her taxi and Laura had parked her car in one of the garages. Then, after cocktails with the Bishop parents, they had been swished away to the Wellesley in the Daimler, with Andrews at the wheel as always.

They looked around them now in disbelief. The enormous hall had been transformed into something resembling a Christmas party, with banners and glitter everywhere. Considering the normal dignified ambience of the Wellesley, it was incredibly vulgar. All around the hall there were sections set aside for group photographs, which would be sent to local newspapers to record the occasion. And *Class of '85* was where Laura, Penny and Gemma were being enthusiastically shepherded now.

'Do you get the crazy feeling we've never been away?' Penny muttered. 'Are we in *Brigadoon*, do you think? I swear we've landed right in the middle of a time-warp. Any minute now we're going to be hauled off to the head-mistress's study for some minor misdemeanour.'

'Or in Gemma's case, a major one,' Laura put in.

'It's definitely a kind of quantum leap,' Gemma agreed, her new American twang very evident. 'The teachers are showing a few more wrinkles, and maybe the dresses have changed. But not that much,' she added with a grin. 'I'm sure some of them have been brought out of the Ark especially for tonight.'

'Well, nobody's likely to be saying that about you, Gem.' Penny eyed the black and gold sequinned dress that made everybody else look dowdy by comparison.

'Do you like it? I picked it up in New York. It cost the earth, but who's counting?' Gemma drawled carelessly.

On anybody else it would have looked appallingly tarty, but somehow Gemma got away with it. She'd grown her heavily-fringed hair longer again, to go with the new image of jazz singer she was portraying these days. And the heavier, more dramatic make-up she now wore hid some of the strain in her face, that was only evident to those who knew her best.

'Is she all right?' Laura murmured to Penny, when Gemma was dragged away and surrounded by an admiring group of girls from a younger class than themselves.

'I think so. Why, would you say otherwise?'

'I don't know. It's just a feeling. She's almost too bright to be true. She's like an everlasting flame that's got to burn itself out or explode.'

'Good grief, that's almost poetic. I'm sure nobody has to worry too much about Gemma, Laura. She could always take care of herself. Look at her now, lapping it all up like a cat with a bowl of cream.'

'I wonder what happened to Eddie, and if she ever misses him,' Laura said thoughtfully. 'I liked him.'

'I don't know if she misses him, but I'm damn sure he misses her. When we met him at your wedding, it was easy to tell he was crazy about her, and she was the only one who couldn't see it.'

Laura hadn't seen it either, but then, she'd been far too busy getting married at the time to concentrate too much on anybody else.

They were being summoned to their various sections for the group photographs now. It was exactly how they used to be organized for their traditional end-of-year photos, and they expected to be told severely to stand up straight and lift their chins, and that Wellesley young ladies never slouched.

But after all, it wasn't the ordeal Laura had feared. A few weeks ago, she'd gone into Bristol and bought a new black dress that allowed for her more ample curves, and she didn't feel as hideous as she'd imagined. Not when there were plenty of others who didn't seem to portray the Wellesley image any too well, either. Penny and Gemma were two of the exceptions, of course, but Laura had cheerfully known they would be.

Penny was simply stunning in a white dress that had probably cost the earth, and the three of them unknowingly complemented each other in their choice of colours.

But when it was all over and they were back at the Bishop place, they could kick off their shoes and drink coffee, and talk until the early hours of the morning. And for all of them it was like stepping back in time in a far more companionable way. Even though the night was warm, the house was heated to its usual hot-house temperature. And it was a time for relaxing and renewing old ties and telling secrets.

'Come on, Gem, tell us what it's really like to be a star,' Penny encouraged her. 'And how do you get on with this LaFarge person?'

To her surprise Gemma screwed up her nose. 'To be honest, I don't like him at all, and thankfully I rarely see him. Rube travels with me as my manager, and that suits us both fine.'

'So he's still on the scene then?' Laura said.

'Oh sure, and before you ask, he's like a father figure to me. I have a minder too, and he's about as sexless as a eunuch. I suppose they think there's safety in numbers.'

'I wasn't going to ask,' Laura protested, and Gemma laughed.

'No, but I bet you were curious, remembering the little sex-pot I always was.'

'*Was?*' Penny echoed in surprise.

Gemma shrugged. 'You learn a thing or two in this job, Pen, and one-night stands can land you in a whole lot of trouble. Not only healthwise, and we all know about that these days, but contract-wise as well.'

At their puzzled looks, she went on, her voice suddenly brittle and resentful at being so manipulated. To a freedom lover like Gemma, it was like being stifled.

'It's written into my contract that I don't do drugs and I don't bring any scandal to the LaFarge Agency.

Any hint of sleaze in the newspapers and I'm out. Dumped. At a minute's notice.'

'They wouldn't do that to you, surely?' Laura said. 'You must be making plenty of money for them.'

Gemma looked at her pityingly. 'You're such an innocent, Laura, and you always have been. Everybody's expendable, even me, and the LaFarge empire's always been squeaky clean, and intends to stay that way. It might be a novelty in the music world, but there it is. It's a gimmick they don't intend to lose.'

She couldn't stop the bitterness creeping into her voice. It wasn't even that she wanted to live it up with wild rave parties or get into the serious drug scene, but she hadn't expected to live like a nun either. The small print in the contract had horrified her at first, but she'd agreed to it because it was such a stepping-stone to a glittering career.

But she sometimes felt she would explode with frustration at the way LaFarge controlled her life, even at a distance. And if she wavered one inch, she wasn't foolish enough to think he wouldn't get to hear about it. The newspapers and agency spies would see to that. It was the price of fame.

'Anyway, that's enough about me,' she said. 'What about you two? Come on, Pen, what's new with you?'

Penny spoke quickly, trying to dispel the sudden gloom. 'I don't suppose you've ever heard about gymnastics on horseback?'

'Good God, I can't think of anything more revoltingly energetic! Don't tell me you're involved in anything like that?'

'We're forming a group in the county,' Penny continued serenely, 'and if all goes well we're planning to enter the National Championships next year, so we've twelve months' hard training ahead of us. I don't know whether or not I'll be included in the team yet. I'm not that much of an expert.'

'It sounds pretty dangerous, Pen,' Laura put in.

'It's all part of the game. There's no special kudos in just riding round and round a field. Anybody can do that, and it's great for exercising the horses, but eventually you want something more.'

'I wouldn't,' Laura shivered feelingly.

'That's because you've got no sense of adventure in your soul,' Gemma told her. 'It wouldn't be for me, either, but I suppose everybody's got to have some substitute.'

'What's that supposed to mean?' Penny snapped.

Laura sensed the sudden drop in temperature between them, and it was just as if they were all back in those early days at the Wellesley, and Gemma and Penny were bristling at one another.

She brushed aside the imagery, telling herself not to be so stupid. They had been children then, and they were adults now. But one look at the tense way they had both sat up, and she knew that some things never changed.

'Well, horse-riding, and all that committee work, and all these other activities you get involved in. It's no more than a substitute for the things normal people do, is it? Everybody knows that. Even Laura will tell you.'

'What do you mean – *even* Laura?' Laura demanded.

Sometimes Gemma could be really bitchy without even trying. Maybe it was a kind of defence mechanism. Though, against what, Laura didn't have the remotest idea.

'Oh, come on, Laura, how long did it take for that dishy doctor of yours to get into your knickers? And don't think I'm knocking it. It's natural and normal. And for somebody of twenty-two years old to prefer horses to men, *isn't* normal, in my opinion. Penny must have been the oldest virgin in our year, and probably any other year tonight. This is the nineties, for God's sake.'

Laura got in first. 'I think you should stop right there. What gives *you* the right to criticize the way other people live their lives? We never criticized yours. And just because you feel restricted by this arrogant La-Farge bloke, you don't have to take out all your frustrations on us.'

'Leave it, Laura,' Penny said. 'What she said is probably true, anyway, but as long as it doesn't bother me, I don't see why it should bother anybody else.'

In the face of criticism and bad taste, she was as cool and detached as ever, and her breeding showed. Which irritated Gemma as much as it ever did.

'I didn't say it bothered me. I just think you don't know what you're missing. Ask Laura if you don't believe me. Is it happy-ever-after for you, or what, kiddo?'

'Oh yes! If you count having two over-active tomboy infants fighting with one another all day long, and an exhausted husband who's at everybody else's beck and call whenever they want him, being a happy-ever-after situation, then yes, that's what I've got.'

The words all came out in a sarcastic rush, and when she stopped to take a breath, Laura saw them both looking at her in amazement. She hadn't meant to say any of that. She was perfectly happy with Nick and she loved him as much as she ever did. She hadn't even been aware of such simmering tension in herself until Gemma forced it out, as she had such a knack of doing. She could deal with it adequately on a day-by-day basis, but being away from it all seemed to bring it more sharply into focus. Contrarily, she suddenly longed to be back home, in safe and familiar surroundings, where she didn't have to examine her emotions so deeply.

'Take no notice of me. It just gets to me sometimes, that's all,' she muttered, backing down. 'I love the twins and I love Nick, so I've really got nothing to complain about.'

'And it's what you wanted, Laura. It's all you ever wanted,' Penny said heavily. 'We all got what we wanted, didn't we?'

Driving back to Somerset the following morning, Laura remembered Penny's words. They had all got what they wanted, yes, but for two of them at least, there were uncertainties.

She dismissed her own anxieties for what they probably were – a hangover from the post-natal depression, which Nick had finally told her could linger in small ways for months or even years. His breeziness was supposed to make her feel less panicky about the occasional bout of depression, but it didn't. Not when she still kept the secrets she couldn't tell to the one she loved most in the world.

But Gemma now . . . Gemma worried her. She was the most successful of them all, yet she was truly like a time-bomb waiting to go off. One of these days, Laura was sure that she would. She wasn't being herself. On stage, she acted a part – but in real life, she had always had the capacity to let her hair down and be pretty wild. It was her way of dealing with pressures, and to Laura's knowledge she never did anyone any harm. It was just Gemma being Gemma. And this LaFarge bloke was suppressing her true nature. It wasn't healthy. Dr Laura had spoken.

She smiled to herself, knowing she was thinking in Nick's jargon. And feeling a sudden lift to her heart at knowing she would be seeing him soon. He hadn't been on call this weekend, and by now he would have given the girls their Sunday morning breakfast and put them down to play.

They would all be eager to see her, and she would sweep the twins up in her arms and tell them all about the party with her old friends. They wouldn't under-stand half of it, but they would catch some of the excitement from her.

And Nick's eyes would tell her more than words how glad he was to have her back where she belonged. And she felt a sudden glow in her heart, knowing just how lucky she was.

Penny didn't allow any mild resentment over Gemma's words to stay with her for long. After her friends had gone, she exercised Midnight Sun that morning, knowing that technically, she was no more a virgin than Gemma, or Laura. The constant horse-riding and exercising had seen to that. No matter how the cynics scoffed at such a thing, it frequently happened, and it had happened to her. But didn't they say that virginity was a state of mind anyway?

Physically, she was perfectly normal, but mentally, Gemma was right. She didn't know how it felt to be loved by a man, and she had never felt the need to try it out just to satisfy her curiosity. She wasn't even particularly curious about it. If she ever fell in love, that would be a different matter. But she was in no hurry for that, either.

Her own parents hadn't married until they were both in their thirties, and it had been five years before Penny was born. She smiled slightly, totally unable to imagine her parents in the throes of passion. Certainly not her mother, who was what Gemma had once called a very cold fish.

Perhaps she'd be a cold fish too, she thought uneasily. Perhaps she simply didn't have the capacity for loving, the way Laura did; or for lust, in the way Gemma had apparently abandoned. But in Gemma's case, it was only temporary, she was sure. One of these days it was bound to surface again.

Gemma stayed in her flat for a week before she went back to America. She had been reluctant to let the place go, despite the foolishness of not living there any more, but it had been the first home she had been able to afford with her own money. Rube had suggested she let it out to a selected and well-vetted clientèle on a kind of time-share basis, and the system had worked very well.

Whenever she returned to London, the flat was hers for as long as she needed it. She wandered around it now, feeling as much at home in its glass and concrete ambience as in any country estate. This was her life, and she revelled in it. There was only one thing missing. She hadn't heard from Eddie in months, and every time she came back here, she missed him. If she had any sense, she'd be rid of the place and be rid of his ghost as well.

But such a thought only made her resentful that he could still have any influence over her life. As long as she stayed here, she told herself she was being strong enough to show him she could do without him. Even though it was a futile gesture, since he obviously didn't think enough about her to care what she was up to. Penny had once said he was in love with her, but she refuted the idea completely. Eddie was only in love with Eddie, and when she'd thrown him out of her life, he'd obviously gone looking for pastures new.

She hadn't yet checked the answering machine, and she saw that it was flashing with several messages. It would be Rube, she thought, and just for a moment she wished he'd never got her that appointment with Desmond LaFarge, and changed her life.

And she instantly told herself how stupid she was being. It was seeing Laura and Penny again that made her restless. Laura especially, with her down-home image and her perfect life . . .

She flipped through Rube's messages, and the one from LaFarge's secretary asking her to call on him on Monday afternoon. And then her heart stopped as she heard the first few bars of one of her old songs coming through the machine, along with her old voice, low and intimate, before it had got all jazzed up. Eddie's fingers were caressing the piano keys as seductively as if he was caressing her.

When the few bars of the recording ended there was a small pause, and then she heard his voice.

'How are you, babe? I heard you were back in town. I'm here for a few days too, so how about getting together for old times' sake? If you're interested, call me on this number.'

The message ended, and Gemma stared at the machine for a few minutes before playing it back. She wouldn't call him. It was a mistake to think you could ever go back, and besides, her contract forbade her to do anything to jeopardize the good name of the LaFarge Agency. And remembering the wild nights she and Eddie had spent together, she knew there could never be anything platonic about their relationship.

There had always been passion between them. They had either loved or hated each other, and there had never been any in-between. She loved him still, but she couldn't risk getting involved with him again.

She was still saying the words to herself when she dialled the number he had given her.

'I take it you're quite happy with the New York arrangements, Miss Grover,' Desmond LaFarge stated smoothly the next day, speaking with the usual formality that set him well apart from all his clients. They might be the stars, but he pulled all the strings.

'I could hardly be otherwise,' she said, feeling as gauche as she had on that first day when she had come here with Rube. It was hard to think it was three years ago now, and that part of her was longing for the five-year contract to end, so that she had the choice of renewing it or telling him to get lost.

And if she did that, she might as well say goodbye to her career. She'd always get work, but it wouldn't be the kind LaFarge had in mind for her. He constantly unnerved her, and she hated the way he controlled her life.

Not that he had controlled it last night, she thought, lowering her eyes so that he wouldn't see the change of expression in them. She had dialled Eddie's number, and said quickly that it was best that he didn't come to the flat.

Instead, she waited until dark, then she dressed in jeans and sweatshirt and bundled her hair up inside a baseball cap, and changed cabs twice before reaching the address he gave her, feeling a surge of excitement and adrenaline that had been missing for a very long time. His flat was in a less than salubrious part of the city, but within minutes of arriving here, she was in his bed, and everything was as marvellous between them as it had ever been.

'Why the hell did I ever let you go?' he asked her savagely a long while later when they still lay entwined, desperate not to break apart.

'You didn't let me go. I walked out, remember?'

'So you did. And now you're back – and if I had my way, I'd never let you out of my sight again, let alone my life.'

'Eddie, don't, please,' she said faintly. 'This is just for tonight. You know that. It isn't for ever.'

'Why can't it be? You don't need this LaFarge guy any more. You don't need anybody except me.'

His hands roamed over her body, and she felt the sweet tingling arousal she always experienced whenever he touched her. It had been so long since she had felt like this, and it was so very tempting to abandon everything and stay . . . She hesitated too long before answering.

'So this is the way it's going to be, is it? Giving me your favours whenever you feel the need, and nothing more. Is that it, Gemma?'

'You called me, not the other way around. I didn't get in touch with you.'

'No, that's right,' he said. 'I begin to wonder if you ever would have done, or if I ever meant a damn thing to you.'

'You always meant as much to me as I meant to you, and we always knew where we were with one another, didn't we, Eddie? No commitments, no strings. It was what we both wanted, and it worked. Don't let's spoil it, please.'

She had never begged from any man, and she wasn't begging now. But she was pleading with him to understand, because he was her friend, her dearest, loving friend, and she couldn't bear to lose the deep and enduring bond that took no account of partings or disputes.

He released her and got out of bed, pulling on his clothes again. Gemma snuggled down inside the bed-clothes, watching him, and all too aware of the chill without his warm body beside her. But it was already morning, and it was time to go.

'Why do you think I phoned you, babe?' he asked, when the silence had gone on too long.

'You wanted to see me, for old times' sake. That's what you said. That was it, wasn't it?'

'That was it,' Eddie agreed.

LaFarge looked at her now, sitting on the other side of his vast office, and smiled. Gemma had always hated that smile. It was oily and thick, and for all that he was such a big-shot entrepreneur and, she had recently discovered, very religious, she had never truly trusted him. He might insist on all those clauses in his contracts about his clients keeping clear of drugs and scandal, which made him appear whiter than white, but she wouldn't put it past him to put the boot in any time he liked, and however he liked. As she'd said to Penny and Laura, everyone was expendable.

'I didn't bother asking Rube Steiner to join us today,' LaFarge said smoothly. 'He'll be faxed with any developments tomorrow.'

'What kind of developments? You're making me nervous.' Gemma sensed that was what he wanted to hear.

In reality, he was making her *angry* – and she didn't

like the way he kept her dangling. Could he possibly have found out that she'd spent the night with Eddie? So what if he had. It was her private business, and being with Eddie was hardly the kind of rave-up LaFarge objected to so much.

'Am I also making you curious?' LaFarge countered playfully.

'Not really. I presumed that you'd want to see me sometime when I was back in London,' she said airily.

He banged his beringed hands on his desk, making her jump. 'All right, girlie, I'll stop fencing with you. This is the deal. How do you fancy three months in Las Vegas?'

Gemma gasped. Whatever she might have been expecting, it hadn't been this. Everybody knew that Las Vegas was where the biggest stars performed . . . Her mouth went suddenly dry as he smirked at her stunned expression.

'Before you answer, let me tell you it's not in any huge casino. You're not big enough for that. It's a small hotel well away from the Strip, and you'll be a support act. But it'll be good experience, and I advise you to take it.'

Gemma had conflicting thoughts running through her brain at that moment. Her initial surge of excitement at his words was completely obliterated by the fact that this certainly wasn't the big-time, for everybody knew that all the big casino hotels were on the Strip. That was where the stars like Sinatra and Bassey and Tom Jones had always been the big attractions. Outside the Strip, you might as well be somewhere in mid-Atlantic for all the notice you got.

And there was something else too. He'd said she wasn't big enough for that. And a *support act*? She'd been in this game now almost from the day she'd left the Wellesley, and she knew exactly what that meant. She'd been clawing herself up in all that time, and LaFarge had had her under his wing for three years already. He was supposed to be moulding her, and grooming her, and all the rest of what she called his French poodle act. And he was reputedly the best.

So if she hadn't made it by now, for the first time ever, the logical thought that was sticking uncomfortably in Gemma's mind now, was that *maybe she was never going to make it at all.*

CHAPTER 13

As the twins' fourth birthdays approached, Penny's belated christening present was mentioned again. Laura would have been quite happy to forget it completely, but Nick brought up the subject while they were having a snack lunch before his Monday afternoon ante-natal surgery.

From the first, he'd approved of the idea of buying them ponies, despite Laura's reservations. She had even dredged up a pathetic comment about the fatal accident that had befallen Bonnie Butler, Scarlett and Rhett's little daughter in *Gone With the Wind*, but such fictional dramas hadn't cut any ice with Nick. Between him and Penny, she had known she would eventually back down, but not without a fight.

'I've said I'll agree to it, but that doesn't mean I'm any happier about it than when Penny first mentioned it,' she said at last.

'She's told you often enough she'll teach them the rudiments, and she's promised to find them the best instructor around here,' Nick tried to soothe Laura's fears.

217

'I know all that – '

'And there's a lot to be said for getting children used to animals early. You of all people should know that. Besides, they're already quite fearless when they visit your father's farm. Most folk would be scared to cross a field of cows, let alone one with a bull in it, but that never bothered you, did it? And it doesn't faze the girls.'

'I didn't have to ride the damn things, that's why,' Laura retorted.

'Well, I hardly think Penny's going to sit them on race-horses, or train them for her wonder-gymnastic troupe just yet. I'm sure she'll find the smallest, gentlest creatures imaginable. You shouldn't deny the girls this, Laura, just because of your own hang-ups.'

'Oh, is that what I'm doing?'

'Well, isn't it? Either that, or you're jealous of the fact that once it happens, Penny's going to be flavour of the month with the kids.'

For a moment, she was speechless with annoyance at such a statement. 'Of course I'm not jealous! What a stupid thing to say.'

But maybe she *was* jealous in a funny sort of way. Not of the girls' adoration of Penny, but only she knew how jealously she guarded the safety of her daughters. Sometimes she couldn't bear to let them out of her sight, especially in the summer months when so much holiday traffic trundled through the inadequately equipped Somerset villages. And now that they were about to start infant school, she wondered how she would get through the long days without their chattering company.

She was appalled at herself for feeling so spineless. It was something she had never confided in Nick; he simply wouldn't understand. He'd tell her to go out and get a life, or something equally irritating . . .

At least he couldn't suggest having another baby to fill the gap, as so many of his patients did. And he still didn't know how she truly felt about not having any more children, because she had never confided her guilty relief to him. She doubted that she ever would. Instead, she poured all her energies into the two beautiful children they had, to the extent of almost smothering them with love.

'Has Penny spoken to you about this pony thing lately?' Laura asked suspiciously now, since the topic seemed to be uppermost in his mind.

'She phoned me at the surgery one day last week.'

'What?'

Nick gave a half-smile. 'My God, get that look off your face. You sound just like the outraged wife discovering the husband's affair. She simply phoned to sound me out about the ponies before she spoke to you, that's all.'

'Why would she need to do that? We've already discussed it a hundred times, and she'll be here next week for the twins' birthdays.'

'But what we've never got organized is when it's actually going to happen,' he said.

'So when have the two of you decided it will be?' Laura was unable to stop the sarcasm in her voice.

She didn't want to fight with him, but all too often lately, they seemed to bicker over the most inane things.

She knew all about the supposed seven-year itch pulling couples apart, but they had only been married for five, for God's sake. She couldn't bear this continual scratchiness between them lately, nor did she have any idea how to stop it.

'It's not a decision for Penny and me to take. It's something we *all* have to agree on,' Nick said. 'But if it was going to be this summer, say, then we should start thinking about getting some builders in to convert the outhouses into stables, and levelling out the paddock.'

'So that's it, is it? It's all arranged for this summer.' Laura's response was flat and emotionless.

'It is *not* all arranged, and I've no more time for any more of this idiotic arguing,' he said, his patience finally running out. 'I've an ante-natal surgery this afternoon, and I suggest you call Penny and discuss it with her more rationally than you've done with me so far.'

And then he was gone, banging the door of the cottage, leaving Laura brooding with resentment. Part of it was because he hadn't even bothered to kiss her goodbye. He was always so busy now, with his own little paediatrics niche in the practice, and the fact that all the young women in the district seemed to want their children to be treated by lovely Dr Nick. If she was a *really* jealous woman, she could certainly find something to be jealous about . . .

She punched out Penny's phone number, stabbing at the figures in a sudden fit of temper, and the unflustered tones of Penny's mother did nothing to appease her ragged nerves.

'Oh, hello Mrs Bishop. It's Laura here. Laura Dean. Can I speak to Penny, please?'

(*May* I speak to Penny, she remembered too late . . .)

'I'm afraid she isn't here this afternoon, Laura. She'll be back around seven this evening. Would you care to leave a message, or shall I ask her to call you?'

'Oh no, that's all right. I'll try again later,' she answered and quickly put down the phone.

She always hated it when she was all worked up to do something, and then she was thwarted. And trying to speak on the phone to people who weren't there, was the worst. She could call her father, but he'd be busy on the farm now, and it was just as easy to drive over there, if she wanted to.

For the first time in ages, she wondered if Gemma was in London now, in that swish flat of hers. There had been the usual note tucked into the last Christmas card she'd sent, telling Laura she was still on the road, but would do her best to make their bi-annual get-together in August . . . as if to say she didn't want anybody trying to contact her before then.

Poor Gem. Everything had gone wrong for her in the last year, and Laura had no idea how she was coping with it, because Gemma kept things so bottled up inside. It seemed as if the old days of sharing confidences were gone. And it had begun to dawn on Laura just how vulnerable Gemma really was.

It had never seemed that way to her and Penny. At the Wellesley, Gemma had always appeared to be so brashly self-confident, able to take on the world, but then her world had apparently all but fallen apart . . .

Penny had told her over the phone in almost hushed tones.

'Gemma was really hoping for a big break after her stint in Las Vegas, and she got several more cabaret spots over there, but apparently it all fizzled out. I got the impression that this LaFarge bloke had virtually lost interest in her. Did you know she was working in some club in the North of England now? A bit of a come-down, isn't it?'

'No, I didn't know! But if she was feeling any kind of a failure, I'm sure she wouldn't have wanted us to find out. So how did you hear of it?'

'I was at a function in London last week, and a friend told me he'd seen her name and photo on a club poster while he was in Middlesbrough on business – he'd remembered her as my famous friend. Out of curiosity he went to the club, although it wasn't really his scene.'

Knowing the kind of places frequented by Penny's circle of well-heeled friends, Laura could imagine what it must have been like.

'And?' she asked.

'He didn't say much, just that she looked nothing like her old glamour photos any more. The club wasn't anything special, and it seemed as if she was really on the skids. Those were his words, not mine.'

'I can't believe it. What do you suppose happened in Las Vegas then?'

'I've no idea, but I really don't like the sound of it, Laura. I've got the name of the club in Middlesbrough, and I'm going to write to her there.'

'So will I,' Laura said at once.

They had both done so, yet neither of them had received a reply until the scribbled note in the Christmas cards with the London postmark. So it looked as if she was back. Laura dialled the number, and listened to it ringing out, until the answering machine took over with a breezy message.

'I'm not here now. Leave a message and your number, and I'll get back to you soon. Love, Gemma.'

'Gemma, it's me, Laura. I just wanted to know how you are – and if there's any chance that you can get down here for the twins' birthday,' she added on an impulse. 'Penny's coming, and we can put you both up for a night, or however long you could stay. We haven't seen you for ages. I'll ring you later unless you ring me first. 'Bye.'

She hung up in frustration. Neither of her friends had been available, and despite what Penny had told her about Gemma, it still seemed to emphasize how busy and important their lives were, while hers consisted of child-minding and baking, and being the good doctor's wife, and answering endless phone calls, and sending Nick off in the middle of the night to some irritating woman's bedside who could easily wait until morning to complain of her bloody headache or whatever . . .

She listened to her inner thoughts with horror, wondering what kind of a shrew she was turning into. Then she was distracted by the girls squabbling in the other room and went to separate them.

'Let's take a walk around the lake, and then we'll go and see Grandad, shall we?' she said. 'I expect he'll let you feed the chickens if you behave yourselves, and then we'll cook tea for him.'

Their screams changed to squeals of delight. They weren't habitually naughty children, just boisterous, and it never took much to pacify them really.

She wrapped them up warmly, then strapped them into their car-seats, and fetched one of her Dad's favourite blackberry and apple pies out of the freezer. By the time they were ready for their tea, it would have defrosted nicely. The sun shone thinly, and it wasn't a bad day for early February, but the roads were wintry enough for her to drive extra carefully down to the lake. It was the girls' favourite outing, summer or winter, even if it took them ages trying to count and identify the different birds.

An hour or so later, they were back in the car again and heading towards the farm; Laura's spirits began to revive with every turn in the road. She knew she had it all. She had a husband who loved her, and two adorable daughters. And her father would be as delighted to see them as ever.

She saw the ambulance as soon as she drove into the yard, and her heart froze. Frantic thoughts of the kind of accidents that could happen to farmworkers rushed into her mind with frightening speed. An overturned tractor pinning down its victim; the pitchfork piercing a foot; the rogue animal going wild and turning on the hand that fed him . . .

She braked quickly, and rushed out of the car, yelling at the girls that she'd fetch them in a minute. Her father's farmhand came out of the kitchen to meet her.

'What's happened, Ned?' she gasped in a panic. 'Why didn't you call me?'

But even if he had, she'd have been at the lake, or on her way here, and no convenient sixth sense had told her she might be needed in a hurry . . . Her mouth dried at the stricken look on the man's face.

'I've been trying to, but there was no reply from your place.' He pushed his fingers through the sparse grey hair, making it stick up in unruly spikes, and Laura could see he was in shock. 'It all happened so fast. One minute we were having a yarn over a mug of cocoa, and then he sort of choked up and went blue, and he just keeled over. By the time the ambulance got here it was no good. He'd gone.'

Laura snapped at him, not wanting to hear any of this nonsense. 'What do you mean, he'd gone? Gone where? I have to go to him – '

'Laura, lass, wait!'

But she pushed past him into the familiar old kitchen, where two ambulance men were kneeling down and attending to something that lay very still on the floor. Something with its shirt ripped open from their desperate attempts to revive it. Something with the oxygen mask still over its face. Something that had once been her father.

'I'm very sorry, Mrs Dean,' one of the men said, recognizing her. 'There was nothing we could do, and the only comfort I can give you is that he didn't suffer at all. The heart attack was massive; death instantaneous.'

She looked at him blindly, wondering how anyone

could be so *stupid*. There was no comfort in anything they could give her. She had been down this road before, when her mother died, and now her father . . .

'*No!*' she heard herself screaming. 'He can't be dead. I won't *let* him be dead!'

'Get her out of here, Ned,' the man said tersely. 'We're waiting for a doctor to arrive to pronounce Mr Robinson officially dead, and then we have to take him to hospital.'

'What for?' Laura wept. 'So they can do unspeakable things to him to see why he died? You can't fool me. I know what happens at post-mortems. You people are ghouls. And don't tell me to get out of here. He's still my father.'

She knew she was behaving appallingly, but she couldn't seem to stop. She dropped to her knees, as if all the stuffing had gone out of her. She almost fell over her father, kissing the cheek that was waxy but not yet cold, and hardly knowing what she was doing any more. She heard the ambulance men muttering together. One of them spoke more gently.

'Mrs Dean, I've asked Ned to make you a cup of tea, and if your father's got some brandy somewhere I suggest you put a drop in it. You've had a terrible shock.'

'Tell me something I don't know,' she muttered.

The whole world went stupid at a time like this, thinking that a cup of tea was going to solve everything. And didn't these fools know anything about drinking and driving? What kind of irresponsible idiots recommended brandy to somebody who was driving two infants around the country . . .?

'My children are in the car,' she said tonelessly. 'They'll be cold and frightened. They're expecting to see their grandfather. We've brought him a blackberry and apple pie for his tea – '

She spoke like an automaton, wound up and preprogrammed. Until that instant, she'd completely forgotten the girls. But now they were the only things in her head, her first priority. And they were too little to be confronted with death.

She heard Ned snuffling, desperately trying not to be unmanly and break down. He'd worked for her father for years, and he needed tea and brandy more than she did. She squared her shoulders, suddenly dry-eyed.

'If there's nothing I can do here, I think I'll take the children home,' she said. 'This will be too much of a shock for them. I don't want them to see their grandfather like this.'

She kissed his cheek and stood up. She had no idea which doctor would arrive to officially pronounce him dead, but it wouldn't be Nick. Not one of the family. She choked back a sob and rushed out of the kitchen.

The girls were squabbling in the car, trying to see which one of them could manage to unfasten the belts on their car-seats. They'd hardly missed her . . . and it was all so blessedly normal that for a moment Laura simply stood and watched them, and listened to them, and wished she could be four years old too, and not have to face the realities of life and death.

And then she saw that Sarah had kicked the back of the front passenger seat in her frustration. And the defrosted blackberry and apple pie had slid to the floor, oozing a sticky red mess all over the car mat. It looked like blood. She averted her eyes. It would have to be dealt with, but not right now. It was such a minor thing, compared with . . .

'Stop that fighting, you two, and listen to me. Grandad's not here right now,' she said brightly. 'Shall we go and see Auntie Hall instead?'

'Yes, yes!' they chorused. They liked the Halls' farm almost as much as their grandfather's, and in any case, people had to be told. Nick probably knew already. He'd be ringing her at home too, trying to break the news gently. Or maybe he was already there, wondering where the hell she'd got to. Her thoughts moved on in small, jerky sequences, and got her nowhere.

Mrs Hall gave Sarah and Charlotte milk and home-baked biscuits, and as soon as she'd passed on the news, Tommy took them out to see the cows and feed the chickens, as they'd been promised.

'We'll help in any way we can, my dear, you know that,' Mrs Hall said, in her practical and no-nonsense way. 'We're family now, and there'll be a lot to see to.'

'Will there?' Laura suddenly wanted to get away. She was in no mood to discuss details. She'd barely arrived, and now she wanted to leave. She was like a spring that couldn't be still. But she couldn't leave yet, because Tommy and the girls were busy with the animals.

'Well, the farm and the stock and all,' Mrs Hall sniffed delicately. 'But you won't want to think about all that yet, will you? Our Nick will sort it all out.'

She insisted on giving Laura the brandy-laced tea she'd refused at her own farm, and the young woman felt the heat of it trickling down her gullet. A short while later, they heard the screech of car tyres, and then Nick was there, pulling her into his arms and holding her tight.

'I've been trying to get hold of you for hours,' he told her, his voice harsh. 'I had no idea where you'd gone when we got the call at the practice. Dr Varley's doing the business at the farm, and I was told you might be here. Are you all right, darling?'

'Of course I'm not bloody well all right! I feel as if I've been punched in the stomach and there's nothing left inside me, but apart from that – '

Apart from that, she had begun to feel the most fearful sense of responsibility. There was no one above her in her own family hierarchy now. No parent to turn to, or rely on. Only her. She didn't know if everyone felt like this, but the dawning realization made her feel suddenly sick, and totally inadequate. It was rather like the way she'd felt after having the twins, when she knew she'd never be able to cope . . .

'Tommy's bringing the twins back,' Nick said quickly, hearing their high, chattering voices. 'I think we should go home and tell them together.'

'I can't – I just can't – '

'We'll do it together.' He touched her cheek gently. 'Just as we do everything important.'

She swallowed, knowing he was being strong for them both. The girls rushed at him, delighted to see their daddy so unexpectedly. Above their heads, Laura gave a small sad nod, knowing they were about to destroy the children's innocence. There was nothing anyone could do to stop it.

229

She hardly remembered driving home, or sitting the girls down on the sofa between them, and letting Nick take over. She knew it was done, because she heard the girls crying, and Nick was trotting out all the usual platitudes of Grandad being so happy to be with Grandma again now.

All of which meant nothing to them, since they had never known Laura's mother. She let him get on with it, though. She also let him get their tea and bath them, and tuck them into bed, because he was used to dealing with grief, and he'd know the right things to say. And she refused to think that she was simply ducking the issue.

Nick was still occupied with the children when the phone rang. She listened vacantly to Gemma's frothy voice.

'Lovely to hear from you, Laura. February's a pretty flat month for me, so I'll be able to get down to Somerset for the twins' birthday. It's the end of next week, isn't it? So tell me which day will be best for you, and what I can buy for them.'

'Gemma, something's happened,' Laura said, as soon as her friend paused for breath.

'Happened? What do you mean?'

'My father died this afternoon.' She said it for the first time, tasting the words, forcing herself to believe them.

There was a momentary pause, as if Gemma needed time to digest the words, and then she spoke in a rush.

'Oh God, Laura, I'm so sorry. Well, of course, that

changes everything. Look, you know I'm no good at saying the right things at a time like this, but if you want me, I'll come. You know that.'

She was brisk and businesslike, reminding Laura that she wouldn't want to be in on anything that was too emotionally fraught. She normally tried to avoid such things.

So why did she think Gemma was almost desperate for her to say yes to her offer? That she needed to get right away from things? Or maybe it was just Laura feeling especially sensitive now, and picking up nuances that weren't there.

'Come down any time if you can bear to be around for the funeral,' she said deliberately. 'Or you could look after the girls for us instead on that day. Whatever. I haven't thought that far ahead, and naturally, no arrangements have been made yet either.'

'Well, I don't suppose they have. Anyway, we can sort out whatever way I can be of help when I see you. I'll come down on Thursday then.'

She hung up, and so did Laura. It was the first hurdle. No, the second. She had already told the Halls. She was beginning to realize that telling people made it more real. And it *was* real. This was something you couldn't hide behind. She rang Penny next.

'I was just about to call you, Laura – '

'Something's happened.' She was repeating the words she'd said to Gemma as if they were a mantra.

'Go on.'

'My father died this afternoon.'

'Oh Laura darling, I'm so sorry.'

She and Gemma said virtually the same thing that everyone automatically said. But Penny's voice was infinitely warmer and more caring, and it didn't hold back from being too involved, the way Gemma's inevitably did. Laura thought she had never fully realized the difference in them until today.

'I know how much you loved him,' Penny went on softly, 'and you'll be feeling lost and dreadful now, and in need of friends. I can be there tomorrow afternoon.'

'Thanks,' Laura responded in a choked voice, knowing how tightly Penny's life was organized. 'Will you be able to stay?'

'For as long as you need me, darling.'

Laura hung up slowly. Her two best friends would be here when she needed them most, as she had always expected them to be. But she had the strangest feeling that it was Gemma who needed consoling as much as herself.

CHAPTER 14

The local newspaper did a splendid write-up on the funeral. Farmer Robinson had been well-known and well-respected in the district, and there was a fine turn-out, Mrs Hall said with satisfaction. They held the bun-fight, as Gemma irreverently called it, at the Halls' farm. Mrs Hall had suggested keeping Sarah and Charlotte with her to help out, which pleased them immensely.

By now, the twins had been told that their Grandad had gone to Heaven, in the same way that he'd explained to them about his old dog a few months ago. They'd never known their grandmother, but they'd known Skip, and with the sweet logic of children, they accepted that if Skip and Grandad were together again now, then that was all right.

They knew more about death than Laura gave them credit for, and accepted it more naturally than she did herself. There were tears, but their natural curiosity forced Laura into explaining things in simple terms, and she discovered that the telling helped her come to terms with it herself.

'What's going to happen to the farm now? I take it that you and Nick won't be moving there?' Penny asked her in a quiet moment when the funeral was all over, and they were back at Lilac Cottage.

It was a relief to Laura to be home again after the rituals of the day, to pull back the curtains that had been kept closed, and let in the daylight again. By mutual accord they had all changed out of their various mourning clothes, and had dressed in casual jeans and T-shirts. It was for the children's sake, Laura told Nick, but knew it was for her own sake, too. You never realized how precious normality was, until something out of the ordinary happened.

It was a deep thought, and she had become prone to deep thoughts in these last days. She was twenty-four years old, a wife and mother, and yet she had never felt as fully or as unwillingly adult as she did now, when both her parents were gone.

She looked at Penny vacantly for a moment, finding it hard to get her thoughts in gear to answer a perfectly practical question. The farm . . . She shook her head.

'We wouldn't move there. Nick's work is here, and it's always been a working farm, Pen. We're happy where we are, and I'm not sure I could cope with all the memories, anyway,' she answered at last. 'You see, Dad never actually owned the farm. He was a small-holder and a tenant farmer, and only the livestock was his. Whoever else takes it on will presumably want the stock, and the proceeds will come to me. But it's all in the hands of the land agent.'

She was irritated by her sudden sense of defensiveness, because it all sounded so narrow and rural, and emphasized the contrast between her own situation and Penny's. When Penny's parents died, she would inherit that great mansion and the land, and all the wealth that went with it. While Laura would receive whatever savings her father had put by, his insurances, and the proceeds from the stock. Everybody thought farmers were rich, but it wasn't true. Not unless you were one of the big boys.

Her brief moment of envy died, and she thought instead of how much her parents had loved her, and how her father had doted on Sarah and Charlotte. She had lacked for nothing, and of the three of them, it was Gemma who had been left out in the cold as far as relationships were concerned.

Laura looked out of the window now, to where Gemma played in the garden with the girls, who were well wrapped up, although the day was mild for February. Gemma pushed them high on the swing, letting them take their squealing turns, and revelling in the way they clearly adored her.

Somewhere along the line, Laura thought, Gemma was still missing out – but Gemma would be the last person to admit it. Nor would she thank anybody for suggesting she might yearn to have a family of her own, one day. It had never been Gemma's style to settle for domesticity.

'Actually, as far as the farm goes, I've a feeling Tommy might be sniffing around,' Laura said, turning away from the window. She'd thought it several times, but it was the first time she'd put it into words.

'Tommy Hall?' Penny asked.

'Well, I don't know any other Tommies around here, and you needn't look so sceptical. We all thought he was a bit of a prat when we were kids, but he's a damn good farmer, and he's got quite a business head on his shoulders. I think he'd make a go of it. And, of course . . .' She paused, and Penny waited for her to go on.

'You may think this is daft, but in a reassuring sort of way, it would keep it in the family. He's Nick's cousin, after all. There's a great sense of continuity in the farming world, Pen, and I know Dad would like to think the farm was in the hands of someone we knew and trusted.'

'I never thought I'd hear you say that about Tommy Hall,' Penny said with a smile.

'I never thought I'd be saying it, either. But the more I think about it, I know I'd be quite pleased with that solution. And once Tommy's got a place of his own, I daresay he'll get married. You saw the girl with him at the funeral, didn't you? She's a farmer's daughter too, so she knows the ropes.'

'Like marries like, you mean.'

'Well, that's how it would be in this case, but I didn't, did I?'

'No. You just got the best catch in town,' Penny drawled breezily, in perfect Gemma-speak. But it made Laura laugh, and somehow brought the day into perspective again. And when Gemma came inside with the children, all sparkling eyes and red noses, she was openly relieved to see her two friends smiling again.

Funereal gloom didn't sit happily on Gemma's shoulders.

Both Gemma and Penny were prepared to stay for as long as they were needed. It was clear that Gemma had no engagements, even though she never made much of it. Penny simply cancelled all her appointments. The administrative details for the new Equestrian Centre she and her father were setting up together could safely be left in his capable hands.

Penny and Gemma stayed for ten days in all, keeping up their usual, if somewhat guarded repartee, until they left to go their separate ways. Then, for Laura, everything fell apart.

She had never felt so alone in her life. Dealing with ordinary, everyday things seemed as impossible as having a mountain to climb. In her heart she knew that coming to terms with her father's death was her own personal mountain.

Nick was wonderful, taking everything from her shoulders as far as the solicitors and farm dealings were concerned. And he was there to help clear out her father's personal belongings and sending the unwanted furniture to the local salerooms.

Mrs Hall was a staunch ally as far as the children were concerned, and other friends and neighbours rallied round. Superficially, life went on, and the first traumatic shock soon passed. But still Laura felt alone. It was the kind of loneliness that nobody else could penetrate, and something she couldn't explain.

She clung to Nick in the way a child clung to a parent,

wanting nothing from him but hugs and reassurances, and knowing that it was a situation that couldn't go on for ever. Nick was a normal, healthy male, and six weeks after Farmer Robinson died, he pulled her into his arms and told her quietly that it was time to come back to the real world.

She looked at him mutely for a moment, circled in his arms in their bed, aware that he knew just how she had been holding him off. But he must also know why. He was a doctor, and doctors were supposed to understand all about the various ways in which people handled grief . . .

Laura was suddenly angry with what she saw as his crass insensitivity, and pushed him away.

'I *can't*, Nick,' she said in a brittle voice. 'You have to give me time.'

'And you have to give me back my wife,' he stressed deliberately. 'You can't go on behaving like a zombie for ever, darling. You go through the mechanics of everyday life, but in your mind you're not even here. The kids may not notice it, but I do, and it's got to stop. It's not healthy, Laura.'

'Are you trying to tell me I'm having some kind of breakdown? Is that your diagnosis, doctor?' she asked, still in that strange, hard voice that didn't sound like her own.

'I'm not saying anything of the sort. I'm just pointing out that you have to accept reality. Your father is dead, but you're not. *I'm* not. And he'd never want you to go into a perpetual state of mourning for him. He was too large a character for that. He loved life, Laura, and he gave you the capacity for loving it too.'

Her anger died away as she listened to the cool, barely controlled passion of the professional man. It must be a torment for him to see her wallowing in self-pity, indulging herself in a torrent of private grief.

'I know you're right,' she mumbled. 'We should celebrate his life, not mourn his death, however hard that may seem right now. But somehow it seemed all wrong to even think of making love so soon after –'

'Does it still seem wrong?' He spoke gently against her mouth, while his hands began to caress her in the sweet, familiar way.

'No.' She took a long, deep breath. 'Oh Nick, no, it doesn't seem wrong. It's what I want, more than anything else, right now . . .'

Making love had been a kind of catharsis at a critical time, Laura thought later, and from that moment on, she felt more able to face the future again.

Spring was just around the corner, and new life was budding everywhere. The twins loved this time of year, and if starting their new 'proper' school had been something of an ordeal for Laura, she found that the taking and fetching, and the company of other young mothers took up more of her time than she had expected. The hours between were busy ones.

The girls had started school in mid-term to get them used to it. They did afternoons at first, then mornings, and then all day. They came home bursting with excitement, with early Easter cards and posters they had painted, and started growing things from seeds and pips in yoghurt pots that lined the kitchen windowsill.

Spring was a time of regrowth and rebirth, and Laura couldn't help but be affected by it, and thanked whatever god was smiling down on her for not letting her sink too deep into the trough.

The girls were already clamouring for Nick to get started on the paddock and stables for the ponies Penny was to buy them. There was no escape from their enthusiasm, and Laura wouldn't quench it.

'You've worn me down between you,' she said with a rueful laugh, when Penny sent them half a dozen photographs of ponies, and told them to say which ones they liked best. 'Just as long as you both know it won't happen until the summer holidays.'

Their howls of protest had no effect on Laura.

'Penny's going to be far too busy until then to think about getting ponies organized for you. And besides, nothing's prepared here yet, so you'll just have to be patient.'

Which was a near-impossibility for four-year-olds, who wanted everything to happen instantly, and saw no reason why it couldn't. But it was true; Penny had plenty of personal business in hand and finally, she told Laura what was happening.

'It's like a dream come true,' she said on the phone, her usual sophistication completely swamped by girlish excitement. 'Dad's funding it all of course, but it's going to be in my name, as a gift to me. He's such a darling.'

And so rich, Laura thought dryly . . . and so astute in

putting the Equestrian Centre in Penny's name from the word go. The more assets a person had, the more the government swooped on them in taxes and eventual death duties . . . she quickly steered her mind away from the thought.

'The work's all going ahead,' Penny went on, 'and we've got an absolute army of people in to clear the land and build the indoor arena. It's going to be such fun, Laura.'

Everything was such fun for Penny, and Laura felt a twist of envy for the serene way her life never seemed to falter.

'I won't forget about the ponies for Sarah and Charlotte, though,' she added. 'There's a very good man in your area who's promised to give them lessons, though I'd obviously like to give them some instruction myself whenever I can. It will be – '

'Such fun?' Laura supplied with a grin.

Penny laughed. 'Right! And you sound much better, darling.'

'I haven't been ill.'

'No, but you've been in shock, and now you sound as if you're out of it. I hope so. Life has to go on, and all that rot. But you know it's true, don't you? And talking of rot, is there any news on the Tommy Hall scene yet?'

In her exuberance she flitted from topic to topic as breezily as Gemma, but Laura was glad to keep the discussion away from her own feelings.

'He's taking on the farm, as we thought, and he's getting married at Christmas, so that's something to look forward to.'

Though just how she would feel, when she inevitably had to visit her old home at some stage, with Tommy and his buxom bride installed in it, Laura didn't quite know.

'Oh well. He tried all of us, though he always had a softer spot for you than Gemma or me, so I hope he'll be happy. I still think it's funny that the two of you are related by marriage after all.'

She prattled on, quite un-Penny-like, and Laura felt exhausted when she finally hung up the phone. But at least the pony question was put off until August, and the 'good man' Penny had suggested as their instructor would come highly recommended.

If Penny was floating on some cloud somewhat higher than the proverbial nine, Gemma was taking stock of her life. April had seen the end of her five-year contract with LaFarge, and it hadn't been renewed. Her great potential as a star had plummeted, taking every bit of her self-esteem with it.

Only she knew the toll it had taken on her. On the surface, she was as bright and confident as ever. You had to be, in this business. Once you let your guard slip and showed the world that you were desperate for work, grasping at every piddling little club date you could find, you were lost.

She sometimes thought she was lost, anyway. She had rubbed shoulders with the greatest in Las Vegas. She'd had a few singing spots on TV and made some records and personal appearances whose reception was comparable with the shrieking kids on *Top of the Pops*.

But over the past three months there had been nothing worth mentioning. No phones constantly ringing. No LaFarge – not that she considered *him* any great loss, she thought with a shudder. Not even any Steiner, since she'd dispensed with his services after an almighty row over her refusal to sing in a strip club.

And she hadn't seen Eddie in months. She didn't know if he was still in the country, or even if he was still alive. Though if anything bad had happened to him, she presumed she'd have got to hear of it on the grapevine. He hadn't cared enough to keep in touch, it seemed – and that hurt.

After all the times she'd fought with him and thrown him out of the flat, he'd surely always known that the bond between them was too strong ever to be broken. Or maybe she had simply been deluding herself in this, the way she'd deluded herself about so many other things.

She sat by the window of the flat, looking out at the beautiful moonlit panorama over the Thames, and saw none of it. All she saw was the reflection of herself, curled up on her sofa with a half-empty bottle of booze by her side, and felt nothing but disgust.

The phone jerked her out of her reverie so harshly that she slopped whisky all over herself. She didn't bother to answer it, letting the machine do it for her. Once her message had been relayed, her heart stopped at the sound of a familiar voice.

'I'm not speaking to any bloody machine, babe, except to say that I'm in town, and I'll call you again.'

Eddie . . . Gemma felt suddenly weak at the knees,

wondering if there was something in ESP after all, because his name had been the last one on her mind. So he was back. He was here in London, and she didn't have a clue where. Eddie-like, he'd left his old place without any forwarding address.

She was sick with frustration, knowing how much she had missed him, even though she didn't trust the thought, all too aware that she was maudlin with whisky and self-pity. All the same, he was like a breath of fresh air, and she got up unsteadily and turned off the answering machine for the first time in days.

Maybe Steiner would know where he was, she thought suddenly, although it was a long shot. She dialled his number with unsteady fingers; his wheezy voice answered at once.

'Rube. It's me, Gemma Grover,' she announced.

There was a slight pause, and then: 'My God, Gemma! I thought you'd emigrated,' he said with false heartiness. 'How are you?'

'Good.' She was trying to sound as bright as he did. 'And yourself?'

'As ever,' he said. 'But I'm damn sure you didn't call me just to ask after my health, darlin'. So how are things with you and LaFarge?'

'We've split, and good riddance to him,' she said. 'He was no good for me, Rube, with all his false promises of the "Big Time". But never mind all that. Eddie called me but he forgot to leave his number. Do you have it?'

She tried to sound casual, and to disregard how fast her heart was thudding.

'Eddie? No, I ain't seen him in months. Last I heard

he was doing the clubs, but then he went to ground. I'll put out some feelers if you like.'

'No, don't do that,' Gemma said quickly. 'He said he'd call me back, so I'll just have to be patient.'

She heard Rube give an amused laugh. 'And that ain't easy for my little gal, is it? Look, it's good to hear you again, Gemma. Why don't you come round to my place for a coupla drinks and a laugh? I could do with some company.'

'Now, you mean? Tonight?' she asked stupidly.

'Of course now, tonight. Hell, it's only ten o'clock. Since when did you ever go to bed at this hour? Unless you had company, of course.'

She hesitated, and he spoke easily again.

'Don't worry, I'm not making a play for you, kid. But I'd like to see you again, strictly legit, for old times' sake. Hell, we go back a long way, don't we?'

He spoke in his usual clichéd fashion, but coming from Rube, it sounded safe and familiar and reassuring. And when he said something, she knew him well enough to know that he meant it. He wouldn't be trying to get her into bed.

'I'll jump in a cab and be right over,' she decided in a rush. 'I don't need to dress up, do I? You don't have people there, do you?'

'Come as you are, babe, and I promise it'll be just you and me. We'll have a good old drinking session and then I'll tip you back in a cab and send you home, okay?'

And if he was going to be shocked at the way she'd let herself go, with her glossy black hair unkempt and wild, and wearing jeans and a skimpy T-shirt, then so be it, she thought grimly.

However, her pride wouldn't quite let her relinquish the image she'd always shown in public. She dragged a comb through her hair and painted on some eye make-up and lip gloss, then swapped the T-shirt for a red silk blouse, and slid her feet into high-heeled shoes. It was no more than a token gesture, but it made her feel surprisingly better.

He let her into his flat with his arms opened wide, and she had a job not to cry and ruin the heavy make-up. He was a sharp-nosed old fool, and she'd had plenty of run-ins with him in the past, but he was also a friend, and right now she badly needed a Dutch Uncle kind of friend.

There were times, like now, when her pride was so badly battered that she was totally unable to confide in her dearest and best friends. You always thought they were the only ones you could turn to, but it wasn't always so.

Laura had had enough worries this year, and would still be getting over her father's death; and Penny was far too involved with this new venture of hers to want to be bothered with Gemma's problems. Sometimes it was better to have a near-outsider . . . Maybe that was what counselling was all about, though Gemma always backed off from the thought of telling any pseudo do-gooder her innermost secrets.

'You're looking great,' Rube flattered, when they were settled in front of the mock-flame electric fire that had long gone out of fashion. But, in Rube's words – *if it ain't broke, don't fix it . . .*

'Bollocks,' Gemma said briskly. 'I look awful, and you know it.'

'And still the silver-tongued sweetheart, I see,' he chuckled, not taking offence. 'Just how much have you had to drink already tonight?'

'I don't know. I wasn't counting,' she said, her mood turning irritable in an instant. 'Why? Does it matter?'

'Not to me. Just making conversation, but maybe you'd better keep to the same grog if you don't want a tongue like a wrestler's jockstrap in the morning. So what was it? Whisky, vodka, wine?'

'Whisky.' She sank into an armchair in front of the dancing flames. 'How much have you got?'

'More than you could take,' Rube said calmly, pouring the drinks. 'So, to what do I owe the pleasure of your company?'

'You invited me, remember?'

'I remember,' he grinned, handing her a generous glass of spirit and keeping one of his own to match. 'But you must have been desperate to call me, since I don't kid myself I'm your favourite person.'

'I've always been fond of you, Rube, you know that,' she argued, taking a great gulp of whisky and feeling it course comfortingly down her throat.

'Oh yeah – when it suited you,' he laughed. 'But that's okay, darling. It goes with the territory.'

She hadn't heard those words in a long time. Eddie used to say them sometimes. *Dress tarty tonight, babe, we're doing a gig in a working men's club, and it goes with the territory . . .*

'So why are you trying to track Eddie down? Looking for work?'

Gemma took another sip of her drink. 'You can be a right bastard, Rube, you know that?' she said companionably.

'Why? Because I hit the nail on the head? It's the only way to succeed in business, babe.'

'Don't call me babe.'

It was Eddie's name for her; coming from him, it sounded sweet and romantic, and all the things a hard-headed career girl wasn't supposed to care about . . .

'So why do you want to find him?' Rube said again.

She stared at him, finding it hard to concentrate on more than one thought at a time. She'd been too busy remembering how Eddie used to fold her in his arms and call her babe, in that gorgeous, sexy voice, and how he used to make love to her in such erotic, inventive ways . . .

She pulled herself up short. Was she mad, clinging onto the past, when the past was over and done with? She should be looking forward. She fought to recall what Rube had just said.

'Looking for work, of course. What else?' She was unable to stop herself saying the humiliating words to Steiner. 'Eddie and me were always good together, and we could be again. You know that, Rube.'

'Especially if you had a good agent to handle things for you. You should think about that, Gemma. There's a lot to be said in sticking with people you can trust.'

'Even somebody who sold me down the river to LaFarge?' she whipped back, not prepared to let that go.

'LaFarge was a mistake, but we all make them, and I promise you it wouldn't happen again.'

'No, it bloody well wouldn't,' Gemma retorted sharply.

They clinked glasses in a kind of mutual acceptance of one another, without any real commitment. It wasn't what she was here for, Gemma thought. By now, she wasn't quite sure why she was here at all, and the whisky and the fire were making her so muddled that all she wanted to do was sleep and not have to think at all.

She had no recollection of sliding down on the armchair and of Steiner putting her feet up on a stool and covering her with an eiderdown while he turned the fire down low. She had no more recollection of anything until she awoke the next morning, with what Steiner would undoubtedly call the father and mother of all headaches.

CHAPTER 15

Gemma couldn't think straight for a minute, nor could she decide just what had woken her. She turned her head a fraction, wincing as the light from the window hit her eyes, and closed them again. Then she smelled the aroma of instant coffee and hot toast, and opened her eyes a further notch.

Rube Steiner was putting a tray down on a table beside her. He wore a shiny Paisley dressing-gown that made her think of somebody in a Noël Coward play. Only the cigarette in the elegant long holder was missing. And she . . . As the wheels of memory slowly began to turn, Gemma felt her heart give an enormous jolt.

'How the hell did I get here?' she croaked.

She was in Rube Steiner's bed. Even though she was still fully dressed except for her shoes, she was still *in his bloody bed*. And she couldn't remember a damn thing about how she got there . . .

'Don't worry, your honour's still intact, though it's probably a bit late in the day to be saying that, kid,' Rube quipped, with an attempt at a joke.

He might fancy himself as a Noël Coward clone, but he didn't look so good himself, she registered. He was even more rat-faced than usual, his complexion a sort of yellowy-beige colour, and she wouldn't mind betting he had a hangover as well. She vaguely remembered that they'd had a lot to drink last night.

'How did I get in this bloody bed?' Gemma snapped.

'I put you there when you fell off your chair and threatened to do yourself an injury,' he said coolly. 'I reckoned I was safer sleeping in the chair, and you'd do better in here. If you don't believe me, you can look in the bathroom mirror. You've got a fine old shiner coming up there, gal.'

Gemma's fingers went automatically to her left eye, and she winced as she felt the swelling there. He had to be speaking the truth. Besides, even if he'd wanted to do anything, she doubted that he'd been in any condition to ravish her – and anyway, nobody could get her out of her tight jeans without a proverbial tin-opener, and she'd surely have remembered that. But in the distant past there had been times when he'd tried it on more than once.

'You're not kidding me, are you, Rube? Nothing happened? You know what I mean,' she persisted.

'Cross my heart and hope to die – but not just yet,' he said with a ratlike grin. 'I might have plans for you, gal, and they don't include puttin' you in the puddin' club.'

The thought of anybody having a child looking remotely like Rube Steiner was enough to put a weak smile on Gemma's lips, and fully awake now, she was suddenly, ravenously hungry. It seemed a very long time since she'd eaten anything, and she reached greedily for the breakfast tray.

'What plans?' she mumbled through the thick, lavishly-buttered toast, thinking that not even a Las Vegas breakfast had ever tasted quite so good.

'I've been on the blower for the last half hour,' Rube responded conversationally, sitting on the end of the bed as casually as if they were flatmates.

'Should I be interested, or are you just making polite conversation?' She took a long swig of the strong black coffee, in the vain hope that the blinding headache might miraculously go away.

'Yes, you should be interested – seeing as how I've been trying to locate a certain mutual mate of ours, kid.'

'Eddie!' Gemma spoke with her mouth full, and swallowed quickly. 'Have you found him?'

Her swift moment of elation faded as Rube shook his head – and then she felt a secret satisfaction as she saw him wince too. Obviously, his head wasn't any more secure on his shoulders than hers this morning.

'Nobody's seen or heard of him, but if he called you, he's gotta be somewhere,' he reasoned with profound logic. 'Maybe he called you from outta town. Didn't he tell you anything?'

'It was just a message on my answering machine, and he said he'd call again.'

She suddenly scrambled out of the bed, feeling her head rock as she did so, but knowing that she had to get back to the flat. Eddie might be calling at this very minute, and she wouldn't be there. He might not call a third time.

'Look, Rube, I've got to go. Things to do and all that. You know,' she said vaguely. 'Thanks for the breakfast, and everything. And I'll be in touch, shall I?'

He'd said something about having plans for her, but she wasn't pinning any hopes on that just now. Not if it meant sleazy clubs and late-night gigs where she was ogled by guys with one hand around their beer mugs, and the other one God alone knew where . . .

'You do that. And if Eddie comes around, I'll be glad to see the two of you together sometime. Maybe we can work something out.'

'All losers together, eh, Rube?'

She bit her lips hard, unable to believe she'd just said that. It was letting herself down. It was letting Eddie down, and he had such talent. It was letting Rube down, too – and he'd always done his best for her, even with the awful LaFarge.

'Never call yourself a loser, darling. Once you start thinking that way about yourself, other people will pick up the vibes and start thinking it too.' Rube had his own special brand of philosophy. 'Always think of yourself as a star, see? You've had the breaks before, and there's no reason why they won't come again, even if they ain't exactly been knocking at your door lately.'

'Thanks, Rube.' Gemma smiled gently. 'You've got a big heart underneath it all, haven't you?'

'For God's sake, don't let anybody hear you say that,' he said quickly, in mock indignation. 'Once I get that kind of reputation, I'm finished in this business.'

Gemma laughed, even though it hurt like hell to do so. She swayed a little on her feet, but she leaned forward and gave him a quick kiss on the cheek before heading for the bathroom to repair the damage to her face.

Her left eye was pretty bruised, but thankfully she had her habitual dark glasses in her bag, and once she'd washed and applied fresh make-up she'd just about pass in a crowd. It was a pretty poor assessment for a so-called star who had always attracted plenty of attention and revelled in it. But not today. Today, she just wanted to get back home and take stock of herself and her life.

And to think that maybe, just maybe, there was still a chance for her to get back some of the glory that had once been hers . . . A star with any backbone went on for ever, didn't fall to pieces as soon as things went wrong. A successful comeback was what made a star a superstar, and it was ironic that it was a small-time, often overlooked agent like Rube Steiner who had made her see things that way. But it was like she said. He had a good heart underneath it all.

She wished now that she'd left the answering machine on. At least then, she'd have known if Eddie had called or not. She waited in for three solid days and nights, willing him to ring, until she was driven nearly mad with frustration and annoyance.

There were calls from several charities, and some-body called Sharon offering double glazing yet again, (didn't those people ever check the properties they were calling?) and a prissy voice that sounded neither male nor female, asking if Garth or Jonathan was available.

And finally some earnest voice inviting her to join the

254

Church of the Avenging Angels, which seemed like a total contradiction in terms.

'Get lost!' Gemma snapped, slamming down the phone, then picking it up and shaking it to check that it was still working. She put it back on its rest, and it rang again almost immediately.

'What do you want?' she shrieked into the receiver.

'I want to talk to you,' Eddie's voice said calmly. 'Can I come over, or am I likely to get my head blown off?'

The joy of hearing him was so intense that Gemma couldn't speak for a minute. Her throat felt so thick she was certain she was in danger of choking, and then she heard him speak again.

'I take it you're still there, darling. Either that, or I've got a heavy breather at the end of the line, which is a bit of a twist, since they're usually the callers – '

'Eddie! Oh Eddie, it's so good to hear you!' Gemma said explosively at last, feeling as if she had been holding her breath for ever.

'Well, good. But you knew I was going to call. I told you so on your machine.'

'That was three days ago, you bastard!' she yelled into the phone. 'Do you know how I've waited in for this phone to ring, and had to talk to the whackiest people in London every time I thought it was you?'

'Hey, from those dulcet tones at least I'm sure it's my one and only on the other end,' she heard him say with a laugh in his voice. 'I'm coming round, okay? I'll be with you in fifteen minutes.'

The line went dead, and Gemma stared at it. Fifteen minutes? And she looked like hell! She rushed into the bathroom, stripping off her clothes as she went and turning on the shower. While on the road she'd become adept at taking a shower, getting dressed and doing a passable make-up job in twelve minutes flat.

She didn't stop to question why it was necessary to make herself fresh and fragrant for Eddie, when he'd been out of her life for so long, and had made no attempt to come back to her when she had needed him. She just knew it was the right thing to do. It was only when she had wrapped herself in her bathrobe and studied her face in the steamy bathroom mirror that she remembered her left eye.

It was puffy, an interesting shade of purply reds and yellows. Dear God, she looked such a sight, she thought in a panic, and spent so much time trying to repair the damage with make-up that he had arrived before she was ready. He'd said fifteen minutes, but he was there in ten. And she still looked a sight, wearing no make-up except to cover her bruises, and still in her bathrobe . . .

She threw open the door to him, and he enveloped her in his arms at once, kissing every bit of exposed skin on her face and neck.

'You smell as gorgeous as ever, babe,' he said in his most seductive voice, kissing the crook of her neck. 'And all ready for me too.'

God, but he had a nerve to think he could walk back into her life and straight into her bed . . . He *always* assumed she'd be ready and waiting, she thought madly.

'You didn't give me enough time,' she snapped,

refusing to be aroused by him. 'I wanted to be all cool and collected when you got here.'

'What the hell for? I don't want you cool and collected. I want you hot and horny!'

'Eddie, don't do this,' she ordered angrily.

'Don't do what?'

'Don't make me fall for you all over again, and then leave me. I've had it with that kind of relationship.'

She had never said anything so self-deprecating in her life before. There she was, practically begging him to stay, and yet she had never considered wanting him to stay permanently in her life before. Not seriously.

When things were going well between them, he'd always been marvellous to have around. Dependable, if that wasn't a crazy thing to say about a guy like him – a musician, who drifted in and out of people's lives whenever it suited him. How could anybody ever hope to have a permanent relationship with a guy like that? Only a fool would do so.

She realized he was standing back from her a little now, although he was still holding her. Holding her up, she thought weakly. And he was studying her face. Her un-made-up, oh-so-vulnerable face. She felt his fingers lightly touch the bruising beneath her eye.

'Who did this to you?' he asked softly.

She flinched, and he let his fingers drop at once as if he had hurt her. But he hadn't hurt her. He'd just got it all wrong.

'Nobody. It wasn't like that, Eddie. I just fell, that's all.'

And the fact that she couldn't even remember how it

happened brought the swift, embarrassed colour to her face. Waking up in Rube Steiner's bed wasn't the happiest memory in her life, either, even though she believed him when he said he hadn't touched her.

'You just fell,' Eddie repeated.

'I'd had too much to drink.' She knew she sounded defensive, but couldn't help herself. 'You know how it is. You of all people know how it is, Eddie, so don't stand there looking at me with that self-righteous expression on your face!'

Anger was creeping into her voice again, but she didn't want to fight with him. She wanted to take things slowly, to renew what had always been between them. To feel loved and cherished and part of a couple again. To belong to somebody. To belong to him.

He backed off, holding up both palms towards her.

'Okay, if you say so, babe. You'd had too much to drink and you fell. Are you with anybody now?'

She looked at him steadily, knowing what he meant. It was the standard kind of question. Was there some other guy on the horizon? And if there was, then he'd clear off and no harm done. Did she mean so little to him? Some people might think he was being generous in acting this way. To Gemma, feeling as she did right now, it was the ultimate in frustration to know that he hadn't changed.

But she knew she had choices. She could tell him to go to hell, and that she had somebody special coming round at any minute, and that she was heavily involved with him. He'd take her word for it, and that way she could keep her pride intact. Or she could do what her heart wanted to do.

'There's nobody else,' she assured him huskily.

'Then what are we waiting for? Or have you gone off sex as well?'

'As well as what?'

'As well as me. Or am I reading the signs all wrong?'

She wanted to laugh. But not as much as she wanted to cry. Was this all there was between them then, nothing but this overpowering, sizzling physical attraction? It had always been enough, until now.

'Well? Do I go, or do I stay?' Eddie demanded.

She looked at him, as unkempt as ever with those dark gypsy looks that added to his smouldering sexuality, and infinitely dear to her. The one person who really understood her, or so she'd always thought. The one who took her the way she was, without question or censure. Part of herself.

'Stay,' she said simply.

A long while later, lying in his arms in her bed, with nothing but skin between them, she spoke lazily against his shoulder.

'Rube Steiner wants to see us sometime.'

'Good God, is he still around? I thought he'd have been swallowed up by the big boys long ago. What does he want with us?'

'I've no idea. It wasn't a message from him that brought you around here, then?'

He cuddled her more comfortably against him. 'I haven't heard from him in years, and I didn't think you'd want to get tangled up with him again after he threw you to the wolves. So what happened to LaFarge?'

Gemma winced. 'It turned out I wasn't star material.' She was being honest for the first time in ages. She hadn't even admitted it to herself, but here in the warm darkness, she could say it to Eddie, because he was the only one who would understand.

He kissed her nose, and then her waiting mouth, and then his lips went lower, seeking her breasts.

'You've always been star material to me, and you always will,' Eddie said.

'Maybe . . .' Gemma began hesitantly, knowing she should mention Rube's vague suggestion of plans for her, and presumably Eddie too, but finding it hard to think logically when he was doing such delightful things to her.

'Maybe we'll talk later. Right now, this is more important,' Eddie growled from somewhere deep beneath the bedclothes, and Gemma closed her eyes and gave herself up to pure pleasure.

Later, they talked, and she discovered he had been in the south of Spain for several months, working in the bars and clubs frequented by Brits. He didn't look affluent, but Eddie never did. He always got by, and was too bohemian to ever conform. She doubted that he'd ever change his looks for society's sake, but she could imagine how he appealed to holidaymakers and British ex-pats, and felt a brief jealousy that she hadn't been there to see and hear him.

Her sense of failure was unimportant to him, and went a long way to restoring her feeling of self-esteem. She hadn't even realized how low it had got until he came back.

Nor had she ever admitted or really appreciated how much she needed him. It was a thought to alarm her now. Because Eddie never really needed anybody, and if she were to start going soft over him, she was heading for disaster. Hearts and flowers and wedding rings were definitely not on Eddie's agenda, any more than they had ever been on hers.

'You've gone very quiet,' he said.

'I was just thinking,' she retorted quickly. 'Shall we call Steiner this morning and see what he wants?'

'You're in a mighty hurry to get out of here.' Eddie was lazily running his finger around the perfect curve of her cheek. 'You and he haven't got a thing going, have you?'

'Are you crazy?' Gemma said, with a laugh. 'But I'd better tell you something before you get the wrong idea. You know how Rube always likes to get people going.'

'Go on.'

'I stayed at his place a few nights ago. I drank too much and fell asleep on a chair. When I woke up I was in his bed. Nothing happened, I swear it. I was fully dressed and had this shiner. He said I fell off the chair, so he carried me to the bedroom for safety's sake. And that's all there was to it. You believe me, don't you?'

Once, she wouldn't have cared whether he believed her or not. Once, they would have shared lurid tales of one-night stands, each trying to outdo the other. But in those days, she hadn't realized she truly loved him, and she couldn't bear to listen to any more stories of his conquests.

'Of course I believe you, babe. You've never lied to me about anything.'

She hadn't, but right now there was a secret between them, and if she divulged it, she had the feeling he'd be gone, out of her life for ever. She had to be content with knowing he always came back when it suited him. It was an arrangement that had once suited them both . . .

'So shall we see what he's got in mind? Maybe he's thinking of some gigs for the two of us, like the old days, Eddie. What would you say to that?'

And it would keep him around . . .

'Why not?' he shrugged easily. 'Let's call him and arrange a meeting.'

Rube eyed them both with an expansive smile. They were what he called 'tarted-up' for the meeting, and his expert eyes told him they were desperate for something to come out of it. At least, Gemma was. Eddie . . . well, from what he'd heard of Eddie since putting out feelers in the last couple of days, the guy hadn't done so badly for himself in Spain. He was looking tanned and sexy enough to attract the punters and make the women go wild over him. With Gemma's dramatic dark looks and transparently pale skin, they could still make a good partnership. There had always been a definite charisma between them, and it was still there.

Rube could suddenly see the potential in these two, now that they were in a more pliable mood than of old. They weren't exactly coffee and cream, and anyway, that had been done already . . . but together they exuded a hot sexiness that was reminiscent of Sonny and Cher in the good old days.

That was it! Rube thought. The gypsy and the

lady . . . With the right backing and hype, the public always went for that in a big way.

'Let's have a drink before we talk,' he said.

Gemma knew well enough that when Steiner offered his clients drinks before a meeting began, his professional mind was already working overtime. For her and Eddie together. Her spirts lifted. Eddie had always represented the something good in her life, and this was going to be no exception. Thank God for Eddie.

A month later, Laura answered the phone without much enthusiasm. It had been a bad night, with three calls for Nick, and both the twins were disturbed and fretful with heavy colds at the start of the school summer holidays. Nick was still out on a visit, the curtains were still drawn, and Laura was sure it must be some unearthly hour in the morning. And she had neglected to switch the emergency calls through to the surgery.

She felt like death, and was in no mood to deal with any more queries or trifling ailments that should be referred to the surgery. She squinted at the kitchen clock, and saw with a shock that it was actually gone nine o'clock, which was a respectable enough hour for anybody. For some reason, it made her feel even more annoyed to know it.

'Good morning,' she almost snapped. 'This is Dr Dean's home number. If you need the surgery, will you please call the following number – '

'Laura, it's me,' came Gemma's excited voice.

'Gemma? Good God, you sound hideously cheerful

for so early in the day. I thought you never got up until noon when you were working.'

Gemma resisted saying that such a situation had hardly been on the cards for months now, because everything was about to change. She laughed into the phone, feeling Eddie's arms around her and his lips nuzzling into the nape of her neck.

'Well, that's how it often is,' she said jauntily. 'Anyway, I wanted to talk to you, as we're not having our regular meeting this year since we met in February – and oh God, Laura, I should be asking how you are – '

'We're all fine,' Laura answered automatically, the way everybody did, and couldn't be bothered to elaborate.

'That's good. Listen, I can't get hold of Penny. She's away at some horse meeting or other, and I can't talk to that snooty mother of hers. So will you let her know my news as well? Something's come up . . .'

She giggled as Eddie whispered a sweet obscenity in her ear, and clamped her hand over the receiver so that Laura wouldn't hear.

'Have you got somebody there, Gemma?'

'Only Eddie,' she explained. *Only the love of my life* . . . 'That's what I'm trying to tell you. We're going to be working together again, and we're flying off to Spain tomorrow.'

'*Spain!*' Laura repeated, beginning to feel like an echo.

'Yes, *Spain*,' Gemma giggled again. 'It's not outer space, you local-yokel! We've teamed up again, and our old agent-manager has got us a season of engagements from now, and right through Christmas and the New Year. We're calling ourselves "Cherish", and with any luck we might be making a CD under the new name. You're the first one to hear about the official comeback, darling!'

In the slight pause before Laura answered, Gemma realized she had never told either of her best friends that she was virtually on the skids, or had ever needed a comeback. But it didn't matter now. Nothing mattered now, except being positive for the future.

'That's wonderful, Gemma. I'm really pleased for you,' she heard Laura say.

'Yes, well, that's all there is to tell you at this stage, except I'll send you a postcard now and then to let you know how things are going. And watch out for the new team. Me and Eddie are really going places this time.'

She hung up before she crossed her fingers for luck, since it could almost be construed as a bad omen to think they needed it. She knew Rube had worked his guts out, getting them this deal with several big hotels on the Costa Del Sol. It helped that Eddie's reputation had already got around the area, and that her name was still remembered on record labels.

All the old confidence was back, and Gemma wanted to keep it that way. She twisted around in Eddie's arms, pressing tightly against him, and looking provocatively into his eyes.

'Well now, was I right to say that something's come up, or was I just dreaming?'

'You're not dreaming, babe,' Eddie said with a grin.

CHAPTER 16

By the end of August, the Penny Bishop Equestrian Centre was up and running. Penny had been touched and delighted when her father proposed handing over the deeds and title of the entire place to her. Even though it was his backing and finance that got it started, it was hers. There was to be a grand opening ceremony and party in the indoor arena, with local celebrities and many friends and well-wishers invited, as well as members of the horse-riding fraternity.

Penny had dearly wanted her two best friends to be there, but only Laura could attend; she had sent Gemma an effusive letter to her new address in Spain, promising to write again later and send photos. If she was faintly worried about Gemma's sudden departure and the assurance that everything was coming right this time, she dismissed it from her mind. Besides, Gemma always came up smelling of roses in the end.

Laura, Nick and their daughters were Penny's special guests. Nick had arranged his rota so they could all stay overnight, and the following day they would be taking a horsebox down to Somerset, containing the two ponies that were Penny's gift to the children. They drove up in the Land Rover that Nick habitually used whenever he had to visit some of his patients in outlying areas.

The children were ecstatic that the ponies were actually going to be a reality at last. They had already met their local instructor, Jeff Rawles. Penny had advised them all of his credentials, and he'd called at Lilac Cottage several times, and instantly won over the girls. He certainly had a way with females, Laura thought, young or old.

'It's important for any novice riders to have complete trust in their instructor, Mrs Dean,' he said on his first visit. 'Ponies can be as unpredictable as any other animal, although I'm sure Penny will have selected the most docile ones for Sarah and Charlotte. There also has to be a feeling of confidence between pony, rider and instructor. The animals sense it, you see.'

'I do see, but you make it sound even more exacting than I thought,' Laura said, unsure whether or not to be nervous of this good-looking man with the rugged look of the great outdoors written all over him.

He oozed confidence, in the same way Penny did. Perhaps it went with the vocation, she thought fleetingly. When you worked with animals, you had to show them who was boss, however kindly . . .

He had very strong hands, she noticed, as he finished his mug of coffee. She noticed hands. Nick's were strong too, sensitive doctor's hands.

'If it's not too impolite to ask, is there any more coffee going?' Jeff asked with an engaging smile, since she had suddenly gone quiet.

Laura flushed, annoyed with herself for being found lacking in her role of the good hostess, the way a doctor's wife should be.

'I'm sorry. I was dreaming for a moment – ' Oh God, that made things worse, since he must think she was being inattentive now, and that was appallingly rude.

'I do understand your reservations,' he said, to her complete surprise. 'Penny told me about your reluctance to let the twins have riding lessons, but I assure you they'll come to no harm, Mrs Dean. I hope you'll trust me in that.'

Laura laughed, to cover the small confusion she felt. He was probably not much older than herself, yet he made her feel like Methuselah by calling her Mrs Dean. Although, of course, she was well-known around here as the respectable doctor's wife and mother, and given to wearing Laura Ashley skirts, which probably put her in a certain category; while she knew that he was single, and considered a real catch . . .

Such inconsequential thoughts were quite ridiculous. She'd never looked at another man since meeting Nick, and she wasn't looking at one now, she thought in a fury. At least, not in *that* way.

For some mad reason, she had a sudden long-ago memory of Gemma's brash voice in her head. At the time she had been sneaking out of the Wellesley nightly to meet boys from the neighbouring school and taking every known risk of expulsion.

'For God's sake, you don't become a nun when you find a guy you fancy, do you?' (To Laura and Penny this had been one of Gemma's hilarious reasonings that was a complete contradiction in terms.) 'As long as you only look, and don't touch, it's one of life's great pleasures, not to say a girl's *duties*, to flirt with anything in trousers. You two should try it sometime.'

The others were pretty sure, even then, that Gemma hadn't restricted herself to the 'look, don't touch' formula.

And why she should even think of such a thing right now, when Jeff Rawles was here, cosily drinking coffee in her kitchen, she simply refused to analyze.

Laura's nerves jumped when Penny brought up his name quite casually, just when she'd been thinking about the incident. By then, they'd been given an early tour of the vast arena of the Equestrian Centre, already bedecked with balloons and streamers and Chinese lanterns for the evening, and Nick had taken the girls off to inspect the ponies yet again.

'So what did you think of Jeff Rawles, Laura? He's a super bloke, isn't he?'

Laura laughed. 'I suppose he is.'

'Oh, come on, you're not so married that you can't recognize a hunk when you see one,' Penny grinned.

'Are you interested then?' Laura countered at once.

'Not in the least, but there was a certain sparkle in your eyes when I said his name that reminded me of Gemma when she was on the hunt.'

'Honestly, Pen, you've got horses on the brain!'

'Well, we all know that, don't we?' Penny said cheerfully. 'But no, darling, there's still no man on my horizon, so you can stop fishing for clues.'

'What about Gemma's news, then? Were you surprised to hear she'd teamed up with Eddie again?' Laura asked as they linked arms and began to stroll back to the Bishop house across the fields, breathing in the scented country air.

Everything was so green and beautiful at this time of the year. Blossom was everywhere, and the hedgerows were humming with bees and insects, busily seeking nectar. The summer had truly been glorious, with the kind of warm and mellow weather that you felt was never going to end.

'I was more surprised to think he'd take her back after the way she ditched him without a second thought.'

'Well, I suppose I was too, although I never thought they'd be able to stay apart for ever, Pen.'

'That's only because you wanted it that way. The trouble with you, Laura, is that you've always wanted people arranged in neat little compartments, like yourself.'

She spoke in the matter-of-fact way people did when they'd known one another a long time, and could say what was in their minds without rancour.

'Well, thanks for making me feel so darned dreary and predictable,' Laura said with a grin. 'And I don't, anyway.'

'Yes, you do, darling. It niggles you that I don't have a man in my life, because you think I'm missing out. And you'd dearly like to see Gemma finish with the wild life, settle down with her Eddie and live happily ever after with a houseful of little Eddies. You can't deny it.'

'Does that sound so awful?' Laura was aware that it encapsulated her thoughts in a nutshell.

Penny squeezed the arm holding hers, realizing it had suddenly gone very tense.

'Not if we lived in an ideal world, but we don't, do we? We each have to go where fate leads us. Just be glad that we all ended up with what we wanted, Laura.'

Penny's words made her feel vaguely uncomfortable. And anyway, *she* hadn't had to try very hard to get what she wanted. Daddy had simply provided it all . . . But Laura couldn't argue with what either of her friends were doing with their lives. It was what they had both been destined for, regardless of the hiccups along Gemma's way.

And hadn't they always said that she'd be the home-bird with the houseful of kids? The awful, depressing clichés kept tripping through her mind, just when she should be celebrating with Penny on the success of her new venture, and sharing in her daughters' excitement over the ponies. She hugged Penny's arm to her and made an effort to sound cheerful.

'Take no notice of me, Pen. Sometimes I think life's just been too good to me, that's all,' she lied glibly, pushing the lingering grief of her father's death firmly out of her mind. Life had to go on. And for the twins' sakes, she'd refused to let her own sadness invade their young lives. She added slowly, 'I've just always felt that there has to be a comeuppance sometime.'

'Only if you do something terribly wrong, darling – and that will never happen to you.'

★　★　★

271

Once the opening formalities of the Equestrian Centre were over, and the evening festivities had begun, Nick was far more at ease with the horse fraternity, as Laura dubbed them, than she was.

In his job he met all kinds of people and had always been able to mix easily. The twins were too excited and too young to feel in the least inhibited by all the important people around them; they tore around the arena with the children of the other guests, bursting balloons and making patterns with spilled orange juice in the sawdust with the toes of their once-immaculate patent leather shoes. And Laura didn't have it in her heart to chastise them.

'Hello, Mrs Dean,' a voice said behind her. 'How nice to see you again.'

She had felt momentarily alone, the way people sometimes do at a party, and she turned around quickly, to see Jeff Rawles smiling down at her. She gave him a frankly delighted smile back, just because he was a familiar face among the crowd who were mainly strangers to her.

'I didn't know you'd be here!'

'I've only just arrived, and I didn't think I'd be able to make it at all. I've been out of the country for the past couple of weeks. But Penny left a message on my answering machine, urging me to come if I could. So here I am.'

The conversation died away, and Laura couldn't think of another thing to say to him. They were acquaintances, nothing more, drawn together through her daughters' needs, and now they were in a totally different environment. She'd been in control in her own home, despite the Laura Ashley skirt and her sense of homeliness. Now, even in the lovely new velvet dress and long gold ear-rings Nick had bought for her, she felt ridiculously nervous, wishing she had some of Penny's aplomb, or Gemma's small talk.

'Can I get you a drink of punch?' Jeff said easily. 'I should warn you I've been told it's pretty lethal stuff, but I'm about to fight my way through the crush to get one for myself.'

Laura laughed. In her experience, hot punch was usually little more than lemonade with a dash of spirits.

'Thank you, Mr Rawles.'

'The name's Jeff, and I refuse to go on calling you Mrs Dean. It's Laura, isn't it? Do you mind?'

She shook her head, feeling as gauche as a teenager, and aware of a sudden spurt of adrenaline in her veins as this handsome man gave her all his attention. When he leaned slightly towards her, the look in his eyes made her feel she was the only woman in the room at that moment. It was probably just to make himself heard above the hubbub of noise in the arena, she thought, but it was flattering, all the same . . . and she realized now that it was a knack some men had, whether or not it was natural or cultivated. In her kitchen at Lilac Cottage, she had been unconsciously aware of it . . .

'Of course I don't mind,' she smiled.

'Come on then. We'll fight our way through to-gether.'

He caught her hand, and she found herself being propelled through the mass of people to one of the long trestle tables, where Penny's father had donned a chef's hat that sat incongruously above his immaculate evening suit, and was doling out hot punch in enormous glasses.

'Come along, you two, I don't want any of this left by the end of the evening. The callers will be starting the square-dancing soon, and my special punch will put a zip in your steps,' he said jovially. 'So this is the handsome doctor husband, is it, Laura? Sorry I've been busy all day, my boy, and haven't greeted you properly – '

'This isn't my husband, Mr Bishop. Jeff is actually a friend of Penny's,' Laura said, scarlet-faced. 'Nick's around here somewhere – '

'Oh, well then, he's probably giving an impromptu diagnosis to one of the ladies, eh?' he chuckled, unperturbed. 'I'm told it's the price doctors have to pay once they've been rumbled. But you've got no worries about an escort or a dancing partner, Laura, m'dear. A lovely girl like you . . .'

They moved away while he was still rabbiting on, clearly having had more than a bellyful of hot punch himself. Hired waiters were meant to be doing this job, but Gregory Bishop liked to let his hair down and be one of the crowd when it suited him, which was more than could be said for his wife, currently holding court with several other county matrons.

Laura took a long drink of the delicious punch, immediately spluttering and giggling at the heady taste of it, and wondering what Jeff had made of the little encounter with Gregory Bishop.

'How did you come to meet Penny?' she asked him, taking a smaller sip this time, and trying to define just what mixture of spirits had been put into the innocuous-looking concoction to make it taste like fire-water.

'It was at a Pony Club bash she organized near Badminton. I was one of the judges,' he explained. From his casual tone, Laura knew at once that it would have been one of those elite 'horsey things' as the twins had begun calling them, which they took in their stride, and which she still felt were outside her experience or needs.

'Have you known her long?' she went on, thinking the conversation was going to come to a dead end if she didn't say something halfway intelligent. And knowing that she wanted to prolong it, if only because all the other guests seemed to know everybody else and were talking nineteen to the dozen, and she had felt oddly isolated until Jeff came along.

'We go back a couple of years, but not as long as you and she, I gather. Schoolfriends, weren't you?'

'The best,' Laura said with a smile.

She became aware that Nick was approaching with a plate of food. Until that moment, she'd completely forgotten that he'd gone off to the buffet tables, and it gave her a little shock to find how completely her mind had blocked out everything but Jeff Rawles.

It was more than shock. It was a sudden feeling of fright, and she turned to Nick with a great show of affection, putting her hand on his arm to bring him into the circle and end this little tête-à-tête.

'I thought I'd lost you,' she said quickly. 'You haven't met Jeff Rawles yet, have you, Nick?'

'I've never been around when you called at the cottage, but naturally I've heard all about you.' Nick shook hands with the other man. 'It's good to put a face to my daughters' current hero. So how do you think they'll shape up?'

Jeff laughed. 'It's too early to say, but if enthusiasm's anything to go by, I don't think we'll have too much trouble.'

Laura took the plate of food and bit on a salmon vol-au-vent as the two men made small talk. As always, she marvelled at the way men found it so easy to find topics of conversation. Even two such unlikely companions as a doctor and a riding instructor had no difficulty finding a mutual interest in cars and vintage motor-bikes and village affairs, and she turned away gladly as Penny came to claim her.

'Come and meet some more people, Laura,' she invited with a determined smile. 'I know what it's like when men start talking mechanics.'

'Thanks.' Laura was grateful to be rescued. She put the plate of food down on a side table, suddenly losing her appetite. But as they moved away, the fierce drink gave her enough Dutch courage to say what was in her mind. 'Pen, I've got to say this. Even now I'm still not sure about the ponies for the girls.'

Penny looked at her thoughtfully. 'Well, it's your decision, of course. If you want to break their hearts, you just go ahead and change your mind, darling.'

Laura felt a momentary helpless rage, knowing it was

true. Things had gone much too far to back out now.

'You really mustn't worry,' Penny said, more gently. 'Jeff's the best there is, and from the way the girls have been gabbling about him, they already adore him.'

Laura looked at her mutely. They had always been so close, able to read one another's mind, even at the most inopportune moment. So why couldn't Penny see that what was worrying her most, was that she might end up adoring him too? The sheer shock of the thought made her hand jerk, and she spilled some of the punch on her dress. She rubbed furiously at the small spots on the velvet material.

'Oh well, I don't suppose I'll have to see him too often myself,' she mumbled.

'Don't you like him?' Penny was clearly astonished. 'He's got girls falling over themselves to go out with him, and I can't think why he hasn't been snapped up yet.'

Well, that clarified things, thought Laura, holding on to the image of girls fighting off the opposition to go out with the dishy Jeff Rawles. So if he was making up to her, it was simply second nature to him, and meant absolutely nothing. Not that she had believed it did. Not that she had wanted it to mean anything. She was happily married and intended staying that way.

And of all of them, nobody would have predicted that homespun Laura would ever go off the rails . . . even though the look in Jeff's eyes had told her she looked anything but homespun that evening in the soft blue velvet cocktail dress bought especially for the occasion. In any case, Nick had already told her so. But a woman always knew when a man thought she was beautiful, even without the words . . .

It was nearly lunchtime before they finally left the Bishop place the next day. For Laura, it was quite a relief to be on the road again, despite the throbbing headache that refused to answer to aspirin or dark sunglasses, and the sight of the horsebox in the Land-Rover's rearview mirror.

The children didn't dislike the sight of it. They spent most of the journey swivelling around in their seat belts to check that it was still there, until both Laura and Nick were exhausted with yelling at them to sit still.

'Jeff won't be getting back until later this afternoon, but I thought it was a good idea to ask him to pop over this evening just to see that the ponies were okay,' Nick said casually, when they were nearly home.

'Oh Nick, why did you do that? I don't want company! After last night I just want to put my feet up for a couple of hours and enjoy the peace and quiet – '

'For God's sake, Laura, listen to yourself. You sound about ninety years old! The least we can do is show a bit of hospitality to the guy who's going to teach our kids the safe rudiments of riding. What on earth's got into you?'

'Hospitality?' she said suspiciously, ignoring all the rest. 'How much hospitality?'

Nick shrugged. 'Well, I did mention that we'd be having a cold supper tonight, and that he'd be welcome to join us. He probably won't take me up on it . . .'

'He probably will.' Laura couldn't hide her fury.

'Is Jeff having supper with us tonight?' Sarah yelled, breathing heavily with excitement. 'Can we stay up, Mummy?'

'Yes, we can, we can!' Charlotte shouted, as usual taking any query as fact, and overriding any possibility of refusal.

Laura gave in. She couldn't win against all three of them. Besides, it was only a cold supper. It might be a good thing for Jeff to see how united, and domestic, and *homely* they all were. And God only knew why she was having such wild and crazy and guilt-ridden thoughts.

But she had to admit, that just for a while last night, when she'd been square-dancing with Jeff in the vast arena, she'd wondered how it would feel to be smooching with him instead . . . and the headache that had nagged her ever since was as much due to that feeling of guilt as to the quantities of spirit-laden punch she had drunk.

At least the ponies were docile, she acknowledged, switching her thoughts away from the instructor, and back to the animals concerned. They were the gentlest creatures imaginable, and the girls adored them already. They'd have to watch them over feeding and coddling, Laura thought keenly, or the poor things would be killed with kindness.

Nick had hired one of the lads, Sam Godfrey, from a nearby farm on a regular basis, to oversee the bedding and feeding. He'd promised to be at Lilac Cottage when they arrived, to help settle the ponies into their quarters. Nick called him on the mobile phone when they were within half an hour of home, and to Laura's relief

Sam was already there waiting for them, since she could now legitimately leave the task in other people's hands without offering to help.

She saw that they'd all but forgotten her, anyway, as Nick and the girls clamoured to get the ponies out of the horsebox, egged on by young Sam Godfrey, and she filled the kettle for coffee with the mildest feeling of resentment.

The phone rang almost immediately, and she gave a sigh, wondering if all patients had a kind of homing-pigeon sixth sense when their doctor was around.

'Hello Laura,' came Jeff Rawles' voice. 'I'm just checking to see if you got back all right.'

'Oh. Yes, of course. Thanks for asking,' she said, stupidly willing her heart to stop thudding so fast, and wishing she could think of something far wittier to say than banalities.

'Good. Sorry I didn't see you before you left this morning. I'm tied up in Cheltenham until later, but I assume that Spick and Span behaved themselves?'

'Who?'

'The ponies,' he said patiently. 'That's what the twins have finally named them, isn't it?'

'Is it? I didn't think it was settled. They chopped and changed so much.'

God, this was awful. All these jerky sentences, and her hands feeling damp as she held the phone, just as if she was some teenager, unsure how to handle the first call from a new boyfriend.

'Look, Laura, about tonight. I wasn't sure if Nick meant it or not. About supper, I mean.'

Surely he was speaking in jerky sentences now? Laura put on her best doctor's-wifely voice.

'Of course it's all right, Jeff. It'll only be cold meat and salad and pickles, but you're welcome to join us.'

'That sounds great. And would you mind if I brought someone with me?'

Laura stared at an imaginary spot on the kitchen worktop and tried not to feel as if she'd been punched in the stomach. Before she could think of what to say, Jeff had carried on speaking.

'It's just that I'd really like my new assistant to take a look at the ponies as well, and to get to know the girls, since there are bound to be times when I won't be the one to give them instruction.'

'Oh, I see. Well, that's fine – '

'Good. Her name's Barbara, by the way. She's gorgeous, and you'll love her, Laura. See you later then.'

She put down the phone slowly, feeling as though she had run through a lifetime's emotions in three minutes.

There had been a sick dread when she knew Jeff was coming to see them, wondering if things were going too fast towards a place she didn't really want to go . . . then a thrill of excitement at hearing his voice so unexpectedly . . .

She'd felt a sense of despair when he'd asked to bring somebody with him, and then elation at assuming for a moment that the assistant would be a man. And now . . . now she found herself laughing out loud in a kind of crazy relief, seeing herself for the idiot she had been.

Anybody who was around at the time would be

281

gorgeous and wonderful to the Jeff Rawles of this world, and she had been so naively available last night at the Equestrian Centre. She had also been in the grip of some belated midsummer madness . . . and it was just as suddenly over.

Nick came into the kitchen, noisily followed by Sam and Sarah and Charlotte, the girls gaping at the vision of their mother seemingly laughing at nothing.

'What's so funny?' Nick was already starting to smile in anticipation.

She moved into his arms, giving him a quick hug, breathing in the faint whiff of pony and straw bedding on him and all of them, and almost enjoying it.

'You wouldn't believe me if I told you. Let's just say I'm glad to be home. So who wants coffee, and who wants lemonade? And then I'm coming out to see how Spick and Span are settling in.'

'How did you know the girls had finally decided on their names?' Nick asked with a grin.

'Guesswork,' Laura replied brightly.

CHAPTER 17

A month later, Laura began to feel as if a small grey cloud had been lifted from her shoulders. By now the girls were having a weekly riding lesson from Jeff Rawles, and the luscious Barbara more often than not came along with him.

It was obvious that Jeff no longer had eyes for anyone else, and far from feeling affronted, Laura was mightily relieved. She hadn't wanted to feel attracted to Jeff, but she accepted that for a brief time, she'd had her head turned, and now it was over.

She could even feel more sympathy for Gemma's brief flings, knowing now that emotions took no account of good intentions. However saintly you thought you were – and Laura had never considered herself a saint – it could happen to anyone.

Penny had managed to get down to oversee the first of the riding lessons, but since then Sarah and Charlotte had been in Jeff's capable hands. They loved their lessons, and the ponies were extremely docile and obliging. It all helped to make Laura feel magnanimous to the world in general, and she accepted that that, too, was due to the fact that whatever small temptation had been put in her way, she had resisted it.

God, but she *did* begin to sound like a saint, she thought with a grin, as she opened the morning's post, including the letter with the Spanish stamp on it. It was quite a bulky envelope, compared with Gemma's usual scrawled postcards. Laura grinned again as she saw the one-page letter inside, accompanied by a brochure advertizing the star attractions at the Don Pedro hotel and holiday complex.

Her eyes widened.

'What is it?' Nick asked, bolting down his breakfast as usual in a way he'd undoubtedly scold his patients for doing as she made a small exclamation.

'Look at this! It seems as if Gemma's going places at last, Nick.'

'Again?' he said dryly. By now, Laura knew he didn't have too much patience with Gemma's erratic career.

'Don't knock it. She's had enough ups and downs in the past couple of years, and she's still survived. Now she and Eddie are topping the bill at this hotel. Take a look if you don't believe me.'

She handed him the brochure almost defensively, feeling an absurd need to protect Gemma from any undue criticism. Nick took the brochure with a shrug, and saw the name CHERISH in large letters at the very top. He read aloud the elaborate wording beneath:

DON'T MISS THE SMASH HIT OF THE SEASON.
HERE TONIGHT, AND ALL THIS WEEK, SINGING FOR LOVERS
EVERYWHERE, THE SWEETHEARTS OF THE COSTA DEL SOL,
GEMMA AND EDDIE.

'I'd say there's a good bit of poetic licence there, isn't there?' Nick teased his wife.

But Laura was too busy reading the scrappy letter to heed him. Gemma sounded positively ecstatic.

'It all happened so suddenly,' she wrote. 'Eddie just starting singing along with me one night, just a few phrases here and there, so I played up to him sexily on stage, and the audience went wild. Until then, he'd just accompanied me on the piano, but the whole thing began to buzz, and now we make a fantastic double act, Laura.'

Laura smiled. Modesty was never Gemma's middle name. But the bubbling enthusiasm almost crackled off the page, and she felt a warm glow, knowing that Gemma was fulfilling her potential at last. And maybe in time, she and Eddie would want to make the arrangement even more permanent . . . She stopped those thoughts, remembering how Penny had reminded her that she liked to put people into neat little compartments.

And she was doing just that, she thought ruefully. She and Nick and the children were a complete unit, and so could Gemma and Eddie be. Everybody nice and neat and matched up. Penny was another matter, and even though she was perfectly happy and successful with her life, Laura's romantic heart still wished she could find the kind of happiness that only came from being in love.

Nick finished his coffee and dropped a kiss on her neck in passing. She twisted round and caught him to her, winding her arms around his neck and kissing him properly. He responded at once.

'What have I done to deserve this?' he said, smiling down at her, just as if he had all the time in the world, instead of already being half an hour late for surgery after being on call to an emergency during the night.

'You've just been you,' Laura smiled. 'And I love you.'

He kissed the tip of her nose, and held her against him more tightly.

'Tell me again tonight,' he spoke seductively. 'And I'll bring home a bottle of wine. If you play your cards right, you could be in for a good rave-up.'

Tommy Hall and his fiancée came to call on them that evening. Delia Parrish hadn't lost any weight since the last time Laura had seen her, and looked ready to burst out of the frilly blouse and old-fashioned dirndl skirt she wore. She was a nice girl, a real farmer's daughter in the accepted mould, but her dress sense was nil. Tommy certainly didn't seem to mind how she looked, though, and was pretty porky himself these days, Laura noted.

'Come on in, both of you,' Nick said, while Laura mentally kissed goodbye to any thoughts of a romantic evening. They both knew that once Tommy got dug in with a few cans of beer, there'd be no moving him before midnight.

'Would you like some coffee, or a glass of wine?' Laura offered hopefully.

'Coffee for me, please, Laura,' Delia responded quickly. 'I'll be doing the driving home later.'

Tommy let out a self-satisfied chuckle. 'Hear that,

our Nick? It's good to let 'em know who's boss right off, isn't it?'

'If you say so,' Nick responded with a grin, while Laura marvelled how the two of them could ever be related. Considering they were cousins, they were like the proverbial chalk and cheese, and yet they always got on remarkably well.

'So what's the occasion? No problems with the wedding arrangements, I hope,' Laura prompted, since the pair of them rarely left their own doorsteps, even to drive these few miles.

'There's no problems at all, but we've come to ask you both a favour, and you especially, Laura.' Delia's face was becoming even redder than its usual ruddy hue.

'Delia wants to know if your little 'uns would be bridesmaids when we get wed at Christmas,' Tommy explained.

Laura was thankful the girls were safely in bed by now, or the excitement at such a prospect would have had them awake and chattering all night.

'I think it's a lovely idea. And I know they'll be thrilled when I tell them. But are you sure you know what you're doing? They're still a bit young – '

Delia broke in quickly. 'Well, I thought you'd say as much, and that's partly why we'd like you to be Matron of Honour as well, see, and Tommy wants Nick for his Best Man.'

As she went on talking, Laura began to wonder if Tommy really knew who was going to be the boss in this marriage, but whatever Delia said seemed to be all right with him. And it was rather sweet, the way each of them spoke for the other. She suddenly felt very much older than the pair of them, and she didn't care for the feeling.

But by now, Nick was shaking Tommy's hand and saying he'd have felt deeply hurt if he hadn't been asked to be Best Man, and Laura found herself saying she'd be very happy to be Matron of Honour. It made a lot of sense too, because Sarah and Charlotte weren't yet five years old, and they'd be just as likely to turn turtle and run out of the church in a fright if she wasn't right there beside them.

'Have you bought your dress yet, Delia?' Laura said, and felt immediately ashamed of her sudden image of this great whale-like girl waddling down the aisle in layers of tulle and lace. She'd be bound to go for frills and fuss, which was totally wrong for her shape – or lack of it.

She reminded herself that every bride was beautiful on the day, and refused to catch Nick's glance.

'Not yet. I wondered if you'd come into Bristol with me sometime, you and the girls.' There was a note of desperation in Delia's voice now. 'I'm never any good at choosing the right thing, and you always look so elegant, Laura.'

'Do I?' she asked in some surprise.

''Course you do, darling,' Tommy said, unbelievably already into his third can of beer, while Laura watched the empties lining up on the side table, as if mesmerized. 'Why do you think I always fancied you for myself, kiddo? You know you broke my heart when you fell for our Nick instead.'

288

'Don't be daft, Tommy,' she remonstrated, starting to laugh, and wondering what Delia would make of all this.

'Don't worry, Delia knows all about my youthful fantasies,' Tommy said, waving his arms about as he sprawled in his armchair. 'But she knows she's the only one for me now, don't you, sweetheart?'

'I'd better be,' Delia warred. And from the sudden sparkle in her eyes, Laura knew exactly who was going to be boss in the Hall household.

'I think it's a very good idea for me and the girls to go to Bristol with you, Delia,' she put in now. 'Then we can all be sure our outfits will complement each other.'

She felt a small dart of pleasure as she spoke. A wedding was always an occasion to celebrate, and for the four of them all to be a part of it was something that bound them together even more. She warmed to Tommy for the thought, more than she had ever warmed to him before.

'So much for the sexy evening I'd planned for us,' Nick said drowsily, when they finally got to bed in the early hours of the morning. 'I'm not going to be much use to you now, darling. More of a damp squib than a rocket, you might say.'

Laura giggled, her own head befuddled with the several bottles of wine they'd finally got through between them.

'It doesn't matter. It'll keep. That's the best of being married, isn't it? We've always got all the lovely tomorrows.'

'Did I ever tell you how much I love you, Mrs Dean?' he said, nuzzling his lips into her neck.

'Frequently, Doctor,' she murmured.

The wedding was upon them before they knew it. It had taken half a dozen trips to Bristol before all the outfits were chosen and altered to fit, with a good bit of subtle advice from Laura and the sales assistant as to which dress Delia should wear. She was so addicted to frills and layers of material that she fondly believed covered all the rolls of blubber, that at first she refused point-blank to try on the sleeker-fitting matte silk dress that Laura pointed out.

It was in a delicate shade of cream that was much kinder to her ruddy complexion than the harsh, glittering white of some of the other models. The bodice had a small basque which flattered the waistline, and it was an ideal style for the larger bride.

When she finally emerged from the fitting room, Laura drew in her breath. Delia was never going to be beautiful in any Hollywood sense, but right now she looked wonderful.

'What do you think? I rather like it, but is it really me? She was clearly full of doubts.

'I think Tommy will absolutely love you in it,' Laura said. 'But you're the one who'll be wearing it, Delia, so you have to feel happy in it. I don't want to influence you, but I do think it's the nicest one you've tried on so far.'

'But I *want* you to influence me,' Delia assured her quickly. 'Everybody knows I'm hopeless about clothes. The cows don't care what you're wearing on the farm, but I don't want to let Tommy down on our big day.'

'You won't let him down,' Laura said softly. 'Why don't you walk up and down a bit in it, and imagine you're in church and that he's waiting for you at the altar. Doesn't that make you feel special already?'

Delia began to smile, following Laura's instructions.

'You're right,' she said at last. 'I feel different from usual, but I'm not in the least uncomfortable about it. The dress gives me confidence, and so do you, Laura. I'm glad we're going to be cousins.'

Laura gave a small sigh of relief. Next, Delia agreed to a smallish veil that wouldn't defeat the whole object of the sleek lines of the dress, crowned by a small tiara of pearls and feathers. The effect was surprisingly stunning.

Then it was the turn of the twins and herself. They had decided on blue velvet for the girls, with matching muffs; and they found a dress in a similar hue for herself, in the same fabric as Delia's dress. This particular boutique took every care in creating an entire bridal ensemble, the assistant said with smug pride.

Once the astronomical bill was paid, which Delia had insisted was Tommy's gift to them all, and no arguments, they took the bridesmaids' outfits home, leaving the rest for alterations and collection in two weeks.

'The girls would never have forgiven me if we'd had to leave their dresses behind,' she told Nick later, when their daughters had paraded in their finery for him at the cottage that evening.

'You both look beautiful,' he told them, 'and so will your mother.'

'And Delia,' Sarah and Charlotte chorused. 'Delia looks beautiful in her dress too.'

Laura gave them both a hug, blessing their childish innocence that hadn't yet seen the flaws in people.

'If this is only the start, this wedding's going to cost a pretty penny,' he said, practical as ever.

'I know, and I offered to pay for our dresses, but Delia wouldn't hear of it.'

'Oh well, it only happens once in your life – at least, it does to the lucky ones.'

Laura knew he was referring obliquely to the latest scandal in the village, where the vicar's daughter had run off with his married sidesman. Such things might not cause a stir in the anonymity of the city, but in a tight-knit village community it was big news indeed.

She was really looking forward to the wedding, egged on by her daughters' excitement. It would be two days before Christmas. Between them, Tommy's farm-worker and Farmer Hall would manage to keep things going on the old Robinson farm for a week, while he and Delia went off to the Canaries for their honeymoon. Farming didn't stop for weddings or funerals, and cows still had to be milked and livestock fed.

On the day, Delia looked absolutely glowing and full of an inner happiness that shone right out of her. Laura still marvelled at how Tommy Hall could put such a sparkle in anybody, remembering back to their Wellesley days when he'd tried it on with her and her friends in turn.

For all his nonsense about being madly in love with her, Laura was under no illusions about that. If she, or Gemma, or Penny, had once given him the old come-on, it might even be one of them walking down the aisle to be joined in matrimony with him now.

She hid a smile. For there was no way that Gemma would ever have tied herself down to a homespun farmer. Imagine those stilettos mincing about in farm-yard mud!

As for Penny, she was in a totally different class – her Christmas and New Year holidays were being spent skiing in Aspen, Colarado, rubbing shoulders with the rest of the rich and beautiful people.

She hadn't heard from either of them for a few weeks until the Christmas cards arrived with their usual letters. A long and effusive one from Penny, with a parcel of presents for everyone, followed by a phone call wishing them all a happy holiday season, and passing on good wishes to Tommy and his bride.

An even scrappier note than usual accompanied Gemma's card. Their contract giving them the run of the best hotels on the Costa Del Sol had been renewed for the whole of next summer. She and Eddie were taking a welcome month's break in February and she might even get down to Somerset, unless it felt too much like the North Pole after Spain, in which case she'd simply hibernate in her flat until it was time to go back. Life was clearly on the up and up for Gemma.

'. . . For better for worse, for richer for poorer, in sickness and in health, to love and to cherish, till death us do part . . .'

Laura brought her thoughts back to the present, realizing they had been wandering for a few moments, and that Tommy was being about as reverent as she had ever heard him, in making his responses.

She caught Nick's glance, and his half-smile told her he too was remembering their own wedding day, nearly six years ago. She thought it with a little shock. Six years of knowing and loving him and being part of him . . .

'. . . I now pronounce you man and wife.'

As the final words of the ceremony were said, there was nothing reverent about the way Tommy grabbed Delia to him and planted what Laura could only describe as a smacker on her eager mouth. It didn't matter. Nothing mattered but the happiness of the occasion, and the fact that, thank goodness, the girls had been so overawed by it all that they had behaved like little angels. And there couldn't be a more wonderful beginning to a Christmas season than to have friends and relatives sharing in that happiness.

Christmas and New Year passed in a haze of celebrations for Gemma. Every night was party night, and each one began to merge into the next. New Year's Eve was the most spectacular, with the British contingent flooding the streets of the town and bursting balloons and sending up fireworks with the natives, to herald the start of another new year.

On the first day of the year, Gemma awoke slowly, trying not to notice that her head no longer felt as if it belonged to her. It was floating somewhere above her, attached more to the ceiling than to her shoulders, and her arms and legs felt like rubbery mush.

She didn't even try opening her eyes, knowing the merest flicker of daylight would be as shocking as forked lightning racing through them. She tried to swallow, but somehow her tongue didn't quite fit her mouth and she couldn't manage it. Her teeth felt as large as tombstones, and at the ghoulish thought, she knew she must be dead, and on the pathway to Hell . . .

'Where am I?' she muttered through woolly lips.

'Anywhere you wanna be, darlin',' a voice said beside her. 'Anywhere your imagination takes you.'

Whoever he was, he wasn't Eddie. She could just about register that much. And he should be Eddie, since Eddie was the only one she slept with these nights, and the only one she ever wanted to. She'd finished with all that sleeping around long ago. Besides, it was no longer safe. Everybody knew that.

'Do you want something else?' the voice tempted. 'We got pills or booze or whatever you want, doll. Just name your poison.'

Her tongue managed to push past her lips and lick them enough to let her speak.

'I don't do drugs,' she said hoarsely.

The voice's owner laughed, and it wasn't a pleasant sound. 'Oh yeah? Well, you sure did last night.'

The shock of his words made her eyes fly open now. She was lying on the floor on some unsavoury old blankets in a darkened room, and she could sense that there were other people sleeping and snoring all around her. The guy lying beside her was a complete stranger.

Not that she could see him clearly. Everything seemed to be swimming about in a water-colour kaleidoscope in front of her eyes.

'Who the hell are you?' she said angrily, scrambling as far away from him as possible, while the weird, multi-coloured images in her brain almost made her throw up.

'I'm Paul, and you weren't so bloody frigid last night, darlin'. You weren't so bloody friendly as you might have been, either,' he added morosely.

'What happened? Tell me, can't you? I didn't really take anything, did I?'

But of course she had. Why else would she feel like death? Ecstasy, maybe. Or any one of a dozen other pills. But not voluntarily. Never voluntarily. It was like she said. She didn't do drugs. Not knowingly, anyway. She'd seen enough of the effects on other people to get caught up in that scene.

'Where's Eddie?' she asked thickly.

'I don't know no Eddie. There was a guy with you earlier, but I think he went off to the beach with some girl.'

Now she really did feel sick. She wanted Eddie so badly it frightened her, and the thought of him with another girl instead of her was enough to make her retch.

'Bloody hell, bitch, you just keep away from me if you're going to throw up.' The guy was furious.

'Do you know who I am?' Gemma questioned faintly.

'Just another piece of skirt,' he said. 'We don't ask for names in my line of business.'

She closed her eyes thankfully. Whatever guardian angel was looking after her right now had saved her from one thing. This lout didn't know her or Eddie, and wouldn't be likely to sell any drug-related story about her to the gutter Press. She doubted if he'd remember anything about her in a little while, because, drug-pusher or not, he looked pretty much under the influence of something himself. There had been a party, she remembered, fighting hard to recall *something* of last night, and then they had all gone off to some other place in cars or scooters, and got separated . . .

'I've got to get out of here,' she muttered, and stood up carefully. The room swayed badly as if she was in a flimsy canoe in a raging sea, but she gritted her teeth and walked unsteadily towards the door, picking her way between the recumbent bodies. The guy made no attempt to come after her.

'Hey, I do remember something,' he called after her as she reached the door. 'The guy who brought you in said his name was Jake. I dunno nothin' about no Eddie.'

Gemma stumbled out of the room and down the rickety stairs, registering the fact that it hadn't been Eddie who had gone off to the beach with some girl. It was a grain of comfort, but it still didn't explain where he was, or why he had abandoned her. It was still dark outside, but she sensed that it was morning, and pretty soon the town would be full of determined holiday-makers, and she had better get off the streets quickly if she didn't want to be recognized.

She went into an all-night café and tidied herself in

the toilet. She didn't look too bad, considering, and her dark glasses hid her frightened eyes. She tried to be positive. She was still fully dressed, and besides, the guy in the shabby room hadn't looked the type to bother with women.

She didn't hurt anywhere, except for her throbbing head, and she was pretty sure she hadn't been raped, or molested, or beaten up . . . and if she could just manage to get back into the Don Pedro without anyone seeing her . . .

The all-night receptionist was dozing when she slipped in through the swing doors. So much for security . . . but for once she was thankful for the anonymity.

She ignored the lifts and sped up the four flights of stairs to her room adjoining Eddie's. She was totally out of breath by the time she got there. Her chest hurt; she was perspiring heavily; there were spots dancing in front of her eyes and she seriously thought she was in danger of expiring. And then her heart leapt.

'Where the hell have you been?' came Eddie's voice from where he sprawled, fully-dressed, across her bed. 'I looked everywhere for you when we left the club, and then some guy said you'd gone off with somebody called Jake, so I called it a day and came back here. But I never even reached my room before I passed out. Are you OK?'

The room was very dim, with the curtains still across the window to keep out the blazing Spanish sun, and only letting in a chink of pre-dawn light. Gemma looked at Eddie's tousled head almost stupidly.

God only knew what had happened in the intervening hours since she'd last seen him; she didn't even want to think about it. Drugs weren't her scene, nor Eddie's, and the shame of allowing herself to be persuaded, or tempted, or however else the pusher had got the stuff down her, was making the sobs well up in her throat.

She almost fell across the room and into his arms. His warm, loving, familiar arms . . .

'Don't ask,' she said thickly. 'Just hold me, Eddie.'

He responded immediately. He was always dependable, no matter what she did. And she didn't deserve him.

Hardly knowing what was happening, she realized she was feverishly tearing off her clothes, if only to strip away the shame of whatever had happened last night. Her first instinct was to take a shower and wash away all the evil . . . but even that could wait. All she wanted now was for Eddie to love her, and make her feel needed and desirable again.

She heard him give a low chuckle, and she paused in her frantic undressing.

'Are you laughing at me?' she said fiercely in the dimness of the room.

'Would I ever? I'm just grateful to whatever made you so randy, and for sending you back to me just when I was having a great erotic dream about you, babe.'

He grasped her hand and thrust it down to give her clear evidence of his meaning. He got out of his jeans with all the skill of a Houdini, and without any preliminaries he was forging into her and holding her savagely to him.

CHAPTER 18

New Year's Eve in Aspen, Colorado, was a world away from a sordid Spanish hotel room. Penny dressed with extra care for the evening in her suite at the wickedly expensive hotel her father had generously paid for. Like something out of *The Student Prince*, it was set against the snow-covered mountains that formed a breath-taking winter playground for the élite and elegant people who flocked there every winter.

Like many of them, Penny had come alone, feeling the need for a certain freedom after the hectic events of the past year. It wasn't the first time she had holidayed alone, and she enjoyed the exhilaration of meeting new people and exchanging small talk, without any need to get too involved.

Her hands shook for a moment as she adjusted the long emerald earrings her parents had given her for Christmas. They flashed and glittered against what poets would call her swan-like neck, and were the only jewellery she wore with the dark green off-the-shoulder taffeta ballgown.

The whole effect was stunningly dramatic, but not even the emeralds in her ears could compare with the way her green eyes shone and sparkled. And it was for one reason only, however unlikely, or unexpected, or unbelievable it was . . .

A smile curved her lips as, from somewhere way back, she seemed to hear the echo of her friend Gemma's cynical voice.

'You're no more immune than the rest of us, Penny Bishop. Horses aren't going to satisfy you for ever, not unless you're a damn sight kinkier than we thought you were.'

And then there was Laura – sweet, romantic Laura . . .

'Of course she's not. And knowing Penny, when it happens, she'll think she's been struck by lightning and that nobody has ever been in love before, nor fallen so quickly . . .'

'*When* you've both stopped analyzing me,' Penny had said with a superior laugh. 'You can both forget such crazy ideas, because that kind of Superman only exists in the movies . . .'

She drew in her breath, as the memories of the Wellesley Penny faded from sight in the hotel mirror, to emerge sharply as the beautiful image gazing back at her. Because now she knew that such things could happen, and *did* happen, and they had happened to her. It was just as Laura had said. As if she had been struck by lightning, with the feeling that nobody could ever have been so much in love before – and with a man she had only known for a week . . .

However logical and sensible she tried to feel about it, however often she told herself that this was no more than a holiday romance, and that she'd be a fool to take it seriously, she knew it went far, far deeper than that. Because Hank loved her too. Gloriously, and wonderfully, and for ever.

She gave a small shiver as she thought the words. Because nothing was for ever. It was a proven fact. Her old science tutor had sternly reminded them all that even the molecules that made up all human existence were in a constant state of change and alteration and reconstitution, like the hairs on one's body that were shed and regrown – and other, far more disgusting things.

Why she should even think of such things now, she didn't know. Or maybe she did. It was all to do with trying to keep her feet on the ground, when in spirit, she was actually flying with happiness. Up to the moon and back would be no exaggeration . . .

She heard a knock on the door of her suite, and flew across the room to answer it. Yes, flying was the most apt term she could use to describe the way she felt . . .

Henry Devereux the third said nothing at all for a moment. She shivered again as his slow glance took in every sensual curve of her body, but this time the shivering was with a feeling of erotic anticipation. And then he held out his arms to her. She went into them as if in a dream, and then they were inside her room, still holding one another, and Hank had kicked the door shut behind him.

'If I told you you were the most beautiful woman on

303

God's earth, would you believe me?' he said, in the rich Texas drawl that was so very sexy in contrast to her cool, so-educated English voice.

'Well, I don't know about that.' She was only half-teasing.

He tipped her face up towards his. He was tall and powerfully-built, and his dark hair was tinged with grey at the temples. His looks were rugged, rather than conventionally handsome, but to Penny he looked even more dashing in a cream-coloured tuxedo and red bow tie, than in the ski outfits he wore on the slopes. A super Superman, no less.

'Then believe it,' he said. 'I don't say such things lightly, as I'm sure you know by now. And honey, you're not just the most beautiful woman in the world to me, you're also the only woman I want with me for the rest of my life. You know that too, don't you? Or have I been wasting my time all this past week?'

Penny caught her breath. If this was no more than a fantasy, she never wanted it to end. Nor did she want to know if it was all just a line. But there were some people you trusted implicitly, even with your life, no matter how short the acquaintance. Hank was one of them. There was truth and honesty in his eyes, and she believed him.

'You know you haven't,' she answered huskily. 'But Hank, we've only known one another for such a short time, and we need to be sure – '

He held her more tightly against him.

'Honey, I was never more sure of anything in my whole damn life! I want you to marry me and come live with me on my ranch. You want horses? I'll give you horses. You want diamonds? Hell, I'll give you a whole damn diamond mine. I'll give you anything you ask for in this whole wide world. All *I* ask in return is for you to want me as much as I want you.'

He let her go, taking her hands in his and drawing them gently to his lips, in a sweet, old-fashioned gesture that made Penny's eyes prickle. He went on talking in that low, serious voice.

'You know I love you with all my heart, don't you? We've spent so much time in one another's company now, and I know everything about you that I need to know. So don't give me that old chestnut about only meeting each other a week ago. Anyway, how long does it take to fall in love? I knew it from the moment I saw you – '

'So did I. From the very first moment,' she said, as breathless as if she'd just raced Midnight Sun against the clock and come out a winner.

'Well then, will you marry me – please? I give you my word that I won't stop asking until you say yes. And if I have to fill this damn hotel room with every red rose the town has to offer, I'll do it.'

'I wish you'd stop!' Penny laughed in protest as she glanced around the room. It was already overpoweringly heady with the sweet scent of roses. There were roses everywhere, in baskets large and small, in intricate floral arrangements, in posies and in simple containers. When Hank Devereux did something, he did it in style. And when he wanted something, he went all out to get it.

'Then give me the answer I want,' Hank prompted simply.

Penny felt a sudden fright. She'd met enough Americans to know how fast they operated, but Hank was sweeping her along with the speed of light.

'Give me time, Hank, please,' she pleaded. 'I want to really savour getting to know one another properly, and not rush into things.'

'Okay,' he said cheerfully, after a moment. 'You can take all the time you want, honey, but I'm coming back to England with you until you say yes. Now that I've found you, I don't aim to let you out of my sight for some goddamned chinless wonder to pick up.'

Penny laughed. 'I'm not in the habit of letting men pick me up.'

'You let me,' Hank said.

'So I did.' She remembered with a smile how she'd been enjoying a breakfast of blueberry pancakes and maple syrup, and this hunk of a man had paused by her table and said what a delight it was to see a woman enjoying her food instead of just pushing it around the plate.

Her first instinct was to wonder if he was implying that she wasn't as stick-thin as some of the Hollywood starlets and beautiful models who flocked here in search of rich husbands every year. And then she'd looked up into his eyes, and she was lost.

'May I join you?' he asked.

'It's a free country,' Penny retorted coolly, trying to ignore the way her heart was doing somersaults.

The waitress hovered near. 'What'll you have, sir?'

'Whatever she's having,' he said.

And that was the start of it. Breakfast lingered for over two hours, white their coffee cups kept being refilled. Like every other boutique and establishment in town, the hotel restaurant glittered with lavish Christmas decorations, and the atmosphere everywhere was one of crackling excitement. But none of it was as vibrant as the leaping excitement in Penny's heart as she got to know this delightful man.

Skiing was the icing on Aspen's Christmas cake, from the wonderful beginner slopes of Buttermilk Mountain, which Penny had long since abandoned, to the more challenging black runs of the Aspen Highlands and Snowmass. She was thrilled to discover that Hank too, was an expert skiier; they were more than a match for each other.

They spent all of that first day together, and their leisurely dinner that evening, Christmas Eve, was the first of all the ones that followed. Dinner, and then dancing in the softly-lit ballroom, to slow, romantic music that created its own atmosphere of sensuality.

'I want you to know that I'm thirty-five years old, that I've been a widower for six years, and that there's been no other woman in my life since my wife,' he said quietly in her ear as they moved slowly around the floor, as close as if they already wore one another's skins.

Penny swallowed. 'You didn't have to tell me that. We're just ships that pass in the night, Hank.'

'We both know that we're not,' he answered, and he let the words sink in before he spoke again. 'May I escort you back to your room?'

He spoke with all the olde-worlde courtesy that to English ears sat so oddly on brash American shoulders, yet she sensed a note of desperation in his voice too, as if he couldn't bear to have her refuse him. As if this night had to be the start of something wonderful, or the start of nothing.

They stood almost still in the middle of the dance floor now, and all the other couples around them seemed to merge into shadowy shapes. There was no one else for either of them but each other, and they both knew how this night was going to end. Penny nodded slowly.

'I think you should,' she whispered.

It had been the beginning, and on that most magical of Christmas Eves, Hank had stayed with her until the early hours of Christmas morning, and she had learned the erotic pleasures of lovemaking for the first time.

From then on, all their nights had been spent together, and for Penny it was like opening a window on a whole new, beautiful existence. She had no other lover to compare him with, and that was an added joy to her, but even if she had, she knew instinctively that now she had the best.

In her room on New Year's Eve, ready to go down for the gala dinner now, Penny looked at Hank, and gave a small, incredulous laugh.

'You're not coming to England! Hank, be sensible! What about your ranch, and your business, and all the people you employ – and, well, your life?' she finished weakly, suddenly realizing that however close they had been this past week, they were truly worlds apart in practical, material things.

'What life do I have without you?' he said simply. 'I mean every word I say, darling girl. As for the rest of it, it only takes a few phone calls to say I'm on an extended vacation. My housekeeper and staff run the place anyway. The ranch-hands will take care of the horses, and as for the oil business – hell, it practically runs itself. We're not talking J. R. Ewing and his devious ole boys here, honey. The Devereux Cartel has the highest reputation and the best profits in the state of Texas, and it can manage very well without me for a coupla weeks more, or however long it takes.'

'For what?'

'For me to persuade you that your place is with me, and that you'll blossom in the Texas sun like you were made for it.'

'You want me to marry you and go to live in Texas,' she stated woodenly, just as if she'd never heard the words he'd been saying to her all week now.

'Yes,' he answered, just as flatly. And then the emotions broke through as he pulled her to him again.

'Penny, I've already lost one woman who meant a lot to me. Don't let me lose another because of a crazy convention that says we have to go through some outdated courting ritual before we can be together. And I promise you that's the last time you'll hear me refer to Dorinda.'

'Because she still means a lot to you?' Penny felt bound to ask.

'Because she's part of my past, and you're my future. And if you can't see that – '

'I do see it. I'm just not the sort to make rash promises. Please, Hank. Give me time,' she asked again, and then she spoke more quickly. 'But if you mean to come to England, then I'd like you to meet my parents and get to know them. And then maybe I could go to Texas and stay with you for a while before we make any long-term commitment.'

'Sounds good to me,' he nodded after a moment or two's deliberation. 'I'd like to meet your folks, but I shan't stay at your place. I'll stay in a hotel and come visit. I've always wanted to see London anyway.'

'Why won't you stay with us?'

He laughed shortly. 'Do you think I could be in the same house and not want to make love to you every damn hour of the day and night? No, honey, we'll do it my way. And tomorrow, I'll make those phone calls home and see about fixing a plane reservation to England.'

It all sounded so simple. But in the end, it didn't work out that way, because Hank received a message to say that one of his most valuable horses had broken a fetlock. Serious complications had set in, but nobody was prepared to take the responsibility of having him put down without Hank's say-so. And in any case, he couldn't get a flight to England for at least another week.

'This delay was probably meant to be.' Penny was sick with disappointment as he drove her to Denver Airport. But she knew too, that he was as devastated as she would be at the thought of losing a cherished animal. 'You wouldn't find much use for ski outfits in England, and you probably don't have enough luggage for an extended visit.'

It was a pathetic argument, knowing he could walk into any high-class clothing store and buy whatever he needed without a second thought. But small talk was suddenly all they had between them as the front-wheel drive hire-car, complete with ski rack, left the town with its luxury, Hollywood-style houses, and the Country and Western saloons and Japanese sushi bars, where women lounged away the après-ski hours in exquisite designer clothes, or in fur coats and cowboy hats and expensive thigh-high boots on their slender legs.

Penny had loved it all, and now she was numb, knowing it was over. And realizing at last, how much she had wanted Hank to be with her on the flight home. What had begun as a routine skiing holiday for her had turned out to be something more magical than she could ever have dreamed about. For one glorious week she had had everything, and now, suddenly, she felt as if she had nothing.

Hank's hand sneaked across to cover hers. He'd said nothing for a few minutes, and she knew his thoughts had echoed hers.

'It's not over, honey. It's only just begun. I'll call you as soon as I get back home and let you know what's going on. The minute I can get over to England, I'll contact you. You know that, don't you?'

'I know,' she murmured.

Gemma might say it sounded like a bloody good get-out line, and she'd never see the guy again. There might not even be a valuable horse or any necessity for Hank to get back to the ranch *post haste*. There might not be any bloody ranch, for that matter, *or* rich-yielding oil wells . . . Gemma would tell her to put it down to experience, and having a damn good time . . . but Penny knew in her soul it wasn't like that. They belonged together, and she would see him again soon.

For two days after she reached home, Penny was jet-lagged and miserable without Hank, but needing to be exuberant and talkative to her father who wanted to know everything, and her mother, whose polite interest was a sober reminder of her *Englishness*. She hadn't even realized she'd picked up a little of Hank's Texas drawl until her mother pointed it out. And she certainly wasn't telling them *everything*.

'I suppose you meet all sorts there, darling,' Helena Bishop commented.

'All sorts,' Penny nodded. 'I met a very nice man, as a matter of fact. A Texas oil-man called Hank.'

'Good gracious, he sounds very rough. I hope you didn't have too much to do with someone like that, Penny?'

As a matter of fact, I did. We made passionate love every night, and he asked me to marry him, and I can't get him out of my head or my heart, and I wish he was here now so I could go to bed with him –

Penny blinked, but no, she hadn't said it, or her mother wouldn't be looking at her now with that polite question still on her lips and in her eyes.

312

'I spent quite some time with him, actually,' she said lightly. 'He's coming to England soon, and naturally, I invited him to come and meet you. It was the correct thing to do, wasn't it?'

She looked wide-eyed and innocently at her mother, knowing there would be no objection to that. Helena gave the slightest of her elegant shrugs, and said of course she would be happy to meet any of Penny's friends.

Later, in the stables and checking on the horses and ponies, her father caught up with her.

'Come clean now, darling. Just how much time did you spend with this Texas oil-man? I think I know you better than your mother, and this wasn't just a casual invitation on your part, was it?'

For a second, she was tempted to laugh it off. To say when did any man ever come close to the companionship of her beloved horses . . . but to do so would be to deny all that had been between them. Her voice was muffled as she spoke.

'I love him, Daddy. I know it all happened too quickly, and Mummy would be scandalized, but I have never felt this way about anyone before, and I know I never will again.'

'And does he love you too?' her father said gently.

'Yes. Oh *yes*,' she said, and then she felt her father's arms around her, and he kissed her cold cheek.

'Then that's all that matters.'

He left her alone then, and she fought to stop the tears filling her eyes. He understood far more than he ever said. He wasn't as stiff-upper-lipped and starchy as her mother, and he'd never dream of asking how far this relationship had gone, but he knew. She was perfectly sure of that. Penny had never been the sort to go for half-measures, and when she fell in love, it would be for always.

Hank phoned early that evening, even though it must be the middle of the night in Texas. Her parents were both out, and the minute she heard his voice she clung to the phone.

'How are you?' she asked.

'Missing you like hell,' he answered. 'Do you know how long the nights are when there's nobody to share them with?'

'Yes. I do know,' she replied softly.

'I'm coming over on the fifteenth. It's the earliest I can make it after all, but I'll speak to you before then.'

'What happened about the horse?'

'We had to have him put down, and it was all pretty traumatic, but I'll get over it. Listen, honey, I'm checking into a London hotel when I get to England, but I'll hire a car and get down to your neck of the woods just as soon as I arrive.'

'Hank, why don't you stay somewhere nearer instead of London? I know you'd prefer not to stay here – '

'Well, maybe I will,' he said. 'I've a yen to see Oxford as well. I told you my grandfather graduated there, didn't I?'

'No, you didn't! You mean he was English?'

'Sure he was. You oughta know that most Americans have a European ancestry of one sort or another.'

Of course she knew that, but the thought that Hank's

grandfather had actually been an undergraduate at Oxford charmed her.

'Why didn't you tell me before?'

'I thought I had, but then, we didn't have too much time for stuff like that, did we?' She could hear the smile in his voice now. 'And I haven't called you to discuss it right now. I'm far more interested to know if you're missing me as much as I'm missing you.'

'More. MUCH more!'

'That's impossible, honey. But just as long as I know it. I love you, Penny.'

'I love you too.'

'Call you soon,' he promised, and the line went dead.

She hung up slowly, instantly bereft that he'd gone, and wondering how she could ever contemplate living the rest of her life without him. It was almost frightening to know how much one person could depend on another. It was even more frightening to Penny, who had never needed anyone before now.

Almost without thinking, she found herself dialling Laura's number.

'Penny!' She heard her friend's delighted voice. 'You're back, then. Happy New Year, by the way, and how was it? Did you have a marvellous time in America?'

Hearing the eager questions, Penny couldn't even speak for a few seconds. When her voice reasserted itself, the words were almost explosive.

'The most marvellous time of my life. It was wonderful, stupendous, the best time ever.'

'My God, you've met a man!' Laura almost squeaked.

Penny laughed, self-conscious with Laura for almost the first time since knowing her.

'What makes you say that?' she hedged. 'You should know me by now – '

'That's exactly why I'm saying it! There's not a horse on earth that could put that kind of tone in your voice. You can't kid me, Pen. Tell me everything.'

Penny laughed again. 'Don't you have children to put to bed or something? Or Nick's dinner to cook?'

'They can wait. Well, actually, he's taken them to see a pantomime, and I opted out of it for once. So there's nobody listening but me, kiddo.'

'You sound more like Gemma – '

'For pity's *sake*, Pen, stop messing about and tell me who it is and when you're seeing him again.'

'His name's Hank – '

'I *knew* it.'

'Well, if you want to know any more, darling, you'd better shut up and let me tell you,' Penny broke in, in her more usual calm and controlled manner. 'His name's Hank, or to be accurate, Henry Devereux the third. He's got a ranch in Texas, and he's the head of a huge oil business called the Devereux Cartel.'

'Good God, it sounds just like *Dallas*.'

'It's funny you should say that, because Hank assured me he's nothing like J. R. Ewing. No evil plotting, or other women in his life – only me.'

There was a slight pause. 'And he's not married or anything? Pen, you haven't got yourself into something you can't handle, have you?'

She sounded apologetic, but looking at things logically, Penny was far more of an innocent when it came to men than herself. Gemma's experiences were legion, and Laura had been a married woman for all these years, and could almost, *almost* have had a fling with a good-looking hunk . . . She switched her thoughts hurriedly from Jeff Rawles.

'No, he's not married. He was, but she died . . . I love him, Laura,' she heard Penny say. 'And he loves me. We spent every minute together while we were in Aspen, and he's coming to England on the fifteenth of the month, and I can't wait to see him again. In fact, I don't know how I'm going to hold out until then, with nothing much to do here at the moment, and the Equestrian Centre practically taking care of itself with the staff we've employed.'

'You know you're welcome to come down here any time. The girls would love to see you, Pen.'

'Thanks, but not right now, darling. Hank will be calling me every day, and I have to be here when he comes over. You do understand, don't you?'

'Oh yes, I understand,' Laura said softly.

She put down the phone. She couldn't be happier on Penny's account. It was just as she'd always predicted: when it happened to Penny, it would be like being struck by lightning. Just like it had been for Laura.

The door opened, and Nick and the girls came inside, rubbing their cold hands together. The girls were still chattering excitedly about the pantomime; Laura shooed them upstairs to take off their coats, promising to make them cocoa and biscuits for supper, and then they could tell her all about it.

And then she put her arms around Nick's neck, pressed him close to her and kissed him hard.

'Well, if that's the reward I get for taking the kids out, I must remember to do it more often,' he said with a grin. 'What brought all that on, anyway?'

'Just love,' said Laura.

CHAPTER 19

Penny's good news did a lot for Laura's morale. It was a tired old cliché, but perfectly true, that children made Christmas, and Sarah and Charlotte were now of an age to shriek with anticipation every time the postman brought another batch of cards, and they had nearly wet themselves with excitement when Nick brought home a real tree from the woods for them to help decorate.

But for Laura, it was also the first Christmas without her father, and all the old familiar rituals could no longer take place. Tommy and Delia's wedding was over, and everything had suddenly gone flat. New Year's Eve too, was tinged with sadness, knowing it was the start of another year when her father was no longer with them.

She knew she was being maudlin, but seemed unable to drag herself out of it. And then Penny had phoned, and life was suddenly sparkling again. She wondered if Gemma had got to hear of it yet, and presumed that she hadn't.

She was tempted to call the hotel in Spain, but it

seemed an imposition to forestall Penny's news when she should be the one to tell her. So, once the girls had finally gone to bed that evening, she told Nick instead.

'Well, it's about time too. I always hated to see a good woman going to waste,' he said.

'You arrogant pig,' Laura accused with a laugh, throwing a cushion at him. 'Do you think women are just put on this earth to pander to men's lusts?'

'God, I hope so, otherwise what the hell were they given the necessary equipment for?' he grinned. 'Still, I hope Penny knows what she's doing.'

'Why shouldn't she?' Laura was on the defensive at once. 'It's not as if she's just out of the schoolroom, and she's always been able to see through any social climbers, if that's what you're getting at.'

'She might as well be just out of the schoolroom as far as relationships with men are concerned. You assure me she's never been in love before, and you know as well as I do that love is blind,' he said flippantly. 'Why else should Tommy have fallen for the less-than-delectable Delia?'

She knew he was teasing, but all the same, Laura suddenly felt uneasy. The fact that she'd half-wondered something of the same was one thing. To have sane, sensible Nick voice it so positively, was something else.

'You don't really think he could be some kind of a con artist, do you?'

'How the hell would I know? I'm just putting in my opinion, for what it's worth, but if it's going to start worrying you, I wish I'd kept my mouth shut.'

'It might have been better,' Laura muttered. 'Anyway, there's not much we can do about it, though I hope she'll come down to see us soon, so I can sound her out about it.'

'Mother Teresa putting the world to rights, no less,' Nick said with a grin.

But if she thought there would be more ecstatic letters and phone calls from Penny in the next few weeks, she was mistaken. Nor was there a single communication from Gemma, which made her feel somewhat slighted. Gemma had surely got to hear the news, and Laura had confidently expected a phone call from Gemma, however waspish, to discuss it all. Between them, the three of them had always discussed *everything* . . .

With a small shock, Laura accepted the fact that it was no longer true, nor could it be. Their lives had run along parallel lines while they were at the Wellesley, but gradually and inevitably, they had all taken different turnings. Laura no longer thought of her own life as humdrum. Instead, she considered it fulfilled and happy, and was perfectly content to leave the thrills and excitements of worldly success to the other two.

The weeks went by, January merged into February, and still there was no news from Gemma. There was a note from Penny to say her parents liked Hank and approved of him, and that he was taking her back to London for a week of sightseeing and shows. She hoped to see Laura some time soon, since Hank was going to do some touring around England on his own to give her some space.

'What he means, darling, is that he's impatient for me

to say I'll marry him, and thinks that this time spent apart will make me realize how much I love him. It's what I want more than anything, but I still need to be sure. It's all happened so incredibly fast, and my feet are still off the ground.'

Laura was smiling when she finished reading the note. Penny sounded so happy . . . but she hadn't mentioned Gemma, and there was still no word from her, even though Laura had sent a lavish Christmas card to her Spanish address and had received one from her well before the festive season began. It was starting to be a little worrying.

At that precise moment, Gemma was viciously tearing up her accumulated Christmas cards and throwing them in a bin-bag. Goodwill to all men was at the very lowest point on her agenda right now. She and Eddie had been so busy in January she'd hardly opened any of her mail, and they'd gone away for a rushed weekend in early February, which had been a miserable failure. A slight bickering had turned into the most unholy of all rows, and when she'd finally screamed at him to get out of her sight, he'd taken her at her word, and now she hadn't seen him in two weeks.

She'd been on less than top form all through January while they were finishing their commitments, and now they had this entire month off to relax and enjoy themselves, she was bitterly resentful of the fact that she felt like death, and that Eddie wasn't around to comfort her.

She'd assumed they would spend all their time

together, but now, she thought savagely, she was glad to have this period apart. Although, if it hadn't been for the wretched way she'd been feeling, she could have thrown caution to the winds and suggested they went off to some *really* exotic spot together. The Caribbean, maybe . . . haunts of royalty and the like . . . but as usual, such plans had all turned sour.

Just like the horrible bilious feeling in her stomach that was gnawing away at her again, together with the realization that she hadn't been able to face a proper meal for days now. Not that fasting from a few meals would do her any harm, she thought cynically, still intent on keeping her fabulous figure.

At the thought, a sudden horrible suspicion shot into Gemma's mind. The ripped-up Christmas cards spilled out of her hands onto the floor as she sat on her haunches in the plush hotel suite. Her huge, velvety brown eyes were suddenly wild with dread, and unconsciously her hands went to her stomach. It was as flat as ever, but to her heightened senses, she swore there was more of a mound than there should have been.

'Don't be bloody stupid,' she snapped, as if talking to somebody else. 'You couldn't be pregnant. Pregnancy happens to other people, and you *can't* be! I won't let you be.'

The hell of it was, she knew very well she could be. That early New Year's Day morning she'd stumbled back to her bedroom so disorientated, and straight into Eddie's arms. They had even made silly jokes later, about how abandoned and reckless they had been, taking no precautions, because there had simply been no time when the need for each other had been so overwhelming, outstripping any thoughts of tomorrow . . .

'God, I don't believe this is happening,' Gemma gasped now, frantically counting back the weeks and grabbing a calendar from the wall to flip back a couple of pages. She usually marked the day her period started, and it was regular enough, within a day or two each month. But these past weeks had been so hectic, so exciting, that she had completely overlooked the fact than since the beginning of the year there had been nothing.

Which presumably meant that by now she could be five or six weeks' pregnant.

Gemma caught sight of her ashen face in the wall mirror. She looked as ghastly as on the night the pusher had given her whatever pills she had taken.

'You're panicking over nothing,' she snapped to her reflection. 'You're mad. Totally mad.'

She thought frantically. There was a *Pharmacia* in the hotel, but she daren't go where she was so well-known to ask for a pregnancy-testing kit. Nor could she risk going to a doctor or letting anyone suspect anything until she was quite sure.

Eddie would know what to do, but Eddie wasn't here, and anyway, she wouldn't dare tell him, she thought instantly. It would ruin everything. Horrified, Gemma saw their entire future slipping away because of one reckless, beautiful hour of lovemaking. And he would hate her for it. That was the worst of all. He would blame her, for taking drugs, for bringing it all back on him, for ruining their career. They'd be washed-up for sure.

She began scooping up the Christmas cards again, just to keep her shaking hands busy, and Laura's handwriting seemed to leap out at her. She drew in a shuddering breath as the solution to everything began to whirl crazily in her mind. *Laura*, whose husband was a doctor . . .

Once Gemma made up her mind to do something, she did it. She had checked out of the Don Pedro and was on the first available flight from Malaga before she gave Eddie another thought. Not that what she had in mind was anything to do with him. Not any more. He'd done his part when he'd made her pregnant, no matter whose fault it had been . . . but she couldn't risk any ethical arguments from him.

Anyway, he'd know, as well as she did, that a baby was out of the question. The big-time career they had craved for so long was finally within their grasp, and a baby would be disastrous. She'd never been the maternal sort, and Eddie had never shown any proclivity towards broodiness.

No, it was better this way. Just herself and an obliging doctor, and the whole thing could be disposed of neatly and quietly. And she simply closed her mind to any thoughts of another, less frenetic kind of life. Domestic harmony was for the likes of Laura, not for her . . .

Back in London, she checked into her apartment, still immaculate thanks to her regular cleaner, and whisked up yet more mail that had accumulated. She discarded most of it, except for a letter from Penny. If she felt anything like laughing, she could almost have laughed aloud as she read it.

'I'm sending this to your London apartment, Gem, because I've lost your Spanish address. Anyway, give me a call when or if you get home during February, and we'll get together. I've got such news! I've met a man and we're madly in love. I can almost hear you scoffing from here, but it's all true, just as Laura always said. Bolts of lightning and all that stuff. I may even think of giving up horses for babies in due course – so it must be love, don't you think?'

There was more of the same, but it was that sentence that squeezed Gemma's heart in the most extraordinary way. She screwed up the letter and tossed it in the pristine waste-bin, unwilling to admit, for the merest second, that even the toughest, the most anti-men, and the most career-minded of women had been known to change utterly when their bloody treacherous hormones took control.

Well, they weren't going to control her, Gemma thought viciously, her hands clenched at her sides. She'd worked and fought too hard for what she'd got, and no squalling infant was going to make her change her plans, thanks very much.

She called Laura immediately.

'I'm in London, but can I come down and stay for a few days? I'm badly in need of rest and relaxation, Laura.'

'Of course,' Laura said, when she'd got over the

shock of hearing her friend's voice. 'If you can call it rest with our girls.'

'Just to get away from this rat-race is all I need, darling.' Gemma was trying to sound bright and normal, when her insides were beginning to wobble alarmingly.

'Come any time then. There's always a room ready for you, Gem, you know that.'

'Thanks. I'll be there sometime tomorrow.'

She hung up, suddenly faint. Laura was so wholesome, so much the Earth Mother . . . and what Gemma was about to do would be against everything her friend believed in. No matter how often you told yourself that abortions were carried out every day of the week nowadays, it still had the power to hit you in the gut when you were the one killing your own child . . .

She flinched as the thought entered her head, even though she felt sure that was how Laura would see it.

If only Nick wasn't *Laura's* husband, she thought perversely now. But Laura mustn't get involved. Laura mustn't even *know*, or she'd be sure to try and talk her out of it. And once she fixed Gemma with that horrified, blue-eyed stare of hers, Gemma knew she would feel like less than dirt.

She caught a train out of Paddington early the following morning, and arrived by taxi at Nick's clinic before lunchtime. The receptionist said he couldn't possibly see a visitor at a minute's notice – and her look said that Gemma certainly didn't look like a patient – when he came out of his surgery and stared at her in astonishment.

'Good God, Gemma, what are you doing here? Laura said you were coming down, but we thought you'd have gone straight to the cottage.'

'I needed to see you on a – a medical matter, and I didn't want to worry Laura,' she said huskily.

'You'd better come into the surgery,' he said briefly, and she could see he was none too pleased. He'd never had a lot of time for her, Gemma thought resentfully; he was one of the few men who hadn't.

'Now then, what is it?' he asked. 'I'm afraid I don't have much time, and you should really have gone to your own GP in London.'

His brusqueness stung her into blurting everything out at once. 'I'm pregnant, Nick. I did one of those home test things. It's no more than six weeks, but I have to get rid of it. I can't risk the news getting out either, so I want you to do it for me.'

He said nothing for a minute, and his eyes were cold. 'Have you had an AIDS test?'

Her face flamed. 'It's nothing like that! I know very well who the father is – who it could only be. And anyway, what business is that of yours?'

'It could be very much my business if you've been sleeping around with all and sundry,' he responded crudely.

'Well, I haven't, and I can see I'm wasting my time in talking to you. But your wife is one of my best friends, and I know she'd want you to help me.'

'Does Laura know?' His tone was sharp.

'Not yet.' She felt a glimmer of hope. She guessed that he wouldn't want Laura to become involved, and if it was a kind of blackmail to let him think she was about to pour out all her troubles on his wife, so be it. She stood up straight.

'I'll be staying at your place for a while, Nick. I don't know how long I can safely leave my little problem, but I'll try not to burden anybody else with it, as long as I'm not throwing up all over the place.'

'Sit down,' he snapped. 'You'd better give me some details.'

She felt a small sense of triumph as she told him all he needed to know, while he registered her as a temporary visitor to the practice.

'I presume Eddie's the father, then?' he asked finally. 'And that he's got no medical condition that needs investigating?'

She glared at him. He might be a dish as far as Laura was concerned, but he didn't have Eddie's sexy looks or persuasive charm. However, he was a man all the same . . . She spoke more softly.

'There's nothing more to tell, Nick. Except that if you do this for me, I'll be eternally grateful. *Very* grateful, if you get my meaning,' she said, her eyes all melting softness now.

'I'll try not to,' he retorted, and she felt as if she'd been given a slap in the face. He'd always been one of the few men who seemed to be immune to her, and she still couldn't resist seeing him as a challenge.

Except that she had never felt less like it, she thought, suddenly desperate to get out of the antiseptic atmosphere of the clinic as the familiar taste of bile rose in her mouth.

'I won't do anything just yet,' Nick went on. 'Those tests aren't infallible, and it's very early days. From the look of you, you could just be anaemic, so I suggest a blood test first of all. If things prove otherwise, my advice is to think very carefully before taking any irreversible step. When you have an abortion, it's a child's life you're ending. Once it's over, it can be very traumatic to come to terms with, and cause you all the grief of losing a full-term child.'

She didn't want to hear this. All she wanted was to get out of there, and fast. She spoke quickly.

'I'll keep it in mind. But I'll leave the blood test for now, thanks. I'll tell Laura I checked in here as a visitor for some uppers, all nice and legit, OK?'

'Whatever you like,' Nick said, turning away.

Gemma fled, leaning against the outside wall of the clinic and fighting down the nausea. The taxi driver she'd asked to wait called out to her. Her luggage was still inside as security.

'Lady, do you want this cab or not? Only the meter's ticking over.'

She fell inside, leaning back, suddenly exhausted.

'Lilac Cottage, please,' she mumbled.

Laura stared at her in dismay.

'You look awful,' she said, honest as always. 'You didn't tell me you were under the weather. The last few months must have been awfully wearing, Gem.'

'More than I realized,' she said. 'Actually, I've just called in to see your Nick and got some pills to buck me

330

up. He thinks I may be anaemic,' she added, glad to have something medical to latch onto.

'Well, you've come to the right place. With a doctor in the house, and me to look after you, we'll soon put you right. How's Eddie, by the way?'

Gemma followed her up the stairs to the twin-bedded guest-room she remembered.

'Eddie's fine, as far as I know,' she replied tonelessly. 'But we can't live in each other's pockets all the time, so we're having some time apart before the next season.'

And only Rube Steiner knew her movements. At the last minute yesterday, she'd called him on his answering machine to let him know she was back in England and staying in Somerset for the time being. He'd have been less than pleased if he'd wanted to contact her or Eddie, and hadn't been able to trace either of them. Eddie . . . A sudden wave of misery washed over her. She missed him so much . . .

'How are the girls? Still mad about their ponies?' she asked brightly, dumping her bags on one of the beds.

'I should say they are. And you've heard Penny's news, of course?'

'What news is that? More hobnobbing with royalty at some horse-show or other, I suppose.'

'You don't know!' Laura said gleefully.

'Oh God, of course I do. This man she's met. It had completely slipped my mind for a minute.'

Laura looked at her thoughtfully. Something was definitely wrong here. Gemma would never normally forget such an important piece of news, however bitchily she wanted to chew it over. She noted the dark rings beneath Gemma's lovely eyes and the tension around her mouth, and assumed that this row with Eddie was upsetting her more than usual. If this was what success and stardom did for you, she could keep it, Laura thought fleetingly.

'I think she's really in love, Gem. Can you believe it?'

Gemma shrugged. 'Why not? It happens to the best of us, kiddo.'

Even me . . . And she wanted Eddie so much at that moment she was in danger of flooding this little room with tears. God, what a marshmallow she was turning into.

Laura didn't miss the yearning note in her voice. But then, she'd always known that Gemma was in love with Eddie. She'd known it before Gemma knew it herself, so it was no big surprise. But it was obvious that nothing was going right between them, and she felt too uneasy to ask questions.

Nor did she like the sound of Gemma needing pills to buck her up. She'd always had such energy and zest for life, but it certainly didn't look that way now. Laura had never thought her capable of taking too many pills and doing herself in, but she admitted that you just never knew with Gemma.

Of the three of them, she'd always been the one with secrets, and Laura doubted if anyone really got to know her completely. And right now, the look in her eyes was, well, tortured, was the only way Laura could describe it.

She linked her arm through her friend's.

'What you need is some good country air and proper food, and I'm going to see that you get it. You can forget everything else but relaxing, Gem.'

'I wish I could. And if you dare to say you intend fattening me up, I'll throttle you,' she finished, laughing with a kind of desperation.

It quickly became obvious to Laura that Nick and Gemma were on even worse terms than they had been before. It grieved her that her husband and best friend couldn't get along, though it also dawned on her that it was Nick who was doing most of the avoiding. Gemma seemed determined to be nice to him. Laura might have suspected it was a kind of inverted sarcasm on her part, but somehow she knew it wasn't. Gemma was practically playing up to him . . .

When this dawned on her, Laura felt a real shock. She was perfectly aware of her own naivete in always seeing the best in people, and it was often more of a curse than a blessing. People took advantage. But she was no wimp, to sit back and watch fearfully for her husband to fall under Gemma's spell. She tackled Nick first, after Gemma had offered to take the girls for a walk after Sunday lunch. To avoid the washing-up, Laura thought, with new-found cynicism.

'Say I'm crazy if you like, but is there something you want to tell me about Gemma?'

He started, looking at her cautiously. 'You know all about doctor-patient confidentiality. What goes on between them in the surgery has to be private.'

'I'm not talking about any doctor-patient relationship. I'm talking about another kind,' she said quickly, as he unconsciously reinforced her suspicions.

She leaned against the work-top as if she needed its support, because never in her life had she thought to have this kind of conversation. But she remembered how easy it would have been for her to fall for Jeff Rawles. He had flattered her and she'd been tempted . . . and flattery and flirting were second nature to Gemma, and Nick wasn't immune.

'My God, if I was ever going to fall for anybody, it certainly wouldn't be *Gemma*,' Nick said incredulously. 'What on earth put such a stupid idea into your head?'

'She did. Oh, not consciously, but I've seen the way she keeps looking at you, almost pleadingly. And no man can hold out for ever once a woman like Gemma decides that she wants him. It would probably be good for her ego to have a fling, since Eddie seems to be out of range for the moment.'

Nick took his wife in his arms, hearing the bitter hurt in her normally calm voice.

'I promise you Gemma doesn't want me, and I sure as hell don't want her. She's got a problem, which I'm going to sort out for her, and that's all I'm going to say about it.'

He bent his head and kissed her, and she clung to him fiercely. But she wasn't a fool; she had never been a fool. They broke apart slowly, and Laura looked into his eyes unblinkingly, but her voice was jerky.

'She's pregnant, isn't she? And she wants you to terminate it. Did she bribe you with a quick screw to do it for her?'

'She did not.' Nick was perfectly aware that the invitation had been there, but it was unspoken, so at least he could answer Laura with that much honesty.

'I'm glad. I wouldn't have wanted to end our friendship after all these years.' Laura spoke softly. 'I'm under no illusions about Gemma, but I didn't think she'd ever do that to a friend.'

And you're never going to know, my sweet darling, Nick vowed, *not in a million years.*

'Then listen to me, Laura. She knows your views on abortion, and it will kill her if she thought you knew, or even guessed, so promise me you'll keep this conversation to yourself,' he warned her.

'What conversation?' she said.

CHAPTER 20

Gemma awoke in the middle of the night, feeling that something was tearing her insides out. Without switching on any lights, she groped her way to the bathroom and sank onto the toilet, shivering and sweating profusely. This was nothing like the occasional cramps she'd been having all day, nor the nausea that she hated. This was sheer hell . . . but even so, she was disorientated enough for it to be quite a while before she realized what was happening.

Her first reaction was one of blind terror. She knew she should call someone . . . but if she woke Nick, it would arouse Laura too, and that was the last thing she wanted. If this was a miscarriage – and she couldn't think what else it could be – there were plenty of women who coped with it alone, she thought desperately. It simply took care of itself . . . and once it was over, it would have solved all her problems.

The pain intensified as if in vicious, silent reproach, and her brief elation evaporated as quickly as it had come. She found herself weeping bitterly, as if grieving for something she hadn't known she wanted. She *hadn't*

336

wanted it, she thought fiercely. But it had been a part of her and Eddie, and in her darkest moments now, she wondered if it was the only part of him that she would ever have.

After what seemed an age, she heard Laura's voice outside the bathroom door.

'Gemma, are you okay? I heard you moving about earlier, and you've been in there an awfully long time. Nick had to go out on a call ages ago, but I couldn't go back to sleep until I knew that you were all right.'

Gemma felt her throat close up at the concern in Laura's voice. Darling Laura, her dearest friend, whom she'd been desperate enough to do the dirty on, if Nick couldn't be persuaded to help her in any other way . . .

'You can come in, Laura. The door's not locked,' she said in a choked voice.

Laura came in, half-fearful of what she was going to find. A half-empty bottle of pills, maybe, and Gemma in a stupor and close to death, and without Nick around to tell her what to do . . .

Inside the bathroom, she gasped at what she saw. Gemma was crouched double by the toilet, her nightgown rucked up around her knees.

'Dear God, what have you done?' she whispered.

'I haven't done anything. Good old Mother Nature's done it for me,' Gemma tried to joke, before she broke down completely. Then she was sobbing in Laura's arms before she knew it, and Laura was completely out of her depth at witnessing such raw emotion.

Laura didn't know how long they crouched and hugged one another mutely, but she was never more thankful to hear the Range Rover return. Ignoring Gemma's plea to leave her alone to get over it, she rushed out of the bathroom to forestall Nick and get his help, feeling fervently thankful that the twins were such heavy sleepers.

'It's not me, Nick, it's Gemma,' she said quickly, seeing his horrified eyes at the bloodstains on the oversized T-shirt she wore in bed. 'I don't think she's done anything to herself, but it looks as though the crisis is over.'

It took another hour before everything was restored to normal. By then, Gemma was back in bed in a clean nightgown, having taken a sedative. This had the effect of relaxing her so well that she couldn't stop talking in a garbled manner to Laura before the drug knocked her out completely.

Opening her heart. Betraying everything she'd kept to herself for so long.

'Eddie wouldn't have wanted a kid, Laura. He'd have hated me for it, and I couldn't bear that, so it's far better this way.'

She drew in her breath on a small sob, and her wandering thoughts took a sideways curve as her hand lay limply in Laura's.

'I wouldn't have gone all the way with Nick, darling. I just had to try anything to get help. I was desperate, you see. But I wouldn't have got him to – well, you know . . . you do believe me, don't you? Anyway, I don't really fancy him . . .'

Her voice trailed away, and Laura leaned towards her. 'Of course I believe you. Get some sleep now.

We're all exhausted, and Nick has to be up early in the morning.'

It was morning now, she reflected, as she left Gemma's room, and changed out of her own soiled garment. It hadn't seemed worth it until she'd cleaned up the bathroom while Nick checked Gemma over, swallowing hard to fight off her own nausea, and feeling as if she'd run a hundred miles non-stop.

She crept into bed. The dawn light was already filtering through the curtains, and Nick lay sprawled out between the bedcovers, his eyes closed. Laura slid in beside him, wanting his arms around her and needing his warmth, but knowing this wasn't the time to ask for it.

She was numb with all that had happened, but more so at the shock of hearing Gemma's incoherent confession of her intentions. She couldn't ask Nick about it. She didn't want to know how far this had already gone . . . couldn't *bear* to know.

Good old 'head-in-the-sand' Laura, she thought, bitter at her own ineptness. But she trusted her husband, as she had always trusted him. And foolish or not, she still found herself trusting Gemma too. It would have been a last-ditch attempt to get help when she found herself pregnant, in the only way she knew. Using her body. An enticement, no more.

And now that she knew about the baby, Laura understood exactly why Gemma had come here and sought Nick out.

But when it came to the point, she was convinced in her soul that Gemma wouldn't have gone through with seducing Nick. Not even Gemma would do that to a friend. Her heart thudded painfully; was she being stupid and gullible? Yet she'd rather be that than a suspicious, shrewish, miserably unhappy wife.

She snuggled as near to Nick as she could, while trying not to disturb him, and heard his tired voice as he hovered on the edge of sleep.

'I love you, Laura.'

'I love you too,' she whispered, the way she always did, and felt her eyelids prickle, wishing that life could be as uncomplicated for her friends as it had always been for her.

Gemma wanted to go back to London at once. Nick and Laura would have none of it, despite the awfulness of the previous night, and the fact that she could hardly bear to look at Laura in the cold, harsh daylight.

'You'll do no such thing,' Nick said firmly. 'You've registered as my temporary patient, and I insist that you remain in bed today. What is more, you're to stay here for at least another week. You've had a considerable shock to your system.'

'I know,' Gemma said, and turned her face away from him, so that he wouldn't see the weak tears threatening to slide down her face. The worst shock of all was her ghastly and unexpected feeling of grief. Nick had warned her it would happen, but she just hadn't believed it.

Losing a child through natural means or otherwise, it was all the same. It didn't alter the fact that there had been a child growing inside her, and now there was nothing but a huge void. It was ridiculous to feel the way she did, and she knew the bloody hormones were responsible for it, and there wasn't a damn thing she could do about it.

She accepted without question now that Laura was aware of what had happened, though she couldn't remember all that she'd blabbed. Laura would have known immediately that the horror of last night was no normal period. At least she didn't have to face Laura's accusing face after having an abortion, but she'd fully intended to go through with it, and the feeling of shame and grief still wouldn't go away.

She slept through most of the day with the help of Nick's sedatives, but by the evening her natural survival instinct was beginning to reassert itself, and she began to feel slightly more human. Especially as Sarah and Charlotte were tiptoeing around her, bringing her fruit and drinks as if she was an old woman. She couldn't take much more of it.

Besides, she had to get well quickly. There were less than two more weeks left in February, and CHERISH were due to start their spring season in the middle of March. She had to look her usual glamorous self by then, instead of the weedy ghost she saw in the dressing-table mirror.

Providing Eddie turned up, of course, and there was still going to *be* a duo called CHERISH.

'Penny said she might come down some time this month,' Laura told her when she got up gingerly the following day. 'I thought I'd give her a ring and tell her you're here.'

'Oh, I don't know if I can face her right now.'

'It'll do you good,' Laura said, surprisingly firm. 'You can't live like a hermit just because of what's happened. You've got to start looking forward, not back.'

'Still philosophizing, are you?'

'Why not? It makes sense, and you know it. So do I call Penny and invite her down?' she demanded.

'It's your house,' Gemma said noncommittally. 'But I daresay she's off somewhere with Hank the Yank, anyway.'

The thought didn't give her any pleasure. Instead, it filled her with acute envy, because Penny had what she didn't.

As for Laura . . . dear Laura had it all, Gemma thought, with sudden inexplicable fury. All these years she had slightly looked down on Laura for her homely needs, her jam-making and her country cottage . . . but now, she'd give the earth to make this kind of a home with a man who really loved her.

And dear God, she must be a bloody sight weaker than she'd thought, if she could wallow in such sentiments.

Penny wasn't off with her Yank, Laura informed her, after she'd spoken to her on the phone for ten minutes.

'Hank's staying in Oxford for a while, spending time at one of the colleges, and keeping out of her way, she said, so she's coming down tomorrow for a week. Actually, I suspect it's make-her-mind-up-time. She's coming by train, by the way, so I said I'd drive up to Bristol to meet her.'

'So that you can talk about me on the way back?'

'So that you can come with me, if you're up to it,' Laura said coolly. 'And don't be so bloody touchy.'

Gemma eyed her warily. 'You can be pretty forceful when you want to be, can't you, Laura?'

She laughed. 'What took you so long to discover it?'

'I don't know,' Gemma answered thoughtfully. 'I guess Penny and I were so busy carving out our Careers-with-a-capital-C, that we managed to overlook the fact that you had a will of your own.'

'Well, I'll overlook the fact that you thought me such a dumb-bell then, and get us some lunch, okay?'

'Oh God, now I've offended you,' Gemma said.

'No, you haven't. I learned long ago that you frequently barge in feet first, and I take it all with a strong pinch of salt.'

'You mean I frequently talk a lot of garbage?'

'Something like that. And by the way, I haven't told her anything.' Laura swished quickly out of the sitting room and starting to bang pots about in the kitchen.

They met Penny off the train at Temple Meads, and if Gemma was still feeling fragile, she was making a determined effort not to show it. She'd piled on the make-up and fixed her mouth into the smile she usually reserved for ogling male punters in her audience. To outsiders she was glamour personified. But Penny had known her too long to be taken in.

'What's been happening to you, Gem?' she asked, once they were on the road, twisting round from her front-passenger seat in the Mini. 'I thought everything was on the up and up again, but it's not, is it?'

343

'Yes it is,' Gemma countered irritably. 'CHERISH is becoming a huge success, and I adore living in Spain.'

'So what's wrong? And how's Eddie?'

'Leave it until we get home, Pen,' Laura put in uneasily, knowing how persistent she could be in that superior way of hers, and that Gemma was ready to explode. She should have said something, after all . . . but now it was already too late.

'No. She might as well hear it all in one fell swoop,' Gemma suddenly said in a loud voice. 'If you want to know, Eddie walked out on me after a blazing row, and I don't know where he is. If he doesn't turn up in the next couple of weeks, we'll have blown it again. And oh yes, I've just had a miscarriage, and luckily it happened while I was staying in a doctor's house. I've always been lucky like that.'

She oozed sarcasm, and Laura knew she was near to breaking point all over again.

'I told you to leave it for now,' she snapped unreasonably at Penny, who ignored her, reaching back to grab Gemma's cold hand.

'Darling, I'm so sorry. So very, very sorry,' she said in a soft compassionate voice.

It was too much for Gemma; she crumbled in the back seat. Penny ordered Laura to stop the car, and she got out and sat in the back, holding Gemma in her arms as if she were a child, while Laura crashed the gears and gritted her teeth in a fit of pique she couldn't seem to control.

But for once Penny's genteel upbringing wouldn't come to her aid, and she couldn't think of a thing to say

344

to comfort her. Nor did she think Gemma wanted to hear meaningless platitudes, so they drove the rest of the way in the most intensely awkward, embarrassed silence the three of them had ever known.

The twins were due to be collected from school soon after they arrived at Lilac Cottage, and Laura was glad to escape from the house and let the others get on with repairing a relationship that had become strained, if not damaged.

But why? she raged. Why should she be feeling like the scapegoat, while the other two took whatever solace they could from one another? None of them had ever been jealous of the others' closeness. The bond between them had always been too strong for such pettiness to last for more than moments.

She had recognized long ago that she was somehow always destined to be *piggy-in-the-middle*. The childish words slid annoyingly into her mind as she crunched the gears of the Mini and drove grimly through the lanes that were already becoming misty, even though it was barely three o'clock in the February afternoon.

Always Good Old Laura. Always on hand to help. The thought made her sound like a wimp. It did nothing to mollify her, even though she knew that being Good Old Laura wasn't such a bad thing to be.

It dawned on her that she was feeling more restless than ever before, but it went far deeper than that. She was uneasy, with the sense that something bad was about to happen; was just around the corner . . . It was what the others used to say scornfully was her grand flash of intuition that usually came to nowt. But sometimes it did.

She brushed aside her forebodings as the school gates came into view, and she saw the crowd of young women, like herself, waiting to collect their infants. She parked the car and forced a smile as one and another greeted her. They all knew her, of course. She was the doctor's wife. Good Old Laura. Always on hand to help in village affairs, big and small, the way a good doctor's wife should be.

She scowled inwardly. Good Old Laura . . . *God*, she must stop this! she thought in alarm.

At this moment, her two best friends were probably laughing over old times and making coffee in the cottage, and Laura was the only one with this dire gut feeling of impending doom . . .

The twins came hurtling out of the classroom, waving drawings and bringing home Early Readers for her to go through with them. *Janet and John* and *Rosie and Jim*, who knew nothing about how life was going to turn out for them . . . She was definitely going bonkers, she thought, if she could get so worked up about imaginary characters in children's books!

'Did Auntie Penny come?' Sarah shouted. 'Is she going to give us a pony lesson today?'

'Maybe not today. Tomorrow's Saturday – '

'Why not today?' Charlotte howled.

'Because you'll have all day on Saturday.'

'It's not fair!' they yelled in unison, and Laura sighed, giving up the argument for the sake of peace, and deciding to let Penny sort it out. Yes, she was definitely acting like the world's worst wimp, she thought.

It was just as she'd thought. The atmosphere in Lilac Cottage now was one of harmony; Penny's serene presence had done its work. Laura had half-expected her happiness to backfire on Gemma, owing to her miscarriage, but she saw that for the moment, at least, Penny was keeping quite low-key about gorgeous Hank the Yank, as Gemma called him.

And once the twins arrived home, the talk was all about ponies and horses, and how soon Penny could give them an extra lesson, and come and see how well they were doing. They didn't give up until they had worn her down and extracted a promise of an entire morning spent with them tomorrow.

'Good Lord, don't you ever stop?' Penny said with a grin. 'How do you cope with them, darling?' she asked Laura, after the girls had gone up to their room to change out of their school clothes.

'Sometimes I wonder. Anyway, you still haven't told us why you didn't bring Hank down for our inspection.'

'She was afraid I'd pinch him, of course,' Gemma said, with a burst of her old spirit.

The others laughed, but Gemma realized she couldn't look at Laura. The minute the words left her mouth, Gemma remembered that it was exactly what she'd planned to do with Nick. Not that she'd have wanted him for ever . . . just while he suited her purpose. What a bitch she was.

These self-condemning thoughts kept intruding into

347

her mind, filling her with shame. It was as if something inside her – a belated attack of conscience, she supposed – wouldn't leave her alone, and insisted on reminding her as brutally as it could of what she had been prepared to do to her best friend.

'You won't pinch him.' Penny's voice was softly confident. 'But I have to be sure of what I'm doing.'

'You love him, don't you? And he loves you, so where's the problem?' Laura was brisker than usual.

'Of course I love him. More than I ever thought I could love anybody,' Penny replied, catching her breath as the force of it hit her, as always. 'I love him so damn much I can't stop thinking about him for a single minute.'

'Well then,' Laura persisted. 'You know you're going to say yes in the end, so why are you waiting?'

'She has to be sure it's not just sex,' Gemma said lazily. 'Though now that we've mentioned it, how was it, Pen?'

'*You've* mentioned it, and since you ask, it was fantastic, and that's all I'm going to say about it.' Penny went suddenly red in the face.

'Oh, for Christ's sake, we're all adult, and we always used to tell each other everything, didn't we? Give us the lowdown,' Gemma said, seeing the closed, dreamy look on Penny's face, and filled with the most unreasoning anger.

Her moods were so mercurial since finding out about the baby, and then the miscarriage, and all the bewildering mixture of emotions that wouldn't let her be, that the words had spilled out of her before she knew it.

348

'It's private. Besides, that was then, and this is now,' Penny answered, so quietly that it had the effect of sobering them all up. Laura cleared her throat. A fine time they were all going to have, she thought, if Gemma kept putting her foot in it every time she opened her mouth, and if Penny was determined to keep everything about Hank to herself.

Not that Laura wanted to pry; she remembered how it had been when she first met Nick, and everything was sweet and new, and she hadn't wanted to share even a single thought between them with anyone else. All the same, she did have a bit of sympathy for Gemma. They had always confided in each other, and now there were so many secrets.

'Is he going to call you here?' Laura asked casually. 'I only ask, because you won't get much privacy until the twins are in bed.'

Penny shook her head. 'We're staying completely *incommunicado* for a week. He doesn't even know I'm here – it was a spur of the moment thing to come down. I wanted to give him space, as well, just to be sure.'

'God, what a pair of idiots,' Gemma said. 'If you want something badly enough, you should grab it with both hands, no pun intended.'

Penny didn't even smile. 'That's the difference between you and me, Gemma. I always knew that if I ever found the man I wanted to marry, it would be for keeps.'

'Who said anything about marriage?' Gemma snapped back rudely.

* * *

By the time they went to bed that evening, Gemma knew she couldn't stay at Lilac Cottage much longer. Nick had insisted she stay a full week to recuperate, and she'd reluctantly agreed, but that was before Penny arrived. And despite her decision not to overwhelm them with talk about Hank, his name cropped up so often that Gemma felt she could scream.

Laura seemed totally charmed by Penny's descriptions of the man. She'd brought quantities of photos from the Aspen skiing holiday; most of them were of Hank, or Hank and Penny together, on the slopes in skiing gear, in the hotel restaurant, dancing on the moonlit terrace clasped in one another's arms. And there was no doubt what kind of a New Year's Eve Penny had had.

All of which only served to remind Gemma of how she'd woken up in some sordid room with a lot of unwashed bodies, with some guy called Paul telling her she was into drugs. And how she'd fled, praying no one would recognize her, and fallen into Eddie's waiting arms . . .

By Sunday, she knew she had to leave Lilac Cottage. It wasn't that she didn't care for them any more, and she knew they gave her every loving support that they could. But after the initial awkward fencing, the sparkle of the other two couldn't be subdued. They both had an assured and happy future, and for Gemma the whole atmosphere became just too cheerful and upbeat for her to cope.

On Monday morning, Laura took the twins to school as usual, and drove Penny on to Jeff Rawles' stables, where she was dying to have a ride on one of his new Irish-bred horses. Gemma told them cheerfully she'd be quite happy pottering, if Laura wanted to do anything else.

'Are you sure? I don't like leaving you alone, Gem.'

'For pity's sake. I'm not a baby – I can amuse myself for a couple of hours. Go and watch Penny do her stuff, only count me out. I can't stand the smell of horses,' she added with a grin to show them she was quite happy.

The twins gave her a hug as usual when they left for school, and Gemma resisted the urge to hug her friends as well, knowing it might give the game away if they saw how moist her eyes were. The minute they left, she phoned for a taxi to take her to Temple Meads Station, and by the time it arrived, all her stuff was packed, and the note she'd written to Laura was propped up prominently by the telephone.

Laura stayed a little while watching Penny ride, and then decided she didn't want to leave Gemma alone too long after all, so Jeff promised to drive Penny back later. It wasn't a very nice morning for riding, Laura thought, and the mist wasn't clearing at all. But Penny knew what she was doing, so she didn't give her another thought as she drove carefully back through what was developing into quite a fog as the lanes dipped towards the cottage.

She saw the note and registered the silence at the same time. Knowing Gemma always had the radio blaring out, she snatched up the note and read it quickly.

'Thanks for everything, darling,' it said. 'Thank Nick for me too, and tell him I'm sorry, but I'll be okay now. Give Penny my love, and tell her to hold on tight to that man of hers. That's advice from an old hand at the game. It's been good to see you, but I can't stagnate any longer. And I think you understand, don't you, Laura? You always seem to have a sixth sense about things, anyway.

Love to all, Gemma.'

There was something wrong here, Laura thought, frowning. It was too slick, too carefully worded, and too damn enigmatic for Gemma, as if she wanted to say more, but didn't know how. It just wasn't Gemma.

And it told her nothing of where she was going, though Laura assumed it would be straight back to Spain. Gemma needed warmth and sun and bright lights and adoration, and Eddie . . .

The phone rang while she was still pondering. She grabbed the receiver, wondering if Gemma had had second thoughts about leaving her a note, and was calling from the station, or the train, to apologize in person. Or it would be a call for Nick, wanting advice, or his services, or his undivided attention . . .

'Laura, thank God.'

She heard the strangled voice, and for a minute she couldn't make out who it was.

'Jeff, is that you?'

'There's been a terrible accident. I've sent for an ambulance. It's Penny – '

'Oh, my *God*. She's not – '

'No, but – '

'I'm coming over.'

'There's no point. The fog's closing in fast, and the ambulance will be here before you. I'll let you know as soon as they tell me where they're taking her.'

He hung up, and Laura burst into tears. All she could think about was her intuition – her famous sixth sense that the others had always teased her about. Now, at last, it had proved itself to be so terribly, terribly right.

CHAPTER 21

It was mid-afternoon when Gemma let herself into her apartment with a sense of relief. She'd spoken to no one on the train, and the taxi driver at Paddington had been surly and silent with dyspepsia, which had suited her fine. He'd dropped her at a foodstore where she'd bought the basics to last her a week. He'd waited for her while his meter ticked up and she tipped him generously, which went some way to cheering him.

And then she was alone at last. She didn't want company. She didn't want to see anybody, or to speak to anybody. She just wanted some time completely alone to let her mind and body recover slowly from these past harrowing weeks. There would be time enough to face the public – and Eddie – in a week or so when she booked her flight back to Malaga.

She instructed the porter at the desk downstairs not to let anyone near her apartment and to hold all her mail until she collected it. If anyone asked for her, he was to say she was out of the country and he didn't have a forwarding address or telephone number.

The first thing she did inside her flat was to pull the

plug on her telephone and answering machine, before stripping off all her clothes and taking a lengthy shower. Then she pulled her bedroom curtains and went to bed, curling up in the foetal position and hugging her pillow to her chest. She set about deliberately making her mind a total blank, so that she wouldn't register for an instant how or why her heart was breaking.

'Nick, at *last*. It's me,' Laura gasped incoherently on the phone, having finally got hold of him on his mobile. 'Gemma's gone, and Penny's had some kind of accident at Jeff Rawles' stables. He's sent for an ambulance. Can you track down what's happening and get back to me?'

'Hold on a minute and slow down,' came his reassuring, professional voice. 'I can't make head or tail of what you're saying. Gemma's gone, did you say? Gone where? And what exactly happened to Penny?'

Laura clenched her free hand until her nails bit into her palm, wondering how men could be so stupid, and why they couldn't grasp the essentials of a conversation right away.

'Never mind about Gemma. I want to know where they're taking Penny,' she yelled into the phone.

'You'd better calm down, or they'll be taking you away too,' he said, still in that infuriating doctor-patient voice. 'If you don't give me any details, there's not much I can do.'

'I don't *know* any details, that's why. All I know is that Jeff sounded terrible on the phone – ' She suddenly choked up, unable to go on.

'Right. I'll get on to the ambulance people,' Nick

said, more briskly. 'I've nearly finished my morning rounds, and if it sounds serious I'll hand over to my locum for the rest of the day and come and fetch you. I presume you'll want to be with her, wherever she is. Can you organize somebody to collect the girls from school, just in case?'

He was so practical, the way Laura had always believed herself to be until now, before she had gone utterly to pieces.

'Yes, I'll call Mrs Yard and ask her to take them home for tea. I know she'll do it. Hurry, Nick, please.'

She put down the phone, checked with Mrs Yard that she could take the girls, without giving anything away, except to say that they might be gone quite a while, and confirmed the arrangements with the school. Then she rang the stables again, and heard Barbara's hysterical voice.

'Oh, Mrs Dean, it was awful. I mean, you don't expect it with such an experienced rider, do you? Poor Jeff's in a terrible state – '

'Will you please tell me what happened?' Laura asked, suddenly calm in the face of this girl's obvious panic.

She heard a huge gulp at the other end. 'Miss Bishop was out riding – oh well, you knew that, didn't you? She was trying out some of the new jumps that Jeff's installed, and the horse skidded on some ice. You know how slippery it is here right now, what with the freezing fog and all. Jeff did try to warn her, but she's such an expert rider – '

'So what *happened*?' Laura snapped, thinking that

this defensive bleating on Jeff's behalf could go on for ever.

Another gulp, bordering on a sob. 'She was thrown off, but somehow her leg got caught in the stirrups so she wasn't thrown free when the horse fell.'

'And?' Laura prompted again, trying to control the wave of sickness surging through her.

'She fell clear of him, more or less, except for her foot that was stuck beneath his weight. And the horse never moved off her. The vet said it broke its neck, Mrs Dean – '

'I don't care about the bloody horse,' Laura yelled into the stupid woman's ear. 'What about Penny?'

She didn't even care if she affronted Barbara either, considering the valuable bloodstock Jeff was trying to introduce into his stables. But Barbara obviously registered the fury in Laura's voice, because she rushed on heedlessly.

'She was unconscious when we reached her, Mrs Dean, and Jeff sent for the ambulance right away. He's gone with them to Southmead now, but they said – they said – '

'*What?*' Laura said harshly.

'They think it's almost certain she'll lose her foot because it's so badly crushed. I'm so sorry, Mrs Dean,' she ended on a whimper.

But by then Laura had gone, her mind in turmoil. Her darling Penny was going to lose her foot . . . that beautiful, elegant girl, whose whole life revolved around sport and riding and healthy exercise. And skiing . . . Laura's horrified eyes glazed. How was Hank going to take this?

357

Her first instinct was to get out the Mini and drive herself to Southmead Hospital in Bristol, but Nick wouldn't thank her for driving crazily through the fog, and maybe ending up in a bed next to Penny. She clenched her hands, helpless and impotent.

Then her fingers were dialling Gemma's apartment number before she realized it. But Gemma wouldn't be home yet, even if home was where she intended to go. She slammed the phone down again. She should probably call Penny's parents . . . but maybe not yet. Not until she knew the extent of the injury. Maybe the paramedics had been exaggerating, she thought, with a sliver of hope. Anyway, the Bristol hospitals were renowned for their expertise in mending broken bones and limbs. Maybe it wasn't so bad as everybody feared . . .

She prowled around like a hunted animal until Nick came home. Underneath, she knew she was fooling herself. Her sixth sense had been spot on. Disaster *had* been waiting around the corner – but it hadn't been waiting for her, nor even Gemma, who had always seemed the most likely candidate. It was Penny, destined to go through life so serenely, with everything that money could buy . . .

She fell into Nick's arms, babbling out what Barbara had told her. He held her very tightly, and she knew it was going to be bad news.

'I know. I've been on to Southmead, and they'll be taking her straight to theatre as soon as she arrives. The signs aren't good, darling, and it's no good pretending otherwise.'

She almost hated him for putting into words all that was in her heart. She wished, just for once, that he'd bother to pretend, to fake it. But that had never been their way. They didn't keep secrets from each other. Only two. Only the fact that she'd been half-tempted by Jeff Rawles' flattery. And the fact that he'd never told her how Gemma gave him the come-on to get him to perform an abortion.

The brutal thoughts raced through her mind, and she simply threw them out. They were unimportant. They hadn't been life-threatening, and were totally meaningless, compared with this far more appalling tragedy that had happened.

'Will she be all right?' she sobbed against Nick's chest.

'Let's go to Southmead and find out,' he said, which told her absolutely nothing. But how could he? He was only a doctor, not a bloody miracle worker, and he wouldn't be the surgeon who took away all Penny's dreams.

At least she could be thankful for that, she thought, and then had a wild desire to laugh at such a nonsensical thought. Fancy being cheered by the idea that it would be some anonymous hospital surgeon who operated, and not your own husband who had to amputate your best friend's foot. She flinched as the hated word swept into her mind, and all desire to laugh died away.

'Can we go then? I'm beginning to feel stifled by these four walls,' she ordered shrilly.

'Have you called Mrs Yard?' Nick asked.

She stared at him. The children, of course. They

would be heartbroken when they knew. They adored Penny so much. And what of her parents? That stiff-necked mother of hers, and her doting father, who would be heartbroken too . . . they had to be told, but she balked from the idea of being the one to do it.

'The girls will stay with Mrs Yard until she hears from us. Nick, should I have called Penny's parents?'

'No. Not until we know what's happening,' he said, to her huge relief. 'Right then, let's go.'

Laura didn't like hospitals. She hated the antiseptic smells, and the many less acceptable smells that permeated the wards; she hated the polished floors where the nurses' shoes always squeaked, and the swish of starched aprons; and most of all she hated the moment when you were the patient, and they pulled the curtains around your bed, and the po-faced man in a suit who you knew was the Big Man around here, came and told you things you didn't want to hear . . .

Nick was used to it all, of course. It was part of the job to be thick-skinned and immune to getting too involved with patients. But it was surely another matter when the patient was someone close, if not to you, then to your wife.

She felt his constant glances on her as they drove without speaking through the fog; she knew he wanted to reassure her, but for once he couldn't find the words.

'I suppose I'll *have* to phone Penny's parents this afternoon, and try to catch up with Gemma too,' she muttered, when she began to find the silence unbearable.

'What about the boyfriend?' Nick said.

She wished he hadn't mentioned Hank. Penny was so vulnerable right now. She was in love for the first time in her life, and everything was rose-coloured and spectacular . . . and Laura simply couldn't bear it if all her dreams were to be shattered because of this accident.

Because she was going to be *disabled* for the rest of her life, no matter how many politically-correct labels you put on it. Some men simply couldn't handle that, and it wasn't as if Hank had known her for very long. Maybe Penny was in for an even greater pain than just losing her foot.

She wouldn't even think about it. From all that Penny had told her about Hank, he was the most wonderful guy on earth, and he'd stand by her. Ludicrously, she wondered just how Penny was going to stand by *him*, with only one foot . . . At the awfulness of the image she began to wonder just what the hell was the *matter* with her to be having all these crazy thoughts in the midst of something so dreadful.

'I don't know where Hank's staying in Oxford, but I'll get the phone number from Penny as soon as she's able to tell me, and get on to him as well,' Laura said numbly.

Because, of course, it would all be down to her. All the trauma of telling Gemma, and the Bishop parents, and Hank the Yank. Good Old Laura would find the right words somehow. Good Old Laura would do all the donkey work and be the shoulder for everybody to cry on . . .

She was suddenly bitterly ashamed of her own secret resentment. It wasn't everybody who had the ability to deal with people the way she did. Call it instinct, or the years of being a good doctor's wife, or simply habit because it was her nature to be generous-hearted and not bitchy – well, not too often. Whatever it was, she unashamedly tried to bolster up her own self-esteem now, knowing that she couldn't have the luxury of going to pieces, when so many people needed her to be strong.

'I'll do that, if you like,' Nick offered 'Call Hank, I mean,' he added, when the silence between them lengthened. 'And darling, you know this could have been a lot worse.'

Laura stared straight ahead, rigid with fury at such a lack of sensitivity and perception. Or did everybody become thoughtless and stupid at a time like this, resorting to pointless platitudes in order to make everybody else feel better? Just like when somebody died. *Well, dear, it could have been worse* – oh yeah?

If so, she could tell him right now – if only she could have trusted herself to speak to him at all – that it wasn't bloody-well working.

'She might have been beneath the horse's body when it fell, and had a spinal injury. She could have been paralysed, Laura,' Nick went on relentlessly. 'You've got to be thankful that it wasn't anything like that.'

'Have I?' She couldn't keep the shrillness from her tone. 'Well, you try telling that to Penny when she wakes up and discovers that some bloody butcher has cut off her foot!'

'She won't just discover it. She'll either be conscious enough to give permission herself, or her parents will sign the necessary form.'

'Whatever,' Laura said, incapable of thinking about such banal formalities.

She knew Nick was doing his best to be patient with her, when all she wanted was to scream at somebody for what was happening. At God for letting it happen, or Jeff Rawles, for buying the horse in the first place, or herself for saying to Penny, *Yes! Come on down*! – as if she was some bloody game-show host . . .

For the first time in her life, she thought savagely that best friends were more trouble than they were worth. What with Gemma with her erratic life-style and troubles, and now Penny with hers, and they all expected her to cope . . . The spiteful thought ran through her like a knife, and she smothered a sob in her throat. But, God dammit, it was the only way she could deal with this situation right now.

At Southmead Hospital, they went directly to the right department. It was one advantage of having a doctor for a husband, Laura thought, being able to cut through the red tape and knowing exactly where to go. He was a familiar face here, anyway, having often sent patients here for treatment and visited them. He tracked down the consultant who was looking after Penny to find out what was going on, while Laura was given the inevitable cup of tea by a nurse who looked young enough to be taking her GCSEs. There was no sign of Jeff.

'It's all right,' Nick explained briefly, when he

returned. 'She's regained consciousness, though she's heavily sedated, and she's signed the consent form. She wants to see you, Laura. You can have a couple of minutes before they take her into theatre.'

She realized how much she had been dreading this moment. How could she face this beautiful girl, lying helplessly on a hospital bed, having just given her permission for an amputation? And how could she not, when Penny had expressly asked for her?

'I'm ready,' she said huskily, trying not to let her whole body shake with nerves.

Nick took her into the little room where the anaesthetist hovered impatiently to give her the final knockout injection. Penny was as white as the sheet beneath her, her lovely hair in disarray, her eyes dark and huge, and her lips bluish with shock. There was a cradle over her legs, from which Laura quickly averted her eyes, and she grabbed her friend's limp hand.

'Oh Pen – ' she began in a choked voice, then felt the weak squeeze on her fingers, and bent down to catch the thready words.

'You have to promise me something, Laura,' she whispered.

'What, darling?' Laura asked.

'Hank mustn't know. If he tries to contact you, you know nothing. And don't tell my parents until this is all over. When you do, tell them the same: Hank mustn't know.'

The brief words exhausted her. The anaesthetist told her she'd done enough talking, and took over, injecting the back of her hand and instructing her to count backwards from ten. She didn't reach eight before her voice slackened and then died away.

And then there was nothing to do but wait. More cups of tea appeared in a little side-room for Laura and Nick, and she babbled out Penny's instructions to him.

'I can't believe she meant it about not telling Hank, but I'll have to do as she asked until she recovers. He'll need to know, and he'll be devastated, but more so if he thought she was keeping it from him for any length of time.'

'Maybe she'll never want him to know,' Nick said.

'How can you say that?' Laura demanded angrily. 'He means everything to her.'

'Yes, but maybe she's scared that she'll mean less to him now. It happens, my love. Not all men are knights in shining armour. Some of them can't handle disfigurement. And Penny may prefer not to face his pity.'

Laura felt total shock at his words, but she had to suppose that he'd seen such things happen.

'From all that I've heard of Hank, it wouldn't be like that,' she protested.

'But you don't *know*. You've never met the man. Penny hardly knows him either, and in any case, her view of him is distorted by their passionate affair.'

'Why must you make it sound so cold and clinical?'

'I'm not. I'm merely being practical, and trying to tell you that she may need a lot of counselling to come to terms with what's happened. And pity is the last thing she'll want, or accept.'

'So what about love?' she demanded again. 'Hank loves her, I know he does. And she'll need him.'

He gave a deep sigh. 'Leave it, Laura. It's their problem, not yours. You can't be little Miss Fix-it for the whole world.'

'And you can't be the most patronizing man on earth, though right now you're doing your best to prove otherwise,' she snapped. She stood up, suddenly stifled by the whole atmosphere in the place. 'I'm going for a walk if that's all right with you?'

'Of course.' He hesitated. 'Look, if you want to stay here for a night or two I'll see if it can be arranged. Once Penny's back in recovery, I'd better get back home and see about the girls. I daresay Mrs Yard will let them stay at her place. They'll enjoy that.'

Guiltily, Laura knew she'd completely forgotten the twins, and she was prepared to let him arrange anything he liked. She couldn't spare thoughts for anyone but Penny right now. Penny, and Hank, and what was going to happen to their fragile relationship.

She went outside the wards and walked aimlessly around the grounds, in and out of the car parks, seeing nothing but her own troubled thoughts. She was hardly aware of the cold seeping through her clothes, nor the patchy fog that was insidiously coming down again. Nick found her later, leaning against the Range Rover, and he tucked her cold hand in the crook of his arm.

'It's all over, and it went well, with no complications,' he said quietly. 'She'll be out for the count for quite a while, then she'll be put in a private ward. There's a bed for you if you want it. I've phoned Mrs Yard – she's happy to look after the twins for a couple of days. And now I'm taking you to a restaurant for some hot food.'

'I couldn't eat a thing.'

'You can and you will. Doctor's orders,' he said.

He had to leave her eventually, of course. She couldn't expect him to stay on for the sake of her friend. He had work to do, and his own patients to attend to tomorrow. The children would need a bag of clothes to be taken to Mrs Yard's house, and to have their Daddy reassure them that Auntie Penny was in good hands. He'd also have to contact Jeff, who had been sent back home with the ambulance when it left, since he was too distraught to do anything but be a nuisance to everybody around him.

How she forced some food down her throat, Laura hardly knew. But Nick insisted; by now it was evening, and she'd had nothing at all since breakfast. She had to admit that her stomach felt slightly less nauseous with something inside it.

Nick didn't stay to see Penny come out of the anaesthetic. He was more anxious to get home safely out of the fog, and to see the children. Life went on. God, how many times had she heard those words in her lifetime, Laura wondered?

She clung to him before he left, needing his strength when she faced Penny, but knowing she couldn't have it. Not physically, at least. She could only draw on the inner strength that grew within a good and solid marriage. Right now it didn't seem anywhere near enough. But it was all she had.

'How will I find the right words when she awakes?' she mumbled into his familiar shoulder.

'You'll find them when you need them,' he said. 'You always have, darling.'

At least he didn't call her Good Old Laura, she thought, with the first glimmer of humour since arriving here. That title was reserved for her by Penny and Gemma.

'I'll be all right,' she told him huskily now. 'I've got to make some phone calls, anyway. I'm sure the Bishops will want to visit as soon as possible, but I'm going to tell them it's best to wait until tomorrow. What do you think?'

'I think it's just as I said. You've already found the right words.'

He kissed her, holding her very tightly for a long moment, and then he was gone, leaving her to find the pay-phone and dial Penny's home number.

Her father answered, and she could hear the polite pleasure in his voice when he recognized her voice. Laura closed her eyes briefly, knowing she was about to shatter his ordered life.

Actually, she reflected later, he took it very well – and with far more dignity than she had done herself. The much-maligned British stiff-upper-lip, no less, had come very much to Father Bishop's aid in those first awful moments. His crisp and businesslike manner disguised his obvious distress, and if he felt like weeping into the phone, he was both too manly and too gentlemanly to betray it.

'It's very good of you to tell us; it can't have been easy for you, my dear. I know how close you and Penny have always been,' he said, and his concern for her feelings made Laura the one who wanted to weep. 'I'll break the news to my wife when she returns from her meeting, but tell Penny we'll be at the hospital some time tomorrow.'

'All right. And Mr Bishop, there was one more thing. Penny doesn't want Hank to know anything about this for the present. She was very insistent about it. So if he should call your home . . .'

'I understand. She'll want to tell him herself,' he said. 'I'll see you tomorrow, Laura. And thank you.'

Thank you for telling me my daughter's had a devastating accident while visiting your home . . .

She swallowed hard, pushing such useless thoughts out of her head. It was going to help nobody to think that way. Nor was she as confident about Mr Bishop's assumption that Penny would want to tell Hank herself.

The glint in Penny's eyes, despite her trauma and semi-conscious state, had told Laura it was definitely all over. If it was humanly possible, Hank was never to know the reason she intended to disappear out of his life. But just how she thought he was going to let her do it, Laura had no idea.

She dialled Gemma's home number again, and just as before, there was no reply. Gemma must have gone straight back to Spain, Laura decided. Her little bit of recent trouble was over, and she'd be ready to resume her successful career in a couple of weeks, no worse than before. Somehow or other, Gemma always came up smelling of roses.

By now, Laura began to feel totally wrung out; there was no way she felt inclined to find the telephone

369

number of the Spanish hotel and ask to speak to Gemma. The delay would only aggravate the tension she already felt from speaking to Penny's father. She would write to Gemma instead; it would give her something to do, to help pass the time here until Penny awoke properly.

But first she called Mrs Yard's home, telling her that Nick was on his way back. Hearing the woman's guarded voice, she guessed that Sarah and Charlotte were nearby, and Laura was filled with an eager longing to speak to them.

Their sweet, childish voices in the background, as they squabbled over who was going to talk to her first, were the most beautiful, the most normal sounds Laura had heard in the whole of this traumatic day.

CHAPTER 22

After five days of her own company, Gemma began to hate the sight of the four walls in the apartment, but she was still too lethargic to move on. She felt weird, as if she was in a permanent state of vegetation, waiting for some metamorphic miracle to restore her to the way she was before – or rather, to the way she wanted to be. But since she didn't know what that was, she couldn't help herself.

She was a wreck, she thought in disgust, a miserable, self-destructive wreck. And she was so lonely she could scream. So alone. So desperate for Eddie. They were so good together, so desolate apart, yet still they somehow managed to destroy one another.

She was wallowing in the bathtub when she heard someone crashing into the apartment. She went rigid. The door opened and slammed shut, and a million possibilities raced through her mind. It wasn't a break-in. Somebody had used a key. So the porter had probably called the police to investigate the continuing silence from her apartment, fearful that she'd taken an overdose . . . and oh, it would have been so easy . . .

'Gemma! Where the bloody hell are you?'

Her throat closed, hearing his voice. Loving his voice. Aching for him. But she couldn't speak. Could only sit there in the cooling bathwater, with bubbles of foam bursting all around her while she heard him moving from room to room, looking for her.

She'd run the shower over her face and hair, with this new and constant need to cleanse herself, and she simply sat there, dripping, until he found her.

'My God, what have you done to yourself?' Eddie said, anxiety making him harsh and accusing.

It was too much. Gemma found her voice, screaming abuse at him.

'I've done nothing, you bastard. What have *you* done? And where have you been? Where were you when I needed you most? Don't come in here looking like a bloody plaster saint and accuse me of – '

She couldn't finish. Because by then he'd yanked her out of the bath, wrapping her up in a bath towel and holding her close to his chest, regardless of the way she was soaking him through.

'Shut up. You talk too much. You always did,' he commanded.

He strode through to the bedroom with her and dumped her on the bed. He gave a smothered oath as she bounced, momentarily as limp as a rag doll. She was still wrapped in the bath towel, looking up at him numbly as he began to strip off all his sodden clothes.

When he was naked he pulled the bath towel from under her and climbed on top of her. There were no preliminaries, no foreplay, no 'can I?' or 'do you want to?' It was arrogant and presumptive, as if he had never been away.

And he was thrusting deeply into her before she could gather her breath, like a man starving of oxygen and finding in her his only respite from dying.

It was insulting, degrading . . . it was Eddie . . . and the most erotically exciting happening in ages . . .

When he finally twisted against her, gasping as they climaxed spectacularly together, she realized she was sobbing. He didn't move away from her. He stayed exactly where he was, warm and soft inside her now, and his fingers were gentle on her cheek.

'What the hell's wrong now?' he said, Eddie-like. 'Isn't that what you wanted? What you and I always want from each other?'

'Oh sure,' she cried, suddenly bitter with remembering. 'And maybe it will happen all over again, and I'll have to go through it all again – '

'What are you talking about?' he asked. But he was nobody's fool. He could see by the pain in her eyes that she'd been through something hellish.

He was always so cocksure of himself, Gemma thought furiously, ignoring the *double entendre* of the words, which would normally have had them both laughing deliriously. But maybe the time for truth had come as well. *Oh God . . .*

'I keep forgetting to take my pill,' she said woodenly, thinking how very stupid that sounded. 'I forgot it before, around New Year.'

'So?' He wouldn't help her, forcing her to say it.

She could hear herself screaming again. She wondered if she was ever going to have control of her voice, and just what the hell it was doing to her precious vocal cords.

'So I got pregnant, you bum, and I went down to Laura's place to try and persuade her husband to fix me up with an abortion. I even hinted that I'd sleep with him if he did it. Only I didn't need it, because I lost it anyway.'

She suddenly crumbled, unable to look at him. Her eyes closed tight with the pain of it.

'Eddie, I lost my baby. Our baby.'

He was quiet for so long that she knew it was over for ever. They'd compared lovers in the past, often jokingly, but that was years ago, *aeons* ago, and it hadn't ever threatened their relationship . . . but this was different. This was betrayal, and they both knew it.

She was holding her breath, and it felt as if Eddie was doing the same thing. It felt as if they were suspended in time, with some mischievous devil deciding which way her fate was going to go.

'*Our* baby?' he said at last.

Her eyes flew open. He was still above her, studying her face, but he had slid out of her now, and they were two separate beings again. It seemed awfully symbolic . . .

'Of course *our* baby,' she said, on a sob.

'Would you have gone through with the abortion?' he demanded next, suddenly the inquisitor, when he had always been so casual, so laid-back and uncommitted.

'Yes,' she whispered. 'I knew it would have messed up everything. It wouldn't have been right for us.'

'So you're the only one to decide what's right for us, are you?'

'Oh, come on! Don't go all broody on me, Eddie. It's not your style.'

'Was it yours? How exactly did you feel when you lost it, anyway?'

It was like being on a psychiatrist's couch. He had no right to try to examine her innermost feelings. Some daft know-all once said that confession was good for the soul, but nobody ever warned you that it could ruin everything in the process.

'All right,' she said tiredly. 'I was gutted when it happened, though I couldn't think why. The miscarriage solved everything, but it was as if – as if I was losing part of you. And at the time, I thought it might be the only part I'd ever have.'

He gathered her to him, rocking her in his arms as if she was the child they never had.

'You're a fool if you think you can lose me that easily. You obviously need tethering.'

'Thanks! That makes me sound like a prize pig,' she said, smiling crookedly for the first time.

He wasn't smiling back. He pulled the bedcover over them, enclosing them both in a cocoon.

'So how about it?'

'How about what?'

'Us. Marriage. The whole bit. So that I can keep proper tabs on you in the future.'

At his cool arrogance she knew she should be mortally offended or laugh in his face. It was hardly the most romantic of proposals. But then, it wouldn't be, not from Eddie. His idea of romance happened between the sheets, or under them, or over them, or wherever . . . but this commitment was all she ever wanted, and she had never even known it, until now. But she wasn't giving in that easily.

'You've got a bloody nerve,' she snapped. 'What makes you think I'd want to be married to you?'

'Because I love you, and you love me. Otherwise, why the hell do I keep coming back to you? And maybe it's time we got respectable, babe.'

Now she really did want to laugh. *Respectable?* She wanted him the way he'd always been, wicked and gypsyish, and exciting. But although he was as macho as ever, there was something in his voice that told her he wanted this. He wanted her to say yes, because the time was ripe. It was truly, beautifully ripe.

And he'd told her that he loved her. Gemma caught her breath; she mustn't let this moment go.

'Okay,' she agreed, as casually as she could. 'So we'll get married. When?'

'Just as soon as I can get a special licence,' he decided, taking control. 'And I'll fix us up with a week's honeymoon somewhere exotic. So what if we blue all our earnings? We don't have to be back in Spain for another few weeks, so we may as well go the whole hog while we're at it.'

'Yes – why not?' Gemma echoed, wondering if this was really happening.

But life was like that, at least, hers had always been thus. One minute you were down and out, and then you were soaring to the stars . . .

'Do you want to tell those friends of yours?' Eddie asked. 'Or Rube? He promised to leave us strictly alone this month, but should we let him know?'

She thought for all of ten seconds. 'No. It's nobody's business but ours. No fuss, Eddie. Just you and me.'

And after the way she'd thrown herself on Nick's mercy, and nearly betrayed Laura, she knew she'd be far too embarrassed to face them for quite a while.

Friends were all right when you needed them, but there came a time when they weren't needed any more. Even Penny, who had everything anyway, had shown the kind of sickly compassion for Gemma that had almost stifled her, and she'd felt like telling her to get lost. They'd all moved on.

It would be just her and Eddie from now on, the way it was always meant to be. She'd send Laura and Penny a postcard in the summer, same as usual, to tell them their news. Or she might just send them one from Barbados. That would *really* shock them, she thought, smiling at the idea.

With her spirits leaping by the minute, Gemma was back on form. She stretched languorously, reaching out for Eddie, and pulling him down to her again.

Penny stared at the ceiling in the private room at the hospital, wishing her parents would go away. They'd been down to Bristol every day for the past few days, and she didn't want them there. Her mother simply didn't know what to say to her, and her father was so full of grief that for once he'd clammed up as well. The silences between the three of them were interminable, and if it hadn't been for Laura . . .

Penny was stronger than she realized, and not just physically. By now she had not only come to terms with what had happened, but she'd come to some very important decisions. Her instructions to her parents had been adamant.

'If Hank calls, you're to say I've gone on an extended trip abroad with friends, and I don't want him trying to contact me. You're not to tell him what's happened. Do you promise me, Daddy?'

'Are you sure that's what you want, darling?' he said, uneasy at her feverish eyes.

'I'm perfectly sure. I don't want him here, and I won't let him see me like this.'

'But when you're well . . .'

'When I'm well I'll have an artifical foot and I'll be disabled,' she said deliberately, ignoring the way her mother flinched at the bald statement. 'I won't be the girl he remembers, and I'd rather he kept the memories intact. *Promise* me, Daddy. If you don't, I'll never speak to you again.'

She knew nothing would drag it out of him once he'd promised, and that her mother wouldn't condescend to be badgered by a brash American.

'All right,' her father promised slowly. 'But I think you're wrong. You need all the support you can get right now.'

'I have it. I've got Laura. So *please* don't feel you've got to keep on coming down here. You both have such busy lives, and I'm perfectly all right. I don't mean to be cruel, but once they give me the okay, I plan to go to a private nursing home to convalesce. Naturally I'll keep in touch, but it's best that you don't know where I'll be, then you can't let it slip.'

And only when she and Laura were alone did the defences slip. She clung to her helplessly.

'I love him so much, Laura, but how can I let him see me like this? I don't want his pity. You wouldn't, if you were me, would you?'

'I don't know,' Laura said. 'But you're not giving him a chance to decide for himself. You're like Gemma, keeping things from Eddie. You love him, and you know he loves you – '

'But for how long? I know his life-style, Laura. He's got everything that money can buy. I could see that the minute I met him in Aspen. He surrounds himself with beautiful things, *perfect* things, and I've no intention of being the only flawed object in his life.'

'Then you're a fool.' Laura spoke bluntly. 'You think you're being strong, but you're not. You're a coward, Pen. God – I never thought I'd be saying that to you.'

'Then don't say anything at all,' she replied angrily. 'I don't need your advice.'

'Why ask for it then?' Laura retorted.

Variations of this conversation made up most of their intercourse, and Laura began to feel exhausted. Penny didn't want Hank in her life, she said, but Laura knew damn well that Hank was *all* she wanted. Penny couldn't stop talking about him, as if speaking his name brought him close in a way she was determined to deny herself.

She was already having physiotherapy sessions and discussions about her prosthesis, and there was plenty of encouragement about the flexibility of her ankle ligaments and so on. The surgeon told her there was no reason why she couldn't ride again; she'd be almost as good as new by the time they'd done with her.

The hospital team were cheerfully optimistic that she'd be able to resume her activities with the minimum of distress. Nobody ever asked her if it was what she wanted.

After three days, Laura wondered how much longer she could stand it. She wanted to go home. Daily phone calls to Nick, and evening chats with her children were not enough. She missed them, and longed for the chaotic normality of family life. It had never been suggested that she stayed for any length of time. Penny knew that wasn't possible.

As if she too sensed that this close contact in these abnormal circumstances was stretching friendship to the limit, Penny spoke abruptly late one morning.

'I know you want to go home, Laura, so don't think you've got to wetnurse me for ever,' she said, and then went on doggedly: 'I've written a letter to Hank and I want you to post it for me. It confirms what I told my father to tell him, that I'm leaving on an extended trip abroad, and it's best that we don't see one another again. It's really just in case he starts thinking my parents are blocking my relationship with a headstrong Yank.'

She tried to smile, but her mouth wobbled.

'I think you're completely mad,' Laura said flatly.

'So I'm mad. Just post the bloody letter!' Penny ordered.

'Yes, my lady. Is there anything else I can do for you?' Laura's voice was full of sarcasm.

Penny's eyes brimmed with tears. 'I'm sorry, Laura, but it's the rest of my life we're talking about, and I have to deal with this in my own way.'

'And spending the rest of your life without Hank is the best way, is it?'

'Yes. The only way,' Penny said.

Laura almost snatched up the letter and ran out of the room. She badly needed fresh air, and even though there was a hospital post box she wanted to walk and to think. All she could think of was Hank's stricken face when he read the Dear John letter.

She knew how he'd look, because she'd seen the photos. She also knew how they looked together – so ecstatic, as if they had just invented love. This idea of Penny's just wasn't right.

The address on the letter in her hand came into focus. It was the hotel in Oxford where Hank was staying now, with an instruction on the envelope to forward it if necessary.

She felt a great compulsion to do something she'd never done in her life before, and was finally unable to resist. She opened the envelope and read somebody else's letter. When she'd done it, she wished she hadn't. It was all so sad, so cold, and yet so supercharged with emotion for anybody with the eyes to see it.

But *would* Hank see it? Would he know there was something wrong, and sense the heartbreak beneath the crisply written words? Or would he take the letter at face value, cut his losses and go back to Texas with nothing but a fistful of memories? She listened to herself thinking in clichés, and she couldn't help it. Sometimes they were the only things that made sense.

She walked out of the hospital grounds and down the street until she found a public phone-box. There were always too many people walking around in the hospital, and besides, this call needed privacy.

She got through to Directory Enquiries and gave the name of the Oxford hotel. Once she had the number she put in plenty of coins and asked the receptionist if she could speak to Mr Henry Devereux, praying that he'd be there.

After what seemed like an age she heard a deep American voice at the other end, and her nerve almost failed her. But somebody had to do it, and there was nobody else. Good Old Laura would do it, whatever the consequences . . .

'Is that Mr Devereux?' she asked nervously. 'Hank Devereux?'

'It surely is.' He was clearly mystified. 'Who am I speaking to?'

'You may have heard my name. It's Laura, and I'm a friend of Penny's.'

'Oh yes, of course! I'm happy to make your acquaintance, Laura.' The surprise in his voice suddenly turned to suspicion. 'But is there something wrong? This isn't just a social call, I fancy.'

She told him carefully and painfully, trying to gauge his reaction at the other end of the line. She told him everything, especially Penny's resistance to pity. And she still didn't know if she was doing the right thing, or just being an interfering busybody.

She hung up quickly when she had finished, shaking all over. It was Penny's life. But it was Hank's too, and his reaction had told her everything she wanted to know. Then she dialled Nick's mobile number and said she was ready to come home any time he could fetch her.

'I'll be there right after lunch, darling,' he said, and she could hear the relief in his voice.

Two men, two voices on the telephone. In each of them Laura had heard love and concern, and her jangling nerves began to unravel, just a little.

'I've called Nick to come and fetch me this afternoon,' she told Penny. 'I hope that's all right with you. The children are starting to play up and I suspect Mrs Yard's had enough.'

The little white lie slid glibly off her tongue, but she avoided Penny's eyes as she spoke.

'It's all right, Laura. I think we've both had enough, and I can't hang onto your apron-strings for ever.'

'I don't wear aprons,' Laura said at once, and stopped as Penny caught hold of her hand.

'Laura,' she said softly. 'You've been the best friend anyone could ever have, but I'm afraid that every time I look at you, I remember how and where my accident happened. We need to be apart for a while, darling, so give me space, and don't think badly of me for saying it.'

'I don't,' Laura whispered. 'I could never think badly of you, Pen.'

But she was able to smile now, knowing Penny was right in one thing. Space was what they both needed, and maybe Laura had dabbled in her friend's life for the last time. But hopefully it was the best of times, and for the best of reasons.

By the time she was back home, Hank would be here, and from then on, it was up to them. Laura wouldn't be a fly on the wall to see and hear them, and she didn't want to be.

Some things were just too private, and the shared confidences of the Wellesley days were far behind them.

All the same, she couldn't help trying to picture the reunion, while she and Nick drove home together in the Range Rover. She was unusually quiet, and every now and then, his hand strayed across to cover hers for a moment, warm and reassuring, and infinitely dear. She was going home, to where she belonged, with everything she had always wanted.

'You've got a visitor, Miss Bishop,' the nurse announced.

Penny kept her eyes closed tightly for a minute, smothering a sigh. Not her parents again, when she'd expressly asked them *not* to keep coming to Bristol . . . and she hardly expected it to be Jeff Rawles, since all she'd got from him was an emotional letter telling her how sorry he was, but that he just couldn't bear to see her in hospital. She had torn the letter up. Not that she blamed him in any way. But she hadn't wanted to see him either.

The heady scent of roses wafted across her private

room, reminding her instantly of Aspen, and of the way her hotel room had been filled with flowers and gifts and love. Reminding her poignantly of Hank . . .

She felt the touch of someone's lips on hers. Not her father's. Certainly not her mother's.

'Hank,' she breathed against his mouth, sure that she was dreaming, and wanting to hold onto the dream for ever.

'That's right. Hank,' she heard his voice say. His loving, half-accusing voice . . . and her eyes opened wide as he sat down on the bed and pulled her into his arms.

'What are you doing here, and how did you know? I *told* them not to tell you,' she stammered, totally disorientated.

'They didn't tell me, if you mean your parents,' he said tersely. 'But how dared you try to keep it from me? Did I mean so little to you that you couldn't trust me to know?'

'Oh Hank, you meant – you mean everything to me. You know that,' she whispered against him.

She couldn't even weep. She had a strange sensation of watching herself, dry-eyed, infuriatingly dignified, the way she'd been brought up to be. And she had never hated that inborn stiff-upper-lip business more.

'Then why the hell all this subterfuge?' he said, his hands hurting her shoulders. 'Did you think I was so shallow that it would make one damn iota of difference to my feelings for you?'

'I'm sorry,' she whispered again, wondering why he was so mad with her, when all she wanted was for him to say he loved her. If he did, he had a strange way of showing it.

'Anyway, who told you?'

But the minute she had said the words, she knew. Laura. It had to be Laura. She felt a blistering, disbelieving anger, and then she saw Hank's eyes soften, and his fingers caressed her cheek.

'Someone who loves you, honey, who's got a lot more sense than you. So just get it into your head that I'm not here out of pity. It was love that made me want to marry you, and it's love that's going to make me nag you until you damn well say yes. I'm not leaving your side from now on until you do, and you're crazy if you think I'm going to let you run away from me now.'

She stared at him speechlessly for a minute, and then felt the slow tears slide down her cheeks.

'How could I run?' she asked huskily.

'Hell, I hadn't thought of that. But I guess that's one advantage,' he said, with a wicked grin, before he gathered her close again, kissing her with all the passion she remembered and thought she had turned her back on for ever.

When they came up for air, he spoke seductively.

'So you'd better agree to marry me, and come live on my ranch with me, sweetheart, or I'll shock all these good hospital people and ravish you here and now. What do you say?'

Penny smiled weakly. 'I'd really like to say yes to the last part, and thanks for asking. But since my proper English upbringing wouldn't let me go that far, I'll settle for saying yes to the first.'

She caught her breath at the look in his eyes, and her facetiousness died away as she clung to him.

'Oh *yes*, I'll marry you, Hank. Just as soon as I can walk down the aisle.'

It was strange, how being away for just a few days made everything look so different. Nick had relieved Mrs Yard of her duties, and he and Laura collected the twins from school, to rapturous screams of delight. They breathed down Laura's neck all the way home, wanting to know all about Penny's new foot, since Nick had broken the news to them gently by now.

They didn't seem at all fazed by it. They seemed to think it was quite an exciting thing to happen. So much for trying to shield them from the curves that adult life could throw at you. You couldn't do that, not indefinitely.

It hadn't put them off wanting to ride their ponies, either, and Laura had really struggled with herself before acknowledging that she had to give them their independence and let them go. That was something else she and Penny had thrashed out. She couldn't baby her daughters for ever.

By the time they had gone reluctantly to bed that evening, she and Nick were finally able to relax on the sofa, listening to music. She desperately wanted his approval of what she'd done after reading Penny's letter, but it hadn't seemed the right time to tell him while they were driving home, nor while the children were around. But it was the right time now.

She told him simply, without trying to dress it up at

387

all, or to excuse herself. She just told him the facts, and her reasons for doing what she'd done. His arm was loosely around her shoulders and she leaned her head against him.

'Was I wrong, Nick? Ever since I did it, I've wondered if I should have interfered. I've never tried to manipulate anybody else's life, but Penny was really suffering, and once I heard Hank's voice on the phone I was convinced I'd done the right thing. But how can I be sure?'

'You could always call and ask her,' he said, but she shook her head adamantly.

'No, I can't do that. I can't speak to her just now. It's her life, Nick.' She looked down at her hands, lying limply in her lap. She went on slowly.

'You know, I feel that for the first time since we've known one another, our lives are finally separating. Penny's got to stand on her own feet – and I'm not trying to be funny – and Gemma's got to sort out her own problems. We shouldn't always rely on one another. I just want to get on with my life here, with you and the girls.'

'That's some momentous decision, Mrs Dean.'

She spoke more clumsily. 'I know. And we'll always be friends, but being "best friends" suddenly seems so juvenile. Do you know what I mean?'

'I do. And for what it's worth, yes, I think you did the right thing for Penny, darling. It would have been a crime to keep Hank away from her.'

Laura took a deep breath. 'And did you do the right thing for Gemma, Nick?'

His brief pause did nothing to still the furious beating of her heart. He might think she was being enigmatic, or arch, but because they were on the same wave-length, she sensed that he knew exactly what she meant.

Gemma had offered him sex, and Nick was a virile, highly-sexed man. And he was *hers*, Laura thought passionately. He caught one of her hands and raised it to his lips. His eyes were clear and honest, as always.

'There isn't a woman alive who could tempt me to stray from the one I've got in my arms and in my heart,' he said simply. 'So you knew?'

'I know Gemma. And I guessed.'

'So now forget it. Nothing happened, and it never would have. It's history. Believe me?'

She gave him the first genuine smile that day.

'Of course I believe you, dammit,' she said fiercely. 'Why else do you think I married you, if I didn't know you fancied me rotten?' And she knew too that she could finally get rid of her guilt over being happy not to have more children. *She* was the one who was vital to Nick's existence and, much as he adored the girls, he would have gone on loving Laura even if they'd never had a child.

Nick laughed, and she could see the urgent flare of desire in his eyes. They had only been apart for a few days, but already it seemed too long. Far too long.

'Is that any way for a well-brought-up Wellesley girl to talk?' he teased.

His hands had begun to unfasten the buttons on her blouse, interspersing the movements with a kiss on every bit of her exposed flesh.

THE EXCITING NEW NAME IN WOMEN'S FICTION!

PLEASE HELP ME TO HELP YOU!

Dear *Scarlet* Reader,

As Editor of *Scarlet* Books I want to make sure that the books I offer you every month are up to the high standards *Scarlet* readers expect. And to do that I need to know a little more about you and your reading likes and dislikes. So please spare a few minutes to fill in the short questionnaire on the following pages and send it to me. I'll send *you* a surprise gift as a thank you!

Looking forward to hearing from you,

Sally Cooper

Editor-in-Chief, *Scarlet*

P.S. Only one offer per household.

QUESTIONNAIRE

Please tick the appropriate boxes to indicate your answers

1 Where did you get this Scarlet title?
Bought in Supermarket ☐
Bought at W H Smith ☐
Bought at book exchange or second-hand shop ☐
Borrowed from a friend ☐
Other _____

2 Did you enjoy reading it?
A lot ☐   A little ☐   Not at all ☐

3 What did you particularly like about this book?
Believable characters ☐   Easy to read ☐
Good value for money ☐   Enjoyable locations ☐
Interesting story ☐   Modern setting ☐
Other _____

4 What did you particularly dislike about this book?
_____

5 Would you buy another Scarlet book?
Yes ☐   No ☐

6 What other kinds of book do you enjoy reading?
Horror ☐   Puzzle books ☐   Historical fiction ☐
General fiction ☐   Crime/Detective ☐   Cookery ☐
Other _____

7 Which magazines do you enjoy most?
Bella ☐   Best ☐   Woman's Weekly ☐
Woman and Home ☐   Hello ☐   Cosmopolitan ☐
Good Housekeeping ☐
Other _____

cont.

And now a little about you –

8 How old are you?

Under 25 ☐   25–34 ☐   35–44 ☐
45–54 ☐   55–64 ☐   over 65 ☐

9 What is your marital status?

Single ☐   Married/living with partner ☐
Widowed ☐   Separated/divorced ☐

10 What is your current occupation?

Employed full-time ☐   Employed part-time ☐
Student ☐   Housewife full-time ☐
Unemployed ☐   Retired ☐

11 Do you have children? If so, how many and how old are they?

_____

_____

12 What is your annual household income?

under £10,000 ☐   £10–20,000 ☐   £20–30,000 ☐
£30–40,000 ☐   over £40,000 ☐

Miss/Mrs/Ms _____

Address _____

_____

_____

_____

Thank you for completing this questionnaire. Now tear it out – put it in an envelope and send it before 31 March 1997, to:

Sally Cooper, Editor-in-Chief

SCARLET
FREEPOST LON 3335
LONDON W8 4BR
Please use block capitals for address.
No stamp is required!   WIFRI/9/96

Scarlet titles coming next month:

SUMMER OF FIRE – Jill Sheldon
When Noah Taylor and Annie Laverty meet again, they are
instantly attracted to each other. Unfortunately, because of
his insecure childhood, Noah doesn't believe in love, while
Annie has trouble coming to terms with her terrifying past.
It takes a 'summer of fire' to finally bring Annie and Noah
together . . . forever.

DEVLIN'S DESIRE – Margaret Callaghan
Devlin Winter might *think* he can stroll back into Holly
Scott's life and take up where he left off – but Holly has
other ideas! No longer the fragile innocent Dev seduced
with his charm and sexual expertise, Holly is a woman to be
reckoned with. Dev, though, won't take 'no' for answer, and
he tells Holly: 'You're mine. You've always been mine and
you'll always *be* mine!'

INTOXICATING LADY – Barbara Stewart
Happy in her work and determined never to fall in love,
Danielle can't understand what Kingsley Hunter wants
from her. One minute, he is trying to entice her into his
bed . . . the next he seems to hate her! 'Revenge is sweet'
they say . . . but Danielle, Kingsley's 'intoxicating lady', has
to convince him that passionate love is even sweeter.

STARSTRUCK – Lianne Conway
'Even ice-cold with indifference, Fergus Hann's eyes demand attention' and they make Layne Denham realize an
awful truth! To be starstruck as a film fan is fun . . . but to
be starstruck in real life is asking for trouble . . . with a
capital 'T' for Temptation.